Land's End

FREDERIK POHL and
JACK WILLIAMSON

Two of the best known science fiction writers in the
world today, Frederik Pohl and Jack Williamson, have
collaborated to create a compelling novel of the drama
and heroism of courageous humans in the face of a natural disaster that could destroy all surface life on Earth. In
the near future, when a meteor shower penetrates the
Earth's atmosphere and strips away the precious layer of
ozone that protects all life from death by ultraviolet
rays, the only survivors of this tragic cosmic event are
those who live underground in protected enclaves, or in
cities beneath the surface of the sea. The death of millions on the surface and the electronic disruption
caused by the meteor barrage create chaos that shatters
the lives of the survivors.

Graciela Navarre and Ron Tregarth are two survivors
who, on the point of marriage when their world is broken, are separated and must overcome tremendous obstacles in order to regain their love. Among those
obstacles in The Eternal, an alien life form dormant for
eons beneath the sea, which is awakened by the meteor
bombardment and which seeks to absorb all Earth life
into its single consciousness. But as "ozone summer"
begins to wane, and life on Earth starts to return to normal, humanity rallies to regain control of its birthright
and Ron and Graciela, against all odds, are reunited.
Their story is a saga of breathtaking adventure and excitement that will thrill readers to the very last page.

FREDERIK POHL is the winner of all the major science
fiction awards. His novels, including *Gateway*,
Man-Plus and the recent *Chernobyl* (Bantam, 1987) have
received critical acclaim as well as being bestsellers. He
and JACK WILLIAMSON have collaborated on several
previous novels. Williamson, a Grandmaster of SF, has
written numerous classic SF novels, including *Firechild*
(Tor, 1987) and *The Humanoids*. Pohl lives in Chicago,
Illinois; WILLIAMSON lives in Portales, New Mexico.

Science Fiction   384 pages   5½ x 8¼
August $18.95a   0-312-93071-2

Published by Tor Books
▶ *A sweeping novel of adventure*
and human courage in the face of
natural disaster

**THESE ARE UNCORRECTED ADVANCE PROOFS BOUND
FOR YOUR REVIEWING CONVENIENCE.**

Land's End

FREDERIK POHL and
JACK WILLIAMSON

TOR

A TOM DOHERTY ASSOCIATES BOOK
NEW YORK

LAND'S END

Copyright © 1988 by Frederik Pohl and Jack Williamson

A TOR Book
Published by Tom Doherty Associates, Inc.
49 West 24 Street
New York, NY 10010

ISBN: 0-312-93071-2

Library of Congress Catalog Card Number: 87-51406

First edition: August 1988

Printed in the United States of America

0 9 8 7 6 5 4 3 2 1

This book is dedicated to the memory of
Judy-Lynn del Rey.
She lived from 1942 to 1986.
It was not nearly long enough.

In the mind of the Eternal, all things live eternally.

In the mind of the Eternal live molluscs and men, a sea captain and a child. Many live in the mind of the Eternal, with all their joys and terrors and loves, forever.

In the mind of the Eternal live the memories of the collision of worlds and the terrible death of stars. Planets grow cold. Races perish. The great bubble of the universe swells endlessly outward. Tiny flakes of being dance around each other, are born, die—all in the trillionth of a second—but live on, in the mind of the Eternal.

In the mind of the Eternal is even a place for everything that ever was . . . for the thrusting of raw mountain ranges and the slow wearing away of their roots . . . for seas to spread and close.

In the mind of the Eternal there is even room for love, for love that invites all things to enter and live eternally . . . in the mind of the Eternal.

The
Last Year

Chapter

1

When her giant squid tried to eat the Ambassador from PanMack, Graciela Navarro had never heard of the Eternal.

Graciela's life was going very well. She had an important and rewarding job to do: running City Atlantica's training school for squid. She had a lover, Ron Tregarth, who was in every way dear to her. She lived in City Atlantica, the finest and most free of the Eighteen Cities under water, and she was certain that life under the sea was better than anything on the teeming, stinking, oppressed land surface of the Earth.

The only thing wrong was that her prize student, the squid Nessus, reached out to pull the fat lubber, Dr. Ambassador Simon McKen Quagger, into the vast squid pool, and indeed into its own huge, menacing mouth.

It couldn't have happened at a worse time. It was graduation day for her first class of trained—no, Graciela would have argued, not trained but *educated*—squid, and everyone who mattered was there. All six graduating squid had been showing how they could operate the harvesting and tilling and planting machines. Mayor Mary Maude McKen herself was giving the commencement address. Besides Her Honor, the Mayor, there was the even more honored and very old Eustace McKen, visiting Atlantica from his regular tour around the rest of the Eighteen

Cities—he had no regular home, because all the cities wanted him. There was the Ambassador from PanMack, with his secretary. And there was one person who mattered more to Graciela than any number of dignitaries, because he was the man she loved. More than a hundred of the leading citizens of City Atlantica crowded the narrow walkways around the immense pool. Even Ambassador Quagger, the huge fat man with nasty little eyes, had pretended to be affable as he donated the ugly, glowing, copper-colored bust of himself as a momento of his state visit . . . and then this!

It was unbelievable that Nessus should be the culprit. Nessus was the biggest squid among Graciela's charges. He was also the smartest and, ordinarily, the most reliable of them. Graciela was shocked when, without warning, Nessus dropped the torpedo-shaped tilling machine he was towing along the pool and propelled himself toward the ambassador.

Until then, it had all been going so well! The six squid slithered back and forth in the pool at her words of command. Through the implanted voice box each wore, they spoke their own names and greeted the mayor by name. Ron Tregarth, the man Graciela intended to marry, beamed with pride at her. The ceremony would have gone without a hitch, if only Nessus had not tried to eat their distinguished guest of honor, the Ambassador from PanMack.

The sequence of events was very clear. At one moment the mayor was delivering her valedictory address as she stood at the feeding board over the wide, deep squid pool inside the school dome. The audience was sitting politely on rows of benches at the side of the pool. The six squid who were the graduating class, Nessus biggest and nearest among them, were writhing restlessly just under the surface. Ambassador Quagger was in the first row, absently stroking the ruddy bust of himself, leaning forward and frowning into the pool.

A moment later there was a splash.

Dr. Ambassador Quagger was in the pool, sinking right into the tentacles of Nessus. Half a second later, all eight long and two short arms of the squid were curled around the Ambassador from PanMack, pulling him toward the great, torpedo-shaped body, and the ambassador was squawking with fear as he was drawn near the immense, gaping mouth.

Half a second later still, Graciela Navarro hit the surface of the pool in a clean dive. "Nessus!" she spluttered. "Nessus, no! Nessus hurt man, not!" And then she could speak no more because she was under water, thrusting and pulling at the great arms at their roots, where there were no sucking disks to hold her, while her face stared into one of the squid's immense, unblinking eyes. The eye was larger than Graciela's entire head, round and bright and inhuman.

But Nessus recognized her. Reluctantly—it seemed—the squid straightened the tentacles. The ambassador broke the surface with a frightened, angry, squawking whoop of air-starvation. A dozen hands helped him out of the pool—no more than was needed, considering his bulk.

The incident was over.

It was the worst thing, Graciela decided, that had ever happened in her whole life; but she hadn't heard of the Eternal, then. Neither had anyone else. Neither had she ever heard of Comet Sicara, yet, though there were a few people on Earth who were aware of its existence, and one or two who thought of very little else.

In this, the twenty-fifth year since the foundation of the first of the Eighteen Cities, there was no better place to be on Earth than in one of them. Let the lubbers of Earth's land areas fight their petty, destructive wars and destroy its soil and atmosphere! The sea bottom was pristine and pure. Like every other "webfoot"—the people of the Eighteen Cities did not scorn the lubber nickname—Graciela Navarro envied nobody else in the world. The land people were rich and terribly strong in a military sense, and they were vast in number. But the Eighteen Cities had what no lubber ever had. They had freedom.

It was by no means clear to Graciela Navarro that this Dr. Ambassador Quagger deserved any more respect or deference than did the humblest filter-scrubber in City Atlantica. So when she was summoned to the mayor's presence—in Graciela's own office!—she did not hurry.

She had other things on her mind, and most important was her school. She had to soothe the graduating squid, now thrashing about worriedly in the pool. As soon as Quagger was safe and the rest of the audience had begun to disperse, Graciela was back in the water. She swam among them, clicking and whistling lovingly to them, speaking their names, stroking the tiny suction disks at the tips of their tentacles with a gentle touch, roughing up the strong, smooth hide of their mantles and siphons.

When they seemed calmer, she guided Nessus and a medium-sized squid named Holly into the repressurization chamber. She did not go in with them—not without a pressure suit!—but when the chamber was sealed she watched them through the crystal wall as the valves admitted the pressure of the deep sea into the lock. The squid stirred slightly as they felt the change. It was neither painful nor bothersome to them; their buoyancy was achieved chemically, rather than through the gas-filled swim bladders of other forms of marine life, so there was nothing in their bodies to cause discomfort by being compressed or distended with changes of pressure. As soon as the chamber's gauge showed normalization with reference to the pressure of the deep sea outside, the gates unfolded. Nessus and Holly swam out slowly with gentle thrusts of their siphons. They hung just outside, fins and tentacles rippling to hold them in place, while the pumps eased the pressure in the chamber to admit the other four. When they were all gone, Graciela Navarro swam to the edge of the pool, where Ron Tregarth was waiting. Beside him were the two women who had been his executive officers in his submarine command, Vera Doom who had gone with him on his last trip to the mainlands, and Jill Danner who would second him on his next. Both were extraordinarily good-looking young women, and Graciela wondered, sometimes, what it was that Ron Tregarth saw in her to prefer her above them. She didn't know the answer; she only was grateful that he did.

Tregarth's arms were already stretched out to her. She reached up and grasped his wrists and, with an easy, fluid motion, he lifted her out of the water to his side. "Her Honor's waiting for you in your office, love," he said, grinning. "Beginning to stamp her little feet by now, I'd guess."

"You've got nothing to worry about. After all, you saved that fat lubber's life," Jill Danner put in. "Want us to come with you to testify?"

"She wouldn't like that," said Graciela, "but thanks."

"Here," said Tregarth. "I brought your robe so you won't have to face her in your skivvies."

Tregarth was half a meter taller than his fiancée and twice as heavy, Viking fair where she was Mediterranean dark, even though all of her nineteen years had been spent kilometers away from sunlight. He helped her into the robe and stood by while she slipped her feet into buskins. She could see that his eyes were past her, gazing out past the crystal dome walls to where the tiny lights of the submarine jitneys were dwindling away as they bore some of the guests toward the distant glow of the main dome of City Atlantica itself.

She said, not knowing she was going to say it, regretting it as soon as it was out of her mouth, "You'd rather be on your ship than here, wouldn't you?"

He said quickly, "Not while you're here, Graciela." Then, for honesty's sake, he conceded, "But everything else being equal, yes, I'd rather be on a ship than in a city. Cities crowd me, love. Might as well be topside with the lubbers."

She nodded soberly, knotting the belt of her robe, and sighed. That was the greatest problem Graciela faced—so she believed, at least, in that time before she learned of Comet Sicara and the Eternal. She and Tregarth had seldom even discussed it, because both knew that there was no good solution.

Graciela's work was in the school dome, with the squid. Ron Tregarth's was to command his great long-distance submarine, tracking all the seas of Earth in voyages that could last for months at a time.

Was it ever going to be possible to reconcile them? Was there any point in marrying if they could not be together? If they did marry, which of them would yield to the other? Could Graciela leave her precious cephalopods and the great work she was doing with them for a gypsy life as a submarine captain's wife? Was it possible for Ron to swallow the anchor and find some sort of job in City Atlantica or around the school?

If there was any good answer, Graciela had never found it.

"Graciela," said Vera Doorn tentatively, "I do think Her Honor expects you right away—"

"Yes," said Graciela Navarro. "I'd better not keep her waiting." She put her lips up to Tregarth's for a kiss and waved good bye to the three of them before, biting her lip, she turned toward the lifts to her office. Her mind was not on the Mayor. It was on the great decision she and Ron Tregarth would sooner or later have to make—the greatest decision, she thought, she would ever face in her life. But she did not then know about either Comet Sicara or the Eternal.

The mayor glared at Graciela Navarro. "You've taken your time," she complained irritably.

Irritated the mayor surely was. She was kicking her heels fretfully against the leg of the table she was perched on, its load of journals on molluscan anatomy and behavioral psychology and linguistic translation programs pushed to one side. The chair at Graciela's desk was fully occupied by the bulk of Dr. Ambassador Simon McKen Quagger. Behind him stood a slim, fair young man Graciela had noticed in the ambassador's entourage. Now he was moving about the room to snap pictures of Graciela and his boss with a wrist camera.

"I'm sorry. I had to let the squid out," Graciela said.

"Sorry," cried the mayor. "The ambassador and I have been waiting for you to apologize for the danger you allowed him to experience. Do you realize that that animal of yours could have eaten him?"

"No, no. That's impossible," Graciela protested. "If Nessus had wanted to eat Mr. Quagger, he certainly would have done it. Do you have any idea how strong he is?"

"It surely looked that way!"

Graciela said, temporizing for the sake of diplomatic relations, "I can only think that the ambassador must have accidentally triggered Nessus's feeding reflexes—just partially, of course! Just enough to start to draw him in. If you'll look at Mr. Quagger's arms—do you see?—you'll see there are no scars on him. Nessus is a full-grown adult male squid. If he had been really serious there would have been circular sucker marks all over your body, Mr. Ambassador, the size of a saucer. But I do really apologize," she remembered to add.

The apology didn't come easily. Graciela didn't like

people from PanMack—or, indeed, from anywhere on the dryland surface of the Earth. They were so violent! The lubbers were always quarreling with each other—the land-McKen PanMack domains against the AfrAsians, the European states against both of them. Even the McKens themselves were known to settle their differences with a staged riot or a "border incident" between the four great fiefdoms of the PanMack empire. So far that was all. The McKens had at least prevented the outbreak of a full-fledged nuclear war for decades now.

And that, Graciela reflected with a shiver, was all to the good, because if a big war broke out it would mean trouble for the Eighteen Cities. One lubber empire or another would surely seize the chance to acquire an underwater city or two to add to its domain.

The ambassador was glowering at her. There was something thoughtful in his expression, a kind of interest in her that Graciela liked even less than his anger. Then the look on his face changed. It smoothed itself into a great, false smile. He glanced at his side with the wrist-camera to make sure it was turned on him and said, "My dear young lady, there is no need to concern yourself. Accidents happen! And I certainly understand your attachment to that, ah, that animal. I myself have a dear pet named Angie who is most precious to me; I quite sympathize with your loyalty to your—ah—your mollusc."

He was carefully presenting his best profile to the camera as he spoke. Graciela saw that, in addition to the camera on one wrist, the other man had a voice recorder on the other; the ambassador's generosity was being preserved for posterity. "I should," said the ambassador, "introduce you to Mr. Newton Bluestone. He is helping me to write my memoirs; I'll send you a copy when they're done. I'm sure you'll find them interesting. But," he added with a sigh, "I confess that I am just a little fatigued from this, uh, this experience. With your permission I'd like to withdraw to my quarters. Come, Newt!" The man clicked off recorder and camera and sprang to help pull Dr. Ambassador Quagger out of the chair. Wheezing and smiling, the fat man waved off the mayor and lumbered toward the door.

As he left, he turned to wag a fat finger at the mayor. "Now," he chided humorously, "please don't be too harsh on the young lady when I've left, Madam Mayor! I'm sure she meant no harm. And I'll be fit as a fiddle again as soon as I've had a good night's sleep, I feel certain of it."

"Sleep well, Mr. Ambassador," called the Mayor. "And thank you for your generous gift! Good-bye, sir!"

And Graciela Navarro, with the Mayor's eyes on her, said, "Goodbye," and, unwillingly, added, "sir."

When the door had closed the Mayor got up and paced around the room, looking at Graciela. "What am I going to do with you?" she demanded fretfully. "Can't you speak decently to the ambassador?"

Graciela took possession of her own desk again, testing the chair to see if its springs had been ruptured. "I did speak decently to him, Mayor. Why do you call him "sir"? He's just an unpleasant fat man who treats us all like inferiors!"

The mayor plumped herself onto the sofa next to the desk. "He's an unpleasant fat man who's here to negotiate a trade contract, Graciela. And from his point of view we *are* his inferiors. His mother was a McKen!"

"You're a McKen, too," Graciela pointed out.

The mayor shook her head. "I *married* a McKen. It was a mistake on both sides, and nobody feels that more strongly than Quagger. How he thinks of us has nothing to do with it. We need that trade to survive. Do you have any idea how hard it is to make steel under the sea?"

Graciela shrugged. "Electrical refining is more expensive, yes—"

"It is *terribly* expensive, and we need the money for other things. So we've got to export foods and pharmaceuticals to the lub— I mean, to the surface people, along with ores from the thermal springs. That lets us buy their steel, and some of their manufactured things, and we're all better off. We don't have to like them, Graciela! We certainly don't have to accept their politics or their stupid class system. But we need their trade. Therefore," she said decisively, "I want you to make friends with the ambassador."

"Me? Friends? With *him?*"

"You will take Ambassador Quagger on a tour of the sea-bottom," the Mayor said firmly. "Be nice to him. Make. him like you. Make him like your pet squid, even, if you can. Make him understand that we people of the Eighteen Cities are trustworthy and decent and know how to repay favors with favors."

"But, Mayor," Graciela wailed, "there are plenty of people in City Atlantica better fit for that kind of thing."

"But you have the squid," the Mayor said thoughtfully. "Did you hear what he said? He has some kind of a pet of his own. He understands your feeling for the squid."

"My squid are not *pets!*"

"It's better if you let him think they are, Graciela; he can understand that. So requisition a couple of pressure suits and a sea-sled and take him out tomorrow. Show him our farms, our power stations, the thermal springs—especially show him how the squid actually work for us. And when you get back don't forget to show him our museum."

"Museum?" Graciela made a face. "Do you think a lubber cares about our submarine archeology?" She took a deep breath, then exploded, "Mayor McKen, I've got all the work I can handle right now! Graduating that first class was only the beginning. I've got fourteen other squid to teach—to fit with voice implants—to train in using the communicators. That school is important to the future of City Atlantica, and the whole thing depends on me!"

"Wrong," said the Mayor politely. "What the school depends on is financing from the City Atlantica budget. That depends on money, and that depends on our balance of payments with PanMack and the other large dry-land trading partners. With Ambassador Quagger, for instance. And what the budget contains, Graciela, depends on what I request as mayor!"

"But, Your Honor, the school is important to our future! The squid can help us earn much more by expanding our farms and mines—"

"Future talk, Graciela. I have to live in the present."

"And in the past!" snapped Graciela, and regretted it the moment the words were out of her mouth.

"Ah," said the mayor, nodding, "I see. You're talking about the small amounts we spend on archeological surveys of the sea floor. But that is for the good of the city, Graciela. The museum shows some of the wonderful things we've discovered already, wrecked ships from the Spanish treasure fleets, twentieth-century nuclear submarines, sunken liners—even a Carthaginian trireme! The future of the museum and the work associated with it is not in question, Graciela. Your school appropriation is. Earn it."

Graciela took a deep breath and said reasonably, "All right, your honor, I suppose someone has to be nice to the ambassador, but why me? Eustace McKen would be better. After all, he's the ambassador's great-uncle, isn't he?"

The mayor shook her head decisively. "In the first place, the bad McKens don't have much use for Eustace. You know that! And anyway, he's already on his way to City PanNegra. So it's up to you to make things right with the man—"

She hesitated, looking somberly at Graciela. Then she added reluctantly, "It's not just your squid, Graciela. There's something else."

Graciela waited patiently to hear what was coming next. She knew that Mayor Mary Maude McKen, however fussy and petulant she might sometimes seem, always had a reason for whatever she did. The woman was tiny and plump, with hair and skin so pale that she seemed almost albino, but inside that diminutive body was a courageous heart and a sharp mind.

The mayor unlocked her shoulder bag and pulled out a sheet of communications printout. "You see, my dear," she said, "he's already filed one diplomatic protest." She flipped the printout sheet to Graciela. "He says his diplomatic security has been violated by illegal and criminal acts of search and seizure."

"No one would do that!" Graciela cried, horrified, but the Mayor only shook her head and pointed to the printout.

Graciela bent her head to read it, frowning. It was in the form of something like an encyclopedia entry, and it said:

The PanMack Consortium
The brothers Angus and Eustace McKen divided their assets on the death of their father. Eustace McKen then foolishly dissipated his resources on the pointless venture of establishing the so-called "Eighteen Cities", an ill-conceived program of colonizing the ocean bottoms which has proved to be of no practical value to the human race. His brother Angus McKen, on the other hand, devoted his immense talents and energies to the welfare of the Earth's land dwellers. The children of Angus McKen, three sons and one daughter, inherited his brilliant management skills, and their own descendants have continued their wise practices. The PanMack Consortium is Angus McKen's lasting legacy to the people of the entire Western Hemi-

sphere. It provides the benefits of enlightened social institutions to more than ten billion people on two continents, from Greenland to Tierra del Fuego. Under PanMack their lives are unclouded by fear of violence, for they are protected by the unflagging vigilance of PanMack's Peace Forces—the Peace Wing in the air and in space, the Peace Fleet resolutely patrolling the seas and waterways and the Peace Guards protecting the land against external enemies and subversives of all kinds. The long-range Peace Wing aircraft—

It broke off there. Graciela looked up wonderingly. "What is it? Besides being PanMack propaganda, I mean?"

The Mayor said heavily, "According to Ambassador Quagger it's classified material, illicitly retrieved from his personal datastore by means of illegal electronic surveillance through our communications network."

"That's insane!"

The mayor shrugged. "There's the document," she pointed out. "It's real enough. It's incomplete, of course. It seems that when the readout got to the military details an automatic alarm stopped the transmission. So as soon as Quagger found out about it he started screaming at me on the intercom, early this morning. And I checked the transmission logs, and, sure enough, we found this."

"But who did it?" The mayor shrugged again. "And *why?* Who would want to plug into the ambassador's datastore for this kind of junk?"

"The trouble is," the major said sadly, "that this isn't the first time. Sandor Tisza's been complaining to me for weeks about unauthorized transmissions on his communications net. I didn't take it seriously. Maybe I still shouldn't —perhaps it's just some bright child, or a prankster. But the ambassador does, and you see why I don't want him to have any further ground for complaints. So I want you to soothe him, Graciela."

"Soothe him?"

"Make him happy. Take the damn lubber out to see what we are doing, and don't let him drown! At least," the mayor finished, "not this time. If he ever comes back as a plain tourist instead of a trade ambassador, why, that will be quite a different story, and I'll help you drain his air tanks myself!"

Chapter

2

The next morning Dr. Ambassador Simon McKen Quagger kept them waiting. All of them were standing around the sea-sled dock, not just Graciela Navarro, but Ron Tregarth as well, and Sandor Tisza, come to see them off, and even the slim young man who was Quagger's own—what was the word?—yes, "amanuensis."

Whatever an amanuensis was, Tregarth thought, studying the man. In physical appearance, the "amanuensis" was a young man. His name was Newt Bluestone. Actually, he didn't seem like a bad fellow—for a lubber, of course. He was neither as fake-jolly nor as blustery as his boss, and certainly he was nowhere near as physically repulsive. Apart from the tanned skin, he might even have looked like any decent citizen of the Eighteen Cities if he hadn't been wearing a curious travesty of a military uniform.

Tregarth thought the suit was a lot more comical than

impressive, especially in its present surroundings. You didn't see many military uniforms in City Atlantica. Still, Tregarth had seen plenty of them in his travels. He knew what they looked like. They were made of a supple carbon-fiber fabric that was almost like armor against enemy weapons. (*Enemy*, Tregarth grunted to himself. What a lubber word that was!) There was a helmet that curved down around the chin and throat, and great gauntlets with their built-in keypads for weaponry. But what Newt Bluestone wore was a mockery of the real thing! The fabric was silk. The gloves were soft leather. The outfit looked, more than anything else, like the scanty costume a chorus girl might wear for a musical military revue.

To the man's credit, he seemed embarrassed to wear it. "Are you coming with us?" Graciela was asking him politely, and the man grinned and shook his head regretfully.

"Don't I wish! No, I'll have to stay here and complete the photo-documentation of the ambassador's visit—that means taking pictures of everything he saw or touched," Bluestone explained. "But I wish I could go! I've always been fascinated by the sea, and this is my first chance to see it."

The man had the makings of a decent human being, thought Tregarth. He said gruffly, "See it? Good lord, man! You're not seeing a millionth of the sea! Do you have any idea of how big the sea is?"

"Well, of course it has to be large—"

"It is *immense*," Tregarth corrected him. "Let me give you an idea. If you add together the area of every continent —Europe and Africa and the Americas and Antarctica and Australia—and then add in all the islands everywhere, from Greenland and Spitzbergen to the tiny rocks along the coast of the Antarctic, the total is a little over a hundred and thirty million square kilometers. The Pacific Ocean alone is bigger than that! It's a hundred and sixty-five million, and even so that's only about two-fifths of the area the sea covers."

"That is big," Bluestone agreed politely, "but—"

"But that's only the beginning. The sea has three dimensions! On the land life only occupies a thin skin on the surface—call it a hundred meters, from the deepest penetration of any organism to the top of the tallest tree; a total volume of about thirteen million cubic kilometers. The volume of the oceans is more than one and a third *billion* k-cubed—a hundred times the volume on land— and nearly all of it inhabited by life of some sort. Do you understand what I'm saying? We have *room.* There are only a few hundred thousand of us in all the Eighteen Cities combined. That's why we're free and you're—"

"Now, really, Ron," Graciela cut in, just in time to prevent Tregarth from getting out whatever the unflattering rest of the sentence might have been. "That's not entirely fair, you know. Half of the sea is deeper than three kilometers, and we can't go down that far."

Tregarth looked surprised and indignant. "But we can! We're getting ready to right now! Vera Doorn's going to take an exploration sub down to explore some of the deeps as soon as it's fitted out!"

"Oh, yes," Graciela nodded, "we do try to explore— some—not very much, and not very successfully. But at least for now we can't stay long down below the three-k depth—not," she smiled at Newt Bluestone, "that that changes much of what Ron was telling you. I mean, we *do* have a lot of space to maneuver in!"

Bluestone had not taken offense. "I envy that," he said thoughtfully. "On the land it's—well—different. There are so many of us, you know. And so much conflict, and—" Then he looked up and abruptly cut himself short. "But here comes the ambassador," he said instead. He turned on his wrist camera. "Would you mind, Miss Navarro? The two of you together, you and the ambassador, just for a couple of pictures? And then I'd better get along to finish up my documentation!"

If the ambassador's man, Newt Bluestone, had seemed a little better than Tregarth had expected, the ambassador himself went all the other way. The man was a nuisance, and an obnoxious one. When Graciela politely addressed him as Mr. Quagger, he corrected her sharply: "I am *Ambassador* Quagger, young lady! With all diplomatic privileges and immunities!" When Tregarth managed to ask a civil question about whether he had had a decent breakfast, the man complained that everything was too salty. When the helpers from the squid school tried to fit him with a suit, he cursed at them and was as clumsy and as nastily comical as he had seemed when Nessus dragged him into the pool.

Except that, really, he wasn't comical at all. He was unpleasant. He was the only son of the only daughter of Angus, the bad McKen. Clearly he took after his grandfather, because he was a gross balloon of a man. Not all of his bulk was fat. He stood well over two meters tall, half a head taller than Tregarth himself. What made him grotesque was that he had the facial features of a much smaller man. His eyes were close-set. He had a tiny, up-tilted nose, and a pouty mouth that might have looked very sweet when he was a small child.

But that had been a long time ago. Now Quagger was huge. When the helpers found the largest size suit available he complained that it was still too tight around his arms and legs. He dismissed Newt Bluestone peremptorily as soon as the "amanuensis" had taken enough pictures, then turned to Graciela with an oily smile. "He has much to do," he sighed, "making a photographic record of my visit here. I have been asked many times to tell my life's story to the world, and Newt has been very useful. And this should make quite an interesting chapter—my visit with the mermen, down on the sea bottom with the crawling things." Then he turned to glare at Tregarth. "But, tell me, what is this man doing here? You did not tell me that this was to be lovers wandering arm in arm!"

It was a shock to Graciela to find out that the ambassador knew so much about her private life, but she said steadily, "Captain Tregarth is a qualified pilot, Ambassador. It is standard practice to go with two pilots when conducting an important person like yourself."

"Humph," he said again, but sounded mollified. Then he squawked at a sudden twinge and turned his glare on Graciela. "You hurt me," he accused.

"I'm sorry," she offered, trying to get the sea-boots on his immense feet.

He only grunted again. Then, "Must we go through this foolishness?" he demanded petulantly. "I've often done skindiving in lakes and streams and I've never had to put up with this!"

Tregarth grinned internally as he saw his lover bite her tongue. She said as politely as she could, "But this isn't a lake, Mr. Ambassador. The dive suits must be very strong. Perhaps you don't know what sort of pressure the suit has to keep out for you. We are twenty-two hundred meters below the surface of the sea. That means that your suit must be strong enough to support a column of water twenty-two hundred meters tall and as thick through as the thickest part of your body—oh, sorry," she said, hiding a grin as the ambassador looked indignant. "I didn't mean anything by that. But that means there's something like forty tons of water pressing on you. Squeezing you. The only thing that keeps it from crushing you is your suit, and if it sprang a leak—" She paused there, and Tregarth listened with interest. Was she really going to tell Quagger just what would happen if twenty-two hundred meters of water hammered into his suit to crush that soft, flabby body into a thin film of grease? She didn't. "It would be instantly fatal," she finished.

"That," sighed Quagger, "I suppose is true. Very well. Have the servants seal this thing up."

Tregarth had another smile to suppress as he saw the expressions on the faces of the "servants". Quickly he slid into his own suit and nodded to Sandor Tisza, acting as lock keeper for them.

"Ready for entry," Tisza called, his faint accent still audible after all his years under the sea.

There was something interesting there, Tregarth thought. When Tisza spoke the lubber ambassador looked up sharply. There was an expression in Quagger's eyes that Tregarth could not quite decipher. Did he know Sandor Tisza? And if so, from where? But then the helpers eased the helmet down over Quagger's head, and the three of them entered the lock that led to the great deeps outside the dome.

Outside the dome of the squid school, Graciela Navarro tried to lash the bulk of Ambassador Quagger firmly in place on their sea skid. The ambassador was muttering to himself as he looked around. He seemed not to like the darkness.

Of darkness there was plenty. The larger dome of City Atlantica was a dim yellow and green gleam in the distance. Behind them the school dome was bright and busy, and two submarine jitneys were coming in from the city dome, their red and green navigation lights blinking monotonously on their sides. Above the distant city dome they could barely make out the three narrow pillars of blue-green light that stretched upward from the communications center at the top of the dome, as far as the eye could follow. And all around, from both domes, even slimmer beams joined the two domes and extended out in all directions to the repeater stations that led to the farm centers, the power stations, the ore springs. "Our communications system," Graciela explained proudly. "We can't use radio under the sea, so we use pulsed blue-green laser beams. We'll follow one of them as a guide."

"Get on with it," said Quagger irritably. "I don't like this darkness!" For that was all there was to see. There was no other light. Not up, not down, not to any side. The sun might have been blazing brightly overhead, but none of the Eighteen Cities ever saw it. The sea soaks up light. Ten meters down the red is gone. Yellow can still be faintly seen at two hundred meters, and the sun's own blue-green wavelengths reach down almost a kilometer; but City Atlantica and its satellite domes were more than twice that far beneath the surface.

Ambassador Quagger, grunting and struggling as Graciela secured him to the skid, found the switch of his helmet speaker. Peevishly he demanded, "Why aren't there any fish? I thought some of them were supposed to be luminous!"

Tregarth winced at the assault to his eardrums. Graciela begged, "Please, Mr. Ambassador! Turn your volume down!" The helmet's external speakers were capable of being heard across half a kilometer of the dense, cold waters at their level; at close range and full gain, they were deafening.

Quagger's amplified voice grumbled to itself as he fumbled with the volume control. Then he repeated, his voice now merely unpleasantly loud rather than ear-destroying: "Why aren't there any fish?"

Ron Tregarth laughed softly. "There used to be, Mr. Ambassador," he said, "but they don't come around any more. Graciela's squid eat them."

Graciela aimed a kick at the man she loved, but Tregarth had already moved away. "Captain Tregarth is joking," she assured the ambassador. "Not exactly a joke, I mean, because the squid do feed on fish. But not on people. There is absolutely no danger to us. In any case—Ron, show him your air-bow—Captain Tregarth is armed, although he has never needed to use that weapon here. Have you, Ron?"

"There's always a first time," Tregarth observed cheerfully. Although Graciela couldn't see his face she could hear the grin in his voice. She thought, *When I get you back in the dome—*

But the Ambassador had recognized Tregarth's tone, too. "Get on with it," he ordered testily. "I am very uncomfortable in this stupid suit."

And making us even more uncomfortable, thought Graciela darkly as she helped the gross man into the skid. She was panting as she strained against the dead mass of his hundred-odd kilos of blubber, even supported by the water all around them.

"Slide in under the shroud—that's right," she gasped, shoving with all her might. "Now let me fasten the straps and the intercom cables—" Touching his body, even through the pressure suit, made her skin itch. Worse, Quagger's bulk was almost more than the space under the sea-skid's shroud permitted. The skid was a very rudimentary vessel; it did not amount to much more than a squid's siphon reproduced in plastic and steel. The skid was basically a simple hollow tube, containing turbine drivers powered by hydrogen fuel cells. The crystal shroud that surrounded it protected its riders from the rush of water, as their suits saved them from the terrible crush of the abyssal deep.

"That's done it," she said, breathing hard with exertion as she snapped the last catch. She plugged the intercom cables into their jacks and announced, "That's better; now we can talk to each other without the external speakers. And now we'll be on our way to see our farms, our power sources and a few other places of interest, but first we've got about six kilometers to travel."

"Six kilometers!" Quagger bellowed indignantly—his voice only inside her helmet now, though, instead of blatting out into the surrounding sea. "Why so far? Were your people too stupid to locate your cities near the power plants?"

Graciela bit back the first words that came to her lips, and twisted her head in its two-hundred-seventy-degree helmet to give Tregarth a glare of warning. Through clenched teeth she said, "It isn't stupidity, Mr. Ambassa‑dor. It's a safety precaution. There's tectonic activity near the hydrothermal vents—that's where the hot water co‑mes from, you see. There is a considerable risk of minor earthquakes, and that's not what you want right beside even a Nexø dome!"

"Nexø?" the ambassador repeated doubtfully.

"The glassy material our domes are made of. There's nothing else strong enough to keep the water out at his pressure. Not even steel."

He grunted. "Get on with it, then," he ordered.

"Yes, yes." Tregarth mimicked, latching himself in next to Graciela. "Can't waste the valuable time of important people, Graciela, so let's get on with it!"

Graciela sighed. Perhaps it had not been a very good idea to bring the sub captain along, after all—though the idea of being alone with this land pig turned her stomach. She advanced the speed lever slowly forward. The skid shuddered and then crept ahead.

"What you will see on the way, Mr. Ambassador," she lectured, "is basically undisturbed sea bottom, just as it has been for millions of years. It looks dead, but in fact there are countless organisms near it, in it and beneath it, surviving on organic matter that drifts down from the photic layers twenty-two hundred meters up. . . ."

Tregarth relaxed, listening to the familiar lecture. Every child of the Eighteen Cities learned it in his first school years, because it was what made their life possible. The soil their crops grew in was sediment, and it accrued very slowly—perhaps a millimeter in a thousand years—but the old sea bottoms had had time for it to grow thick and rich.

What made the sediment, and what fed the creatures that lived on the sea bottoms, was refuse from the many meals of the organisms above. Fish are sloppy eaters. When a fish catches, say, a shrimp, it drools blood and other fluids, as much as a quarter of the mass of the prey. This oozes into the sea and is taken up by microorganisms, or by the kinds of creatures that have sheets of mucus to trap their food; and then they, too, become prey. Some organisms died natural deaths—not many, in the endless hunger of the sea!—but even they usually got eaten somewhere in their slow drift to the bottom, perhaps years on the way for the smallest of them. Fecal pellets fell with them; the excreting animals don't have perfect digestive systems, so there is nourishment in the pellets, too, and all that enriched the oozes that City Atlantica farmed for its crops.

"Ah, yes," Ambassador Quagger boomed cleverly, "but if that is so, why don't we see bones below us? After all, nothing eats whale bones, does it?"

"A very good question," Graciela complimented the man. "But, you see, we're below what is called the carbonate compensation depth! That means that under these pressures even the bones dissolve and there is nothing left. . . ."

Tregarth yawned, wishing he could see the expression on Ambassador Quagger's face as he heard all this. Tregarth himself was at ease, content to leave the piloting of the sea-skid to Graciela as they followed the narrow blue-green laser beam toward their first destination. He was well aware that, sub captain though he was, Graciela had many more hours at the controls of a sea-skid than he ever would have. He felt almost tolerant toward the odd-looking, unpleasant man from landside. Lubbers couldn't help being lubbers, he thought charitably. It was the nature of lubbers to rub you the wrong way. In the interests of a scrupulous fairness, Tregarth admitted to himself that it would be pleasant enough to rub Quagger the wrong way in return—preferably with something that would do a decent job of maiming him, like the sandpaper-rough skin of a shark. But as long as Quagger got no worse than he had been so far, Tregarth resolved not to provoke him. After all, the man was a McKen! From the bad side of the McKens, true, but still a blood relative of that wonderful Eustace McKen who had made the Eighteen Cities possible in the first place.

So Ron Tregarth, scudding over the sea-floor ooze, allowed himself to relax and feel at peace with the world.

After all, why not? The world was being very good to Ron Tregarth—always excepting the presence of that bundle of nastiness Graciela was required to treat like a decent person. Everything else was fine! The rush of water past the crystal shroud was soothing; he was with the woman he loved; he was on the eve of a major voyage in his sub—why, he thought with pleasure, he really had a great life! And so did everyone else, in those easy days in the Eighteen Cities beneath the sea . . . and no one dreamed that it might ever change, since they had not yet learned about Comet Sicara and the Eternal.

As they approached the West Rise of the great Mid-Atlantic Ridge Tregarth began to feel a little less at ease. They were so *naked*.

Free-sailing over the black and in hospitable deep made Tregarth uncomfortable. He was not a free-swimmer. He had spent as much of his life two thousand meters under the sea as any average inhabitant of the Eighteen Cities— which was to say, almost all of it. But Tregarth was a ship's captain. Although the deeps were the seas he sailed, there was always a stout submarine's hull between him and the crushing pressure of the blind dark. Tregarth was well able to handle the knowledge of the pressure, and that little itch of claustrophobia that twitched at the nerves of almost any normal human being when he let himself think of the two thousand meters of ocean between himself and the air. If you couldn't do that, you simply didn't ever become a sub commander.

But this was entirely different! The little sea-skid was already dodging among jagged, kilometer-high undersea peaks! Subs didn't stay near the sea bottom when they could help it. Who could know when some unsuspected sea-cliff or guyot might suddenly loom up in the sonar and rip through your plates? He stared uneasily into the black depths, and then back at the vast shapes sliding by on the sonar screen.

Then it got worse. The things they were approaching were no longer foothills.

The lubber ambassador had been complaining almost non-stop for the last four kilometers. When he caught a glimpse of the great peaks that lay ahead in the sonar screen he spluttered, "Stop! Are you trying to kill us? We'll crash into those things!"

"We're quite safe," Graciela assured him cheerily. "Aren't we, Ron? Tell him that we just have to follow the laser beam. . . ."

Tregarth managed a reassuring croak as he stared at the screen. His heart wasn't in it. What he saw was a submariner's nightmare. Peaks loomed before them like the Rocky

Mountains rising before the old covered-wagon pioneers, awesome, huge. But these peaks were closer, and far more deadly. Tregarth swallowed a warning noise that rose in his throat.

Graciela, hearing, gave him a perplexed glance, then said, "There's the pass we take. We'll go right through. Just be patient another moment—" She guided them expertly into an angled crevice in the cliffs. Tregarth no longer needed the sonar; in just the light from the skid's lamp he could see the vast cliffs they were snaking through. The sea-skid weaved and twisted. . . .

And then they were in the great deeps again.

The sonar showed the range they had passed behind them. Dimly ahead was the East Rise, just as huge and threatening. And in between, below them, was—nothing.

They were in the great central valley of the Mid-Atlantic Ridge.

Graciela cut the thrust. They hung there in their neutral-buoyancy suits, suspended over nothingness. She clicked the skid lights off. Apart from the blue-green beam off to one side, the only illumination was from the faint glow of instruments.

It was like being buried alive.

They were alone in an empty universe of blackness. Tregarth could not see what Graciela was doing, but he felt the sea-skid shudder as the valves admitted sea water to the flotation chambers, reducing its buoyancy. He felt the little craft sinking, bearing them with it. . . .

Then Graciela said, "Look! You can just begin to see the farms below us!"

Just emerging from the dark below them were faint, orange-yellow hints of light. Graciela powered the skid's thrusters just enough for steerage way. She spiraled them down, closer and closer. The lights became huge, free-floating globes of radiant energy, sunshine bright, and below them—

Below them were the broad hectares of farmland that made City Atlantica possible.

The undersea farms lay in wide, elevated valleys between the rises of the Mid-Atlantic Ridge. They were high enough to avoid the killing pressures of the great deeps themselves, where even Ron Tregarth's submarine dared not go. Their "soil" was ocean-bottom muck, rich with the detritus of eons of organic particles drifting down from the seabirds and the plankton and the masses of living things in the photic zone near the surface of the sea. Trapped in the bowl of this valley, the muck was full of life-giving chemicals, waiting only for light to make things grow through the miracle of photosynthesis.

The people of the Eighteen Cities had brought that light to the sea bottom.

With electric power generated from thermal springs, they rationed out "sunlight" that had never seen the sun. Twelve hours of light, twelve hours of darkness; even the sea bottom now had its diurnal rhythm. They were in the daylight half of the cycle now. The great globes shed life-giving illumination over the broad fields of the farm, letting the three voyagers see the regular rows of growing things that stretched out of sight.

Undersea plants did not have to struggle to grow, as land organisms did. They flourished. Given light and proper seeding, these subsea farms produced more biota per hectare than any Kansas wheatfield or shoreline marsh.

"Humph," said Ambassador Quagger. "What are those metal things? They look dangerous."

He was staring at the heavy machines the farmhands used—now, the squid would use—for repairing and building powerplant machinery, and to plow and tend and harvest the farms themselves. They did look almost like weapons, as Graciela thought, but hastened to reassure him. "No, they're simply tools," she began to explain, but the ambassador wasn't listening.

"And what's that thing on wheels?" he demanded.

Now he was pointing with one fat arm toward the wheel-hose pouring its cloudy material onto the farms.

"Oh, that's fertilizer, Ambassador Quagger. It's the wastes from City Atlantica, you see. We replenish the minerals we take from the sludge."

"With *sewage?*" he cried in horror. "Dear heaven! I've always known webfeet were filthy! But this is terrible; I don't see how I can eat another mouthful here!"

"But Ambassador Quagger," Graciela wailed, struggling to keep her tone reasonably polite, "there's nothing unhealthful here. Everything is irradiated before it leaves the dome. Not a single disease organism is left alive."

"It is disgusting," Quagger said severely. "Is there much more I have to look at?"

Tregarth bit back the remark he was eager to make. This lubber was not only offensive, he was *bored!* He didn't have the wit or understanding to realize what a triumph these subsea farms were! He seemed to be barely listening as Graciela proudly explained the facts of the benthiculture tracts below them. "Ten thousand hectares of farmland in this plot alone," she was chattering. "Five crops a year— there's no winter here, you know! And almost all the produce is edible, Ambassador Quagger. We're underwater, you see. The crops don't have to waste energy on building strong stalks and roots to fight the pull of gravity; there are few unusable parts to what we grow!"

"Yes, yes," whined the ambassador testily. "It's all very interesting, but, really, I am not at all comfortable in this confounded suit! Can't we get on to the next thing?"

But the next thing seemed no more interesting to the ambassador. Graciela took them over the area where the thermal springs broke through the surface. "This is our power," she announced proudly, pointing down at the flat bubble of Nexoø that covered half a hectare of sea bottom. "Inside that dome we trap the hot water from the thermal springs. We use the energy to generate electricity, which makes the oxy-metal hydride fuel cells that power everything we do; also, the springs are very rich in minerals of all sorts, which—"

"Which we buy from you," finished the ambassador, "because of course you people don't have the technology to refine the ores yourself. Yes, yes. But tell me something. If you use the electricity from these springs for everything, why do you demand fuel uranium from us? Are you secretly making bombs?"

"Bombs?" Graciela gasped, aghast at the shocking thought. "Oh, no, Ambassador Quagger! It's just that most of our long-range subs are still nuclear-powered. We certainly wouldn't make *bombs*."

"I hope not." The ambassador glowered. "It would be very unwise."

Graciela nodded and tried to resume her train of thought. "The ores from these springs are very rich in—"

"Oh, spare me," Quagger grunted testily. "The mayor has already provided me with detailed studies of the springs and so on. Young woman, is there anything else that is *worth* seeing? So far you've shown me nothing I didn't know about already!"

There was a distinct pause before Graciela answered. When she spoke, Tregarth could hear the strain in her voice as she made the effort to remain civil, and through the two-seventy helmet he could see the look of loathing on her face. But all she said was, "Very well, Mr. Ambassador, we'll start home. There is only one more thing I'd like you to see, and that's another farm—this one actually under cultivation."

She advanced the speed lever and sent the skid up and away from the thermal-springs dome, which quickly disappeared below them. In the sonar screen Tregarth saw those undersea peaks rising before them again and braced himself.

Then he saw something else and cried, "Graciela! What's that?"

The girl gave him a perplexed look and then bent her helmet to gaze at the screen. "Yes, there's a bright reflector there," she said. "Oh, wait—it's just the repeater station for the laser net, don't you see?"

Tregarth insisted, "Not that! I know a repeater when I see one. A moment ago there was something else—a little work submarine, I thought. But it's gone now."

"Oh, I don't think so," Graciela said doubtfully. "These are my farms, Ron. There's no work crew scheduled here now."

"I saw *something*," he insisted grimly; but peer as he might, whatever it was was gone from the sonar screen.

And the peaks were closer than ever. Graciela seemed hardly to notice them as she resumed her talk for the ambassador:

"In order to farm the sea bottom it must be planted and harvested, and, of course, the growing crops must be protected—otherwise the organisms that live there would simply eat them as fast as they grow."

"I suppose so," groaned the ambassador absently. "Is it much farther?"

"Just a few more minutes, Mr. Ambassador," Graciela promised. "This is where the squid come in."

Tregarth grinned to himself at the change in Graciela Navarro's tone. Now she was talking about her favorite subject, and her voice was excited, pleased—it did not matter that her only audience was Tregarth, who had already heard it all a thousand times, and their intrusive visitor from landside. She said proudly, "We've already trained them to patrol the farms while the crops are

growing. The squid aren't vegetarians; they eat the creatures that are pests for us. But now that we've actually
taught a few of them to communicate we can do better than
that! So far all our planting and harvesting has been done
by human beings, driving tractors and combines across the
sea bottom. But soon we'll have squid doing that! And
soon—but here we are, Mr. Ambassador. Just a
moment. . . ."

And she switched to the external speakers and called:
"Nessus! Graciela here! You come, yes!"

She had cut the thrust. They hung over the floating
lights of this new farm, the ripe crops visible in rows far
below.

"I don't see any squid," grumbled the Ambassador,
peering down.

"They're not here yet," Graciela explained, using the
suit speakers again. "Just past that rise the bottom falls off
sharply; there are deeps there we don't go into, but the
squid live there. One moment—" And as she turned back
to the external circuits her voice blasted through the sea:
"Nessus! You come, yes!"

Even though she was using the directional speakers, her
amplified voice, many decibels louder and an octave
deeper than her normal sweet, clear contralto, hurt
Tregarth's ears. He winced; and over the suit circuits the
Ambassador yelped, "Are you trying to deafen me?"

"I'm sorry, Mr. Ambassador," she said politely. "I'm
simply calling one of the farmhands."

"Farmhands," Quagger snorted. "Monsters, you mean!
And why are you lying to me?"

"Lie?" Graciela repeated wonderingly. Her tone wasn't
angry or offended, it was simply puzzled. But Tregarth was
suddenly furious; how dare this lump of blubber from
landside call the woman he loved a liar?

"You say you are calling him," Quagger sneered. "You

think I am so ignorant you can tell me anything at all, but I happen to know that squid are deaf. I have been well informed that they can't hear anything at all!"

"Oh," said Graciela, trying, but not quite succeeding, to repress a giggle. Tregarth too was smiling inside his two-seventy-degree helmet. "That's true enough, Mr. Ambassador. They are really deaf. They not only don't have ears, they don't even have an optic nerve area in their brains. It's impossible for a squid to hear anything at all—in fact, that has been an evolutionary advantage for them."

"What rot," the Ambassador snorted. "What sort of fool do you take me for? How can deafness be an evolutionary advantage?"

"Whales," Graciela explained succinctly. She went on to amplify: "The squid have one great natural enemy, the toothed whales. They feed on squid whenever they can—as well as anything else they can catch. Squid are their favorite prey, but the squid have the natural defense of deafness. You see, the toothed whales catch most of their prey by emitting loud bursts of sound—you've heard how much noise whales can make under the sea? Squids are harder for them, because they're deaf. The sounds don't stun the squid, as they do fish. If the squid could hear, those loud sounds would shock and disorient them, too, and perhaps the whales would have hunted them to extinction long ago."

"Humph," growled the ambassador. "Then, if you admit they can't hear, why do you expect me to believe you're calling one of the beasts?"

This time Graciela's laugh could not be repressed. It came loud and clear through the helmet speakers. "Sorry, Mr. Ambassador," she apologized, "but I thought you knew about the implants. Every one of our student squid carries a (sonic conversion implant). It's that metal boss on their mantles; you must have seen it. The implants convert sound into electrical nerve impulses, which are fed directly into the squid's brain. They don't perceive them as sound, of course—they don't even know what sound is. But they do receive complex patterns of stimulation, and after training they learn to interpret them. They can even talk back, as you've heard—that's what our squid school is for. Mr. Eustace McKen mentioned it when he introduced the mayor's valedictory address, but perhaps you weren't listening."

There was an irritated snort from the ambassador, as though he were preparing to say something even more insulting. He stopped in mid-breath, though. He became aware, as Tregarth had become aware a fraction of a second earlier, that something was happening below them.

An image appeared on the sonar screen. It flared brighter, hurtling up toward them, large and growing fast.

It moved so fast that Tregarth instinctively pawed the harpoon bow that hung by his side. He didn't draw it. He wouldn't have had time, even if that had been necessary. There was a quick, hard thrust of pressure from the water around them, and six meters of slate-blue, boneless flesh, followed by a stream of tentacles three times as long, torpedoed up out of the abyss and joined them. Where the tentacles joined the great head a staring eye, huger than Tregarth's helmet, contemplated the three human beings on their sea-skid.

One of the shorter tentacles curled back to manipulate a metal object embedded in the mantle. From the device an inhuman voice addressed them.

"Nessus here, Graciela," the voice of her favorite student announced. "Sea-jelly man here, why?"

There was an infuriated sputter from the ambassador, drowned out by Tregarth's bellow of laughter. *Sea-jelly man!* How well the name fit!

But Quagger was not at all amused. Before the spluttering could erupt into a roar, Graciela said hastily, "Nessus! Man friend, yes! You be friend, too, yes!"

The great, unwinking eye studied them, the tentacles wriggling slowly to keep their owner in position next to them, while the squid pondered that. Tregarth thought that Nessus in the school tank and Nessus here in the open sea were two different things. This was Nessus's own territory, and human beings, even the sea-dwelling people of the Eighteen Cities, were only interlopers. Then the tentacles stroked the communicator and the voice announced, "Sea-jelly man friend, not! Stink bad hot, yes!" And the squid, with a flirt of the rudimentary fins and a jet from his siphon, spun away. It hovered in the sea at the limit of visibility, the great tentacles writhing loosely.

"Graciela," Tregarth asked, "don't let him get away! Ask him if he knows anything about the work sub."

Graciela looked at him, perplexed. "What work sub? Oh, you mean the one you thought you saw back there? But I've already told you, dear, there couldn't have been a sub there—"

"Ask him," Tregarth said harshly.

"Oh, very well." She keyed in her speaker and called to the squid: "Nessus! I ask you question, yes! You see person steelfish this day, yes?"

"Nessus see person steelfish, not," the squid replied, the hollow voice booming sepulchrally.

"Ask him if he's sure," Tregarth said, but Graciela shook his head.

"Of course he's sure," she said. "Nessus would never lie."

"Get him to come a little closer, at least—"

But at that, at last the ambassador found his voice. Stabbing at the speaker controls, he hit the outside button and his furious words exploded into the sea. "Don't you dare!" he bellowed. "Don't let him get a bit closer! What do you mean by calling that dangerous creature here in the first place?"

"I only wanted you to see the squid out in the free ocean," Graciela said apologetically. "There's no danger, I promise—though I don't quite understand what Nessus means. Still, I thought—"

"You didn't think at all! That monster has already attacked me once! I warn you, if anything happens to me my government will surely retaliate!" The squid edged interestedly closer, listening to the unfamiliar words. Quagger flinched away. "Take me back to the dome at once!" he commanded. "I will make a report on this in the strongest terms. I promise you, you will regret this insult to the PanMack Consortium!"

Chapter

3

Once he had joined them, Nessus seemed reluctant to leave. He paced them as they rode the sea skid, all the long way back to City Atlantica, just inside the limits of visibility.

Tregarth didn't mind. Ambassador Quagger obviously did. He kept stubbornly silent, no matter what polite conversation Graciela offered. A true heir of the bad McKen line, Tregarth thought, the ones who had tyrannized the land areas of the Earth with their immense

PanMack complex of interlocked holding companies that were the true governments of all the western hemisphere.

As they saw the yellow-green lights of the dome begin to appear Tregarth said: "Graciela? Let's go by the dock area. I'd like to take a look at my ship—that is, if the ambassador doesn't mind."

Quagger said petulantly, "This trip is not intended for your sightseeing, Captain Tregarth! I wish to get back inside as quickly as possible."

"But it's as quick one way as the other," Graciela explained, changing the angle of the approach minutely. "Look, we're almost there."

And indeed they could already make out the spidery pipes and columns that surrounded the huge Nexø dome, lighted from behind by the lights of City Atlantica itself. Nestled in the clutter were half a dozen submarines, tiny shuttles and huge ocean-going transports, all locked to the dome by hatch-to-hatch seals. The nearest was the largest. It was a sleek, dark vessel more than a hundred meters long. Its running lights were on, indicating that there was a crew inside and its nuclear motors were being turned over for maintenance checks.

"That's mine!" Tregarth announced with pride. "The *Atlantica Queen*. She's loading now, and in twenty-four hours I'll be taking her to Baltimore Harbor. Want a ride home, Ambassador?"

"Certainly not," the fat man declared indignantly. "When I return it will be on my own air-yacht, *Quagger One*. And I won't be going to Baltimore—that's the domain of my cousin, General Marcus McKen. I'll fly nonstop to my own capital."

But he wasn't really looking at the cargo vessel. He was peering past it, at a stubbier, rounder vessel that gleamed with the bright shine of Nexø armor. Figures in neutral-buoyancy suits were moving around it, meticulously checking every joint and seam in the hull. The ambassador drew a shocked breath.

"Treachery! Wickedness!" he cried. "You've got an armored vessel there! That is an illegal weapon of offense! You have violated your pledged word that none of the Eighteen Cities would maintain a war fleet!"

The man seemed on the verge of apoplexy. Tregarth said soothingly, "Oh, no, Ambassador, that's not military armor. We don't have warships in the Eighteen Cities— what would we use them for?"

"I can see it with my own eyes!" Quagger cried. "Next thing you'll be using it for treacherous attacks on our peaceful PanMack surface vessels!"

Peaceful surface vessels! When everyone knew that the PanMack fleet carried rocket launchers and laser-guns! Tregarth opened his mouth to respond bitterly, but Graciela was ahead of him. "But the *Thetis* is a research vessel, Mr. Ambassador," she said reasonably. "It's going to dive deeper than any of our regular ships can—why, Ron's own executive officer, Vera Doorn, is going to command it. To study the deeps, you know—don't you remember, I told you about it? That's why it needs the extra armor. Any of our other ships would be crushed at once."

"Really?" sneered the Ambassador. "Supposing that what you say is true, can you guarantee that none of your malcontents would seize it and use it for military purposes?"

"We don't *have* any malcontents," Graciela offered, and Tregarth cut in:

"That couldn't happen," he said positively.

"But I think it could," the Ambassador said. "You people are terribly careless. Where are your security forces here? Anyone could simply come in. You've already let some unknown persons steal a work sub, after all!"

The man was full of surprises, Tregarth thought darkly. Graciela said worriedly, "Oh, you mustn't think that. It's true that one of the work subs is missing, but it was almost certainly a mechanical failure—the moorings must have parted, and it drifted away. That was weeks ago—"

But Tregarth had a more important question. "How did you know that?" he demanded harshly.

"Oh, one hears stories," Quagger said evasively. "And then you were quite interested in the sub you thought you saw, out in the deeps, weren't you?"

"I did think it might be the missing one," Tregarth admitted.

"Anyway," Graciela put in, "it couldn't have been *stolen.* Someone would have had to steal it, and no one is missing from City Atlantica."

"Humph," said the ambassador. It was his favorite word, it seemed, and what it meant was that he did not wish to pursue the discussion any farther. Then he gasped. "That animal of yours—what's he doing now?"

There was genuine alarm in his voice. As Graciela and Tregarth turned they saw the reason for it. The squid, Nessus, had drifted close to the *Thetis,* and he was acting oddly. The long tentacles were jerking spasmodically as he slid dangerously close to the suited workmen, who were now maneuvering stress-testing instruments across the hull of the research ship. But it was not the workmen that Nessus's great eyes were fixed on; it was the stubby cylinder of fuel that was being guided into the engine-room hatch.

"No, Nessus!" Graciela shouted. "No touch! Danger here, yes! Go away, yes!"

The squid writhed convulsively. The torpedo-shaped body turned, the great eyes now fixed on Graciela, but the tentacles still struggled toward the cylinder of fuel.

Then, slowly, Nessus turned and slid away.

Graciela drew a deep breath. "They're refueling the ship," she explained. "It's high-energy nuclear fuel, and for some reason the squid are very sensitive to the presence of radionuclides lately. It seems to confuse their reflexes. I'm really sorry if it frightened you, Mr. Ambassador—"

But Quagger was in high dudgeon. "Sorry! Just as you were sorry when the beast attacked me in the pool! I've had enough of this, young woman! I want to go back inside the dome at once!"

Since they had entered by the cargo docks, Tregarth took advantage of the chance to pay a fast trip to the *Atlantica Queen*, promising to join them in the undersea museum.

When he did there was a new look in his eye. He listened quietly to Graciela's running account of the exhibits, but his eyes never left Quagger.

The ambassador was clearly bored. He kept glancing at his watch as Graciela pointed out one bit of salvaged treasure after another. When she reached the seventh amphora, the Mediterranean wine jugs of classical times, he erupted, "No more pots, I beg you! No rotten wood that once might've been a ship's keel, no rusty metal. Trash is trash, young woman. On the land we know enough to throw it out. We don't fill museums with it."

"But, Ambassador," Graciela protested, "these relics are precious. Look at this display, for instance!" And she pointed to a holographic picture, cloudy and remote. The picture certainly showed something. Whatever it was, it glittered, in that abyssal gloom where everything else was dark. It was surely an artifact, but the picture was so fuzzy no one could quite say what. "Taken with a robot sub," Graciela said proudly. "It may be a century old or more— perhaps a piece of a broken-up naval submarine from one of the great World Wars!"

The ambassador scowled at it. "I wonder if its nuclear

warheads are still operational," he said. "But you don't really know if it's a war sub at all, do you? You're just guessing."

"We won't be guessing much longer," Graciela declared. "That's one of the things Vera Doom is scheduled to examine, when she takes the *Thetis* down deeper than any of our subs has ever gone before . . ."

Ron Tregarth had almost stopped listening. This whole discussion could have been written out in advance, he thought; Graciela was certainly making no impression on the ambassador. And there was the question that he had to ask Quagger.

Lost in thought, Tregarth hung back as Graciela and the fat lubber moved away along the rows of exhibits. He gazed at the hologram of the mysterious derelict vessel the robot sub had photographed. It was certainly worth investigating, thought. He almost envied his former executive officer her opportunity to command the *Thetis* on its voyage of exploration. But what his mind was full of was what Jill Danner had told him on his quick trip to the *Atlantica Queen*. What were the PanMacks up to this time?

He caught up with the others. They were still arguing. Graciela was showing Quagger the skeleton of the Carthaginian trireme they had recovered only a year earlier, on the Iberian Abyssal Plain, far on the eastern side of the Rise. "—a warship," she was saying, "probably escorting a convoy of freight galleys from the tin mines in Cornwall. That's history, Mr. Ambassador! Your great-uncle, Eustace McKen, founded this museum. He used to call the deeps the time-vault of the world—colder and calmer than the shallow seas, with no wave action and few currents to demolish sunken objects—"

"My great-uncle Eustace McKen," said Quagger coldly, "was crazy. Just like you people, with your silly museum and your foolish deep-sea explorations."

"But—but that's scientific *research*," Graciela explained. "There are things in the sea that have never been properly studied, especially below the three-kilometer level. Our scientists say—"

"Scientists!" he scoffed, the kewpie-doll face contorted in a grimace of disdain. "No wonder you people are so backward! You waste your resources on idle curiosity." He glared at Graciela. "We keep our scientists *useful*," he barked. "None of this airy-fairy egghead foolishness about science for science's sake. We want *results*. Better fuels! New machines! More powerful weapons! That's what science is good for, not wasting time and money poking into things that don't matter to any sensible person."

And Tregarth saw his chance. He stepped forward and cleared his throat.

He asked politely, "Does space travel matter?"

The effect on Dr. Ambassador Simon McKen Quagger was shattering. His pudgy little jaw dropped. His tiny eyes bulged. "Wha— What are you—" he gasped, and tried again: "What the devil are you talking about?"

"It's just that I've heard some rumors," Tregarth said easily. "My friends on the *Atlantica Queen* were telling me about radio reports from one of our other ships. They say you people are going to send up a space exploration probe again, only this time you're sending a ship to a comet."

He saw that Graciela was staring at him in wide-eyed wonder. "A space probe, Ron? After all these years? And to a comet? Oh, no, the lubbers wouldn't—"

Tregarth gave her the faintest shake of his head. She stopped in the middle of the sentence, waiting to hear what Quagger would reply.

The fat man blustered, "Where did you hear that? That's classified information, young man! You could be arrested just for mentioning Comet Sicara. It's a clear violation of every security regulation—" He broke off, remembering that he was where the security regulations of the PanMack Corporation had no effect.

He changed tack, making an effort to be good-humored. The strain showed. "Well, anyway," he said, smiling unctuously, "of course we are not such savages as to stop *all* scientific research. We simply insist that it be important."

"And this comet—what did you say its name was, Sicara?" Tregarth persisted. "Is there some reason why it is important?"

The ambassador's poise had returned. The little pig face was bland as he said carelessly, "Oh, you know how it is. One can't keep up with all the technical details. But, yes, there's some reason why it is worth the expense. I'm not sure I remember what the reason is, exactly."

Then he glanced at his watch again. "My," he said affably, "it's almost time for me to make my presentation —another little bust of myself, just a token of thanks for the wonderful hospitality you people have shown me, this one for the City itself instead of just your dome. So I think I'd better go get a copy of my impromptu remarks from my amanuensis, Newt Bluestone, ha-ha."

But Ron Tregarth didn't laugh.

He didn't even follow the ambassador as he waddled away on his tree-stump legs. He was deep in thought.

It was the first time he had ever heard the true name of Comet Sicara.

And neither he nor anyone else had yet heard of . . . though they had very nearly seen . . . the Eternal.

Chapter
4

Graciela Navarro's duty as tour guide to the lubber ambassador ended when the man made his final official appearance. For a wonder, Quagger did not complain about a thing. Appearing before a small gathering of the leading citizens of City Atlantica, he made a point of thanking Graciela politely. "Not only did she show me everything of any importance," he declared, "but Ms. Navarro was unfailingly courteous and informative throughout—as well," he added, beaming at her, "as being outstandingly beautiful." Graciela wriggled uncomfortably; she did not like the way the man was looking at her. Tregarth, by her side, liked it even less.

Quagger went on: "Since I must leave early in the morning I would like to thank all of you for your wonderful hospitality. And so I would like to leave you a small token of my appreciation—a bust created by one of our most capable sculptors. Newt!" The ambassador snapped his fingers and Newt Bluestone came forward with the gleaming metal object.

Tregarth could not make up his mind whether to laugh or scowl. The effrontery of the man! As if anyone would want to look day after day at that petulant small face on the huge, blubbery head! The bust was an exact copy of the one he had placed in the squid school; and, in the same way, Quagger insisted on placing it where he was standing. "Not in a so-called place of honor in your museum," he said, his oily smile directed at everyone in the audience, "but here, at the base of your dome, to symbolize how fundamental it is to all of us that our relationships should continue in friendship and cooperation forever! Pictures, Newt!" he added sharply, beckoning to the mayor and to Graciela. "Mustn't forget our responsibility to posterity! Make sure you get good ones of me with these two lovely ladies . . ."

An hour later Graciela and Ron were back at the squid school, and Graciela was splashing industriously about the pool, trying to rinse off the memory of that pudgy arm held so familiarly around her waist. Only two of the squid were with her, the young female, Holly, and an even younger male who had not yet. been given a name.

Tregarth waited patiently. He had already visited his ship and knew that everything was proceeding well without him. He was impatient to get back to it—not so impatient, however, that he was willing to give up any more of these last few hours with the woman he loved. How pretty she was in her brief swimskins, lalluping in and out among the swirly tentacles of her students! Tregarth marveled at how important Graciela Navarro had become to him, in so short a time. It was less than six months since they'd first spoken to each other in any personal way. Nowhere nearly as much as six months spent together, either, because for four of those months he had been away on one of his voyages. In that time they'd been with each other hardly more than a couple of weeks. They had become lovers on his next stay in Atlantica, would become more than that if only she would listen to him.

Well, she did listen. Carefully and lovingly. But the answer was always the same.

Graciela spoke sharply to the squid. Obediently they

began practicing with the heavy agricultural equipment. She pulled herself up in front of Tregarth, shaking water from her hair, and said, "Ron, I've been thinking—"

"So have I," he interrupted, and tried one more time: "Let's get married. Today!"

And one more time she said, fondly and regretfully, but firmly all the same: "Oh, Ron. If only we could! But you've got your life and I've got mine. . . . No, I mean I've been thinking about Ambassador Quagger. He's up to something, I'm sure of it. He wasn't really interested in anything I showed him, or anything else in City Atlantica. There's some other reason he came here."

"Quagger," Tregarth said definitively, "is a loathsome animal. I wouldn't trust him as far as I could throw him, and heaven knows that's not far! But what could he be up to here?"

Graciela said positively, "I don't know, but I'm *sure.* What about that space rocket? There's something false about that. I know it isn't pure research, whatever he says. And then he's always digging into things. How did he know about the missing work sub?"

"Someone could have mentioned it to him," Tregarth said justly. "It's not really a secret. Anyway, I reported my possible sighting to Sandor Tisza, so he'll put it on the communications net and everyone will keep an eye out for it."

"Well," said Graciela. "I just don't like him. I'll be glad when he's gone and we can—oh, damn you, Holly!" she cried, seeing where one of the squid was trying to take away a sea-plow from the stubborn tentacles of the smaller one. "Be right back!"

And she splashed away, shouting orders at her charges.

Tregarth watched her longingly. She was so wonderful with the squid—well, wonderful in every way there was, to be sure, but particularly with the animals. They would obey her when they would listen to no one else.

And they would talk back! That was the true marvel. For the first time in all the ages the human race had another species to talk to! Mankind had tried and failed with dogs, apes and dolphins; had attempted to unravel the simple languages of migratory birds and the food-locating dance vocabulary of the honeybees. But with the squid there could be actual *conversation!* True, between *Homo sapiens* and *Architeuthis dux* the dialogue permitted only a sparse vocabulary and a restrictive grammar. But it was still a wonder.

The language had started partly as Ameslan and partly as symbols—the natural communication of squid to squid, it seemed, (was almost) entirely through changes in the coloration of their skins. But they had learned to communicate with symbols, flash cards and blocks in the beginning. For a time, like Gulliver's Laputans, the first linguists among the squid carried much of their vocabularies on their backs. (But the improved voice box implants) had eased that.

Tregarth wondered if the squid had any idea of what they had got themselves into when they finally established communication with mankind.

Certainly they gained little from it! The squid were kings of the deep sea; only the toothed whales were dangers to them, and the squid could go where even the whales could not follow. He watched Graciela dart between the two squid, tugging the plow away from Holly, shouting orders as she did so. Either one of them could destroy her in a moment, he knew. There was so much strength in those vast, inhuman bodies! And they seemed nearly indestructible. Every time one of them entered the lock of the school dome they suffered a quick reduction of pressure from the two-thousand-meter depth to sea-level. Why didn't their whole bodies explode? A human being in such a drastic transition would die instantly; so would any of the other sea creatures, fish or jellies or crustaceans. . . .

He turned to see Jill Danner, his new executive officer, coming toward him with a list of waybills to sign. As she greeted him she glanced at the bust of Dr. Ambassador Quagger, the petulant little face scowling down at the molluscs being trained. "Oh, God," Jill exclaimed. "Did he put one here, too?"

"Afraid so, Jilly," said Tregarth, handing the sheaf of documents back to her. "Any further word on that PanMack space probe?"

She shook her head. "The mayor has asked the monitors on the surface platform to check all message logs for the past two days. Maybe there's something there. But if so I haven't heard about it; just that first report from a City PanNegra sub off Port Canaveral that the people from *Atlantica Princess* passed on. All they knew was that a space rocket was being prepared for launch, and there was some talk about a comet."

"So the lubbers were trying to keep it secret," Tregarth said thoughtfully.

"I guess," said Jill. "Captain? Maybe they got it wrong about the comet. Isn't it possible it was just a regular supply rocket for one of the oneill habitats?"

"Not a chance," Tregarth said positively. Only four of the original habitats had ever been launched, only one entirely finished and fully staffed. That was the first, Habitat Valhalla, and even it had never fulfilled the bright hopes of the more generous age that built them. Few of those eager early settlers of space had learned to enjoy all the limits and discomforts of existence in the big air-filled containers they came to call tin cans; most had lost heart and come back home to Earth. Only a few hundred were left even in Valhalla, where there was room for tens of thousands. "You saw the report yourself," he said. "This is a deep space rocket. Wherever it's going, it's out past the Moon. Chasing after a comet is as likely as anything else. And anyway," he finished, "if it had been any normal kind

of launch Quagger wouldn't have acted so shaken up about
it."

"I guess we're all a little shaken up," Jill sighed. "What
was that about one of the squid going crazy outside the
Atlantica Queen?"

"Oh, nothing serious. You were loading a fuel capsule,
and I guess it sensed the radioactivity. So it went all weird,
the way they do when they feel radiation."

He frowned out over the pool, where Graciela had
persuaded both squid to put the plowing and harvesting
tools away. Now they were taking up an array of sensing
instruments—sound amplifiers that fed into the stimula-
tors on their mantles, stubby telescopes built to the structure of a squid's eye and optically filtered for maximum
vision in the murky deep.

Graciela swam up to them. She greeted Jill Danner and
lifted her face to Tregarth's for a moist kiss. "I'll just be a
few more minutes," she apologized. "They've been
spooked about something and I want to calm them down
before I leave."

"Ron's going to get jealous of those things," Jill Danner
laughed, then sobered as she caught a glimpse of the
expression on his face.

But it was not anything she had said that had prompted
it.

The two squid had followed Graciela, puppylike, to the
far end of the pool. Now they were acting spooked indeed.
The unnamed young one had dropped its sonic system and
was twisting erratically, like a man trembling with anger.
The other, Holly, had rocketed directly to the head of the
pool, just under the ugly bust of Dr. Ambassador Simon
McKen Quagger, and its longest tentacles were creeping
out of the water toward the greasily smirking bust.

"Holly, no!" Graciela cried. "Stay in pool, yes! Touch
metal person thing, not, *not!*"

She splashed over to the squid and drove them back to

the far end of the pool, then returned to Tregarth and Jill Danner. "Something's wrong," she complained. "I've never seen them act this way except around radiation, like the fuel capsule yesterday—"

She broke off, and turned to stare at the bust of Simon McKen Quagger.

"Oh, Ron!" she cried.

"What is it?" Jill Danner demanded anxiously, and Tregarth said grimly:

"It's radiation, Jilly."

"Radiation? You mean that hideous little bust? Do you think—?"

But Tregarth was already on his feet. "It doesn't matter what I think," he said. "We're going to find out, one way or another, for sure!"

Ninety minutes later the mayor met them at the City Atlantica dome lock. She was seething. Even before Tregarth and the others got out of their two-seventy-degrees helmets she was crying, "He did it here, too! As soon as I got your message I had the other bust sonar-blipped and radiation-checked. The same thing! There's a nuclear bomb inside it, all right. Nuclear! Careful, Frank," she warned, as Frank Yaro, the tech chief of City Atlantica and the closest thing they had to be a bomb-disposal expert, took the ugly coppery bust from Tregarth's hands.

"Piece of cake," Yaro said briefly. "I'll take it to the shop and we'll have it defused in five minutes, just like the other one. But it's a nuclear bomb, all right. If it had been triggered it could have blown the dome right out."

Jill Danner shuddered. "Things are getting kind of nasty," she complained. "I'd better get to the ship, Captain —we're supposed to sail in two hours!"

"Do it," Tregarth agreed, as he watched Frank Yaro bear the deadly thing tenderly away. He said grimly, "At least Quagger's not likely to set it off while he's still in the dome."

The mayor nodded. "He's waiting in the anteroom to my office. Had the nerve to complain about being rousted out in the middle of the night, if you please! But actually he wasn't asleep; he was sending coded messages through the communications center to his plane that's coming to pick him up." She led the way to the lift, pausing to say over her shoulder, "Oh, and I had a response from the *Princess;* I queried them as soon as you told me about this comet thing."

She passed a sheet of flimsy blue paper to Tregarth, who scanned it rapidly. The *Atlantica Princess* was sister ship to his own *Atlantica Queen,* just entering port in Galveston with the remainder of its cargo of sea-grown food and pharmaceuticals, and it had left Port Canaveral two days earlier.

Tregarth read the answer out loud, his voice puzzled: "All anybody aboard knows is that they've launched a rocket to intercept a comet they call Sicara. There is a rumor that the rocket is armed with nuclear weapons. One of the crew remembers hearing something about a Tunguska event, whatever that is.'" Tregarth looked up from the paper, scowling. "Nuclear weapons! And what's a Tunguska event?" he demanded, as the lift stopped at the dome's topmost level.

The mayor led the way through her private entrance into her office. "I asked the same question," she said somberly. "So Frank pulled the data out of my terminal. It's on the screen now."

There was not just a single entry on the screen of the mayor's data terminal, there were three.

The first was headed "Tunguska Event", and it was brief. It said only that in 1908 some sort of comet nucleus, wandering tiny asteroid, or large meteorite had fallen to the Earth and impacted the tundra near Tunguska, Siberia.

It was not a very rare event in the long history of the Earth, since craters all over the planet's surface showed where such objects had struck many times before. As such things went, it was not even a very large one, though it had flattened fifty thousand square kilometers of forest and killed every living thing nearby. The only thing that made the Tunguska event unusual was that it had happened late in Earth's history, at a time when human beings had evolved far enough to be puzzled by it; and the entry ended with, *See Impacts, extraterrestrial.*

"Impacts, extraterrestrial" was much longer. The print-out catalogued thousands of craters—some still visible on the surface, most long since worn away by rain and wind and tectonic activity, so that all that showed they had existed was such minerals like "shocked quartz" that proved something had once struck very hard. And it listed as collateral data something called *K-T extinction.*

The "K-T extinction" was the real shocker. Translated, it referred to the succession of the Cretaceous Period by the Tertiary, during which three-quarters of the large animals on Earth (including the dinosaurs) became extinct. And the extinction was linked with a small, thin deposit of iridium at that geological level, almost world-wide. Iridium that seemed to have come from outer space; brought, it seemed quite likely, in the star-stuff of some large object, like the one in Tunguska, but far huger.

Tregarth looked up into Graciela's eyes. "Comet Sicara," he breathed.

"Exactly," said the mayor somberly. "Do you know what I think? I think Quagger and the rest of the lubber leadership—the ones high enough to be allowed to know anything—are scared witless about this Comet Sicara. I think he planted those bombs as blackmail, to force us to take them in if the danger turns out to be real."

"Bastard," said Tregarth flatly.

"At least," the mayor agreed. "I'll bring him in now. But be careful, please—remember, he has diplomatic immunity, whatever he's done."

"I'll remember," said Tregarth. "But he isn't immune to a punch in the nose!"

But no one punched anyone. No one had any excuse.

Dr. Ambassador Simon McKen Quagger came in with an outsized smile on his undersized face, as though no one had interrupted his sleep or insulted his dignity or caused him any inconvenience at all. "My dear Madam Mayor," he cried, lunging forward to grasp her hand. With the other he wagged a playful finger at her. "It was naughty of you to send guards to bring me here! Remember, I'm an ambassador." He turned to the others, crying, "Ah, here is the sweet young Graciela! And, uh, Captain, uh—I have good news for you today! The menace of Comet Sicara is ended, due to the valor and skill of the PanMack Peace Wing!"

The mayor, whose mouth had already opened to talk frostily of bombs, blinked and closed her mouth again. Captain us— was less polite. "What the hell are you talking about?" he demanded.

"I'm talking about Comet Sicara," Quagger caroled. "Oh, it did give us a nasty turn, I admit. The thing was a monster! It could have caused immense destruction if it had been permitted to strike the Earth. Fortunately, we of PanMack have been aware of the problem for some weeks, and—"

"Hold it," snapped Tregarth. "If the whole Earth was in danger, why didn't you people announce it?"

"Why, because of the danger of *panic*, my dear fellow," said the fat man, looking both surprised and hurt. "We didn't want to spread *panic*. Good heavens, can you imagine what the lower classes might have done if they'd known that there was some chance of destroying the entire land area of the Earth? Riots! Looting! An end to all order!

No," he said, wagging the blubbery head severely, "we could not risk informing the lower classes while there was still danger."

As a member of those "lower classes", he was sure, Tregarth's temperature was rising. "Why do you say 'was'?" he demanded.

"Why, because the danger is over," Quagger said with pride. "That rocket launch you asked about? Yes, there was one. It was successful. Our brave spacemen reached the comet and completely demolished it!"

"With nuclear weapons," said Tregarth.

The smile flickered on Quagger's face. He regarded Tregarth shrewdly. "I see you don't miss much, Captain Tregarth," he said, and this time there was no pretense of forgetting his name. "Someone has been quite thoughtless about speaking of classified matters, and I will certainly have it looked into when I return. However," he said, beaming once more, "the nasty thing is gone. It was spotted several weeks ago. A huge clump of frozen gases—a good many million tons of them, the scientist fellows claim. But now it is just a cloud of small particles." He frowned slightly. "They do say some of the particles will strike the Earth's atmosphere," he added, "but only in small pieces over a period of time. Most will simply burn up and disappear. That too is something I must look into very soon. I don't see why they couldn't simply wipe it out entirely, but they're always making excuses about what they can and can't do, if you let them."

The little eyes looked angry for a moment. Then Quagger beamed. "Well, Madam Mayor," he said brightly, "I suppose that was what you wanted to ask about. So there's no further reason for me to stay down here in this dreadf— in your beautiful City Atlantica. If you have no further questions, then—"

The mayor raised an implacable hand. She no longer looked like a fussy, harassed middle-aged woman. She was every bit a high official, exercising the stern duties of her office, and she was looking as though carved out of steel at that moment. "I do have one question," she said.

"Oh, really? Well, perhaps my amanuensis could help you, but I personally am quite tired after what has been an extraordinarily fatiguing—"

She shook her head. "Not your amanuensis, Ambassador Quagger. You have to answer this one yourself. Tell me. Why did you plant bombs in my city?"

The change in Ambassador Quagger was almost as remarkable as the mayor's. He was no longer a comic fat man. He was something far more sinister.

He stood silent for a moment, peering at her. In her office at the top of City Atlantica's dome, with the black sea with all its might and menace just outside the Nexø shell, there was no sound at all.

Then he said softly, "Bombs, Madam Mayor?"

"Nuclear bombs," Tregarth rasped. "Hidden in those hideous busts of yours. They're defused now, you might be interested to know."

"I see," said Quagger thoughtfully, nodding his great head. Then he smiled, not at all a pleasant smile. "I think," he said, "that there's really no reason for me to wait until morning to take my departure, is there? So if you'll excuse me—"

"After you answer our questions," the mayor said firmly. "Nuclear bombs are weapons of terrorism. People have been shot for far less."

Quagger recoiled. "Don't forget my diplomatic status!" he squeaked.

Mayor McKen said grimly, "Your diplomatic status does not give you the right to blow up our cities. However," she added, glancing at Tregarth, "he does have it, Ron. You may not touch him."

The ambassador took a deep breath. Then the fat little face wrinkled into a condescending sneer. "The worst you can do," he observed cheerfully, "is expel me. That's quite all right, since I was going anyhow. Of course, speaking for the record, I deny all your allegations." Quagger paused for a moment, regarding them blandly. Then his expression hardened. "But, also for the record, perhaps I should bring up the question of your lawless behavior at this time."

The Mayor gasped indignantly. "Our lawless *what?*"

"I am referring," squeaked Quagger ominously, "to your practice of giving shelter to escaped criminals."

The Mayor was caught off guard. She blinked at him. "What criminals?" she demanded.

"The infamous terrorist Sandor Tisza!" Quagger cried in triumph. "He is wanted for many felonies by the governments of Common Europe, as well as outrages against my own colleagues in the PanMack Consortium. Don't deny that you are hiding him here. I saw him with my own eyes!"

The mayor said tautly, "We haven't made any secret of Dr. Tisza's presence here. He is not a terrorist. He is a refugee."

"He's a criminal!" Quagger shrilled. "He assaulted peaceful citizens in Budapest!"

The Mayor said firmly, "He escaped from their prisons, yes. At that time the secret police tried to recapture him, and there was a struggle. He took no lives, Ambassador Quagger! In any case, that is a matter for the Common Europeans, not for you and PanMack."

"Not at all! He committed fraud when he left the PanMack Consortium!"

"No," said the mayor, shaking her head, "that won't wash, either. He slipped past your border guards to escape, but that is no crime in City Atlantica. We have already rejected your request for his deportation. That is ancient history. The question now is what excuse you have for planting bombs in my city."

Quagger stared at her fiercely for a silent moment. Then he shrugged. His expression smoothed back into a bland smile. He said, "But I have already told you that I don't know anything about any bombs, Madam Mayor! No," he added, raising a hand to stifle their protests, "I cannot be certain there was no explosive material in the busts of myself I presented to you. I didn't cast the things myself, after all! There are always malcontents in the lower classes. Perhaps some treacherous factory workers had some imagined grievance against City Atlantica—"

"That's a lie," Tregarth said harshly.

Quagger glanced at him inquiringly. There was silence for a moment, then Quagger smiled. He pressed his pudgy palms together, touching the fingertips meditatively to his lips, and said, "Let me tell you a made-up story. It should be interesting—if it were true, that is. But it isn't. I'm making it up."

"You've already shown us you're good at that," Tregarth snapped.

Quagger shrugged. The movement rippled through his blubbery arms and shoulders almost like the writhing tentacles of Nessus. "Your opinion really doesn't matter, does it?" he demanded sweetly. "In any case, this is the story. Once upon a time—let us pretend—the sovereign administrators of a certain power had reason to believe that they were threatened by a great natural catastrophe. They had an obligation to save their countries, wouldn't you agree? And these people—these made-up people, remember—might have felt it necessary to make sure that certain, ah, other areas which were not in the same danger should accept their natural humanitarian responsibility to offer shelter to the threatened ones. Is it an interesting story so far?" he asked politely.

Tregarth's snort was not an answer, but Quagger nodded as though it had been what he expected. "So they perhaps had two options. One way would be to transport themselves to the orbital habitats. Perhaps they considered that, but life there would be very hard and unrewarding; that would be only a last resort. Better to find places where civilization of a sort did exist, even if only on a rudimentary level. Places where they could live for a few years, while the trouble on the surface sorted itself out—"

"What about the bombs?" Mayor McKen demanded.

The piggy little eyes widened. "Bombs? I haven't said anything about any so-called bombs. I've just been making up a story. . . . But if there *were* bombs, or let us say some way of enforcing justice, would you say they were without cause? Isn't there a sort of law of the sea about such things? If you see a shipwreck, aren't you obliged to help the survivors? Perhaps it might be inconvenient for you, but in that case wouldn't the survivors have a right to insist? Of course," he added virtuously, "no one would expect to have to use a weapon to get simple justice! You would expect that those who could offer aid would do so without question . . . but you might do well to have a weapon ready, just in case they weren't."

Mayor McKen had had enough. "That'll do, Quagger," she said, an edge to her voice. "You are formally expelled from City Atlantica as persona non grata. You are to leave at once, with all your belongings."

"But of course, dear lady," smiled Ambassador Quagger. "I was quite ready to go now anyway."

The Eternal had paused.

Twin necessities had drawn it here: the foreseen predicaments of the planet's life evolving into the shadow of extinction, and its own demanding dilemmas. It was itself truly deathless, its patterns of memory and mind securely stored in cells immune to time and change, but its great interstellar vessel was merely metal, the old hull scarred and eroded from voyaging too far, the drive and navigation gear worn and damaged beyond further service, even the emergency fuel depleted.

Waiting for mind to evolve, for crisis to come, for the aid it required, it had sunk to rest on the floor of an ocean deep, remote from all the freakish hazards of the land. Icy brines made a shielding blanket over it, a safeguard against the accidents of open space and the waves and tides of surface seas, a shelter from suns and storms and any mischief from the not-yet-thinking creatures swarming overhead.

An asylum, almost, from time itself.

The old ship was still secure against tectonic shocks and the pressure upon it. No light could reach it. The brines around it barely moved. All that touched it was the slow particulate rain of cosmic stuff and the wind-borne dusts from the barren lands emerging from the seas and the microscopic debris of dying life drifting down from living waters far above. That accumulating ooze thickened to cover it, slowed the erosion, healed the scars, screened it from any new harm.

It waited there, a long round hill in the dark ocean floor, resting through the fleeting generations evolving in the sunlit surface seas and on the drying land. Sometimes it sensed dim things crawling in the mud or hunting their poor blind prey in the dark water over it, but these were always too dull and dumb for it to reach. It kept on waiting, though the geologic ages while new species rose and fell. Yet never with impatience, because that pause was the merest moment in its Eternal time.

When thinking things came down to reach it, the pause had ended.

Chapter
5

The mayor herself escorted Dr. Ambassador Simon McKen Quagger to the shuttle submarine that would take him away from City Atlantica.

They were not alone. They were in the docks area. Outside the crystal dome of Nexø the shuttle hung next to Tregarth's own *Atlantica Queen,* as well as Vera Doorn's *Thetis* and several smaller craft. Half the crews of the subs were standing in a knot, watching silently. They knew what had happened. The word had spread through City Atlantica like brushfire. Tregarth, holding Graciela Navarro's arm, nodded heavily to Vera Doorn and his executive officer, Jill Danner. His own departure was less than an hour away.

"Goodbye, Mr. Ambassador," the mayor said formally. She even extended her hand to shake his in farewell.

Quagger made no pretense of cordiality any more. He didn't shake the mayor's hand. He didn't speak to her at all. He simply snapped to his secretary, "Get those bags on board, Newt! Oh, I can't wait to breathe the free air of the land once more!" Newt Bluestone staggered after him with the last of the Ambassador's luggage and turned to give the small group from City Atlantica an oddly apologetic look.

Bluestone might have been a fairly decent person, Tregarth thought, if he had happened to live in a decent world. The ridiculous uniform did not make him look fearsome, as a warrior of the Peace Service was supposed to look. It only made him look uncomfortable.

When the lock closed behind them Tregarth snapped, "Good riddance. (That man deserves to be put away, like any dangerous animal.")

The mayor looked at him thoughtfully. "He's evil," she agreed. Then, sorrowfully, "The bad McKens! They're all alike—even—"

She stopped there, firmly closing her mouth. The mayor rarely spoke of the McKen she had married, whose name she still bore. Outside the dome Quagger's shuttle was leaving its dock, slanting sharply upward toward the landing platform on the surface where his plane waited. She stared unseeingly after the craft.

Graciela said tentatively, "But—well, whatever their reasons might have been, don't you think we owe them something?"

"For what? For trying to destroy us?" her lover demanded.

"For what they did in space, Ron. If this Comet Sicara was as dangerous as they say, and they blew it up to make it harmless, then they've helped us too."

"They did it to save themselves! It's the lubbers who would have suffered, not us!"

"I don't think so, Ron," she said. "Maybe we wouldn't have been affected at once, but certainly there was danger. If the comet had landed in the sea anywhere near us—"

She didn't finish the sentence. She didn't have to. She just reached out and touched the chill, crystal-clear Nexø dome, the few centimeters that sheltered them from the crushing sea. Every one of them saw the same mind's-eye picture of the dome split open and the terrible might of two kilometers of ocean hammering in to demolish their world.

Tregarth shook his head. "Don't forget those bombs! We owe them nothing at all."

The mayor sighed, blinked and smiled at them. She put

her hand on Tregarth's arm, looking up at him. "It's over now, Ron," she said. "We can go about our business. And my first business," she declared grimly, "is to make a full report of this to the mayors of the rest of the Eighteen Cities! I wonder how many of them had sudden visits from high-ranking lubbers this week!"

And then, all too soon, it was the *Atlantica Queen*'s turn to leave the docks.

Graciela had not been able to let the sub go without one last peek inside. She could see nothing of the holds, bulging with food concentrates and sea delicacies for the hungry, as well as for the merely gluttonous, dwellers on the surface of the land. She looked into Ron's tiny captain's cabin, a cot barely wide enough for his huge frame, and went with him to the main bridge, where Jill Danner was running through the pre-departure checklist.

As she looked out through the wide Nexø navigation shield she saw the squid, Nessus, hanging just outside, his great eye regarding her emotionlessly. She gestured a greeting. But the squid did not respond, and in a moment it drifted slowly down and out of her line of sight.

Graciela sighed. Clutching her lover's arm, she climbed back out into the dock area of the dome. "I wish I knew what was bothering them," she muttered. "It's not just radioactivity."

Tregarth turned her around and stopped her speech with a kiss. She returned it willingly enough. Then he gently held her away from him for a moment, looking into her eyes.

"There's something I do know, Graciela," he said. "I want to marry you. Say yes!"

"Oh, Ron," she sighed.

"Give me an answer, Graciela!"

"You know I love you. It's just that I don't think it would be sensible—"

But the desolation in his eyes stopped her. Impulsively she kissed him again, then leaned back in his arms for a silent moment. Then she grinned.

"Ron Tregarth," she said formally, "you win. I accept your proposal. I guess we can plan for a future now. Therefore—" She closed her eyes in a moment's silent calculation—"yes! If things haven't gone all sour somehow five weeks from now, when you come back, we'll get Mayor McKen to marry us right here in City Atlantica!"

"Thank heaven," groaned Tregarth. "And just about time, too!" And for the next nearly twenty minutes, until Jilly Danner appeared in the hatch to announce that all the checklist was complete, they were as happy as any two people could be. Five weeks was an eternity, thought Ron Tregarth, but, really, it was one he could live through. And as for things going all sour—well, what were the chances of that? The odds were very high that the world would still be the same in five weeks; he was willing to bet on it. . . .

But that, of course, was a bet that he, and the whole world, was going to lose.

Chapter
6

Dr. Simon McKen Quagger had been a problem child. A spiteful brat, his mother confessed to her psychiatrist. Too heavy for his age, unpopular with his peers, totally impossible. Dragged into the doctor's office the year he was six, he called the man dirty names and tried to kick his shins. Left alone during the consultation, he did a dirty thing on the doctor's couch.

That noted and expensive physician of the mind was careful of Gloria Quagger. He knew she had been the first child of old Angus McKen. He knew about her impulsive marriage to a penniless poet; about her father's consequent rage; her disinheritance; the bitter family feud when the old man died.

"Little Simon is not a bad boy," he assured her. "Your own son of course; I see that he has your own strong will. Perhaps his father pampered him. Perhaps he has been reminded too many times that he's growing up to be one of the world's richest and most powerful men—next to his cousins, of course. Perhaps a few weeks of therapy will be beneficial. That is, if you agree."

"If he does," she said. "What else do you suggest?"

"I'd watch his diet. Sweets and fats especially. Try to ignore the temper tantrums. Don't scold when he wets his bed. And try not to fret about his erratic behavior. Nothing abnormal, considering that he's your son. Just let him grow up."

His private notes were more candid. After one hectic session, he submitted a bill for smashed lamps and soiled carpets and prudently informed her that little Simon need no further therapy. Quagger had grown bitter and fatter in the years since that interview, but the doctor doubted privately that he would ever grow up. Nobody knew whether he still wet his bed.

Now, as *Quagger One* carried him back from City Atlantica to his stronghold in Mount Quagger, his mood was bleak. The stupid pilot had flown him through ten minutes of turbulence—he would pay for that! And his mission had not been, well, an unqualified success.

Those dirty little webfeet had no business discovering

the bombs. Quagger was fairly sure that his colleagues—
well, be truthful: his superiors—among the leadership of
PanMack Consortium would not be pleased.

One of the things that chronically angered Simon
Quagger (there were dozens of them) was that there was
no *Quagger Two* or *Three*. Indeed, apart from a handful of
crop-dusters he had no other aircraft at all. To him that fact
was just one more proof of the fact that Simon McKen
Quagger was not treated with the respect and given the
largesse he was entitled to by right of birth.

Quagger gazed disconsolately at the glorious Rocky
Mountain peaks that were the heart of his domain. He
despised them. What did his domain amount to, after all?
A few million hectares of land, either played-out farms or
useless mountains; a dozen cities, but none of them in a
decent climate; some tens of millions of citizens to pay
taxes to him and do his work—and how reluctantly they
sometimes did those things! He had the smallest and
poorest domain of any McKen in the PanMack consortium,
he thought discontentedly, glowering down at the bright
lights of the landing strip as they rose to meet his aircraft.

The wheels touched down as gently as a kiss. The great
delta-winged jet rumbled to its stand, where Quagger's
personal lift truck was already waiting. Newt Bluestone
ventured out of the crew quarters as they landed, and was
standing by the plane's door as it opened. He hurried out,
scuttling down the mobile steps beside the lift before they
were quite in position. The three stewardesses who at-
tended *Quagger One* put their best smiles on as they moved
quickly to unstrap Quagger from his throne and help him
navigate the few steps to the open door, where the lift was
waiting. The pilot was there, too. "Lord Quagger," he
apologized, "I'm sorry we got bounced around back there.
The downdrafts in these mountains are pretty severe—"

Quagger paused to turn his angry little eyes on the man.

For a moment the pilot's job was in the balance, if not indeed his freedom. But the lightning did not strike.

Quagger turned morosely away. "Get this lift down," he snapped to the girl at the controls. "Be careful! Don't let me drop! Where's my dear Angie? Why isn't she here? If anything's happened to her—"

The lightnings were still playing around the heads of everyone there. What saved pilot, stewardesses and the lift operator at once appeared through the huge metal doors of Quaggerhome.

Hissing and screeching, a creature came bounding out of the tunnel. It looked at first glance like a tiny monkey, perhaps a capuchin. It was no larger than a cat. It scrambled up the lift frame and hurled itself at Quagger. As it clambered to his shoulder his fat little face broke into a smile. "Ah, there's my good girl! Hello, Angie," he murmured, letting it pet and groom him.

It was not a monkey like any other monkey in the world. Its scalp bore long, rust-red tresses; its whole body was covered with short fur of the same color. Its face was almost human, and it had breasts that would have done justice to a miniature version of any voluptuous woman. And it spoke. "Quaggie, Quaggie," it chattered lovingly, tangling its tiny fingers in Quagger's hair. "You were gone such a long time! Angie missed you so!"

Quagger's servants at last dared relax. "How sweet," whispered the pilot, loud enough to be heard by everyone around, though the strained smile on his face did not match the words. The lift operator gently began lowering Quagger's immense body to the ground, where Quagger's little car was waiting to bear him inside.

Lord Quagger was safely home again.

Quaggerhome was carved into the base of a mountain, and it was huge. There were kilometers of passages, thousands of cubic meters of rooms and halls and workspaces. It had its own water supply and its own waste disposal facility. It sucked its air from ten multiply-redundant shafts; some of them stretched twenty kilometers away to the tops of other nearby mountains, and all of the ventilation shafts contained micropore filters and static chambers to remove particulate matter, as well as every other device known to science to insure that the air Lord Quagger breathed would always be fresh and pure, no matter what happened outside.

These were not foolish precautions. Every McKen family took them. In the strained relations between PanMack and the rest of the world—not to mention the ceaseless jockeying for power among the McKens of PanMack itself—you never knew when that outside air might be radioactive, or laden with biological-warfare organisms, or merely full of attacking aircraft.

There were no fewer than fifteen well guarded, very secure hideouts for members of the four reigning families of the bad McKens. The shelters were scattered all over the Americas, wherever ran the law of the tremendous PanMack syndicate. Quagger's was by no means the largest—after all, he had failed to produce any sons to carry on the line even with the aid of the most famous specialists.

Still, Quaggerhome was built to house some twenty-eight hundred people. When there was no special cause for alarm, and Simon McKen Quagger allowed himself to live in one of his luxurious villas on Lake Powell or along the Arkansas River, the standby maintenance staff left inside the hollowed-out mountain was sometimes as few as eight hundred.

Now the mountain was full.

It was not that any armed attack seemed imminent. Quagger had moved inside the armored retreat out of prudence, as soon as he had heard about Comet Sicara. He thought briefly of moving out again now that the comet was only dust and gravel, but decided against it. You never knew if these scientific johnnies could be trusted. They had promised that nothing larger than a few hundred kilograms was left, but the McKens took no chances with their valuable lives.

Anyway, Simon McKen Quagger *liked* Quaggerhome. It was entirely *his*. The staff of servants and attendants were hand-picked, all two-thousand-plus of them—the bare minimum, of course, that a McKen could get by with, to ensure the necessary comforts.

It was not an accident that more than seventy percent of the staff were young, female and quite beautiful. The ranks of the Peace Brigade had been combed for specialists with just those qualities. In other shelters of the McKen family the proportions were different, for the female McKens were not to be deprived of strong, handsome and compliant young men; it was a basic rule of life on that hemisphere of the Earth dominated by the PanMack Consortium that no McKen should ever be deprived of anything he ever chose to wish for.

After all, wasn't that what government was all about?

The heart of the mountain caverns was Quagger's audience room.

Ten minutes after *Quagger One* touched down, Lord Quagger was ensconced there. He lay grunting on a soft table, while two expert masseuses were gently stroking and pounding his enormous body to ease the stresses of his ordeal. The ceiling of the room was a shallow dome, on which three-dimensional projections of summer clouds drifted lazily across a blue sky. The walls were lined with vision screens, slaved to cameras all over Quagger's personal fiefdom; they showed factories, mines, farms—all the enterprises that made Quagger rich and great. No, thought Simon Quagger, not *really* rich and great! Not by the standards of the McKens of the PanMack Consortium, at least. Of the four McKen domains, his was the least. In Family usage, all kinsmen were cousins—and he hated them all. Cousin Marcus to the east had the rich Atlantic seaboard with its great cities and productive factories. Cousin Isaac to the west had all the Pacific Coast, and most of the richest provinces of what had once been Canada, while Cousin Daniel owned almost all of Latin America.

Still, there were compensations.

By Quagger's sides four beautiful women in scanty garments carried silver trays—chilled wine and little hot canapes, icy fruits, confections, anything that might tempt Lord Quagger's appetite. Quagger gazed at the trays dubiously, waiting for someone to put the choicest item between his lips. Absently he reached to fondle the nearest of the serving women.

The women were not usually allowed to feed Quagger themselves. That was Angie's prerogative. The little creature scanned the trays jealously, selected just the right tidbit and put it in Quagger's waiting mouth.

Lord Quagger sighed in the pleasure of being once more where he belonged.

When Quagger was home he felt safe. When Angie was with him he felt loved.

He had reason for both. Angie loved him very much and always would; she had been genetically bred to love, and as soon as she was born she had been imprinted to Quagger. She couldn't help herself after that.

That accounted for love; and safety was what Quaggerhome was all about. If the Common Europeans or the AfrAsians should ever dare to attack . . . if the constant threat of nuclear war should ever occur . . . if, in spite of all the efforts of spy cameras and police control, Quagger's serfs should ever try to rebel against him . . . no matter what happened, the mountain that held Quaggerhome was a secure bastion.

And yet Simon Quagger was uneasy.

This thing of Comet Sicara! How could it have happened? It had been a *threat*. He could have been *hurt*.

It was all very well that the scientific johnnies had finally gotten a ship into space and nuked the comet into harmless dust—well, they *said* the fragments would be harmless. It would go badly with them if they were wrong, he thought darkly. They would not be the first of their kind to feel his wrath. Already Quagger had sent a dozen of his own starveling scientists to the labor camps for impudence, or ignorance, or simply because he hadn't liked to hear the warnings they had timorously tried to give him.

That was wise of him, he informed himself. They needed to be taught their place. Still, he reflected, perhaps a *little* tolerance might be necessary from time to time. It had been the devil's own job to find enough cooperative scientists to figure out how to blow Comet Sicara up in the first place.

And meanwhile—oh, God, did his labors never end?— he had to get back to the business of governing his domain.

He pushed the hands of the masseuses away, lumbered to his feet and mounted to his throne, a whale of a man in briefs that could have held a cow's haunches, grunting and wheezing. Angie tumbled after him, perching on the back of the throne, glaring angrily at the dozen beautiful women who were Quagger's court and awaited his commands. As the massage technicians hastily slid the table out of sight and departed, Quagger grunted, "Let the audiences begin."

The first person to seek audience was Newt Bluestone. "You sent for me, Lord Quagger?" the young man said uneasily, wondering what had come up in the few minutes since they had been in *Quagger One* together.

"Of course I sent for you," snapped Quagger. "It has been a long time since you brought me up to date on your progress with my life story."

"But we were in City Atlantica, sir. I had pictures to take, notes to make—"

"That does not excuse you neglecting your essential tasks!"

Bluestone said humbly, "No, Lord Quagger. Well, I've completed the script up to the marriage of your illustrious parents."

"Ah," said Quagger, gratified. "I want to read your draft right away—no, wait," he added, as Bluestone turned away. "Have the pictures you took in City Atlantica been indexed yet?"

"Certainly, Lord Quagger. I did it on the plane. Would you like to see them now?"

"Not all of them," Quagger said severely. "I have many important things to do first. But I want you to find all the pictures of that webfoot girl—Graciela something?—and bring them to me. Quickly!"

His steward approached the throne as Bluestone was leaving. The steward was male, middle-aged and, of course, a relative—unfortunately for the steward, only on Quagger's father's side, and not of the McKen blood line. Still, he was a powerful person in Quaggerhome. He said with dignity, "Lord Quagger, the affairs of your domain are in good order, with one exception. I regret to inform you that coal production for the quarter is two percent under quota."

Quagger was enraged. "But we need that coal! Fools! Incompetents! I go away for just a few days and everything goes to pieces!"

"We miss your wise leadership," the steward said humbly. "Still, what happened was difficult to predict. A fire broke out in one of the deep mines. It had to be shut down until the burning veins were sealed off."

"Indeed! How many have you arrested?"

The steward licked his lips. "Sixteen, Lord Quagger," he said.

"Only sixteen?" Quagger glared furiously at his steward. "Perhaps I should order another arrest right now!"

The steward stood his ground, though his face was white. He knew better than most what the labor camps were like. "Sir," he pleaded, "the ones most at fault died in the accident—more than forty of them. Now if we arrest more workers we'll be left short-handed."

"Humph," snarled Quagger. He gazed darkly at his major domo for a thoughtful moment. Then Angie turned to whisper in his ear. Quagger calmed. "Very well, my dear," he said to her. He turned to the steward. "I have decided to overlook your incompetence this time. However, you must make up the difference in the next quarter. Do you understand?"

"Perfectly, Lord Quagger," the steward sighed. "Will you wish to hear reports from your captain of the guard and domestic staff now?"

"Now? After you've upset me like this?" Quagger bellowed. "Certainly not!" He dismissed them furiously. "Out! All of you—no, not Angie, of course," he added, fondling the little creature.

When the chamber was empty, Simon McKen Quagger faced the unpleasant task he had put off as long as he dared, but could postpone no longer. He reached toward the keypad on the arm of his throne to call Marcus McKen on the secure circuits.

He shivered as he punched the code. He was not going to enjoy this, but it was better to get it over with.

He was right. He didn't enjoy it. To begin with his cousin, General Marcus McKen, kept him waiting for a full three minutes before he came on the screen.

Quagger squirmed—to be treated this way, like someone who was not even in the Family—but when Marcus's blunt, dark face appeared Angie skipped out of sight fearfully. Quagger managed a cousinly smile. "Well, Marcus," he said playfully, "I hope you're not as angry as your message sounded."

Marcus McKen glared out of the screen at him. He was in full field uniform—how typical of the man, playing soldier! He said, "I called you, Simon, because you botched the job in City Atlantica! First, you planted two bombs without permission from me. Second, you let them be discovered. You are a disgrace to the Family, Simon!"

"But Marcus! You gave me the bombs!"

"And I gave you strict orders to keep them in reserve, in case it was necessary to convince the webfeet that we meant business."

"I judged it was necessary," Quagger pouted. "Don't you see? I only planted one in the main dome. The other was in that stupid squid school. If we'd had to use it it would have destroyed only one small outlying structure. That would certainly have taught them their lesson! The other needn't ever have been used. The city itself would have been intact for us to take over. I thought the whole plan out very carefully, Cousin Marcus, and—"

"You are not capable of thinking anything out carefully! Or of keeping a secret—are we at least on a secure circuit now?"

"Oh, yes, Cousin Marcus! I made sure of that!"

"But you didn't make sure word of Comet Sicara didn't get out. The Eighteen Cities know about it now. What did you tell them?"

"Nothing, Cousin Marcus," Quagger pleaded. "I didn't

tell them, they already knew. I give you my word! They picked up some careless radio transmissions and saw a launch from the sea. That's all! And, really, this isn't fair. I didn't ask to be an ambassador."

"That's good," snarled General Marcus McKen. "You're not an ambassador any more. I'll take personal charge of all future questions concerning the Eighteen Cities. We may need them yet. Now I want you to see if you can at least run your own affairs better than you did this mission —and watch those coal production figures!"

His image flickered and disappeared. The automatic search-and-show program instantly resumed displaying the kaleidoscope of scenes from Quagger's domain. He gazed at them moodily as Angie crept apprehensively back to his throne.

Quagger petted her absently, brooding over the conversation. How dared Marcus McKen talk to him like that! He, too, was a McKen!—but, he acknowledged sadly to himself, never properly treated as such by the Family.

It angered Quagger to think about it. By all the laws of genetics, there was as much McKen blood in his veins as in Marcus's own. It was not his fault that his McKen parent was a female! Only the blatant sexism of the McKen family caused his second-class status. . . .

"Quaggie, dear, see who's coming," Angie hissed in his ear, pointing at the door. He glanced up.

"Lord Quagger?" It was Newt Bluestone, waiting humbly for permission to enter the audience chamber. Quagger waved a fat arm impatiently.

"Have you got them?"

"Of course, Lord Quagger." Bluestone slipped the disks into the reader before the throne and touched the switch.

At once Graciela Navarro's image appeared in the room, life size, just as she had appeared at the squid school. Quagger studied the picture thoughtfully, then commanded, "Run them all." As Bluestone obeyed there was a series of a score of shots of Graciela Navarro, sometimes with someone else, even Quagger himself, more often alone—diving into the pool, wearing the pressure suit, admiring that ill-fated bust.

Quagger said thoughtfully, "I require some new attendants, Bluestone. I want you to match these pictures against the candidates on the personnel list." That was the list, kept constantly up to date, of young women in the Quagger domain who might sometime be eligible to join his staff in Quaggerhome. "Find the one who most closely resembles the webfoot girl—no, better find the closest five. Bring them here and I'll interview them myself to see which are most suitable. Do it right now!" he commanded and, as Bluestone was gathering up the disks to leave, "And inform the chamberlain that I wish to bathe now. Have him send in Greta, Emily—I don't know, two or three others."

And then he smiled. "Come, Angie," he said. "Bath time!"

"Ooh, wonderful, wonderful," the creature cooed, for bath time was always a time of pleasure.

Almost always.

This time, though Quagger lolled in his blood-warm tub, while the bath attendants soaped and scrubbed and oiled him with all the skills they had been trained to possess, Simon Quagger's thoughts were dark.

So many things kept coming up to destroy his well deserved happiness! The reprimand from Marcus McKen. The constant threat from the Common Europeans. The hazy, worrisome possible threat of what was left of Comet Sicara.

And now there was something new to worry about.

Every one of the persons who lived and worked within Quaggerhome was hand-picked and repeatedly checked for loyalty. Was it possible that someone among them placed obedience to an outsider, even an outside McKen, higher than loyalty to Simon McKen Quagger himself?

Quagger could hardly believe it. Yet how had Marcus McKen known so quickly that the coal production had slumped?

Chapter
7

On the day the tiny frozen-gas fragments that were all that was left of Comet Sicara first began to strike the atmosphere of the Earth, Ron Tregarth was glumly threading the silty waters of the approaches to Chesapeake Bay, en route to the PanMack port city of Baltimore.

What made Tregarth glum was that Chesapeake Bay was no place for a deep-sea submarine to be. There were shallows and banks. There were other vessels contesting his right-of-way; worst of all, there was the open sky above. Like any decent human from the Eighteen Cities, Ron Tregarth always felt naked with nothing overhead but air. He stood before his popup controls on the weather deck of the *Atlantica Queen* and squinted belligerently at the bright sun. "Easy, Jilly," he muttered to his second in command as she dexterously circled a lumbering trawler, its net poles out and half its cables dragging in the water.

"Aye, Captain," said Jill Danner politely. She had the conn, and she was fully qualified to guide the *Atlantica*

Queen through any waters anywhere. She didn't resent his unnecessary orders. She knew that the captain was not being critical, only edgy.

This time, the approach to Baltimore was not at all routine. They had both done a little swearing at the orders of the harbor control lubbers that they approach the port in this nasty and unsafe way—"for more orderly handling of traffic," the port captain's orders had said; but they both knew it was only so they could be kept under minute by minute surveillance by the watchtowers on shore.

"They're getting ugly," Tregarth said fretfully. "Wonder why they're tightening up just now?"

"Lubbers are always ugly," Jill said, out of the wisdom of her twenty-four years. But they both knew that the new regulations were even more troublesome and restrictive than ever before.

Tregarth rubbed a hand over his sweaty face, irritably wondering if he was going to get a sunburn—yes, *sunburn*, rarest of all human discomforts for the people of the Eighteen Cities. Thank heaven, it was nearly sundown. He would not have to stand in this bright, hot light all the way in to port!

Of course, he didn't really have to be standing on that narrow weather deck at all. There was barely room for the two of them in any case. The *Atlantica Queen* seldom had use for any external command bridge; most of its life was spent with cool, friendly water above it.

It would not be long, Tregarth reflected, before he would be back in the deeps again. Forty-eight hours in port. Another few hours to get back to the open sea. Then the long run, underwater all the way, to City Scotia, off the tip of South America, before rounding Cape Horn to head north for the cities and the lubber ports of the Pacific. This was a good voyage in many ways after all, he reflected. Only four of his ports of call were on the surface. Six were

undersea cities; and then, when he returned to City
Atlantica—

Jill wondered at the fact that her captain was suddenly
smiling as he gazed out over the unfriendly bay.

What kept City Atlantica prosperous was its trade with
the land dwellers, but seldom did any of its long-range
subs voyage out without visiting others of the Eighteen
Cities on the way. If intramural trade among the Eighteen
Cities was not economically important, it certainly was
politically so.

Each of the Eighteen Cities had its own special attri-
butes. City Atlantica, on the slope of the Mid-Atlantic
Ridge, not far from 40° W and 38° N, was some fifteen
hundred kilometers from the nearest land. Even that was
only islands—Bermuda to their west, the Azores a little
nearer to the east. The ships of City Atlantica rarely visited
either place. Their nearest neighbors that *counted* were not
islands. They were sub-sea city domes like City Atlantica
itself. There was City PanNegra, just east of the ridge and
north of the northern edge of the Cape Verde Basin; in fact
between that and the Canaries Basin to the north, close
enough to the Tropic of Cancer to be easy to find on a map.
Farther south was City Romanche, smack on the Equator,
midway between the bulges of Africa and South America,
on the edge of the Romanche Gap. North was City
Reykjanes, south of Iceland; and that was all for the
Atlantic Ocean.

The Pacific had more. There were the twin cities of
Clarion and Clipperton, in the huge fracture zones of the
Eastern Pacific. There was City Murray, on the Erben
Tablemount, about twelve hundred kilometers west of the
lubber town of Los Angeles. Farther west, City Mahalo, on
the slopes of the Emperor Seamount, northwest of the
Hawaiian chain; farther still was City Caroline, on the

Eauripik Ridge, north of New Guinea. City Caroline was the largest of the Eighteen Cities and the one closest to land, except for City Arafura, midway between New Guinea and the Australian coast. There was City Bellona, east of the Great Barrier Reef in the Coral Sea; and, farther west still, City Andaman, in the Bay of Bengal, north of Sumatra; and City Walvis, west of the Cape of Good Hope. Little City Tarfuk came next, in the east-to-west circling of the globe: it lay in the Red Sea, and was devoted to the mining of heavy metals from its hot springs.

Then there were the cities of the far south. Few of them were near any inhabited surface land; the surface of the Earth is far too cold to support self-sustaining life at the latitudes of City Gaussberg, on the ridge midway between Kerguelen Island and the coast of the Antarctic continent. City Gaussberg was *really* remote—five thousand kilometers from City Nazarene, east of Madagascar, and even farther from any lubber-inhabited lands. (But those deep, cold bottoms were very rich; they were what supported the krill, which supported the larger fish and the whales and squid of the southern seas.) City Scotia was just as far south, south of South Georgia Island, but inhabited land was closer—if you considered the Falkland Islands inhabited. And almost as close to the other pole was City Laurentian, farthest north of all. There was never any open sea over the dome of City Laurentian. There was solid sea ice, winter and summer alike, for seasons made little difference in the Beaufort Sea—but there was oil in plenty under those deep sediments.

Oil and food. Metals and pharmaceuticals. Those were the treasures the people of the Eighteen Cities wrested from the deeps, and oh, how they were valued by the always-hungry masses of the PanMacks, Common Europe and the AfrAsians!

It was no wonder that the lubbers sometimes cast

covetous eyes at the bright Nexø domes that sprinkled the sea bottoms.

There had been tense times when the cities were building, especially when some of Pacific cities came a little too close to what the lubbers were pleased to call "coastal waters"—though often enough those "coasts" were only the barren shores of some useless little island. But the lubbers wanted only what the cities could give them. They did not want the hard life of the cities, especially in those early days when the first thermal springs were still being capped and it was touch-and-go whether human beings could survive in the domes at all.

So the negotiators for the submarine McKens had won the Second Law of the Sea Treaty: Lubber nations and consortia promised not to bother them as long as no city dome was less than a kilometer below the surface. And the treaty had been kept.

More or less. . . .

So far.

Less than a kilometer from its dock, a fussy little PanMack patrol boat scooted across the bows of the *Atlantica Queen* and hailed her. "Stop there!" bawled its commander, voice shrill through his loud-hailer, face hidden by the huge Peace Fleet helmet. "You must remain at anchor until the harbormaster clears you!"

"Anchor!" groaned Tregarth. His ship hardly even *had* an anchor; submarines of the Eighteen Cities had little use for such lubberly devices. He nodded to Jill Danner, who stopped the engines and paid out the slim cable of the tiny umbrella-shaped thing that would be barely adequate to hold the *Atlantica Queen* in even the mildest tide or breeze. Aloud he shouted: "How long?"

He could see the Peace Fleet officer shrug. "Until the harbormaster returns."

"And when will that be?"

"When it happens, webfoot," the officer growled and, bending to his communication tube, turned and sped away.

"Hell," said Ron Tregarth, scowling at the distant city towers. The sun was just setting behind them, turned sickly red by the smokey, sooty air.

Jill Danner nodded. She didn't answer. There wasn't anything to say except to swear a little, and they had both already done all of that they needed. She gazed out at the vessels around them, more than a dozen at anchor nearby. The *Atlantica Queen* had not, at least, been personally singled out for this last annoyance. There was even a great, gray cruiser of the Peace Fleet with its engines off and its crew loafing along the deck. She studied the rocket launchers and gun turrets and shook her head.

"Thank heaven they don't have subs like that," she said prayerfully.

Tregarth followed her gaze and nodded. "But they've got other things," he pointed out. "They've still got robot subs—not very big, but what's to stop them from putting nukes in the head of one of them and crash it into a dome? Even Nexø couldn't stand a nuclear warhead."

"But they haven't used them for years! The robot subs need skilled operators, and I doubt they have any."

"Then trawlers," Tregarth said grimly. "They're still trying to find oil of their own, aren't they? And they've got deep-sea drilling equipment—no, don't feel too safe, Jilly. If the PanMacks want to attack us they've got the tools for it."

"I hope you're wrong," Jilly said.

"I hope so too," said Tregarth, and swatted irritably at some kind of insect that seemed to want to drink a little of his blood. Bugs! Hot sunshine, even nearly at dusk! And the stink of the air as the breezes blew it from the land, so

unlike the constantly recirculated, always filtered, blessed-
ly sweet air of City Atlantica. How did lubbers stand living
like this, anyway?

Then he forgot his annoyance. He gaped upward, marveling.

A bright streak of light, high up, like silent lightning,
blazed across the eastern sky. For one moment it was
almost as bright as the lowering sun.

Then it was gone.

"What was that?" Jilly cried in astonishment.

"I don't know—wait, yes I do," Tregarth corrected
himself. "It's a meteor. Probably it's a piece of that comet!
They said there might be meteor showers as the fragments
hit the air."

"But that bright? And, look, there's another!"

A lesser streak of fire sprouted from the same point over
the eastern horizon. They both stared silently, waiting for
more. None came for a time, and Tregarth, glancing at the
nearest ore vessel, saw some of its crew on their deck, also
silently watching.

"There's another," Jill Danner cried—this one quite
faint and short in the evening sky.

"If we can see them at all while it's still daylight,"
Tregarth said wonderingly, "they have to be pretty big."

"They're pretty," said Jill Danner, who seldom saw
meteors at all—or any other phenomenon of the open
skies.

Tregarth shrugged wryly. "They're interesting, anyway," he conceded. He picked up the phone and called the
wardroom kitchen. "We'll take our chow up here whenever it's ready," he ordered. And, to his second in command:

"We don't have anything better to do. Might as well stay up here and watch the fireworks."

And that was the first (though not the last) that Ron Tregarth saw of Comet Sicara; he did not yet know of the Eternal.

Chapter
8

In the last hours of the last day of the last year, Graciela Navarro saw no meteor showers falling on City Atlantica. Though she was at the top of the city dome, in the mayor's office, there was too much water in the way.

She was in conference with the mayor and several of the section chiefs of City Atlantica. They knew about the meteor showers. The duty crews on the surface platform that floated two thousand meters over the city had reported an unusual sky show, but the meeting was about something else entirely. Old Sandor Tisza had a sheaf of blue flimsies, printouts from the communications system. The mysterious traffic in data transmissions had not stopped with Ambassador Quagger's hasty departure, and they were poring over them, looking for a common element that might explain why anyone wanted them. The one in Graciela's hand was particularly odd; it was simply a technical report on the fauna and biochemistry of the hydrothermal vents:

Oxygen uptake occurs primarily in peripheral organisms, e.g. the hydrothermal vent clam *Calyptogena*, while sulfide consumption is most marked in core animals such as the hydrothermal vent mussel *Bathymodiolus thermophilus*. Tubeworm populations, e.g. *Riftia*, and predators, e.g. the starfish *Bathybiaster* and various crabs and shrimp, are intermediate.

Opportunistic predators (crustaceans, arthropods and free-swimming fish) obtain most (40–65%) of total dietary intake from the vent animals.

Protein production is high but not suitable for human consumption due to residual sulfide traces, which produce unpalatable flavors. *Calyptogena*, however, is a special case. Other cities have harvested and processed *Calyptogena* meat for export to landside markets, and City Atlantica might consider such a program for the near future. . . .

It went on from there, but Graciela had lost interest. "There's no *point* in this sort of thing!" she exclaimed. "Everybody knows this stuff already—if anyone cares! What are the others about?"

"Oh," the mayor said, shaking her head, "what have they not been about? The formula for Nexø. The most productive crop strains for our undersea farms. The bio-chemistry of the human body, if you please! At least a dozen papers on your own squid, Graciela—"

"Yes, I saw those," Graciela agreed.

"And everything else! There was a whole engineering study on Vera Doorn's ship, the *Thetis*—now why would anyone want that? Especially because it's not even here, since she sailed days ago. Another engineering study, this one on the work subs—"

"Like the one that's missing," Frank Yaro pointed out grimly.

The mayor sighed. She was looking older, Graciela thought, her pale hair no longer seeming quite so blonde and more nearly white. "I know you think it's some kind of a plot, Frank," the Mayor said. "But who? For what?"

"At least we can be sure it isn't the PanMacks," Sandor Tisza put in, "since there aren't any left here."

"They could have left agents," Yaro said stubbornly. "Even bugged our communications system somehow—"

"No," Tisza said warmly, "that's impossible. I've got Ector Farzoli out checking all the laser channels now; he hasn't found a thing. I think we're too suspicious of the PanMacks."

Graciela looked at him in surprise. "But don't you know that that horrible fat man called you a—"

"An escaped criminal?" offered Tisza. He nodded soberly. "Yes. The mayor has told me." He looked at the girl pleadingly. "I broke no real laws, Graciela. I only wished to do my work without interference. Therefore I left Budapest for the PanMack countries; when I was not allowed to do proper work there, I came here. But it is true. I did violate their regulations in both cases by leaving without permission. They call that a crime."

"It's PanMack that's the crime," Frank Yaro said bitterly. "Thank heaven we're here and not there!"

"Thank heaven indeed," Tisza echoed. "Of course they are evil—but I do not think we can blame them for everything."

The mayor shook her head. "'Everything' takes in so much these days," she sighed. "Communications leaks, work subs missing—and," she finished pensively, "I wonder why Captain Doorn hasn't reported in for the past thirty-six hours."

And an hour later, secure in her neutral-buoyancy suit and strapped to the speeding sea-skid, with five of her squid sedately pacing her, Graciela still felt the chill of that remark.

It made the trip a long one.

* * *

The sea farm they were approaching, like City Atlantica itself, lay on the rises that approached one of the ranges of that vast underwater chain of newly born mountains called "the mid-ocean ridge."

The ridge is not truly in the middle of all the oceans it traverses. Sometimes its peaks press hard against the continental shores. Nor is the ridge entirely continuous. The great ribbon of underwater mountains and ridges begins under the ice of the Arctic Ocean, north of Spitzbergen. It drops down to the Atlantic—Iceland is only one of the places where it has risen so high that it protrudes above sea level—and continues south through both North and South Atlantics. Other peaks above water are the Azores, Ascension Island, Tristan da Cunha—places that range from the merely remote to the utterly alone.

The ridge sweeps wide around the Cape of Good Hope, avoiding Africa to reach almost to Antarctica, then up into the Indian Ocean. One short spur wanders off to the Red Sea. The main range continues westward, south of Tasmania and New Zealand's South Island, out through the empty South Pacific and then straight north until it comes almost to Baja California.

It stops there.

A few thousand kilometers to the west, another little stretch of ridges makes the Hawaiian archipelago. If that gap were filled in—and if another extension went from the end of the Hawaiian chain up through the Bering Strait and across the Pole—the circle would be closed, and the Earth would be bisected by the mid-ocean ridge.

Even without those, it is the single largest geological feature on the globe.

For the people of the Eighteen Cities, it was also the most valuable.

The mid-ocean ridge gave two great gifts to the people of the Eighteen Cities. For many of them, the ridge made a useful platform—high enough above the abyssal plains that their Nexø domes could withstand the pressure, deep enough to be insulated from the tribulations of the open air. Most of the Eighteen Cities were located on or near it.

That was only one of the ridge's two main uses, and the lesser of the two. The far greater benefit (and one of its great hazards) was its tectonic activity.

The mid-ocean ridge was the most tectonically active part of the Earth's crust. It was where the hot, gummy magma under the rock shell was relentlessly forcing its way out through cracks and crevices, to make new rock . . . and new ores . . . and new sources of heat for the electrical generators of the Eighteen Cities. The ores that seeped out of the magma were what gave the cities their first commercial reason for existence. The hot waters from the undersea thermal springs were what kept them alive. For the sea bottom poured out endless quantities of megacalories in the springs. The ocean's weight forced some of its bottom waters down into the pores of the crust. Heated and enriched by minerals, the water was squeezed out of the rock again as clusters of springs; and the heat engines driven by the temperature differentials of the thermal springs gave the cities never-ending power beyond the dreams of landlubbers.

Still, one could never have too many thermal springs! They didn't last forever. For a few years or decades they would flow steadily. Then the crust would wrinkle imperceptibly. Then the springs died out in one place and reappeared in another, perhaps far away. Then all the organisms that depended on the springs for life would die, too, and all that was left was a bed of broken and half-dissolved shells.

So there was a constant hunt among the people of the Eighteen Cities for new fields of thermal springs. They could deal with the dangers of tectonic activity well enough—the cities were always sited in tectonically "safe" areas, and the strong Nexø domes were proof against most earthquakes. But they could not survive if their sources of power failed them. Then the lights would go out. Then the air pumps would stop.

Then the cities would die.

And so, when the squid Nessus pulled Graciela toward him, with one long tentacle and boomed, in the hollow tones of the implanted voice box, "Have new hot up-water, yes. Graciela come, yes," Graciela Navarro could not refuse.

With five of her squid, Graciela had come to one of the great farm terraces on the western slope of the range, and, of course, she didn't know that the last year was ending. To Graciela Navarro, every day was a beginning of something new, shining with promise and hope; she had no experience of endings.

Down below her, the squid were patiently carrying out orders. It was seeding time, and in teams of two they were guiding the neutral-buoyancy planters along the long, plowed rows of fertile muck. Above the four laborers Nessus swam in slow circles, his tentacles weaving patterns of command.

Graciela's heart was melting in pride. All she had to do was watch! The squid were performing their tasks flawlessly. They were perfect farm laborers for the deeps, as patient and strong as the work-elephants of old Siam. No, far better! Unlike the elephants, the squid could speak. They communicated among themselves with writhings of tentacles and with color changes on the skins of their mantles, and no human being could decipher that code; but with the voice synthesizer they could talk with human beings.

And, once they knew what human beings wanted, they did it! Why was that? Graciela could not guess. In the early stages of training the squid teachers like herself "rewarded" them with bits of food—but, really, Graciela knew, they were more polite than eager when they took the chunks of fish from her. Actually, they seemed to enjoy catching their own food. It was, she supposed, play for the squid to obey human commands. The best reward of all was simply approval. So Graciela activated her downward-ranging external speakers and called to them:

"You do good, yes! Finished now, yes!"

Nessus's croak floated up to her, "Understand, yes!" And, the last row finished, the four working squid began tugging the massive, if nearly weightless, seeders to their storage place.

Graciela gazed happily down at them. Wonderful creatures! They did so much—and could do so much more, she was certain, as they learned more and more of human needs and desires.

There were, for instance, the great deeps to the south and west of City Atlantica. Verna Doom's *Thetis* was even now exploring them—Graciela felt a quick stab of worry at that thought, but quickly repressed it; of *course* Doom's ship was all right!

Yet it occurred to Graciela that the squid visited such places at will.

Suppose, she thought, suppose the squid were fitted with cameras and recording instruments and sent to follow the *Thetis*, even to go to places the *Thetis* would not see.

Those vast areas of the deeps were still almost unexplored. Before the Eighteen Cities, there were only occasional probes with trawls or robot subs, or once in a great while a brief and hazardous trip in a human-manned exploration vessel. Even now, there was simply too much to be fully mapped. The most mysterious regions of the deeps were still too hazardous for easy human venturing . . . and yet who knew what might be found there? The deeps did not change! They might hold wonders of a hundred kinds, preserved there for tens of thousands of years. . . .

She beckoned to Nessus. As the great squid swam up to

join her she said, "Nessus good, yes! Nessus know fat deep person steelfish *Thetis*, yes?"

The great eye peered at her. "Nessus know, yes," he boomed.

"You see *Thetis*, yes?" she demanded.

There was silence. Then the squid said, completely ignoring her question, "Squid finished farm work now, yes!"

Graciela bit her lip in vexation. Down below the other squid had gathered all their implements and moored them to their holdfasts sunk into the sea bottom. As they swam up to join her, she said to each of them, addressing them by name, "Triton good, yes! Holly good, yes! Merman good, yes! Neptune good, yes! All do good, yes!"

They gazed up at her silently, and beside her Nessus startled her by booming, close to her helmet, "All do good, yes!" No inflection of mood was possible with the voice box, but Graciela had not doubt he was expressing pride.

"Now go find new hot up-water, yes," he announced.

"All right," she said, almost as though talking to another human, and then corrected herself. "Go yes. Nessus go first, yes."

"Nessus go first, yes," confirmed the squid, and reached out with the great tentacles, enwrapping not only Graciela but her little one-person sea skid as well.

She sighed silently. Nessus seemed unwilling to believe that she could find her way around by herself. Really, she preferred the sea-skid, but there was, she admitted to herself, something comforting about being borne along in those great, immensely strong tentacles, skid and all. The skid's automatic inertial systems would keep track of where they were going, and there were always the faint blue-green traces of the laser net to follow. She would not get lost. She stroked one of Nessus's arms with her gauntleted hand . . . wishing it were Ron Tregarth she was touching. . . .

She did not want to think of her fiancé just then. Besides, Nessus had not given her a proper answer to her question about the *Thetis*. She called, "Nessus! You see fat person steelfish go deep, yes?"

Pause, while the great, glassy eye stared at her. Then, "Nessus see, no," the voice boomed.

"Nessus sure, yes?" she asked; but the squid vocabulary was not up to such refinements.

"Nessus see, no," he repeated stubbornly.

Graciela frowned. The squid was contradicting himself. She supposed that the squid were probably capable of lying, if they wanted to. What reasonably intelligent animal was not? But why this particular deceit?

It was one more unsolved riddle to add to the hundreds she already had to puzzle over. Like the others, it would have to wait.

They were driving along over the foothills of the range, the other four following along in almost a military V-formation. They cleared a peak—

"Hot place, yes," Nessus announced, and gently settled toward the bottom, fifty meters below.

At first Graciela thought the trip had been a waste of time.

True, there was a cluster of thermal springs there. Certainly it was worth looking at.

It was, in fact, a submarine garden. There were flowers, trees and even fountains . . . though none of them were the same as their surface analogues. The "flowers" were creatures like sea anemones. The "trees" were jointed white tube worms, like the trunks of bamboos; the creatures that made the white shells were peering out of the tops of them, like scarlet palm fronds. And the "fountains" were what made everything else possible. They were jets of "white smoke" and "black smoke", pouring out of invisible cracks in the sea bottom.

It was a typical, unspoiled deep-ocean thermal-spring oasis. Abyssal slopes are only sparsely populated, but where the thermal springs bring heat and nutrients to the sea bottom a hectare or two can become as luxuriant as anything along the Great Barrier Reef. It was the fountains that did it, hot, mineral-rich water; they nurtured the sulfur-compound organics that fed the clams and mussels, the crabs and hydroids and all the other living things clustered in this deep outpost of creation. They were hot, these fountains. The black plumes were hotter than the flame of a match, and laden with dense sulfur compounds and ores. The white springs were comparatively cool—hotter than boiling water, to be sure; but at these depths water was forbidden to boil. There were other springs that were still cooler—no more than body temperature—but as they were not hot enough to dissolve minerals out of the rock they had no color at all, and were visible only as glassy ripples of refraction.

After a lifetime spent undersea, Graciela Navarro was still enchanted by the beauty of the place. She caught a glimpse of a tiny, reddish fish hanging head-down in one of the cooler fountains, waiting for food particles to jet up to its waiting mouth. Near another there was a mass of fibers that looked like spaghetti; and atop them was a clot of red algae that looked like the appropriate tomato sauce.

Graciela sighed. There was only one thing wrong with this undersea garden.

It was not new.

There were hundreds of such spots along the mid-ocean ridge, near enough to City Atlantica to be useful—but only a bare handful of them were useful. The rest were too small to be practical; and this one was small indeed. She craned to study the sonar scope and nodded to herself; yes, it had been charted long since, and set aside as worthless for any useful purpose.

She hesitated, trying to think of a way to convey this to

Nessus, who was stirring restlessly beside her, waiting for a response. His two long tentacles, twice the length of the working ones, were curling around to touch the back of her helmet, as though tapping to remind her.

She said, "Hot up-water old, yes. Know this hot up-water, yes."

The long tentacles writhed irritably. "Hot up-water old, yes. Hot up-water new, yes. Know this hot up-water, no!"

Graciela frowned to herself. What was the squid trying to say? Calling the springs simultaneously both old and new? But that was self-contradictory. . . .

Then she peered down the slopes, past the great black lumps of pillow basalt, and she saw.

"Oh, boy!" she shouted. "It's a big one!"

For beyond the old garden a new and much huger one had formed—no, not a garden yet, she corrected herself; there had not yet been time for organisms to colonize the space. But they would! It was one of the richest fields Graciela had ever seen! The crust had wrinkled again, just enough to close off a few seepage faults and open others, and now there were thermal springs as far as she could see.

They came in two distinct varieties: the warm vents, with fifteen-degree water oozing slowly out, and the hot chimneys, pouring out water at 350 degrees and higher, at velocities of meters per second. Though Graciela could see only a few hundred meters in the brightest light from her sea-skid, she saw that there were literally hundreds of the tall, priceless ones that would turn City Atlantica's turbines—power enough nearly to double the city's present supply!

"Let go Graciela, yes," she ordered.

The great beast obediently uncurled the tentacle that held her. It is an irritation to observe that, although Graciela had asked Nessus not to do it, the arm that held her was one of the animal's sexual tentacles, the smooth-padded ones that were specialized for fertilizing the female squid. It could have been an accident, of course. When Nessus was fully occupied in something, operating a cultivator or tearing at a fish for his dinner, he often used all ten tentacles. He was sometimes forgetful—or acted that way, she thought glumly, though she sometimes believed he forgot nothing at all except what he chose not to remember. She would, she decided, speak to him again about the proprieties of conduct.

But not this time.

This time there were the springs to check and map. She disengaged herself from the sea-skid, turned herself right over and, head down, paddled toward the bottom. The two depth gauges inside her helmet—one pressure, one sonar —confirmed that she was at a safe operating level: so the field could be exploited! She swam across the field, carefully avoiding the super-hot shimmers of rising hot water, and found it more than a kilometer across: so indeed there was plenty of it! She could even feel the difference in temperature. She was becoming almost uncomfortably warm!

A quick glance at her oxygen readout showed that she should not remain away from the dome much longer.

"Help Graciela, yes!" she ordered the squid, as she struggled to unsnap a sonar buoy from the sea-skid. The smallest of them, Neptune, gently edge her aside and effortlessly removed the lance from its clamps. Then, with Graciela giving orders, it carried the long rod to the bottom and steadied it. Graciela fired it. A surge of recoil let her know that its arrow-bladed point had been drilled deep into the bottom. She released the cable, and watched the buoy climb to the limit of its tether. She tugged hard on the cable to make sure it was firmly embedded, listened with her helmet microphones turned far down to hear the buoy's sonar beeps.

The squid, of course, paid no attention to the sound. All four of them hung there, watching gravely—

Four?

She counted again swiftly. It was true. There were only four squid there.

Nessus was gone again.

What a nuisance, she thought, momentarily annoyed. She had not told him to go! And normally he would not have, but now—now, Graciela admitted to herself, he was indeed acting peculiarly now and then.

Yet it was Nessus who had led her to this great new treasure.

She shook her head and, sighing, strapped herself onto the sea-skid and started back to City Atlantica.

By the time she was within signal range she had forgotten her annoyance at Nessus's behavior and was only basking in the warmth of the good news she had for the people of City Atlantica. At maximum distance she began calling.

She was not surprised when there was no answer at first.

A few minutes later, when she should have been well within range, it became a little more puzzling. Frowning, Graciela checked her one-to-five-thousand sonar overlays. Yes. Definitely she was within range. They must be hearing her, so why didn't they answer?

She keyed the palm board again. "Wake up, you people! This is Graciela Navarro reporting in, ten minutes from arrival. I have located a major new thermal field. Acknowledge!"

And still no voice responding.

Was it possible, she asked herself in sudden anciety, that something had gone wrong with her transmitter? (But the instrument readings were optimal.) Or could there be something terribly wrong at the dome? City Atlantica's message center was *always* manned! It was impossible that no one should be there to listen. She peered ahead through the gloom. No lights visible yet. The faint blue-green beam of the laser net was only a few dozen meters away; she could tap into that, of course. But first she repeated her message on the sonar communicator. . . .

And then, just as misty, murky lights far away told her that the dome, at least, still survived, an answer came. "I read you, Graciela—" it began. And stopped.

Ice swallowed Graciela's heart. Had that been Frank Yaro's voice? So strained, so almost frightened?

"Frank!" she implored. "Is that you? Is something wrong?"

No answer.

Worse than no answer at all, actually, because she could tell he was there and the circuits open. She could hear a faint muttering of voices, and all of them sounded as agitated as Frank's own. And that was *wrong!* It was true that the communications center was never left untended, but it was also true that never was it filled with people, except when something very big was happening. "Please, Frank," she begged, "Tell me what's happening. Is it the dome? Is it—have you heard something about Ron Tregarth?"

The mutterings in the background ignored her. Only one strange phrase was audible—or almost audible, anyway; certainly it was not anything she understood. Then Frank Yaro's voice came back:

"We're real busy here, Graciela. Come in, but clear this channel, please!"

"Frank, is it Ron's ship?"

"Nothing like that, no. But I can't tie up the circuits now. Over and out!"

And he did not speak again, though Graciela, in flat disobedience of traffic instructions, tried to raise him again and again, right up to the moment the Tinker-Toy pipes and structures of City Atlantica loomed through the turbid waters ahead of her.

She dove into the port. The closing of the lock behind her, the slow lowering of pressure so she could enter the dome—they took *forever.* Graciela was frightened. She dreaded what she might hear. Most of all, she was bewildered.

That strange phrase!

She was nearly sure she had heard it right. She rehearsed the two words over to herself experimentally. Yes, that was it—but what in the world was an "ozone summer"?

Chapter
9

Before dawn, the terrible display of fireworks over Baltimore Harbor dwindled and stopped. Ron Tregarth swung himself up to the narrow weather deck one more time, red-eyed and irritable. He had not slept more than twenty minutes at a time in any part of that night, and did not see a prospect of catching up ever.

He took the night glasses from Jill Danner, and stared around at the other ships. There was nothing to see there. Nothing had changed. No ship had been allowed to move; but only when Tregarth was sure of that did he swing the glasses to look aloft.

There was not much to see there either, now. The show was over, as the display moved westward and finally set, like the sun before it. But the spectacle had been unbelievable while it was going on. The meteors had showered down in the tens of thousands. More than anyone could count; they had streamed across the sky a hundred at a time, radiating from a central point that moved from east to west as the night advanced, with brilliances that ranged fro bright to preposterous. A dozen times the harbor had been lit as though by day. Ebven in the quieter periods the streams still came, so that the hwble waterway was illuminated, ships and water and shoreline. Everywhere staring faces peered wonderingly at the sky.

And there were no explanations anywhere.

If anyone ashore knew what was going on, there was no way for the crew of the *Atlantica Queen* to find that out. Radio communication was wiped out by static at once, as the incoming fragments of Comet Sicara piled the air before them into dense, furiously hot plasma that radited in every band, including the radio frequency. A dozen times that night Tregarth had signaled by flasher to other vessels, but the conversations were always one-sided. Everyone had the same questions. Answers there were none.

Tregarth put down the glasses and said, "Try the radio, Jilly."

His bleary-eyed second in command shook her head. "Tried it five minutes ago, Captain. It's still bad. I don't understand why, if the meteors have just about stopped coming."

Tregarth sighed heavily, "They may not have stopped everywhere. They're probably still falling, but over the western horizon, so they're out of our line of sight." He glanced around, rubbing his eyes. "The other thing I don't see," he said, "is Baltimore."

Jill Danner blinked at him. "Captain?"

He gestured forward. "Eight miles ahead of us, on the port quarter—that's where the city is. Do you see any lights? Neither do I. Not even along the shore here, except a few places where they probably have emergency generators."

First Officer Danner moved her lips, trying in her fatigue

to work it out. "Power failure? But how could meteorites knock out power stations?"

"They wouldn't have to. There's something called 'EMP'—electromagnetic pulse. A huge burst of radio energy. It just blows out equipment. Long power transmission lines are especially vulnerable; they act like huge antennae. The longer they are, the worse. They collect the energy, send it right along to their switching circuits, transformers—anything that can be damaged. EMP burns them right out."

He paused, glancing over his shoulder toward the east. The first hint of sunrise was brightening the sky over the sand barrier that lay between them and the deep Atlantic. He stared wistfully in that direction for a moment.

Then he made a decision. "We're going in," he announced. "Wake up the engine room."

Jill Danner gave him a wondering look, but she was already on the engineroom line. It wasn't necessary to wake anyone, of course; no one below had been sleeping, either.

Tregarth answered her unspoken question. "We can't stay here," he said. "Look at those surface ships! They navigate by automatic radio guidance. There's not one of them that knows what it's doing without satellite guidance and shore beacons; when they start to blunder around I don't want to be in their way."

"Yes, sir!" Jill Danner, relinquishing the conn to the captain. Under his guidance they crept forward, dead slow, keeping well within the channel markers. As they made the turn past Fort McHenry the bay opened before them.

It was almost empty. The few craft in sight were fast to their moorings.

"Half ahead," Tregarth ordered, scanning the dock area ahead.

There was not much to see at this distance. The tall old buildings of the city of Baltimore were still darkened, only the tops of the tallest picked out in pink and rose with the sunrise light. There were no street lights, no lights in any of the windows. A few cars moved along the waterfront, their headlights blazing, and the channel buoys had their own self-contained power sources. Everything else was darkness.

Jill Danner stole a glance at her captain. Should we be doing this? she asked—but only silently; you didn't ask you captain such questions out loud. There would come a time when she herself would be a sub skipper, and have decisions to make just as tough as this one. But, thank heaven, she told herself, not yet awhile.

As they closed on the dock area she squinted and pointed ahead. "That's our berth, Captain," she murmured.

Tregarth nodded. "You can take her in, Jilly," he ordered. "Get a watch on deck. I don't see anybody there to take a line."

"Yes, sir." A moment later the six of the starboard crew were squeezed in a knot on the deck, standing clear of the officers, ready for mooring.

"Something coming up fast, sir," Jilly said suddenly. But Tregarth was already looking that way, and before the words were out of her mouth the huge whoop of a siren cracked their ears. A port cutter was throwing spray twenty meters on each side of its bow as it raced toward them, dead on.

"Damn fool!" snapped Tregarth, and then swore even louder.

There was a crack and a splat. Something sent up a fountain of spray thirty meters off their port bow.

"They're firing on us!" Jilly cried.

It was not technically true. The shot had been across their bows, but everybody on deck could see the ugly snout of the projectile launcher bearing on them from the bow of the cutter.

"All engines stop," Tregarth grated. Then, a moment later, "Belay that! Engines back full! Hard starboard! Bring her around—he's coming too damn close!"

It looked as though the cutter were indeed going to ram. It would have been a suicidal maneuver, because the flimsy shallow-water vessel would have crumpled like a paper cup against the stout Nexø hull of the *Atlantica Queen*. Tregarth did not let it happen. He was too good a seaman to allow a collision. He brought the engines to full speed astern, twisting away from the patrol vessel.

And then there was a shudder, and filthy black mud spewed up along the flanks of the *Atlantica Queen*. In order to dodge the cutter they had left the channel. The submarine was firmly aground.

The port cutter reversed thrust with a vicious maneuver that might have torn the screws out of some vessels. It bobbed to a stop not ten meters away. The projectile launcher swerved to cover them. A figure on its bridge lifted a loud-hailer to its lips.

"You on the submarine! You're all under arrest for violating the military curfew laws! Come on deck, all of you, with your hands up!"

And an hour later the entire crew of the *Atlantica Queen*, captain, executive officer and all, were in a military prison ashore. Their possessins had been taken from them. They were unfed, without bedding—and left without explanations of any kind.

The only thing they were not without was company. The cavernous holding pen was evidently not planned as a prison—it seemed to have been an underground warehouse of some kind, pressed into service to hold all the curfew violators Baltimore's PanMack police could find. There were at least two hundred persons in that bare, dark pit. Most of them were as furious, and as ill-informed, as the crew of the *Atlantica Queen*.

As far as Tregarth could tell, the only thing they had in common was that few of them were lubbers from the PanMack domain. Most were land people, to be sure, but at least they were seagoing land people, mopped up from the crews of the moored vessels, with an occasional foreign businessman or even tourist for seasoning.

A few were submariners like the crew of the *Atlantica Queen*, people of the Eighteen Cities. As Ron Tregarth was banging on the doors of the holding pen, furiously trying to attrack the attention of a guard, a lanky young black man strolled up to him. "I'm M'Bora Sam," he said. "City PanNegra. You from the City Atlantica sub?"

When Tregarth nodded, M'Bora grinned wryly. "You should have stayed in City Atlantica, friend. It's not going to be healthy here for the next little while. Welcome to the ozone summer!"

I live in the mind of the Eternal, and I remember.

I remember another life. I remember a childhood in the high reaches of the great World Tree, leaping from branch to branch while my mothers waited anxiously on the branches just beneath to catch me if I fell, and I remember the god who came to teach us. We had so much to learn! Not even the oldest of my fathers knew of such things as "planets" and "stars beyond the highest branches at the high crown of the Tree." We never saw such things. We could not know that a "star" unimaginably far away—but very near, by comparison with others "stars"—was about to explode, and destroy itself, and blast our own world with terrible invisible light and unfelt heat.

At first we did not believe.

Then the World Tree itself began to die, as the awful radiation blighted its highest parts.

We died with it.

I died there, on that star-ravaged world, so far away. We all did.

It is more than eight hundred thousand years since I died . . . but I live on still, in the memory of the Eternal.

The
First Year

Chapter
10

In the first hours of the first year of the new age of mankind Graciela Navarro—starved for sleep, starved for food because it was twelve hours since she'd had time for a bite, starved most of all for news, because the news was terribly scant—Graciela Navarro, drafted into emergency duty with her school sub, was piloting the little ferry sub on the long spiral up to City Atlantica's surface platform.

The errand was urgent. Something—Graciela was not sure what—had blinded the platform. All of its delicate electronics were damaged; it had neither radio nor radar, and an Atlantic storm had smothered the platform in cloud and torrential rain. Sandor Tisza, City Atlantica's chief of communications, was with her, but the more important part of her cargo was crates of replacement parts.

As Graciela Navarro slid the ferry sub up in its tight berth between the deep, buoyant legs the platform floated on, the little vessel began to roll hugely in the mid-Atlantic swell. For almost the first time in her life, Graciela wondered if she might be susceptible to seasickness. Then she began to wonder if she might be more likely to drown. This platform was not the dome. Here there was no safe, secure mating of port to port; the size of the waves forbade it.

Here they had to squeeze out through the hatch, clutch the cables of a flimsy-seeming bridge and, soaked with spray, hustle inside the shell of the platform.

It wasn't just Tisza and herself who had to be got aboard. What the platform crew greeted even more eagerly, and handled with far more delicate care, were the crates of electronic components to replace the ones fried by the vast electromagnetic pulses that had smitten every communications facility on Earth. The newcomers were not in the open more than two minutes, but in that time the Atlantic gale had drenched them all.

Graciela was glad to be inside, but what a noisy thing a platform was! As it rode the waves and slewed about under the thrust of the gusting winds, the platform creaked and groaned and crackled. A taut-faced communications technician was feverishly checking the electronics from the crates. "Should be all right," she muttered. "Two kilometers of water ought to be insulation enough—" Then she looked up and spared a smile for her boss. "Welcome aboard, Dr. Tisza," she said. "Come on, let's get this stuff where we can use it!"

She shouldered one of the crates and led them to a tiny elevator. Up they went, fifty meters and more, to the command deck of the platform, and there Sven Borg, the head meteorologist, greeted them. "Sandor! Am I glad to see you! We've got no communications to speak of, no weather station reports, no satellite pictures—and the weather's rotten! Not to mention the damn meteors!"

Graciela peered up at the black, stormy sky. What she saw, beyond the forest of antennae and dishes that were the platform's chief reason for existence, was almost nothing. "What meteors?" she asked, raising her voice to be heard. Even so, it was almost blown away by the wind.

"They're there, all right," said Borg. "Beyond the clouds. Even under them, sometimes—the big ones punch right through. Just keep watching, and you'll—there! Look at that!" And off to the south, just as he spoke, a great line of white fire stretched itself out of the base of the cloud and arrowed toward the earth. Graciela flinched away from the expected noise. It didn't come. Bright as it was, the meteor was silent. "At least two hundred kilometers away," said Borg bleakly. "But that one hit the surface, all right. If one of them hit us—"

He didn't finish the thought. He peered more closely at Graciela's face, fishbelly-pale in the stark light of platform's deck standards. "You're exhausted, woman!" he cried. "Why don't you go below? Get something to eat— get a little rest, too; there's nothing for you to do up here."

Graciela realized she had not been on the platform in a long time—not since she was a small girl, and her father had taken her and a couple of schoolmates to see what a strange thing the surface of the ocean was. It had frightened her then. It frightened her now, if she allowed that to happen. There were *storms* up here! There were *meteors*, there were even, perhaps, *enemies*.

She wondered what it was like to spend long weeks on the surface. It would be almost as bad as being a lubber, she was sure. Yet the platform was necessary. Water was nearly opaque to radio waves. The ultra-long wavelengths used for city-to-city communication could penetrate it, but those wavelengths required such kilometers-long antennae that only a city could deploy them. The platform was also where airborne visitors could land, taking the ferry subs down to City Atlantica's dome two kilometers below. Of course, people from the Eighteen Cities never flew— why should they, when they had their long-distance submarine fleets to carry them wherever they wished to go? But a certain amount of the commerce with the land went by air.

In the refectory a youth with a worried expression served her the food she'd been missing ever since the emergency began. Great mugs of coffee, stacks of sea-soya pancakes, rashers of tuna bacon; she devoured them all, and then sat wearily over the third mug of coffee, thinking of nothing.

She was too tried to think. When the full dimensions of the meteor showers began to register with the people of City Atlantica she had just returned from her expedition with the squid. After that it was all a blur. City PanNegra had broken off communications in the middle of a message, and they had not been able to raise them since. The mayor had instantly ordered an emergency check of City Atlantica itself, securing all external gear, moving all the subs to moorings far away so that any sudden turbidity current or other water movement wouldn't send them crashing into each other, or, worst, into the Nexø dome. There had been something very near to panic. And then Graciela had been summoned from the squid school, where she was trying to calm her charges, to take the school sub to the surface with urgently needed supplies. . . .

How could such things happen, she wondered dazedly.

She glanced up as she became aware someone was joining her. "Mind if I sit down?" boomed the voice of Sven Borg. He was a huge man, hair Viking pale and face reddened with the sun and winds of the Atlantic surface. He was smiling wearily, almost apologetically, as he loomed over her. "I guess I was rude to you when you came in—sorry about that! But the big thing was to get Sandor up here to help out—and the new components, of course! They're working fine—as far as we can use them. We've got one radar back in service, anyway."

"I didn't expect a red carpet welcome." Graciela smiled, and then they both spoke together: "How are things going—" only one said, "—up here?" and the other, "—down below?"

"The city's all right," Graciela finished.

"And so are we—if we don't capsize, anyway," said Borg.

"Capsize? How could the platform capsize?" Graciela demanded incredulously. "It's so big!"

Borg barked a laugh—this time, not a pleasant one. "It's a chip on the ocean," he declared. "This storm's nothing, we're built for worse than that. But there's been one tsunami wave already, and if we got a really big one— Oh, you didn't know," he said, shaking his head. "While you were asleep. There was a wave from the east—not big here, out in the open sea; tsunamis don't look like anything until they hit a shoreline. We don't know what caused it, for sure, but Sandor thinks it was a big chunk of the comet, somewhere far away—hours ago, probably, and the wave just reached here. There was a big pressure reading, too—oh," he added hastily, "City Atlantica's all right. But we haven't heard a word from PanNegra. . . ." He took a swallow of his coffee.

Graciela shivered again. "Do you think PanNegra's—in trouble?" she asked. "We lost communications hours ago."

"Let's hope not. It could be just their comm systems. Anyway," he went on reassuringly, "at least the front's passing, so the weather's getting a little better—I think so, anyway." He grinned ruefully. "I guess we'll wish for an occasional storm like this, if we get that ozone summer." That phrase again! When he saw the question on Graciela's face, Borg only shook his had. "Don't ask me what that means. I don't know anything about meteors! Meteorology sounds as though I should, but, you know, meteorology is weather and meteors are pieces of junk that drop on us out of space—what do I know about space? Sandor knows a little more than I do, just because he's got the kind of mind that squirrels away information, whatever it is. But he doesn't know, either. We just heard the term, 'ozone summer', on some lubber broadcasts before they all went out. And Sandor thinks—" He paused, as though he didn't like what he was going to say. "Sandor thinks it has something to do with the ozone layer. It's delicate, you know. Maybe the meteor strikes might affect it—I don't know!"

Graciela was puzzled. "And if the ozone layer got damaged?"

Borg said somberly, "That ozone layer's the only thing that keeps the sun's ultraviolet away from us, Graciela. The bad ultraviolet. Killing radiation, that would damage plant life and probably every living thing that wasn't protected. Of course, City Atlantica wouldn't be affected—we're two kilometers down! But the surface-dwellers—" He let the sentence trail off. Then he added, "But that's only a guess! It won't happen—I hope."

He touched the beet-red skin of his cheek again absently, and Graciela took a sudden breath. "Your face!"

He smiled crookedly. "That was yesterday," he said. "A little sunburn; I didn't even think about it at the time. But it was still daylight here when the first meteors struck— Still, it may be just a coincidence, you know—"

He stopped in the middle of the sentence, as the speakers in the hall rattled: "Attention! Attention! Emergency stations! All personnel to their stations at once! Unidentified aircraft approaching!"

Graciela Navarro had no assigned emergency station on the platform, of course, but she could not keep herself from responding as rapidly as Borg. The two of them didn't wait for the slow, cramped lift; they pounded up the ringing metal stairways, jostled by others on the same errand, arriving out of breath in the open air.

Sandor Tisza was there on the met deck, surrounded by the instrument shelter, the hooded theodolites, the useless radar dishes; he was peering through great binoculars into the dark sky. It wasn't entirely dark any more; the rain had stopped and the clouds were broken, and it was not dark at all off to the west, where the fireworks display was still going on, bright slashes in a narrow band by the horizon.

He handed the binoculars to Borg at once. "Aircraft, Sven," he said briefly. "High up—twenty thousand meters at least. Radar says there are three of them."

Borg didn't answer; he was already scanning the sky overhead anxiously. Shading her eyes from the lights around her, Graciela tried to see for herself. It was so confusing! There were all these lights in the sky—they were stars, of course, and Graciela knew what stars were though she had seldom seen them before. The stars were beautiful, they were astonishing, but they confused her when she was striving so hard to make out—

Yes, there they were. A couple of tiny plumes of flame. No brighter than the nearby stars—nothing at all, compared to the swords and lances of fire off to the horizon—but she could see them move.

"What are they doing?" she gasped.

The bearded Hungarian gnawed his lip. "Nothing, so far," he said reluctantly. "But they shouldn't be there at all! We're not in the normal aircraft lanes—anyway, their communications must be as bad as ours, so they must be falling back on inertial guidance for navigation. But why? They must have some urgent reason to be there—"

"And whatever their reason is," Borg said grimly, lowering the glasses, "it can't be good for the Eighteen Cities. Have they made contact?"

"No, Sven," said Tisza worriedly. "Of course, their radio is probably fried, like everything else. Our spotter plane took off a few minutes ago to try to make visual contact. But those planes could have been using laser-optics all along if they had anything to say—"

"If they wanted us to hear it, yes," boomed Borg. "They're just orbiting up there." He handed the glasses to Graciela and took a deep breath of the clean sea air.

"Anyway, I think the meteors are getting scarcer, don't you, Sandor?"

The Hungarian shook his head in gloom. "Not for a while yet, I think," he said. "I don't know enough to have an opinion, though. How big was this Comet Sicara? What was its course? How many fragments was it broken into? How far out was it at the time—which means, how long did the swarm of fragments have to disperse before they began to strike? I don't know any of that. But the shower could go on for days!"

Graciela gave up trying to find anything in the glasses and listened to Tisza. "I don't know anything about comets," she said apologetically.

"They're cosmic junk, Graciela. Fragments of stuff left over when the planets were formed. Most of them are out in the Oort Cloud, far beyond the planets—dirty snowballs; frozen gases and cosmic dust. Now and then one comes near enough the sun to boil off a little gas and show a tail—they can be really spectacular, sometimes. Ancient people used to be superstitious about meteors and comets. They thought that when they saw a big one a great disaster was about to happen. Maybe they were right!"

"Come one, Sandor," Borg chided. "He doesn't mean that, Graciela."

"This time," the Hungarian said heavily, "I'm afraid I do. Look at your face! Have you ever had a sunburn like that before? And that was when you were in the sun for just a few hours, at the very beginning of the shower!"

Graciela squinted to see if she could make out the platform's little scout plane, as it climbed to meet the strangers. If it was there, she couldn't detect it among the panoply of Atlantic stars. She stared off to the west, where the narrow band of pyrotechnical meteors still flashed. Strangely, they all seemed to be coming toward her. Sandor explained that meteor showers all seemed to radiate from a common point, now far beyond the horizon;

but even he was startled when one giant object flared bright enough to drown all the rest, coming toward them across the sky like a backwad sun until, abruptly, it died. "That one probably hit the surface," Tisza muttered, eyes fixed on the dreadful splendor. "I don't think it was big enough to do much damage, though." He glanced overhead. "I think the only things we have to worry about right now are those—*what's that?*"

Far above them was a quick, tiny blossom of flame that was neither meteor nor jet exhaust. It was an explosion.

"The plane blew up!" Graciela cried.

"But that's impossible," muttered Tisza, staring up at the bright little flower expanding in the sky overhead. "Aircraft do not blow up for no reason."

And Sven Borg wasted no time in staring or in guessing. He disappeared into the command bridge and came out, his face tight beneath that rosy sunburn.

"Our spotter plane," he said, his tone somber. "We have it on the radar, and it has collided with one of theirs. There are parafoils coming down. Graciela! We'll take your sub—we have to pick up the survivors!"

Pick up the survivors. How easy to say, she thought, and what a terribly difficult job to do!

The sky was growing lighter in the east, precursor of the sunrise—that was good. Everything else was bad. Graciela's sub had never been designed for operation on the surface. Neither had Graciela! As the little sub lurched and wallowed in the swells of the open sea Graciela's fear of seasickness returned—not just the fear, either; she retched and gagged as she fought the controls. She had been stressed so far past her limits that it almost seemed comic now; what, she wondered, did the world expect of her?

It was even worse for Sven Borg, because the huge man had the task of guiding the sub. Instruments could not help. Communication with the platform was non-existent, in any ordinary way. The only options open to them were to guide it visually, which meant that Borg had to spend his time on the sub's upper deck, using the one little dorsal hatch that washed great green slops of water inside every time he opened it, hanging on for dear life, keeping the platform in sight for their lamp signals, straining to see the parafoils overhead.

That took a long time. The parafoils came down so very slowly that they were invisible to Borg until minutes before they reached the surface. It was the one working radar on the platform that followed them, and the directions communicated by lamp from the platform to Graciela's sub that put them anywhere near the impact point.

At least Borg could see *something!* Graciela, hunched miserably over her controls, had no such luck; she could only follow his orders, shouted through the vent hole in the hatch, and pray that they were the right ones. Then he boomed: "I've got them, Graciela! Change course—ninety degrees starboard, right away, and put on the speed—" And then, almost at once, "No! Slow down—I'm being washed away!"

They almost crept for ten long minutes. Then, at Borg's shouted order, Graciela cut the engines and floated, listening for orders that didn't come, bobbing about in the slow, vast seas, wondering—

She heard scrabbling noises on the upper hull, then Borg's voice. "Got two of them," he panted. "Our own boys!" The hatch opened and two men tumbled in; then it was slammed again, Borg staying on the deck. "Now vector forty degrees port!" he called, his voice ragged with strain and exhaustion. "About two kilometers—there's another parafoil. . . ."

At least now she had company in her misery. The survivors were not in good shape. How could they be? Graciela asked herself; they had bailed out at twenty thousand meters or more—no air to speak of, and what there was was terribly cold; their helmets had given them oxygen enough to survive the first free fall until they dared deploy the parafoils, but then there had been the long, slow descent through air only microscopically warmer. They were frozen and half unconscious from the exposure. The taller of the two was the pilot, Larry d'Amaro. He had a huge bruise on the left side of his face where the helmet had smashed into him as he took it off and he was bleeding at the nose. But he managed to say, "Thanks! We thought we were going to drown there until Sven jumped in and pulled us out."

"But what *happened?*" Graciela demanded, crouched over the controls.

"The bastard rammed us," the pilot said bitterly. "We were trying to talk to him by lamp—they didn't respond."

"The collision wasn't on purpose," argued the other. "He was just trying to scare us away and he got too close."

Following Borg's shouted course corrections, Graciela eased the wallowing sub near the one remaining survivor.

But as she cut the engines, Larry d'Amaro cried out, "What's that?"

Graciela felt it too, or heard it—she could not be sure which; it was a series of thudding distant sounds. It was unidentifiable, but it was frightening. Graciela's first thought was that more of the comet fragments had smashed into the sea nearby; yet, she was almost sure, that was impossible, for it was the other side of the Earth that was taking the barrage now; it would not be their turn again until the sun was high in the sky.

There was no time to waste on speculation. She heard Sven Borg's exhausted bellow from the deck: "Can one of you get up here and give me a hand?" Then, faintly, a splash; evidently he had gone into the water again.

Larry d'Amaro was already scrambling up through the hatch, slamming it behind him. Then there was an agonizingly long wait. Then, slowly the hatch opened again. Graciela heard muffled grunts and fragments of words from above. A bucket of green sea water sloshed in to add to the bilge that was already soaking the crew compartment; then, unceremoniously, a man was tumbled in.

He was unconscious. He was a stranger, pale-skinned, hair so fair that it seemed almost white. Something about him looked vaguely familiar—but that was impossible, thought Graciela, tasting the word she had never spoken before, because he was an *enemy*, for he wore the gold and green flight uniform of the lubbers' so-called "Peace Wing".

Danny Lu, the other survivor from the spotting plane, bent over him. He pulled off the great, heavy Peace Wing helmet to reveal a worn young face, its eyes closed. "He's alive," Lu pronounced. "He's swallowed a lot of water, though. I'd better see if I can get some of it out of him." He rolled the stranger over a bench and began rhythmically pressing on his back. It didn't take long for the man to cough rendingly, vomit a huge volume of bloody water and try to sit up.

Then the hatch opened once more.

Silently Larry d'Amaro lowered himself in, turned to help Sven Borg.

"Close the hatch," Graciela ordered. "I'll get back to the platform water, I can make better speed that way—"

"There's no reason to hurry," Borg said heavily. "The PanMacks have sunk it."

For one moment there Graciela was sure she was dreaming. Sunk the platform! Why would anyone do that? But, then, why *anything*, of all the incredible and unjust things that had been happening?

"It's true," Larry d'Amaro confirmed, obviously shaken. "I saw them—two of them, Peace Wing ships with those ogival delta wings—they were diving on the platform, pounding it with missiles. They used nukes, Graciela! There can't be any survivors!"

And from behind Graciela a hard voice choked, "Of course we retaliated! You attacked us without provocation! You rammed my ship, so of course that was an act of war!"

The pilot from the Peace Wing ship was standing unsteadily now, one hand bracing him against the bulkhead of the sub, the other resting at the holster on his belt.

"That's a lie!" shouted d'Amaro. "We were only trying to ask you what you were doing. You tried to scare us away. And came too close—lousy piloting!"

The Peace Wing pilot shook his head. "Untrue," he muttered, wiping dazedly at his face. "It was deliberate suicide ramming on your part— A definite act of war— Anyway," he said sharply, straightening. "That does not matter! I am Flight Commander Dennis McKen, PanMack Peace Wing, and I have captured this vessel under the rules of war. You will set course immediately for the nearest port on the continent of North America—"

Graciela cried, "But that's impossible! We don't have the fuel—we don't have charts—"

"Nevertheless," McKen said coldly, drawing the sidearm out of his holster, "you will do as ordered. "You!" he snapped, pointing the weapon at Graciela. "Set course immediately! Due east, two-seventy degrees. Full speed. I expect—"

But what Dennis McKen expected he never said. He toppled over in the middle of the sentence, an astonished expression on his face.

Behind him Danny Lu put down the iron bar he had struck the man on the back of the head with, and reached to pick up the gun. "It seemed like we could save a lot of arguing this way," said Lu apologetically.

"Well done, Danny! Keep an eye on him," ordered Borg. And then, somberly, "There's nothing to keep us up here any longer, Graciela. Let's go back down to the dome."

She hesitated. "But what did he say his name was?"

"He said it was McKen! That's enough for me!" Danny Lu snorted.

"But he said *Dennis* McKen, and isn't that—"

"Oh, my God, you may be right," whispered Danny Lu, gazing at the unconscious man. "I think I've just coshed the mayor's only son."

Chapter
11

Newton Bluestone had never asked to work for Simon Quagger. The task was impossible, trying to polish that gross public image! He'd laughed when his agent called to offer him the job, laughed at least until she mentioned a salary that took his breath.

At first it hadn't been too bad. The aura of power had a kind of glamor until he began to learn what Quagger did with power. Once he had welcomed the chance to observe and record a curious chapter of world history. And he had met Judy Roscoe.

If Quaggerhome was a trap, they had served as bait for each other. In the beginning, when they might have got away, neither had wanted to leave the other. They had become too useful since, and now it was too late. PanMack officials always denied keeping any sort of blacklist, but bad things happened to those unfortunates who offended any McKen.

At sundown on the second day of the first year, Bluestone was standing before the great doors of Quaggerhome, gazing worriedly at the sky. "There's one!" cried Judy Roscoe, touching his shoulder to point to a quick, faint streak of light in the sky overhead. "And—yes, that's another. But nothing like last night!"

"No," Bluestone agreed. "Nothing like last night." Nothing had *ever* been like that terrible long night of fire flaming down from the sky; he and Judy and half the population of Quaggerhome, it seemed, had stayed there all night, staring at the awful display from the heavens.

"I think it's over," said Judy Roscoe. "And," she added wonderingly, "I'm getting hungry. Funny. I didn't even think about eating before! Let's go back inside."

In the lift to their quarters high inside the old mountain they didn't talk much. They were not only exhausted physically, they had used up all the talk that either could think of on the subject that drove out all others. Judy Roscoe held the title of Science Advisor to Lord Quagger; astrophysicist and nucleonics expert, she had the background to justify the position. But even a woman with two separate doctoral degrees could say very little about the funny thing that had happened to the world when there was no data to deduce from.

In the lift, Bluestone thought Judy Roscoe had been looking at him in an unusual way. When they got to the comfortable staff lounge adjacent to their quarters she went at once to a mirror and peered at her face. "You've got a little sunburn," she announced, "and so have I."

Bluestone felt his own face. It is—yes—just a little tender. "Strange," he said. "We weren't out that long, were we?"

She said grimly, "Long enough, maybe. Newt? Were you listening when I told you about the ozone layer?"

"I was listening, all right. I'm not sure how much I understood."

She shook her head. "I'm afraid we're all going to understand a lot more than we'd like before long. Start with this. We've both been a little sunburned, and yet I'm sure we didn't exceed normal exposure limits. What does that mean?"

"What you said? The ozone layer damaged?" Bluestone guessed.

She nodded soberly. "I wish I had some communications with the rest of the world," she fretted. "I'm just guessing now! But there was certainly a lot more hard ultraviolet in the sunlight today than usual, and I'm afraid it has something to do with Comet Sicara."

Bluestone stared at her. "What does a comet have to do with sunburn?"

"I wish I could say nothing," the woman said. "Wait a minute. . . ." She went to the phone. "Lord Quagger?" she asked, and then, nodding, "I see. Still in executive session." She made a face at Bluestone. "Then let me know at once as soon as he's free, and meanwhile send up some food to the lounge. For two; I don't care what. The best and fastest you can."

She hung up and turned to Newt Bluestone. "At least the internal communications are working," she sighed. "Everything else is fried. EMP." Bluestone nodded; she had already explained electromagnetic pulse to him. "The blackout's total: no radio, no satellite contact. If we weren't hardened in here we'd have no power, either, because I'm willing to bet half the world's without electricity now."

"I don't see what that has to do with sunburn," Bluestone objected.

"They come from the same thing, I'm afraid. Comet Sicara. A comet is a mass of frozen gases. Reducing gases, mostly—hydrogen, methane, carbon monoxide. When the

McKens broke the comet up they kept it from hitting the Earth as one single body—and, God! That was a good thing! But the fragments kept coming. First there was the electromagnetic pulse that fried everything electronic that was exposed. Then—chemical reaction! All those reducing gases hitting the ozone layer! Ozone—the most violently oxidizing form of oxygen. What I think, Newt, is that the ozone combined with those gases from the comet, and we don't have an ozone layer any more."

"Well," Bluestone said reasonably, "that's interesting, but I don't see—"

"With no ozone layer hard ultraviolet from the Sun is not just an annoyance. It's *deadly*." She shook her head. "I can't predict exactly how bad it will be, but it will be bad. For as long as it takes the ozone layer to reform, the whole surface of the Earth is going to be bombarded with killing radiation."

Bluestone swallowed. "How—how long—?"

"I don't know! I don't have enough facts! I don't know how much of the ozone was used up, and even if I did I don't know how long natural processes would take to restore it—it has never happened before, and it's not something you can test out in a laboratory. Weeks? Months? I just don't know! And then the other thing—"

She hesitated. "What other thing?" Bluestone prompted, his nerves twitching.

"I'm not sure of that. But with all that carbon combining with the ozone—will there be an increase in carbon dioxide? I'd have to work out the numbers. But with a carbon dioxide increase there might be a general warming of the atmosphere. That might last a long time, and what it means to the Earth's climate is hard to predict."

"I don't think I'd mind warmer winters in Colorado," Bluestone offered, trying to envision the future.

"How about warmer winters at the Poles? Perhaps

melting the ice caps? How about more storms, Newt? The atmosphere's a heat engine, you know. Put more heat in and you increase the chances of frontal formation— storms; maybe even bad ones—" She stopped there, staring blankly at the wall.

A knock on the door announced that their food had arrived. Two waiters, wearing Peace Force badges on their jackets, wheeled in a table set for two. They whisked covers off dishes, fussed to rearrange the plates and disappeared. .

The meal was roast beef, beautifully cut and aged and cooked, with steamed broccoli and a huge baked potato for each. Bluestone looked at it distastefully.

"I think I've kind of lost my appetite," he complained.

"Eat," Judy commanded, picking up her own knife and fork. "You may regret it before long if you don't."

"Meaning what?"

"Meaning," said Dr. Judy Roscoe, already chewing, "that sunburn isn't the worst part of it, if I'm right. That same ultraviolet will kill vegetation. Take whatever food you can get now, because the time may come when there won't be any more."

An hour later Newt Bluestone was tossing and turning in his bed, aching for sleep, unable to attain it.

It was not that his bed was in any way uncomfortable. As secretary and general factotum to Lord Quagger himself, Bluestone shared with Judy Roscoe and half a dozen other top staffers the luxurious executive level, with its own lounges and refectory and sauna. There were no windows in his room, because there were no windows anywhere in Quaggerhome, but in every other way it was a suite a millionaire might have envied.

And it was his, for as long as he enjoyed Quagger's favor. And not one minute longer.

Bluestone pounded his pillow, trying to find a comfortable position for his head. Reluctant right arm to Lord Quagger! He had never planned such a career for himself. . . .

Time was when Newton Bluestone was a rising creator of video-docs. Not the most famous in the world, no. Certainly not the best paid. But his star was on the rise, and the future looked good.

Then came the call from his agent. "Dr. Simon McKen Quagger," she announced breathlessly. "A *McKen,* Newt! He wants a documentary on his life, and he wants you to do it. Get out there to Colorado; your tickets will be waiting at the jetport!"

And then his first sight of Quaggerhome.

He had expected a multi-millionaire's opulence, of course. Simon McKen Quagger was one of the "Macks" of the PanMack consortium, owners of half the world. A genuine member of the McKen Family, if only on his mother's side; it was to be taken for granted that the place he lived in would be something rich and startling. But Bluestone had not expected *that.* He had not known that Simon Quagger had taken over the old North American Air Defense Command headquarters inside Cheyenne Mountain, and converted it into a citadel of luxury and security.

And then Bluestone met Quagger himself. Not just Quagger. Not even Dr. Quagger. There in Quaggerhome he was addressed as Lord Quagger, and his major domo warned Bluestone sternly not to forget.

Quagger himself had shrugged the title aside. "It amuses my loyal staff to call me that," he said, beaming at Bluestone out of the tiny pig eyes. But he didn't tell Bluestone to forget the title.

What he told Bluestone was his plan. "Our family, the McKens," he said loftily, "has done more for the human race than any other in history. More than the Adamses or the Rockefellers or the Hapsburgs. The McKens have outdone them all. Even the minor members of the family, like my silly great-uncle who wasted his fortune on those absurd cities under the sea. We have made the planet blossom!"

Blossom for the McKens themselves, anyway, Bluestone thought. Their grasping, exploiting policies had made them incredibly rich. But it was a zero-sum game, and most of the rest of the inhabitants of the PanMack empire had paid the price to balance their gains. "However," Quagger went on, waving off a beautiful, scantily-clad serving girl who was offering a decanter of wine, "our family image is tarnished. The world does not know the truth about us, Mr. Bluestone—Newt, may I call you? So I want you to tell the wonderful story of the McKens for all the world to see."

"Actually, Mr., uh, I mean, Lord Quagger, my specialty is impartial documentaries—"

"But certainly you must be impartial!" cried Quagger, the rosebud lips pouting. "No one wants anything else. I want you to set the record straight. Our family is tarred with an unfair label slapped on us by the silly seafaring branch of the family. They call us 'the bad McKens'." He shook his huge head in humorous wonder. "Imagine that! Us! Whose commercial ventures control nearly half the Earth's surface, and fully six-tenths of its gross product! It's that false image I want changed—objectively, impartially and accurately. Of course, any artistic venture needs a focus, so in this case we will tell the McKen story through my own life—not, I promise, an uninteresting one. And I myself will help you get it all accurate!"

Bluestone cleared his throat. He did not need to be reminded that PanMack controlled six-tenths of the world's product. He already knew that all the broadcasters and disk publishers he dealt with were McKen corporations. "The only thing is," he said, temporizing, "it's possible we might find that your point of view and mine disagreed in some respects—"

"Nonsense," Quagger boomed jovially. "Just sign the contract. I warrant I'll make you see the truth of what I see. And— Ah, here she is, my darling Angie!" And the huge man was actually trembling with pleasure as a—a *creature*, Bluestone thought, because he had no other word for her—came bounding and squealing into the room. A monkey, he thought at first, but then he heard it speak. It leaped to Quagger's side, crooning to him, then it spotted Bluestone. It hissed sharply and cried out, in actual English words: "Throw him out! He's not one of ours! He doesn't belong here, Quaggie!"

"Now, now," chided Quagger, chuckling as he stroked the long, rust-colored fur. "It's only our new friend, Newt. He's going to be with us for a long time, Angie dear, so don't be a naughty girl. Kiss Newt!"

Bluestone could not help stepping back at pace when the thing came toward him.

It didn't kiss him. He was spared that. But it touched him, it smelled him, it bounded around, gazing at him, and then it went back to huddling in Quagger's lap, glaring at him.

"So you see?" Quagger demanded. "Angie loves me, and Angie is never wrong—so I must be a good person, Newt. Sign the contract! I'll make you not only rich but famous, as the one true recorder of the glory of the great McKens! —As exemplified, of course, by my humble self."

And so he had signed the contract. . . .

Bluestone got out of his bed and threw a robe on, shuffling aimlessly toward the common lounge. If he could not sleep, he might as well not stay in his lonely bed.

Judy Roscoe was there in the lounge before him. She was bent over the desk monitor, punching out instructions into the great Quaggerhome computation facilities. "What are you doing?" he asked, heading for the table where a coffee pot steamed away.

She leaned back. "Making computer simulations," she said. "Hoping my first guesses about what will happen might be wrong—but the simulations all come out the same way. You look terrible, Newt."

He sat down, sipping the scalding black coffee. It would not help him sleep, he knew, but apparently nothing else would, either. "I was thinking about Angie," he said.

"Ugh! That'd make anybody look terrible," said Judy. "I'd love to get that creature on a necropsy table!"

Bluestone looked at her curiously. "That's a veterinary term, isn't it? Does that mean you think she's an animal?"

Judy Roscoe gave a short laugh. "I think 'animal' is too good for her. But," she added thoughtfully, "I don't know exactly what she is. Quaggie has never said, you know."

"And you don't know?"

Judy shrugged. "There are two theories. I've heard them both. One is that she's a kind of relative of the abominable snowman—Quagger's supposed to have bought her from a Nepalese monk who trapped her somewhere near Khatmandu and taught her to speak."

"Is there such a thing as an abominable snowman?"

"There's certainly such a thing as Angie," Judy said grimly. "But I don't believe that, myself. The other story's more complicated. It says that when Quagger was young he fell in love with a caddy."

"A *what?*"

"A caddy," Judy explained. "As in 'golf'. Long ago, when he was still young enough and not too fat yet to do things like play golf; and he had this young female caddy. Only she had a boyfriend who didn't like her fooling around with the rich gringo McKen—this was in Mexico, they say—and so he tried to kill them both. He must have been a terrible shot, because he missed Quagger entirely. He didn't miss the girl."

"But— But she doesn't look like any woman anybody could fall in love with! Even after being wounded!"

"Oh, the story doesn't say she was wounded. It says she was killed. And Quagger was so heart-broken—after he'd had his private army kill the boy friend, of course—that he took a scrap of her flesh to a genetic-engineering firm, begging them to clone a copy of her. And they tried. But it didn't work right, and that's how we got Angie."

"My God!" Bluestone cried. "Is that possible?"

"Oh," said Judy Roscoe morosely, "I don't believe it for a second. It contains a basic misconception. You see, I know Quagger pretty well. I know he's a woman chaser; why do you think I became his science advisor? There were better qualified people; but they were either male or ugly."

"You're saying the cloning was impossible?" Bluestone hazarded.

"Not at all! The impossibility is something else. What I don't believe is that Quagger could ever really be in love."

"True enough." He nodded and paused to admire Judy, who was completely admirable. "The McKens never love anybody, except of course themselves. Gloria McKen tried to break that rule, and look what happened to her!"

"So? Who was Gloria?"

"Quagger's mother." His voice turned bleak as he recalled her story. "I think she got a decent start. Pretty enough. A mind of her own. People liked her. Just barely eighteen, she broke an engagement old Angus had arranged for her and left the family to live with her lover. He was Alvin Quagger. A bright young poet and dramatist, just beginning to make his name. She got pregnant by him, which made old Angus furious."

"McKen morality!" Judy grinned.

"She did marry," Bluestone said, still a little grim. "The

week before the kid was born. Alvin was just producing his first play. On her money, of course, but the old man put a quick stop to that. Disinherited her. The opening night had got rave notices, but PanMack interests owned the theater. He got the company turned out in the street."

"McKen genes at work!" Judy's voice showed malice of her own. "One legacy he couldn't cut off. It came right on down to Quagger."

"Old Angus!" Bluestone nodded, approving the clean lines of her jaw. "Your basic McKen. Killing the play was just for starters. He dug up scandals, or made them up. Filed false legal charges. Wrecked the poor guy's career. Harassed him to financial ruin and finally suicide. All of which brought out the true McKen in Gloria."

"If she'd ever been different."

"She might have had a chance," Bluestone insisted. "If—" He sipped his coffee and shook his head again. "The way things went, she proved to be her father's daughter. Sued the half-brothers for control of all PanMack when the old man died. Kept the whole estate tied up for years. And Quagger—the Lord Quagger we know—he's the not-surprising consequence."

Judy looked behind them, out of cautious habit, before she murmured, "A hateful consequence, but I don't quite see what you mean."

"That killed the love in Gloria, if she'd ever really been in love. She gave the rest of her life to hate. Hating Angus. Hating the brothers. Hating PanMack. Finally hating her son, I'd imagine, for the McKen she must have seen in him. No actual abuse, so far as I know. There were trust funds and nannies and tutors and private schools, but he must have felt the hate. Nobody loved him. He never learned to love."

"Except to love himself." Judy made a face. "Unless he really loves that disgusting—"

The phone interrupted her. It was the major domo, and

she demanded Bluestone's presence at once. "In the audience room! Immediately! Don't keep Lord Quagger
waiting—what? Judy Roscoe? Certainly not! Lord
Quagger's had his fill of scientists."

"Come in, come in," cried Quagger. "And close that
door! There's a draft coming in here!"

Newt Bluestone hesitated in the doorway. Lord Simon
McKen Quagger was not in his audience room after all; he
was in the great, marble-lined hall that contained his
swimming pool, his potted tropical trees and his steamy
garden of hibiscus and orchids. He sat sprawled in a
throne-like chair at the end of the enormous pool, his gross
pink flesh bulging out of swim trunks, a glass of wine in
his hand and a frown on his doll-sized face. He wasn't
looking at Newt Bluestone. He was gazing with troubled
eyes at a group of three young women—all dark, all tiny,
all quite beautiful—who stood bewildered and weary at
the foot of the pool. There was something vaguely familiar
about all three of them, though Bluestone couldn't immediately decide what it was.

Then Quagger shrilled, "Which one, Newt? Which one
looks most like that cute little webfoot woman?"

At last Bluestone remembered. Of course! The women
Quagger had ordered drafted out of all the corners of his
domain, chosen for their resemblance to Graciela Navarro!

Bluestone said hesitantly, "Lord Quagger, I've just left
Dr. Roscoe, and she was telling me about something she
calls the 'ozone layer'—"

"No, no," cried Quagger crossly. "This isn't the time for
that kind of science mumbo-jumbo. That's not the question
I brought you here to help me with. Which one of these
handsome young ladies should I choose, Newt? I've sent
the other ones away—but I simply can't make up my mind
about these three beauties."

Newt Bluestone persisted: "But the situation is quite
serious, Lord Quagger. As a scientist, Dr. Roscoe says—"

From the back of Quagger's chair the little monstrosity named Angie hissed warningly at him. Quagger scowled. "Don't you see you're upsetting Angie?" he complained. "She doesn't want to hear about scientists. Neither do I! I hold them responsible for not warning us in time of this, ah, this regrettable incident! Their behavior is very nearly treasonable, Newt, and I shall be quite stern with Dr. Roscoe when I have an opportunity to discuss it with her."

"But she says—"

"I know what she says!" Quagger bellowed. "Same old thing! Complaining because I quite properly refused to allow her to waste desperately needed state funds for research to satisfy her idle curiosity! Don't tell me you share her spendthrift ideas!"

Looking around at the lavish life style represented by this one single room, out of all the luxurious rooms in Quaggerhome, Bluestone thought bitterly that a hundred years of research could have been funded for what was spent here. But to think it was one thing. To say it was far too imprudent. "Very well, Lord Quagger," he said submissively.

Angie hissed suspiciously, but Quagger was mollified. "We'll say no more about it," he said generously. "Now to the question. Which one, Newt? The one on the right, in the Peace Fleet uniform? She used to be a gunnery officer, until she was invited to join us here. The one in the middle? Lived in San Antonio, I think; has some sort of degree in languages. And the other is an artist, they tell me—isn't that right, my dear?" He didn't wait for an answer, but turned expectantly to Bluestone. "Well? Which one shall I choose?"

Bluestone could feel his stomach knotting up and churning. To be spending his time on something like this, when the world was falling apart around them! To live in the safety of Quaggerhome was certainly a boon worth having

—but was it worth it if the price was to humor the whims of this tyrannical, petulant madman?

He said diplomatically, "All three look very like her, Lord Quagger. All three are certainly very beautiful."

Quagger stared at him blankly for a moment. Then the undersized face broke into a smile.

"My dear boy!" he cried. "What a wonderful way you have of striking to the heart of a problem! Of course, you are right. I'll keep all three of them! Yes, yes, Newt, take them to my major domo and have her settle them in here in Quaggerhome. I'm really very grateful to you, Newt, but now—" the rosebud lips split in a yawn, delicately covered by a huge, fat hand— "now I'm afraid I really must let myself get some sleep. Good night, Newt—and good night to all three of you, my dears! And send in my masseuses on the way out, if you please. . . ."

But even when the masseuses had come and gone, Lord Quagger of Quaggerhome was not permitted to sleep. "It is the general, Lord Quagger," his major domo reported, looking serious. "He will call you personally in twenty-five minutes."

Quagger sat up on his bed. "Call me?" he demanded. "But I thought all communications were out."

"Yes, Lord Quagger. They've managed to restore a few links—old optical cables and buried ground longlines systems. By rerouting and taking detours General McKen has found a way to reach us here." She waited submissively for an answer, though of course there could be only one.

"Yes, yes," Quagger groaned. "Urgent affairs of state. I cannot let my own comfort interfere. Patch it through to me in my audience room; I'll wait for the call there."

If there was one thing Dr. Lord Simon McKen Quagger really loathed, it was being made to drink coffee late at night. It upset his delicate digestion. It made his sleep, when at last he did get to sleep, uneasy and troubled. It was an imposition.

It was also, however, a very wise precaution to be taken when he was expecting a call from his cousin, General Marcus McKen. Those calls were always annoying, and sometimes they could be downright humiliating, especially when Quagger was not at the very peak of his intellectual powers.

Annoying, yes; humiliating, often—and this time, Quagger thought as he waited with growing rage, downright insulting! For the twenty-five minutes had come and gone, and no call had come from the general. How dare the man treat a full McKen so cavalierly! Quagger fumed. It would serve Marcus right if he simply went off to bed and refused all calls until a decent hour the next day. . . .

But that he did not dare do.

He stared around his room, taking no pleasure in it this time. The banks of vision monitors were all gray and lifeless: the cameras that kept him posted on everything that went on in his domain had been damaged, he supposed, by this ridiculous event—one more thing, he vowed, to take the scientists to task for! He had been *inconvenienced.* Someone would have to pay.

Idly Quagger heaved himself to his feet and stepped out onto the deep pile of the carpet, staring thoughtfully down at it.

The carpet of Simon Quagger's audience chamber had been woven by hand. A hundred skilled carpet weavers had given two years of their lives to display Quagger's domain in tiny tufts of wool and silk, dyed in all the colors of the rainbow, meticulously positioned to show rivers, cities, mountains, lakes. It was unquestionably a work of art.

Quagger hated it.

He glowered down at it, wondering if this were the time

to demand that it be torn out at once, instantly, taken out and burned, destroyed—removed from his sight so that he would be spared the constant humiliation of seeing how tiny and poor the lands he controlled were.

Quagger's domain took in most or all of five former American states, with small nibbles out of two others. Colorado, Utah and New Mexico were his. So was most of what had once been Texas, except for the easternmost (and most valuable!) strip along the Gulf of Mexico. So was all of Arizona except for the part (again, the most valuable part!) next to the California border; so was a chunk of the western part of Oklahoma and a thin strip of Kansas . . . and all of it put together was, in Quagger's opinion, nearly worthless. Fewer than one hundred million subjects! Mines that were played out, farms that had been plowed and eroded until the soil was almost empty of nutrients, rusted old factories that would never operate again, deserts —and a climate that ranged from Arctic in January to Hell in July.

Quagger lumbered over to the edge of the carpet, where the golden hues and features of Quagger's own domain gave way to the unmarred blue that outlined General Marcus McKen's far richer and far more beautiful lands. Angie, bounding in belatedly to see what her beloved master was doing out of bed at this hour, found him there. He gazed at her unseeingly. "By rights this should be mine!" he muttered.

Angie, plucking fondly at his cheeks, soothed, "No, no, Quagger dear, don't upset yourself!"

"I'm not upset!" he shouted. Then, more cunningly, "But I have been doing some thinking, my dearest Angie. These treasonable scientists have let something terrible happen to the Earth, you know. I've seen the reports! I am not ready to discuss them with anyone but you yet, but I know what's happened! Unprotected people dying of sunburn in terrible agony. A few fragments of that disgust-

ing comet large enough to punch right through the atmosphere and do real damage—oh, most of them landed in
water somewhere and who cares what happens to the
oceans? Or the webfeet that live in them? But what they
call 'seismographs' show that at least one may have landed
quite near one of Marcus's cities—Pittsburgh, I think—
and heaven knows what damage it's done there."

"Have them shot at once!" shrilled Angie in indignation.

"Shot? Who? Oh, you mean the scientists," said
Quagger. "Perhaps I will, dear. But I've something more
important in mind. You see—" He paused, as a mellow
chime sounded. Quagger swallowed nervously. "That will
be Cousin Marcus," he said. "Hide, Angie! Don't let him
see you! He's so—so *prejudiced* against you, my dear, and I
don't want to argue with him at this time of night!"

As soon as the little creature scurried out of sight,
Quagger composed his features, activated his communications screen and said heartily, "My dear Marcus! I am so
delighted to see that you've come through this ordeal in
good health!"

The conversation was even worse than he had feared.

The first thing General Marcus McKen did was to sneer,
"Where's that filthy little beast you take to bed with you?
Hiding so I won't see her and remind you how stupid you
are?"

"She's—ah—resting, Cousin Marcus," said Quagger,
hoping that McKen would not spot the long red-brown tail
sticking out from under his throne. "Is all well with your
people?"

"Well?" the general snorted. "Don't be a fool, Simon.
Nothing is 'well' right now. In fact, we have suffered some
terrible losses," Marcus declaimed. "Cousin Dennis's own
plane was stricken down. A true McKen, Simon! He was
lost over City Atlantica!"

"But," said Quagger helplessly, "I don't understand. You told me there would be no fighting. I thought the plan was simply to take possession of the platform, and then compel the city to surrender—"

"Those barbarians," Marcus snarled, "they rammed his ship! Of course the rest of the squadron destroyed the platform."

"Then how will you be able to make the mermen surrender?"

Marcus gazed at his cousin with indignant loathing. "Don't try to think of such matters! You're not competent to."

"Very well, Cousin Marcus," Quagger said humbly. "But I do want you to know that I sympathize deeply for the loss of our beloved kinsman."

"Oh, don't be a hypocrite! Now, pay attention, Simon! I didn't call you to chit-chat. I want you to take measures. Effective immediately, I want you to confiscate every bit of food you can get your hands on. Also fuel; also all the electronic equipment you can find that is still packed in original shielded cartons, or was otherwise protected so that it's still in working order. Grab it all! Store it away. Put armed guards around the warehouses, and tell them to shoot if necessary. Do you understand that?"

"Yes, Cousin Marcus. I will start preparing the operation tomorrow—"

"You will *not*. You won't prepare it at all; you'll simply send out detachments of troops and do it—and not tomorrow, either! Right now. Tonight. Before everyone has time to realize that this stuff will be priceless. I want to make sure that in case I have to come back—that is, in case I need more supplies you'll have them for me. For the *Family!* No," the general added as Quagger opened his mouth, "no more discussion. Don't waste time. Do it!"

The screen went blank.

Dr. Lord Simon McKen Quagger raised his great bulk and capered around his room, grinning.

Angie poked her head out from under his throne, regarding him anxiously. "What is it, Quaggie dear? Don't excite yourself this way! It can't be that bad!"

"Bad?" Quagger shouted. "There's nothing bad! It's all good, because now I know what Marcus is going to do! My dear cousin will certainly not want to live in a world as badly damaged as this one. I think he is planning to leave it!"

"Leave it?" gasped the furry little thing. "I don't understand, Quaggie, dear."

"He would leave it for some place in the Eighteen Cities if he could—that's why he had his stupid nephew out there to get knocked down. But I don't think he'll be able to do that. No," said Quagger judiciously, "I know what Cousin Marcus is going to do. He'll head for one of those terrible tin cans he owns in space—Habitat Valhalla, most likely. Yes, that's it! My cousin is going into orbit, Angie dear!"

"Let him go," Angie chattered viciously. "I hate him!"

"And with every reason, my dear!" Then Quagger added triumphantly, "But don't you see what it means for us? If Cousin Marcus is foolish enough to go gallivanting off in space, there's no reason I can't take over the lands he leaves behind!"

Angie looked at her master with worship. "Oh, wonderful, clever Quagger!" she whispered as Quagger, preening himself, leaned toward his communicator and began bellowing for his generals.

Newton Bluestone had tried hard enough to understand. He'd been hired, after all, to create a more appealing public image of Lord Simon McKen Quagger. It was a dismally hopeless task that was always being enlarged to include other dismally hopeless tasks, all of which he heartily hated and longed in vain to escape. Yet even now he couldn't help asking what had made Quagger the total monster that he was.

"I despise him!" he had muttered to Judy Roscoe, once when he knew no planted bug was listening. "We all do, but I'd still like to know what makes him tick. Partly now, it has to be this ozone inferno. You've got to remember that we're all caught in it. Quagger himself, like all the rest of us. Even old Marcus, out by the moon. Trapped in a cruel new world they can't command or even understand. They're panicked, like frightened animals. No wonder they act more than a little bit insane."

"Animals they are!" Her lip curled. "Let's look for something better to think about."

Judy herself was something far better, at least just then, and whenever Quagger's demands left him any time at all for her. He never tried again to explain Simon McKen Quagger, certainly not to Judy, but the inhuman ugliness of all the McKens kept nagging at him like a splinter festering in his finger.

Some people were evil. Court records and history books held enough appalling evidence of that. But why? Why Simon Quagger? Why all the dryland McKens? One more riddle that he finally lost among all the other haunting riddles of a world gone mad. He never found an answer.

When Newt, sleepy-eyed and worried, reached the audience room, Lord Quagger's four top military commanders and an even dozen of their aides were already there. They looked as though they were even more worried than Newt Bluestone. Quagger darted him a resentful look as he came in the door. "You're late," he barked, and Angie hissed angrily to confirm it. "How can you properly record my life for history, if you sleep through the most important parts?" He paused threateningly, then turned back to the great map on the carpet. He took his stance on the city of San Antonio. "I want two divisions, here," he declared, "ready to strike for Houston and the Louisiana Coast. Three more in Wichita over there, to head up through Missouri and Illinois to the Great Lakes. Air support will be on combat alert, but they won't move until the ground forces do. Then when I give the signal they will move simultaneously; we'll lop off the whole western edge of Cousin Marcus's lands and consolidate, and then—what's the matter with you, Danforth?" he snarled, looking at his senior general.

The officer said bravely, "Sir, their troop strength is twice ours and they will be in defended positions. To attack like that would be suicide. They'll be ready for us, and—"

"They will *not* be ready for us," Quagger corrected coldly. "They will suspect nothing."

"But, sir, as soon as we begin to .mobilize on their borders—"

Quagger gave him a triumphant smile. "But they won't see it in that way, General Danforth. They will understand that our troops are merely moving in to declare matrial law in communities that are rioting, panicked by the damage caused by the comet fragments."

"Rioting?" Danforth looked perplexed. "There isn't any rioting in those areas, Lord Quagger."

"Of course there will be," Quagger said silkily. "That's your job. The first thing you will do is send agents into those cities to get the rioting started. I want panic, Danforth. I want people in the streets, breaking shop windows, looting; I want armed bands roaming the cities; I want at least a hundred civilian deaths—rapes, robberies, fires breaking out—I want such an outbreak of disorder that when Cousin Marcus hears about it the only thing he'll ask me is why I didn't send the troops in earlier. Then, when he's off guard, we'll strike!"

Danforth's eyes narrowed, calculating. "It is true, Lord

Quagger," he said thoughtfully, "that their forces are spread all over. It would take time to concentrate them."

"And time is what we won't give them!" Quagger crowed. "You'll prepare a timetable. So many hours to reach your first objectives, so many hours to consolidate and move on. I want every step spelled out, Danforth, and I want to approve every word of the plan. Make it fast. And make it real, because when the operation begins I will hold you to it! Any unit that fails to accomplish its objective will be decimated—one man out of every ten will be shot; and the first one to die will be its commander! Do you understand me?"

The general's face was like stone. "Yes, sir," he said.

"Then do it! I want a workable plan of campaign on my desk tomorrow morning, the first riots forty-eight hours later, the troops in place twenty-four hours after that. Then we wait for my orders; but you must be ready when they come . . . and, Danforth," Quagger added with a grin, "that battle plan is your first objective. Accomplish it! Or pay the penalty."

When Quagger had dismissed the generals he turned to Newt Bluestone. "They're such children," he sighed. "If you don't rap their knuckles now and then they won't even try. Have you got all this, Newt? Oh, what a grand climax it will make, how I, Simon McKen Quagger, saved the family's interests when even other McKens began to falter! And make sure you tell it well because—" he wagged a humorous finger at Newt Bluestone—"that, after all, is still your first objective, isn't it?"

When Newt finally got back to his bed he tossed and turned, gazing at the ceiling.

Thousands were going to die as the result of the scene he had just witnessed. Cities would be shelled and bombed, homes would be ruined, refugees would be streaming across the country, seeking food and shelter and jobs.

It was so easy to look at Simon McKen Quagger and see a foolish, clownlike fat man . . . and to forget that under the capering mound of blubber was a snakelike, deadly creature that fed on power, hungered for more . . . and knew all the ways there were of gaining and preserving it.

Chapter
12

When the PanMack guards came storming into the prison tank Ron Tregarth was asleep. "Get up!" they were yelling, prodding the sleeping prisoners with stun-batons, kicking them with their steel-toed boots. "Get up and get moving! You've loafed around here long enough!"

Tregarth pulled himself erect, blinking in the harsh glare from the hall. "What is it, Captain?" whispered Jill Danner groggily from the floor behind him.

"Better get up," Tregarth said, peering down at his executive officer. Jilly Danner had stood the confinement as well as anyone else, but it had been hard on them all. They were all squinting painfully in the sudden light. There had been no lights in the great common cell for days—weeks, maybe; he'd long since lost count of time. For the first few days he'd been able to count meals, because for the first few days there actually had been meals. Sometimes there had even been hot ones, and then you could tell what time of day it was because breakfast was always breakfast, burned bread they called "toast" and slimy porridge and something they said was coffee, while the other two meals were always stew. Then the stews had become soup, and the soup had been the only meal they ever got. Then the lights had gone out, and all the guards would say was there was no sense wasting valuable power on criminals, and even the soup was less frequent and thinner, and hardly ever even warm.

A guard in the Peace Fleet helmet swung his baton at Jill Danner, barely missing as Tregarth pulled her out of the way. "Outside!" the PanMack roared. "Time for you creeps to get to work!"

"Work at what?" Tregarth demanded, but the only answer he got was a scowl and a disgusted, "You *stink*." Tregarth didn't argue; he knew it was true of all of them. Forty-one prisoners had been confined in that one room, and Tregarth could not remember when any of them had last had enough water to bathe with.

Helping his executive officer along with one hand, Tregarth joined the other prisoners as they slowly began to move out of the cell, blinking in the brighter light of the corridors.

He looked around him, trying to remember what this place had looked like when he was thrust into it. It wasn't a real prison, it was an underground warehouse, built by the lubber McKens in one of those crazy times of tension when they seemed on the point of throwing nuclear missles at each other to settle some question of dividing the spoils of the looted Earth. Tregarth remembered clearly that when he was brought down there the storage spaces had been filled with stored food. The food was gone. From the bays they passed as they trudged up toward the surface he heard moans, and the glimpses from inside showed him row on row of cots with bandaged-swathed people. Could they be casualties? Casualties from what? Had there been a war after he was imprisoned? If so, a war between whom and whom? Had the undersea cities been involved—and Graciela—?

He put those thoughts out of his mind again, as he had a thousand times since he was imprisoned.

When they reached the surface he forgot those worries. He stood appalled, with the rest of the prisoners, as they squinted out into the harsh sun of the outside world. "What's happened?" whispered Jilly Danner, and from behind them the black submariner from City PanNegra, M'Bora Sam, croaked bitterly:

"It's real, then. It's the ozone summer, and everything's burned!"

Whatever had happened, it had been bad. The grounds around the prison had been landscaped once, almost like a park. Now the space was like a park in—in, say, Hiroshima, long before, just after the dropping of the world's first nuclear bomb. The trees were dead. The grass and flowers were gone. Nothing green showed anywhere in sight. The scorching sunlight parched dry brown stubble.

"Halt!" ordered the guards.

The column of prisoners collapsed, and along under the sheltered colonnade, out of the sun but wearing huge dark eyeshades, a slim, scowling youth with the platinum braid of an officer marched toward them. The guards came to quick attention. The officer swept them with a scowl, then mounted a desk top to look at the prisoners.

It was apparent that he did not like what he saw. He said, voice filled with loathing, "I'm Lieutenant Marutiak. Take note, you are all hereby officially impressed into the service of the Peace Forces under the command of General Marcus McKen. You people have had it easy long enough, while the innocent citizens who put you in prison to punish you for your crimes have been risking their lives every day to keep you fed! Now it's your turn. You're all assigned to work details, harvesting what's left of the crops before this ozone hell destroys them. Work hard! Try to

redeem yourselves! Pay your debt to the PanMack
Consortium—because if you don't work, you won't eat."

As they moved aside an ambulance drew up outside the
loading platform. A man in a white suit and white gloves,
wearing a white, broad-brimmed hat, jumped out of the
cab. He turned his own dark-glassed eyes on the prisoners,
then waved the ambulance driver back until the rear door
of the vehicle was just under the sheltering roof of the
dock, outside the pitiless glare of the sun.

From inside the hospital-prison-warehouse exhausted
orderlies appeared to begin to carry the patients out of the
ambulance. A doctor, who wore not only the broad-
brimmed hat but the same huge, dark goggles as Lieutenant Marutiak, even inside the shelter of the bay roof,
stopped each one to study for a moment before waving the
stretcher-bearers on. Some of the people from the ambulance were moaning like the patients down below, some
writhed silently in pain. When the doctor looked at one
who did not move at all he shook his head. "This one's
dead," he said. "Salvage the bandages."

And as one of the orderlies set the stretcher down near
Tregarth and stolidly, wearily began to unravel the gauze
that concealed the patient, Tregarth saw with horror that
the dead man's face was blistered, puffed, lobster red.
What had killed him was sunburn.

M'Bora Sam whispered bitterly, "Now you know what
they mean by the ozone summer. But I didn't believe it
would be like this!"

"Silence, you," snapped the PanMack commander.
"Guard! Get these first ten prisoners into the ambulance;
it's time they went to work!"

Because Tregarth was the nearest to the vehicle he was
almost the first in, M'Bora Sam right behind him. Tregarth
struggled against the incoming prisoners, craning forward
to call, "Jilly! Come on! We've got to stick together!"

But she was too far back; the guard aimed another swipe at her with the stun baton and she stopped short. "It's all right, Captain," she called. "I'll be in the next load!"

And the ambulance doors slammed shut, and the vehicle took off. Inside, there was no light at all. In the stinking heat Tregarth could hardly breathe, but he felt M'Bora Sam's hand on his shoulder. "She'll be all right, Tregarth," the submariner said.

"I hope so," muttered Tregarth. "Anyway, I'm sure I'll see her soon."

But he didn't believe it when he said it. In that he was right; he never saw Jill Danner again.

The way the prisoners paid their "debt" to the society that had thrown them in jail was by digging through the parched, rock-hard fields for potatoes, carrots, beets—for anything that might be edible, down under the seared ground.

It was terribly hard work, and the baked soil was not the worst of it. It was the sun that was deadly. Even the overseers did not force the work crews out into the worst of noonday. The prisoners were allowed to sleep then—for two or three hours at most, less if there were any clouds, not at all if it happened to rain. Then, if they were allowed the hours off in the middle of the day, they were made to work at night, with the guards all around them with their flashlights, ready to punish anyone who dared eat any of what they were so painfully gleaning.

It was inevitable that someone would put the guards' threats to the test, and perhaps it was inevitable, too, that M'Bora Sam should be the one to try it. They had just finished a night's hard work and were stumbling back to the shelter of the tobacco-curing shed where they slept.

Exhausted as he was, Tregarth turned to look over his shoulder at the dawn. The skies at morning were now brilliantly colored. Tregarth had never seen such sunrises, but submariners were not expert in such matters. Even through the heavy goggles the colors were like a sky on fire. He whispered to the lubber prisoner next to him, "Are they always like this?"

"Shut up," the man snapped under his breath, darting a glance at the guard. Then as the man with the stun-baton turned away, the prisoner whispered, "It's the smoke. Soot! There are fires you wouldn't believe out west, and it's all coming here."

He had not been quiet enough. "No talking, you two!" roared a PanMack guard, lunging toward them with his stun baton. Tregarth tried to duck away, but the wicked weapon caught him on the back of his neck and the shock made him flop his arms and legs like a galvanized frog in an experiment. The pain was indescribable. He fell full length on the searing blacktop road, waiting for the next blow, sure that it would kill him. . . .

It didn't come. He heard a confused shouting, and when he was able to raise his head he saw the PanNegran submariner, M'Bora Sam, borne down by four guards. "Steal food, will you?" shouted one, belaboring him with the stun baton, and another cried harshly:

"Make him scream! I've got something for him to eat!"

And when the PanNegran opened his mouth in a shout of agony, the guard thrust the baton into his mouth, brutally, and thumbed the charge button.

The sound that came from M'Bora then was not a scream. The damned in hell might make sounds like that, but Tregarth had never heard anything like it from a human being before. Even the PanMack guard jumped back, startled. He gazed around almost defensively. "Serves him right! That's what thieves get," he declared; and another guard said roughly:

"You! Pick him up! If he's going to die, he'll have to die at the camp, where we can be sure he's not just trying to escape."

Tregarth obeyed the order. He didn't sleep for hours after that; he spent the time trying to trickle water, a few drops at at time, into M'Bora's mouth. He fell asleep sitting beside the unconscious man, and, as every night, as he fell asleep, he dreamed of Graciela Navarro.

But when the crew was ordered out again M'Bora, though he could not speak, rose with them and, face set against the agony inside, dug in the hot, dry dirt for the last bits of harvest.

Then the rains began.

For days, then for weeks, the rain came down—hot, oily rain that drenched the ragged clothing, turned the fields into mud. It was because of the smoke, the prisoners told each other, but whatever the reason it teemed. The river was chocolate colored now, with the red clay of the naked soil and the soot from the fires.

At least, Tregarth thought, they wouldn't have to work at night any more. The sun's rays were as deadly fierce as ever, but they spent themselves on the far sides of clouds that roiled five thousand meters into the sky.

In this he was wrong.

The rain that turned the fields into mud scoured the surface soil away. The few tubers and roots that were left began to rot in the dank heat—when they were not simply washed down to the full creeks with everything else that was exposed.

Of course, the PanMack Consortium could not countenance this waste of their resources. So the guards were given their orders. "Harvesting" would continue day and night till the last salvagable bit of food was safely in the storage bins. The guards feasted in their trailers on canned goods and frozen food; the moldy roots were for the prisoners. And that night the guards passed the word: "Eat in the fields! You've got two more hours' work before you get your lazy bodies in bed. Eat now-and do it fast!"

But the rations had been cut again. They weren't even cooked! The potatoes the crews had loaded into the trucks before dark were doled sparingly out to them again, two per man. The storm was worse than ever, thunder crashing overhead, lightnings flashing, and when Tregarth begged some water for M'Bora, just beginning to recover his voice but still in pain, the guards laughed. "Water? There's plenty of water!" they roared, grinning as they pointed at the mud-filled creek.

As Tregarth opened his mouth to protest, M'Bora put a hand on his shoulder. "It's no use," he whispered, face contorted with the pain of trying to speak. "Let's go."

In the scrubbed-out fields M'Bora stood in the teeming rain with his hands cupped before his mouth until his thirst was satisfied. Then silently he fell to.

The pickings were sparser than ever. By the time they had reached the very bottom of the field, fumbling wearily through the mud for the last of the tubers, their sacks were still almost empty. A PanMack command vehicle was parked on the road, just below them, its great spotlight on the roof of the cab roaming aimlessly around the field to give them all the light they had. Tregarth heard music playing from inside the cab—dance tunes! A cassette recorder, no doubt; but it astonished Tregarth that on this ruined earth people still had the leisure to play music.

M'Bora coughed rackingly.

One of the guards inside popped his head out, muttering to the other still inside. Then, cursing, they came out in their black rainsheaths and helmets, sending the light from their hand torches around the field. They approached Tregarth and M'Bora suspiciously. "What are you two doing down here by yourselves?" one demanded. "Stealing the nation's food?"

Tregarth didn't answer. Next to him, M'Bora whispered something angry and incomprehensible as the guards walked toward them. "Ah, look," said one guard to the other. "It's the black sailor, the one we caught stealing already. Looks like he wants another dose!"

The second guard snatched M'Bora's sack and peered inside. "He's a thief, all right," he said virtuously. "Look at this sack! Not a dozen rotten little spuds! They've been filling their bellies with the good ones all night!"

Both men were closing in on M'Bora, shining their lights in his face. He squinted at them silently, his face opaque. He did not move at all until one of them, swearing, raised his stun baton.

Then M'Bora swung at him with the sack. He caught the guard in the face. There was not enough mass in the paltry sack to do serious harm, but the PanMack stumbled, shouting angrily, and slipped and fell in the greasy mud; and Tregarth moved, too. He didn't stop to think. He simply could not let M'Bora Sam be punished again. He launched himself at the back of the second guard, his arms around the man's chest, reaching up to lock his hands behind the guard's head. He exerted force—

The PanMack's head snapped forward with a sickening crack.

Tregarth did not wait to see if the man was dead. He flung himself into the bitter struggle between M'Bora and the other guard.

A minute later one guard was dead and the other unconscious from his own stun baton, and M'Bora and Tregarth were cautiously approaching the command vehicle.

They gazed at it in silence for a moment. It was a handsome machine. Bullet-proof tires, four-wheel drive. Even air-conditioning. There was a light machine gun mounted in a flat turret on top, and its motor was an omnifuel that could burn anything from high-test gasoline to wood chips.

Tregarth looked at M'Bora Sam. "What are we waiting for?" he asked.

And M'Bora Sam, for the first time in weeks, laughed out loud. He clutched his throat when he did it, but kept the smile on his face. "After you, my friend," he whispered, gesturing to the driver's seat.

Chapter
13

In the first months of the first year of the new history of mankind Graciela Navarro's squid school had ceased operations. There was nothing for it to do. There was no room for the squid—the great pool had been drained to make room for some of the bunks and pads that were all the fifteen hundred refugees from drowned City PanNegra had to live in. And Graciela herself, like everyone else in City Atlantica, was working eighteen hours a day to deal with the emergency.

When her shift was called she got up, ate sparingly (for food, too, was becoming as scarce a commodity as living room) and made her way across the great open space, now filled by the refugees, to her work sub. Then it was out across the sea bottom to the site of the new satellite dome that City Atlantica was hurrying to build to house its unexpected new population.

There was no choice about that.

City PanNegra was dead. One fragment of Comet Sicara

had struck the sea nearby, and the hydraulic hammer that
resulted cracked the base of the city's Nexø dome. That
was enough to kill City PanNegra.

The city took a measurable amount of time to die, for the
crack only let the sea in at first. That was bad enough (sea
under two kilometers pressure thundering in, destroying
everything it touched; pressure in the dome building fast
enough to crack eardrums.) But there was time for a few of
the inhabitants to get into subs or pressure suits.

Then the crack widened as the lift of the air inside the
dome pulled it remorselessly apart.

Air bubbles the size of a house belched out, pulling
people and things with them; the people and the things fell
out as the bubbles wriggled to the surface; and then the
dome lifted away from its foundations.

That was the end. The dome remained partly attached to
its moorings at one side, tipped crazily, like the top of a
soft-boiled egg in its cup just before the breakfaster dips
his spoon into it. But there was nothing alive inside.

More than eighteen thousand people died in that terrible
half hour, and nearly all of them knew what was happening. And the survivors had fled to City Atlantica.

Graciela Navarro's job was to help build the new satellite
dome. The foundations had been scooped out of the
abyssal muck, the old Nexø plant had been revived and
was already pouring out its thick, colorless ooze that
would harden into the crystalline structure of the new
habitation.

To build a Nexø dome was rather like blowing a soap
bubble. It was already well along. They had found the
perfect site, a few kilometers from the old squid school.
Then jet drills had reached solid rock and the Nexølite
cables were now anchored solidly to immovable holdfasts.
The new dome of PanNegra, at least, would not float away.

As Graciela approached in her work sub she could see

the great liquid-in-liquid Nexø bubble swelling slowly as the hydraulics crews pumped water in. Great hoops of silvery metal were brought to touch it; the Nexø joined to them by surface attraction, as the wire circlet of a child's bubble-blower would pick up a film of soapy water from a dish.

That was Graciela's assignment. She joined the other tugs as they pulled the rings carefully apart, stretching the bubble to make it longer; other circlets pulled out bays and protuberances.

It was dicey work, holding the parts of the new dome precisely in place as it swelled to its full size, but it didn't take long. Blowing the bubble was the easiest part of making a new dome. Once the foundations had been set and the mix prepared, the actual swelling of the bubble took less than a week. A heavy jolt of high-voltage electricity froze the Nexø into a single giant crystal; the rings were needed no longer, nor the sub crews to hold them in place.

Then it was time for the pumper craft to pull their huge Nexøfilm hoses up to the surface, sucking in air; time for the pumps to force the water out of the new dome. Then the construction crews could go in, installing the floorings and the walls and, ultimately, the furnishings and machines that would make the new dome alive for the refugees to occupy . . . but those were not Graciela's concerns. When the Nexø was flashed into its permanent shape she was through—with that assignment at least—and she was allowed twelve long hours of sleep as a reward.

She did not enjoy it.

She woke a dozen times in those dozen hours, fretful and weary. Each time as she woke she reached out to touch the person who should have been slumbering beside her, Ron Tregarth. And each time she found only the tiny, slim

form of the PanNegran woman who had been assigned to
share her room.

Ron Tregarth was not there.

Ron Tregarth, she was beginning to be certain, never
would be there. Sometime in the last months the date they
had set for their wedding had come and gone; and she had
not even been aware of it when it passed.

Her first duty was to report to the mayor for reassign-
ment.

Graciela had seen little of the mayor since the day of
Comet Sicara. No one else had, either. Like everyone else,
the mayor had been terribly busy. But, unlike everyone
else, the mayor had had a personal problem that she
seemingly did not want to face in public.

The problem's name was Dennis McKen.

The captured Peace Wing officer was not only a nephew
of General Marcus McKen, most powerful of the PanMack
overlords, he was also the son of the general's deceased
younger brother . . . who, for a brief time long ago, had
been the husband of Mary Maude McKen, now the Mayor
of City Atlantica. Flight Commander Dennis McKen was
her son.

Since his capture, Dennis McKen had been a model
prisoner. He didn't disguise his contempt for webfeet and
all their works. He contemptuously refused to give his
parole—if he saw a chance to return to his uncle's
domains, he vowed, he would take it at once; escape was
the duty of any officer taken prisoner! But he worked as
hard as anyone else at the endless drudgery of finding beds
and food for the PanNegran refugees; he volunteered to
don a pressure suit and work with the crews digging the
foundations for the new dome; he bore no malice, he said
(and seemed to mean it) against the people who had taken
him captive—least of all, against Graciela Navarro.
"You're wasting yourself here," he told her seriously a day

or two after his capture. "If I escape you should come with me."

"I can't 'escape'," she told him. "I live here. This is my home, and I love it."

"You love it," he said contemptuously. "Don't you know how stupid that sounds? City Atlantica isn't a country! It's a fish tank at the bottom of the sea, only the fish are outside."

Graciela shook her head. "You've been brainwashed," she said. "You've been taught to hate the Eighteen Cities all your life, just like any other lubber. You think we're contemptible peasants."

"Not hate," he corrected her. "The webfeet aren't worth hatred—contempt, yes. It isn't brainwashing, it's just a rational view of the facts. All the Eighteen Cities together don't mean as much as a single town in my uncle's domains."

"If you feel that way," she blazed, "why are you here?"

He looked at her in astonishment. "Why, because you captured me," he reminded her. "I'm your prisoner."

"You're an enemy in our home!"

"Yes," he agreed reasonably, "but trust me not to hurt you, Graciela. As long as I'm here I'll do my share, but I won't stay here forever. The time will come when I can escape. When that happens, I will. You should come with me, you know. You can be an important person in PanMack!"

"But everyone in PanMack seems to be dying of sunburn and starvation," she reminded him—not meanly, but to try to make him face facts.

He shrugged and grinned. "The McKens will survive," he boasted. "My uncle's already in a safe place, I know. And when it's time for him to come back, I'll be there with him—you, too, if you'll come to your senses and join me!" And when she mentioned, as tactfully as possible, that she was going to marry Ron Tregarth he seemed genuinely sympathetic. "But of course he'll never come back," he said—no more meanly than herself. "You have to face facts, Graciela. What's the matter with you webfeet? You're as bad as my silly mother, who won't even see me!"

Graciela resolved to talk to the mayor about that. She quickened her step toward the mayor's office—and then the tiny *brrrk, brrrk* of her wrist communicator told her that someone was looking for her.

It was Doris Castellan, her assistant, sounding distraught. "Graciela? It's Triton! He's in the pressure lock! He's looking for you, I'm sure, only he's—funny."

Graciela blinked. "Triton?" Triton was one of the most docile, if unfortunately also least intelligent, of the students of the squid school. He was also the school's leading truant. What had brought him out of the depths at this time?

But her assistant could not answer that. "He was here, that's all. He wouldn't speak—he looked very odd, Graciela; I can't tell you why. I had to sign to him that you were in the city dome, but I think he went there right away. He's probably there right now!"

He was.

When Graciela reached the city dome, the squid was floating in the water just outside the main service docks of City Atlantica, the great tentacles streaming away into the dark sea, the huge eye gazing at her. The body colors were dire dark blue and pale lavender; but what that meant Graciela could not guess. No human had ever been able to learn the squid vocabulary of skin hues.

Graciela docked her work sub a few meters away and raced back through the corridors to the main service docks. Frank Yaro was standing there, waiting.

"Only a few minutes, Graciela," Yaro said. "We tried signaling, but he didn't respond. Is he—dangerous?"

Graciela withered the man with a look. Triton dangerous! He was the school cutup; he had, Graciela was sure, a sense of humor. And he certainly was not dangerous! He was not only her student, he was her friend.

She squinted into the outside lights. One of the squid's tentacles was curling back, pointing to the metal boss that covered the implant in his head. Why? She seized the microphone to the outside comm speaker and said, "Triton, boy! You look Graciela, yes?"

The tentacles writhed helplessly, but the squid made no other response. "We tried talking to him, Graciela," Yaro said. "He won't answer."

Graciela shook her head, mystified. Since the squid school, perforce, closed, she had rarely seen one of her squid. There was no reason for them to come to the dome. Certainly they didn't need to come for handouts of food— even if City Atlantica had had food to spare. The squid were far better off than the hard-pressed human population. If anything, the squid had benefited, at least temporarily, from the devastation of Comet Sicara. As the hard ultraviolet killed off the surface organisms in vast numbers more and more organic detritus floated down to be consumed by the deep-sea animals—who, in turn, were consumed by the squid.

So why was Triton here? He had always been a puzzle to her—so playful, even sometimes what she could only call downright affectionate; and yet he so often failed to show up for his class—almost never, she had noted, though she had not been able to find out why, when Nessus was there. "Triton need help, yes?" she called.

No answer. She turned to Frank Yaro. "Let him in."

Yaro stared. "You mean it? With everything that's going on, have you time to play with your squid?"

"Let him in!"

Yaro, shrugging, keyed the outer gate open. At the same time the huge third gate behind them grumbled shut; now they were actually in a part of the lock. "He wouldn't be here if something weren't wrong," she said apologetically to Yaro, watching the squid slowly ripple into the lock.

"What *isn't* wrong?" Yaro retorted; but he was already closing the outer gate. When the *ready* lights flashed to show the seal was complete he actuated the alarm squawk, then keyed the inner gate open.

There was a sharp puff of pressure as the water containing the squid spilled into the inner pond. It was not great. Water is so nearly incompressible that it hardly matters, but the entrapped air was not. Graciela swallowed instinctively, then stripped off her outer clothing and dived into the pool.

"Triton boy," she cried. "You talk Graciela, yes?"

Triton's colors were less alarming now, a pale rose stippled with gray. The squid reached out to her with the delicate tip of one tentacle. It did not speak. It merely captured Graciela's wrist—so very gently!—and guided it to touch the boss over the implant.

Graciela glanced up in puzzlement at Frank Yaro, but there was no help there. Carefully she released the seals on the boss and looked inside.

No wonder Triton didn't speak! He had no voice. The implant was intact, but its power cell was missing.

Graciela floated back, stroking the tentacle reassuringly, trying to think. Why would Triton remove his power cell? Squid never did that. Squid seemed to enjoy being able to make and hear sounds, for in their natural state they were totally deaf. It was true that the first implants had been placed, willy-nilly, on terrified captives; but the squid had quickly learned to use them. Then why this?

The only way to find out was to ask. "Frank!" she called. "Are there spare cells in the emergency cabinet?"

"Of course there are." He did not look enthusiastic, but he rummaged through the cabinet and tossed one to her.

As soon as it was in place, the squid curled a tentacle

around Graciela's wrist again, almost like a human hand-shake, and spoke. The voice was mechanical, deep, reso-nant: "Triton glad, yes. Sound thing good now, yes."

"That is good, yes," said Graciela. "Triton open sound box, what reason?"

"Reason no," growled the unearthly voice from the box, as the squid's tentacles curled uneasily. "Triton open sound box, no."

"What?" Graciela was astonished. She tried again: "Tri-ton open sound box, no. Open sound box, who?"

"Other open sound box, yes," boomed the voice.

"Other?" Graciela's attention was distracted by the *brrk*, *brrk* of her wristlet, on a shelf with her outer clothing. "Answer that for me please, Frank? Tell them I'm busy." And to the squid: "Other, who?"

"Squid place other, yes," said the voice of Triton, and his tentacles moved more agitatedly than ever.

"Squid place other—" Graciela began, and then looked up.

"It's the mayor," Frank Yaro said. "She wants you. Now."

"One minute," Graciela begged. "Squid place—"

But Triton was rippling slowly away from her, toward the external gate. "Open box in squid place, yes," his receding voice boomed. "Triton go now, yes."

"Not yet! I mean, Triton stay minute, yes. Please!"

"Triton go now, yes," the voice repeated. The box was not capable of intonation, but there was a sound of finality to the words.

"Triton go now, where?" Graciela pleaded.

"Triton go squid place, yes," said the squid firmly. "Go see other in squid place, yes."

"Other in squid place, who?"

But the squid only thrashed its tentacles about. Its coloration had changed again; now it was an ugly mottled red.

"Graciela!" Yaro called impatiently. "Now!"

"Other in squid place," Graciela repeated, trying desperately to find out what was going on. "Other friend, yes?"

The squid coiled itself around so that the great eye was gazing at Graciela again. Its voice box sputtered for a moment, then said: "Other in squid place friend to Nessus, yes. Friend to Graciela, no."

When Graciela got to the mayor's office the woman had a man in her office. Graciela recognized him—Ector (Farzoli, who had been one of Sandor Tisza's communications technicians.) "You've been spending time with your squid, Graciela," the mayor accused. "How can you do that now, when we need every working minute?"

"It was only Triton," Graciela apologized. "There's something wrong, Mayor McKen. His voice-box power cell was taken out—I can't imagine who would have done it! No one's been working with the squid these last weeks, have they? No one's even seen them—"

"Wrong," the mayor said firmly. "Ector Farzoli here has seen them. One of them attacked him as he was checking the repeater stations, no more than two hours ago!"

Graciela blinked at the mayor. "Attacked him? One of *my* squid? That's impossible!"

"Tell her, Farzoli," the mayor ordered.

The man looked resentful, but obeyed. "It's just like I told the mayor. I was on my rounds—nobody's kept up maintenance the last few weeks, so I was going out on my own time—and I saw something on my sonar screen. It looked like that work sub that's been missing for months, so I went after it. It looked like it had gone behind a peak, and as I turned my sea-skid toward it out of nowhere this damn huge squid came at me. It was a monster! The biggest I've ever seen! I turned around and got out of there—I was lucky to get away with my life!"

"Oh, no," Graciela insisted. "My squid would never attack a human being."

"Oh, yes," he snapped, getting angrier. "It happened to *me*. You weren't there!"

"It could have been a wild one," Graciela offered, but the man shook his head.

"No chance! They all look alike, sure, but I could see something bright attached to its body."

"A voice implant?"

Farzoli hesitated. "Well," he admitted justly. "I didn't hang around long enough to make sure. It was bright, though. Maybe not exactly like the others—more like bright red glass, I'd say. But it certainly wasn't natural, I'm sure of that, and wild squid don't wear jewelry!"

The mayor lifted her weary head. "That's enough, Farzoli; Graciela has the picture. You can go back to work now." She peered pensively after his rebellious back as he left, then sighed.

"Graciela," she said, "do you know how serious this is? We've dug deep into our food stores. If we don't get the crop in on time I don't see how we can feed ourselves and the refugees—and how can our farm people harvest if they're going to be attacked while they work?"

"I don't believe it was one of my squid," Graciela said staunchly. "I'll ask them. Let me take a sea-skid and see if I can find Nessus—he's the biggest of them, and Farzoli said the one he saw was big."

"He's also the one that tried to bite Quagger's head off, isn't he?" the mayor said meditatively. "Of course, now we know the reason for that—at least, we think we do." She sighed and rubbed her eyes. "Oh, Graciela," she said, her voice wearier than ever, "I think I'm getting too old for this job."

"No!" Graciela said sharply. The mayor peered at her inquiringly. "It's not you," Graciela added. "The job is too hard for anyone, maybe—but there's not a soul in City Atlantica who doesn't think you're the right person to be leading us. Only—"

She stopped, trying to find the right words. The mayor waited her out in silence. Finally Graciela said, "Why won't you talk to your son?"

The mayor looked at her without speaking for a moment. Then, "Is everybody asking that question?"

"Everybody's worried about you, yes. They don't mean any harm."

"I'm sure they don't," said the mayor wearily. She stood up and walked over to the table at the side of her office, where a carafe of water stood. She poured some, counted out two pills from a tiny vial, and swallowed them with the water.

"I was married for just two years," she said reflectively. "To a McKen. General Marcus McKen's younger brother. There I was, a little webfoot girl in the big city, and he saw something about me he liked—I never had a chance to say no, Graciela. And that first year! The McKens live like emperors, and I did with them. And then Dennis was born, and—"

She poured herself another glass of water. "I couldn't stand it, Graciela. We were so rich! And all around us there was the PanMack domain, with millions upon millions of people living in poverty, so we could have air yachts and a servant for every need." She grimaced. "My husband had special needs," she said, her tone even and thoughtful. "He had servants for that, too. Pretty ones. And when I objected, he divorced me. Had my residence visa canceled. Threw me back to City Atlantica as an undesirable alien— me, the mother of his son! I tried to get custody, at least the chance to see my baby—but the PanMacks own their courts. Lubber lawyers wouldn't even talk to me. . . .

"I gave up, Graciela.

"I pretended to myself that I'd never had a child—and

then, when you brought Dennis here—Graciela, I don't know what to do about it! I'm afraid."

Impulsively Graciela stretched out her hand to touch the mayor's. "Don't be," she pleaded. "He's your son."

"He's an officer in the Peace Wing! It's because of him and his comrades that fifty-one of my people are dead and our surface platform is a wreck on the sea bottom two kilometers from here!"

"He's still your son," Graciela said softly. "Talk to him. Please. For his sake! He's alone here, among people he thinks are enemies."

"Nobody here will hurt him!"

"But how can he know that, when his own mother won't even see him?"

The mayor pursed her lips. Meditatively she went back to her desk and sank back in her chair. She looked at Graciela appraisingly.

"You're invading my privacy, you know." Graciela shrugged. "However," the mayor went on, "you may be right. I'll invite him up to see me. If he can stand it, I suppose I can—and now," she finished, "get out of here and see if you can keep your squid from eating our farmhands."

After three hours on the sea-skid, Graciela began to doubt that she would see any of her squid again.

She had tried everywhere she could think of—on the edges of the deeps, over the broad farms, in every place where they had been known to go. A hundred times she stopped the sea-skid and called, "Nessus, come! All squid, come! Come to Graciela, yes!"

And never was there an answer. They were gone.

Squid she did see now and then, half a dozen of them or more, lurking at the edges of her sonar screen. They had to be wild ones, she told herself. They not only did not come when she called, they showed no signs of hearing at all—just as any squid without the voice-box implant would have been expected to do. Twice she saw a huger, more menacing shape at the edge of the screen and realized that she was looking at one of the great toothed whales, sounding the depths of the sea in a quest for the food that was disappearing nearer the surface.

Maybe, she thought with a pang of apprehension, whales had eaten her squid. Certainly they would if they could; the squid were an important item of diet for the toothed whales at any time, certainly more so now that other prey was becoming scarce. Would the implants make them vulnerable? That was a discomfiting thought. The whale that would eat a squid would be likely enough to take a nip at a human being, too, and she was alone in the great deeps.

But still Graciela was almost pleased as she soared along over the sea bottom. The mayor had agreed to see her son! And when that happened, Graciela was sure, they would forget the decades of separation and the politics that divided them. Dennis McKen was not an evil man. He had been brought up in an environment that encouraged evil, like the children who became Hitler Youth a century and more before; but he was capable of gentleness and kindness, too, and even forgiveness toward those who had captured him.

Arranging that meeting had been only one small triumph in a forest of defeats, of course. Her squid were still not responding. Vera Doorn's *Thetis* was still unreported and by now certainly lost. The PanNegrans still had nowhere of their own to live. The land surface of the Earth was scorched and dying . . . and, most of all, her dear Ron Tregarth was gone.

But one small victory was more than she had had in many weeks, and she treasured it as she set course to return to City Atlantica.

Halfway there, her mood sobered as she saw a great

irregular shape begin to take form in her screen, because she knew what it was. It was the wreck of the surface platform, sunk by Dennis McKen's comrades and now forever at rest here at the bottom of the sea.

As she approached she saw figures moving about it. Curious, she set the sonar for magnification and when she realized what they were there was a sudden tang of bile in her throat.

They were searching the wrecked mass for the bodies of those who had drowned in it.

She paused, gazing at the shadowy figures, near to tears. Many good people had died in that vicious attack, and it had been near enough to being her own death, too. If she hadn't been ordered out to rescue survivors of the aircraft collision her own body would have been one of those the workers were laboriously pulling out and reverently shrouding in Nexøfiber body bags.

She turned away sadly, her heart going out to those workers. Not only was their task terribly depressing, it was also both dangerous and difficult. They had to get inside the passages of the wreck and search them, one by one—at crazy angles, with debris in the way more often than not. The aftermath of the tragedy was almost as heart-rending as the sinking of the platform itself.

As she mused and started the sea-skid again she saw a new shape on the sonar.

It was a squid.

It hung motionless in the water as though waiting for her, and as she approached it did not flee. She keyed her communicator. "Triton, yes? You follow Graciela, yes?"

And an unearthly voice boomed back, "I follow Graciela, yes. Graciela get hurt, not. I follow, yes."

The wave of feelings that washed over Graciela Navarro were confusing; they almost left her speechless. So Triton was trying to protect her! But from what? And why was he

so stubborn about answering her? Because when she tried
to cross-examined him about Nessus he gave only incomprehensible replies:

"Nessus, where?"

"Nessus, not."

That was a blow! She managed, "Nessus dead, yes?"

But that was wrong. "Nessus dead, not. Nessus Nessus,
not!" And what could that possibly mean? But however
many times she rephrased the question, Trident obstinately
kept denying that Nessus was dead and insisting that there
was no Nessus; and there was simply no way Graciela
could get at whatever truth lay behind the contradictions.

Nor would he speak of any of the other squid that had
been her students. Her air was beginning to get a bit low.
So sorrowfully she started to bid him farewell, and then
paused, struck by an idea. She glanced back at the
shadowy wreck of the platform.

Where the suited humans could go only laboriously and
in great peril, a squid could slide about easily.

It was worth a try. She keyed the communicator again
and said: "Triton! People dead in broken steel place, yes."

"People dead, yes," the squid agreed.

"Triton get dead people bring out, yes."

There was a pause while the squid thought that over.
Then, "Triton eat dead people, yes," the squid agreed.

"No!" Graciela cried. "Eat, not! Triton bring out dead
people, yes. Triton eat dead people, not!"

The squid gazed at her out of that huge, unfathomable
eye. "Triton bring out dead people, yes. Triton eat dead
people now, not."

Graciela was halfway back to City Atlantica before she
realized the significance of that word "now".

Chapter
14

The principal orbital refuge for General Marcus McKen was called Habitat Valhalla. From outside, it was an odd-looking structure.

What it resembled, as much as it resembled anything at all, was one of those ancient German potato-masher hand grenades. It started with a squat cylinder, proportioned about like a soup can, and it had a narrower, smaller cylinder attached to one end that looked very much like the handle of the grenade.

In a sense, the projection really was a handle. At least, it contained the lever that controlled everything on the PanMack L-5 satellite; it was the headquarters of General Marcus McKen. There was no good military reason why McKen had set up his command center there, in the projection from the central barrel of the habitat. True, the few hundred people who had been launched with him to occupy the habitat could not hope to fill it; there was room for many thousands. But the real reason was quite personal: Marcus McKen had discovered that the lesser gravity there did a lot to compensate for the unfortunate bad-McKen habit of becoming grossly fat.

And in a sense, too, it was quite reasonable that the whole satellite should look like a grenade, for it certainly was in a position to release a lot of explosive power on the helpless victims below it.

What made Marcus McKen fume was that he didn't know who to blow up.

It was not that he didn't have enemies. Marcus McKen was about as well supplied with enemies as any Hitler or Jenghiz Khan, and deserved them just as much. He had two and a half billion enemies in the people of the AfrAsian block alone. Besides them—and the Common Europeans, and all the lesser satellite fiefdoms—he had his own stupid relatives who had been left on the surface of the Earth to keep things in order. Above all (or below all), he had the webfeet of the Eighteen Cities, the insufferable outlaws in their stinking silly glass bubbles on the floor of the sea, who had always been an impertinence and now had the effrontery to seem to have survived the cataclysm that had desolated the surface of the land.

It would have given Marcus McKen pleasure to nuke them all.

It just wasn't practicable. As far as the AfrAsians and the Common Europeans were concerned, bombing would have been a waste of good nuclear missiles; Comet Sicara had blasted them more thoroughly than all of McKen's nukes could have done. Even two of his cousins seemed to have suffered some unpleasant fate—at least, they did not respond to his messages—and the third cousin was simply impossible.

Simon McKen Quagger! To think that he had the effrontery to consider himself a real McKen!

To throw one nice little forty-megatonner in through those disgusting heavy armored gates of Quagger's mountain fortress would have been a great pleasure—but *someone* had to stay down there to keep the plebes in order! Even if Quagger was an incompetent, he at least was on the scene, maintaining some sort of order through wholesale punishment. Quagger was good at punishing, Marcus McKen could not deny that.

And General Marcus McKen could afford to be patient, he informed himself. The day would come when this wholly unexpected ozone summer was over (his scientists had promised him that; after what had happened to them because they failed to warn him of its probability, it was not likely they would let themselves be wrong about that). And when, when it was time to come back to the surface of the planet, it would be time enough to enjoy straightening out cousin Simon Quagger.

Which left the Eighteen Cities—seventeen, now, he corrected himself, unless they'd finished rebuilding PanNegra.

Marcus McKen sprang athletically off his couch (how wonderful to weigh only a quarter as much as on Earth!) and danced gracefully over to the great terran globe that hung poised between magnets beside his throne. He waved his hand at it to make it slowly revolve as he studied the subsea city sites.

Eighteen cities. The amber lights that displayed their locations sprinkled the peaceful ocean blue like blemishes, from City Laurentian in the Beaufort Sea to City Scotia, on the edge of the Antarctic Ocean.

For eighteen cities, eighteen missiles.

The attack commanders had complained about the problem of guidance, with the satellites and radio beacons still fried from that terrible wash of EMP. But, grudgingly, they had admitted that even a near miss was good enough: Twenty or thirty megatons trying to compress incompressible water that was already under a pressure of many tons to the square centimeter would produce a hydraulic hammer that would crush those silly crystal domes. . . .

Marcus McKen's foul mood grew fouler. He was caught on the painful edge of a dilemma, between "want to" and "dare not". He had no objection at all to killing off a few hundred thousand lawless webfeet. But destroying the actual domes was something else entirely.

They might yet be needed.

When Marcus McKen was in a bad mood the best cure he knew was to spoil someone else's day. "Fetch Sicara," he grumbled, and in a moment the unfortunate astronomer was groveling before him.

"Dominic Sicara," the general thundered, "you have been tried and convicted before the military court of willful negligence in the carrying out of your duties. It is only because of my own clemency that you have not yet been sentenced."

"Thank you, General," the old man whimpered. "But I couldn't help it! The observatory—the main telescopes were dismantled at your order—"

"The space those telescopes occupied was needed for urgent national purposes!"

Sicara almost choked on that; the urgent national purposes had been the construction of a new gymnasium for the suddenly lightweight general. "Of course, sir," he sobbed. "How can I serve the general today?"

"You can show me the latest surveillance photos of the surface of the Earth—and be quick about it!" snarled Marcus McKen.

The scientist quaked as he hurried to obey. His fingers fumbled at the controls, but even so it was only a moment before he had retrieved the latest surveillance shots and was displaying them on the general's wall screens.

Marcus McKen began to relax. Almost as good as making someone else suffer was to see how vast and inescapable some earlier suffering had been . . . and there was plenty of it to be seen.

Desolation.

Wherever McKen looked, there was desolation. First

there had been the searing blast of the ultraviolet radiation, no longer screened off by the ozone layer. Then the remorseless summer heat as the carbon dioxide levels built up and trapped the infrared as well—carbon dioxide that had been building already for many decades of industrialization and forest burning, but now doubled almost overnight. The carbon monoxide that was part of the comet gases had contributed a mighty share, but greater by far was the carbon dioxide released by the burning of all those millions of hectares of dead and drying vegetation. The American redwoods, the Swedish pines, the Russian birch, the palmettoes and banyans, the trees of the tropical jungles—they had died, and they had burned; and all the carbon that they had sucked out of the atmosphere for the years and centuries of their lives had been returned to the air at once.

And what parching heat and fires had begun, the torrential rains had finished. Where once there had been forested hills, now there were slippery slopes of mud. Where once there had been green river valleys, now there were immense, wide slashes of red and black clay.

"Of course," said General Marcus McKen benignly, "when we are ready to return we will want all this cleaned up, and I suppose you so-called scientists are the ones who will have to do it."

Dr. Dominic Sicara goggled at his master. "But General!" he protested. "That's—well, impossible! Not to mention that my own expertise is in astrophysics, not reclamation of ruined agricultural soils—"

"Excuses, excuses," General McKen smiled. "They don't matter now, Sicara. But when we go back there won't be any excuses. You'll simply do it. Or you'll wish you had."

And he waved the unhappy astronomer away. It had not, after all, General McKen mused in satisfaction, a wholly unentertaining day.

Chapter
15

Time was when a Johns Hopkins student could jump in his jalopy in Baltimore and drive down to Fort Lauderdale for his spring break madness, two thousand kilometers and more, on express highways all the way; if he pushed, or took turns with the other undergraduates who shared his car, he could be there in twenty-four hours.

That time was over.

Tregarth and M'Bora Sam were lucky to make a hundred kilometers a day. They had to detour around cities, to avoid the PanMacks, and they had to cross rivers. Rivers were the harder problem, because most of the bridges were out, swept away in the floods. So there were endless detours; and every day their car used fuel and their bodies food. The fuel could be replaced—anything that burned would do for that engine—but by the time they reached Hampton Roads the armored car's supplies were running out.

If they had a destination, Hampton Roads was it. Any big port was it, because what Tregarth and M'Bora Sam wanted most of all was the hope of a submarine that they could steal or join, to get back to the Eighteen Cities—if any of the cities survived. But when they reached salt water at what the maps said was Hampton Roads there was nothing Tregarth recognized.

The rains had stopped at last. The flooded river had receded somewhat, but where it had been was only a desert of mud flats and a litter of what had once been buildings, first burned, then flooded.

There wasn't any sub. There were surface vessels, a few of them, heeled over in the mud flats and abandoned. But even if there had been some way to raise them there was nothing big enough to venture into the Atlantic—even if there had been any point in trying to find City Atlantica in a surface vessel—even if City Atlantica still existed.

"We're stuck here," muttered M'Bora hoarsely, rubbing his throat.

"We're not," said Tregarth. "There are other ports farther south."

"And how do we get there?" M'Bora demanded, gazing at the broad flood.

"If we have to, we'll build a raft and float the damned car across!"

But the first thing to do was to find a place to hide from the searing sun, already lightening the sky. They found a place—shattered steel and concrete; from the smell of it, it had once been an oil storage depot. Tregarth rolled the car half under a leaning concrete wall—at least it would be in shadow!—and put on the floppy hat and dark glasses to reconnoiter. M'Bora was already half asleep, but he grinned weakly as Tregarth slid out the door into the terrible dawning day. He almost wished for the rains to return. He wished that M'Bora's strength would return, for the injury to his throat had not healed and the man was losing weight every day. He wished—he wished for many things, and most of all for the world to become sane again, so that he could be back in City Atlantica with Graciela Navarro by his side.

But none of his wishes seemed to have much chance of being granted.

He stiffened as he heard a noise behind him. A hard, high voice rapped out: "And who the hell are you guys?"

The figure wore a Peace Force soldier's tattered uniform. Black goggles obscured the face, and a rapid-fire carbine was held dead-center on his chest.

M'Bora groaned, from where he sat against the great wheel of the car, "They've got us this time, Ron."

Tregarth said nothing. There seemed to be only one soldier. True, the PanMack had the gun, and Tregarth's own was leaning against the wall, well out of reach. But still, if he could distract the man for a minute. . . ."I asked a question," the high voice repeated. "Who are you? That's a Peace Fleet car, but you don't look like PanMacks."

"We escaped from Baltimore," M'Bora said miserably. "If you're going to send us back, we'll die there."

The figure stood doubtfully for a moment, then one gauntleted hand reached up and pulled away the goggles and helmet. The face revealed was grinning . . . and it was a woman's face.

"Glad to know you," she said. "I escaped, too, from a lot farther away than Baltimore. Name's Jannie Storm. I used to live around here."

Jannie Storm never let her carbine get far away, but she didn't point it at them any more, either. With Tregarth looking on, she felt M'Bora's head. "You're sick," she told him flatly. "Hang on a minute."

She disappeared behind the leaning wall, returned in a moment with a bulging knapsack. "Real medicine I don't have," she told them, "but I've got aspirin. Start with two of these. The other thing you need is decent food." She counted out two of the little white tablets, hesitated, shrugged, added two more. "No more for a couple of hours, though. You got water?"

"We filled the canteens at a creek last night," Tregarth said, "but we're beginning to get a little short—"

"Creek water! You want to die? You know how many dead bodies are floating around in all those creeks? Here," she said, pulling a corked bottle out of her bag. "That's been boiled. And I've got something you can eat, too." She rummaged in the pack again and produced an old-fashioned Mason jar. She held it up to the light and nodded as she unscrewed the cap. "All right, you," she said. "No more than one third, though. One third's for your buddy, and I'll eat the rest myself."

"What is it?" M'Bora whispered, sniffing the unfamiliar mixture.

Jannie Storm shrugged. "Stew, I think. Maybe horse. I found it in a farmhouse."

Tregarth watched M'Bora gobble it down, then took his own turn at the jar as they talked. After six months in a PanMack work camp he was not fastidious. "Not bad," he said, his mouth full. "You don't know what it is?"

Storm shrugged. "Probably horse. Could be goat—or cat or dog, for that matter. That's enough," she ordered, watching carefully as he reached the two-thirds mark in the jar. "The rest's mine." But, when he set the jar on the ground between them, she made no move to pick it up. "Now tell me exactly who you are, and what you're doing," she commanded.

It didn't take long; all stories were short stories these days, because the long, miserable parts were what everyone already knew. "So we're heading for a port that's still working," Tregarth finished. "Maybe Florida."

"Why Florida?"

"They say PanMack's given up on everything south of Savannah. That used to be General Marcus McKen's, and now he's off in space."

"Habitat Valhalla," the woman nodded. "You want company?"

Tregarth considered. She was a healthy-looking human being; she had a gun, and it was clear she had experience in using it. "How do we know you're not PanMack yourself? You're wearing the uniform."

"And you're driving a Peace Fleet armored car," she grinned. "That's why I pretty near took you both out without talking—but your buddy here looked too sick to be just sitting around here when there's a command post no more than two klicks away."

Tregarth stared. "A PanMack command post?"

"Six men and a tank," she confirmed. "I was just figuring out how to take them on myself when you came along. They've got food, fuel, medical supplies—they've even got a flat-bottomed scow that they patrol the water in."

"Would it hold this car?" Tregarth demanded.

"Maybe. Probably." She turned to M'Bora, listening intently to them as he leaned against the wall. "How are you feeling?" she asked.

M'Bora blinked at her. "Why—well, I guess the aspirin's helped a little," he croaked. "I'm kind of weak, though."

"I'm not talking about weak, I mean sick at your stomach?"

M'Bora considered. "No, I don't think so," he said, and before he could ask why the woman was already reaching for the neglected jar of stew, wiping the spoon off on her filthy uniform sleeve, shoveling it in. Around the mouthful she explained, "This home-canned stuff, there's always a good chance of botulism, you know? But since you ate it and didn't die—" She shrugged, grinning.

Tregarth started to protest, then changed his mind. After all, it was a reasonable precaution. All he said was, "This PanMack post. You say they've got a tank?"

"And six effectives," Jannie Storm confirmed, wiping her lips on her sleeve. "Jesus, what I'd give for a cup of coffee! But they've got coffee, Tregarth, and canned food enough for months. And vitamins. And probably medicine. And they've got ammunition—" She hesitated, then grinned and handed her carbine to Tregarth. "As long as we're in it together," she said, "I don't mind telling you that I fired my last round weeks ago. That's why I couldn't figure out how to take the post out myself."

Tregarth shook his head, admiringly—more admiring than anything else, anyway. This was obviously an unusual woman. "This car can't fight a tank," he pointed out—not discouragingly, just to put the facts on the table.

"But it's a Peace Fleet car," she said. "And I've got a PanMack uniform—what's left of it, anyway. We don't have to fight them. I—" she hesitated, then said, "Tell the truth, I've had enough of fighting, anyway. I'd like to live the rest of my life without killing another person. All we have to do is wait until it gets dark again, and then come in on them when the tank isn't manned. They won't fight, once they see the guns in this car. Why would they? They've got nothing left to fight for!"

Whether the Peace Police still thought they had anything to fight for or not, they didn't fight. The man on guard lowered his machine-gun long enough for Jannie Storm to cover him with her own empty carbine. He might have dared that, but the guns of the armored car backed her up convincingly. When the rest of the details tumbled out, scared, half asleep, they gave no trouble at all.

Their stores were everything Jannie Storm had promised —not just food, but such food! They had obviously looted a gourmet food shop somewhere, and they had jars of paté and cooked snails and macadamia nuts; they had powdered milk and canned hearts of palm; they had sealed boxes of chocolates and a dozen kinds of sweet biscuits and cookies. They had fuel that was better than the moldering splinters of wood Tregarth had collected, and they certainly had ammunition. While the captives lay on their bellies in plain view, M'Bora covering them with their own machine-gun, Tregarth and Jannie Storm labored to fill the armored car. And the scow was small, yes, but it took the weight of the car when they cautiously rolled it aboard. They took two of the men with them to help unload it at the far shore—first disabling the post's radio. And when they were on firm ground again, with a clear road ahead, Tregarth made them a present of the scow. He waited until they were in midstream before he turned away.

"Might as well get going," he said to Jannie Storm. "There's likely to be a Peace Wing helicopter checking them out when they don't report in, and we'd better be a long way from here by then. Let's let M'Bora sleep for a while; you and I can take turns driving."

But that last exertion had been too much for M'Bora's weakened body. When they climbed into the car the PanNegran was still sitting erect at the wheel, but when they touched him they saw that he was dead.

Twenty kilometers down the road, they took time to bury M'Bora Sam. Jannie Storm helped Tregarth dig, stood silent while he spoke a few words into the unhearing darkness, whispered something to herself as they covered him over. But when she took the wheel she drove with reckless haste along the dark roads, daring to flash the lights on only for moments at a time.

If the PanMacks had been up to peacetime standards they wouldn't have had a chance to escape, but the PanMacks were decimated, too.

There was no doubt that Jannie Storm was an unusual person—after all, she was still alive, when all the average human beings had long since given up and died. Even so, when at last they dared stop to rest and hide from the sun, Tregarth was astonished at what she had done, single-handed, in a lunatic world.

Time was when Jannie Storm had been duty officer in one of Dr. Lord Simon McKen Quagger's missile silos near the town of Canadian, Texas. When the comet struck, her team went at once to full red alert. So did their comrades and their opponents in every landlubber base in the world. Miraculously, no one pushed the button; at least the world was spared nuclear holocaust.

It wasn't spared much else. The first shattering strikes of the comet had produced a worse holocaust than anything Jannie's silo could produce. Within a week, the nuclear warheads abandoned, she was guarding a different type of silo, a state farther north and east, on the border of Kansas.

For a time—a very short time, it seemed in retrospect to Jannie Storm—things had been almost normal, except for the terrible intensity of the sun. Military discipline continued unchanged. Rations were issued. If trucks came to take grain from the silos, they were Lord Quagger's trucks, and they were authorized to transport it to places nearer Lord Quagger's headquarters in the mountain—they had papers to prove it.

Then a column of trucks came that did not belong to Lord Quagger.

They made the mistake of coming with reason behind them instead of guns; all they wanted, they said, was food for the hungry cities in Kansas and Oklahoma. The Peace Force drove them off easily enough.

But they returned.

And others came; and now they brought weapons. Jannie's detachment was driven away—the ones that weren't killed in the furious fire-fighting around the grain-storage facility; and after that guarding stopped and search-and-seizure missions began. Her detachment was armed with formal, government-stamped requisitions for every grain of corn, wheat or barley, signed by Lord Quagger himself. But it wasn't long before the farmers refused to accept them—or tried to refuse. Then there were more fire-fights, and Jannie took shotgun pellets in her shoulder one day near Emporia.

After that, anyone her detachment saw who was carrying a gun and not in the uniform of Lord Quagger's Peace Police was fired on at once.

And then it was anyone with a gun who was fired on, no matter what he wore, as the rations stopped and the chain of command disintegrated. Farmers became hard to find. What stores of food they had left were hidden. The search-and-seize missions had to use infrared scopes to detect living bodies—any kind of living bodies. Animals were food; humans might be able to lead to where food was hidden.

It was a long, long way from Jannie's childhood on Virginia's Eastern Shore.

When the sunburned, starving survivors of her battalion began to fight among themselves she stole a gasoline truck and headed east.

"And here I am," Jannie Storm finished. "I thought Virginia might be different—oh, the people would be dead, sure, most of them. But there'd be food, anyway. If worst came to worst, I could catch crabs along the inlets—" She laughed. "Maybe there are still some crabs there," she said. "But I never got that far."

Tregarth sighed. He had already told her his own story, including the fact that he had left behind him a woman he loved, Graciela Navarro. Then there was a pause, before he asked, "How about you, Jannie? Didn't you have a boyfriend or something?"

"Not a *something*," she flared. "I had a *husband!* And a damned good one, too!" Her expression softened. "His name was Peter. We were going to take retirement in a year or two, settle down, raise a family—" She laughed sharply. "I guess everybody has the same problem, Tregarth," she finished. "Gets monotonous, doesn't it?"

He ignored her tone. As gently as he could, he probed. "And Peter? He wasn't with you?"

She glared at him, then looked away. "When the farmer

ambushed us with that shotgun," she said, rubbing her shoulder reflectively, "Peter pushed me out of the way. I just caught the edge of the pattern on my arm. The rest of the charge—the rest of it blew Peter's head away."

There were no ships at any of the ports in the Carolinas. There might have been at Savannah, but there was a Peace Wing helicopter hovering overhead and they dared not chance it. When they crossed the border into Florida there was nothing at all.

The Sunshine State was a vast, sun-seared tomb. Nothing moved in the stagnant oven heat. Birds and animals had vanished, though sometimes the air was still foul from long-dead carcasses.

Florida could never feed its people at the best of times. At the best of times more than half the inhabitants of Florida's towns were elderly. No longer. The old people had died early, unable to stand the heat, the radiation, the hunger.

The palmettoes were gone. There was no Spanish moss dangling from the trees. The trees were bare even of leaves, much less fruit; the old orange groves around Orlando still stood, some of them, but they looked like a Maine hardwood forest in February. Even the swamps and lakes were burned and boiled dry. It would be a thousand years before the Okefenokee Swamp was again the broad, shallow, slow river of water that flowed eternally south to the Everglades.

"You'd think there'd be a few people left," Jannie Storm commented, peering into the wreck of an old amusement park.

"Dead, I guess," Tregarth said. He was studying the stark, leafless trees. Some were burned, others merely dead, though here and there a new sprig of green showed itself where it was sheltered by something larger—and dead. Tregarth was curious; a webfoot by birth, he could hardly imagine what this had been like before Comet Sicara. "I wonder what kind of trees those were?"

"What difference does that make?" Jannie said bitterly. "They're dead, too. Let's get moving—if," she added, the voice even sharper now, "you have some idea where we're going."

Tregarth shrugged. "We used to put into Port Everglades sometimes," he said. "That's down south of here, quite a distance. There's another port near Cape Canaveral; we could check them out, see if by any chance there's any contact with the Eighteen Cities."

"And if there isn't?"

"At least," he said, "we're away from the PanMacks."

She nodded, then pressed his shoulder. "I'm sorry," she said. "I don't have any better ideas than you do—I've got no right to give you a hard time."

"No harm done," he grinned, putting his hand over hers. She withdrew hers quickly. She started to speak, hesitated, then went ahead firmly:

"Tregarth," she said, "two men tried to rape me in the last four months, and I killed them both."

Astonished, he began, "But I wasn't—"

"I know that," she said impatiently. "I just want you to know where I stand. I like you. But I'm not going to make love with you."

"I wasn't going to—"

She cut him off again. "What*ever* you were going to, let me say my piece. You're a pretty good guy. I don't have anybody else, and it looks like you don't, either —but I don't want to get pregnant, and I haven't got any good way to prevent it. Do you know what I'm saying?"

He grinned. "I know," he said, and reached out to pat her hand. This time she didn't draw it back, just looked at him levelly until, still smiling, he got back into the car and started it up.

*   *   *

There were ships in dock at Port Canaveral, all right, but they were in even worse shape than the ones at Hampton Roads. Three great ocean-going surface freighters lay beside their piers, all listing severely. They had simply been abandoned—looted, too, Tregarth discovered.

"They were the ships General Marcus McKen used to supply his space base," said Jannie Storm, looking around at the storm-swept desolation. "I guess when he took off for Habitat Valhalla he didn't bother about what was left behind."

"Shall we give it up here and start south for Port Everglades?"

"Let's look around a little first," Jannie said. "See what's left of the general's space base. It's right up the shore here, I think—"

And so it was. Or something was. Ten minutes later, Tregarth and Jannie Storm were looking at a razor-wire barrier that bore a metal sign, hanging at an angle after the winds of one hurricane or another had not quite succeeded in blowing it away. It was lettered in red paint:

KEEP OUT!
SPACE BASE McKEN
PEACE WING RESERVATION
Trespassers will be
SHOT

"There's somebody still here," said Jannie Storm, her voice perplexed. "That sign wasn't made by General McKen's people. They would have had something a lot fancier—and they wouldn't bother with a warning."

"Maybe they couldn't stand the sun," Tregarth said absently, staring around. People had been there, that was clear. Parts of people still were here. Just a few meters inside the fence a sand-smeared skull leared up at him. Perhaps it had been buried once, and some storm surge had washed it free.

Tregarth, peering through the razor-wire fence, could see faraway structures—or the remains of them, for they too were little more than skeletons. A gantry, stretching toward the clearing sky. A white building so huge that Tregarth thought at first it could be no more than a quarter of a kilometer away—then he saw the tiny, half-buried wreck of an automobile near its base. Scale readjusted; the thing had been a hundred meters tall at one time! The entire dome of City Atlantica could not have held it! A long road led from it almost to the razor-wire fence—then it was washed out or covered with mud from the storm surge; but it had been a highway once, though now all that was left was slashed with ravines.

"There's nobody alive here now," Jannie Storm decided. "What do you want to do now, Tregarth?"

"Find a way in," he said shortly, and began to pick his way over the gullied landscape, along the perimeter of the fence.

She sighed, then grinned. "I'm with you," she observed. "But if you want in, there's easier ways than trying to climb that fence. We could just knock a hole in it with the car."

As it turned out, they didn't have to; half a kilometer nearer the beach the fence was down entirely, and its razor edges were buried under a swell of ocean sand.

What the ozone summer had not destroyed, the hurricanes had drowned in sand and mud. Near the beach there was nothing recognizable. The land lay flat and bare, with only scattered black stumps and naked foundations left to show where trees and buildings had been. It wasn't just the storm that had wrecked the buildings; they had been blown up, perhaps to remove cover that attacking forces might have used.

But as they regained the old road, there were structures that had not been deliberately destroyed. "Careful," warned Jannie Storm from the gun turret. "That's a gun emplacement ahead!" But there was no sign of life around it, and as Tregarth cautiously drove toward it, ready to cut and run if necessary, they could see that the machine-gun ports were half-filled with sand. They passed it gingerly, Jannie swiveling the turret to cover it from the rear. But it was out of action.

More than once they passed bleaching bones, where some animal or man had died in the lethal sun, moving slowly toward the tall spacefield structures. Tregarth made out a yellow-patterned control tower, tiny-seeming beside the loom of the destroyed old hangar. But there were other buildings that were not destroyed.

Still, there were no Peace Wing aircraft or spacecraft anywhere in sight. Nothing moved.

They found another launch pad by the old Banana River, this one with its gantry still tall and complete, though there was no spacecraft anywhere near it. The control bunker by the river was as silent as any other structure on the field . . .

But just beyond the bunker, at the river's edge—

"It's a boat!" Jannie shouted. "And there's somebody in it, just sitting there, looking at us! It looks like—" Her voice faded for a moment in wonder. Then she gasped, "It's a little girl!"

They drove carefully over the cracked pavement around the bunker toward the boat, Jannie tensely swiveling the turret in all directions, alert for any surprise. Tregarth stopped a dozen meters from the river's edge, staring at the child.

She was worth staring at. She wore a great sombrero on her head and dark goggles over her eyes. Her clothing was long-sleeved, but her face, and her hands where they poked out from the cuffs of the blouse, were covered with greasy-looking paint. She gazed up at the armored car and said politely, "Good morning, *señor*. My name is Maria. I was fishing but, as you see, have caught nothing yet." She gestured toward the empty bottom of the skiff and prattled on, "My father thought perhaps that the storm would have brought some fish back. It may be so, but none have taken my bait. Have you seen any alligators?"

"Alligators?" Tregarth repeated, perplexed. To Jannie, scrambling down from the turret to take a seat beside him, "What's she talking about?"

"God knows. Keep your eyes open, though." She cracked the windscreen and leaned out. "What are you doing here, Maria?" she called.

"Fishing, as I have said, *señora*," the little girl said, and added politely, "And good morning to you, too."

"Good morning," Jannie responded, grinning. "What I want to know is where are your people?"

"Oh, they are in the settlement on the mainland, *señora*," said the girl, waving across the river. "The storm blew some of our sun shelters down and they must repair them at once, of course. But have you seen any alligators, please?"

"Alligators? No," said Jannie. "How many people are in your settlement?"

"Oh, many, *señora*," the little girl assured her. "There is Manuel and Sergeant Lucas and my mother, Angela, and my father, Corporal Hagland, and Commander Ryan and many others."

"Commander Ryan?" Jannie frowned. "The astronaut?"

"Precisely, *señora*," the little girl said, smiling with pleasure. "He is the *commandante* of us all, you see. It is a very important job, to keep everything here in order until the General McKen comes back from his place in the sky—though," she added shyly. "I have looked often in the sky, but I have not seen General McKen."

She regarded them placidly, sitting on the gunwale of the boat. "She doesn't look very dangerous," Tregarth said doubtfully to Jannie Storm.

"She doesn't look like she has a submarine in her pocket, either," Jannie snapped. "What's the use of talking to her? Maybe we ought to turn around and get out of here!" Then, as Tregarth shrugged, she said offhandedly, "All the same, I guess we can probably spare some food for her if you want to. If her people have been living on fish they've had some pretty slim times. We could give her some vitamin pills, anyway—we've got more than we need, and they sure aren't getting any fresh vegetables around here!"

"Why not?" Tregarth grinned, and called, "Maria? Do you know what vitamins are?"

"Vitamins, *señor?*" the little girl said doubtfully.

"Pills which make you healthy," Tregarth explained. "To make up for the vegetables you can't grow any more."

"Oh, but we have vegetables, *señor*," the girl assured him. "My mother has explained to me how I must eat the salads and the fruits, and I do not mind the fruits, they are quite good, but I do not much like raw carrots."

"Fresh vegetables?" Jannie said, perplexed. "But how—"

The little girl's eyes flicked away for a moment, then returned to them. "Oh, we have little farm places in the glass houses, *señora*. And there we grow many things—"

Then her expression changed.

Belatedly, Tregarth snapped, "Watch it! There's something going on—"

Too late. There was a scratching noise just under the windscreen, then a man's head appeared. It was covered with the same thick grease as the girl's face, and next to the head there was a hand with a gun, pointed directly at them. "That was well done, Maria," the man called, not taking his eyes off Jannie and Tregarth. "As to you two, I want you to move very, very slowly—open the door—come out with your hands up—don't do anything foolish. Because, you see, you have entered a military zone and you are already subject to being shot without warning."

Although the girl was no more than six, she was quite good at tying knots. She bound the arms of Tregarth and Jannie Storm behind them, while her father held the gun on them. Then when they got into the skiff she started the outboard and took the tiller.

Tregarth and Jannie sat amidships, facing aft, with the girl's father, Corporal Max Hagland, perched in the bow and watching them from behind.

"I do hope you will forgive me," Maria prattled earnestly, "because, of course, it is the first duty of every one of us to protect Base McKen of the Peace Wing. I hope they will not shoot you—though I am afraid," she added sadly, "that this is what usually happens."

"Thank you," Tregarth said.

"You are welcome," she said. "And will you please keep watch on the water? In case of alligators, I mean," she added, frowning in concentration as she steered the boat south through a passage between the beach and a low island as bare as the mainland. "That is Gator Key," she said pointing. "It had many alligators once. Some died, but the ones that are left we must kill if we see them—if there are any, that is—since one of them was possessed of the demon."

"What are you talking about?" Jannie Storm demanded.

"The demon that lives in the jewel," Maria explained. "The chief alligator was one and, oh, *señor* and *señora*, it killed many people before Commander Ryan shot it. Even now that it is dead it is very powerful—you will see!"

Tregarth scowled at the childish prattle. It was an

annoyance at a time when he wanted his thoughts to be as clear as possible. There had to be some way to get out of this! If he flung himself suddenly backward— If he could knock the man with the gun overboard— If then he and Jannie Storm could force the little girl to untie their hands—

But when he started to turn his head to see just where Corporal Max Hagland was, he felt the cold steel of the gun barrel pressing against his neck. "Don't turn around," the man ordered. "Don't even look as if you were *thinking* of turning around. Commander Ryan won't get mad if I shoot you myself, instead of wasting his time bringing you in alive."

For the rest of the trip Tregarth sat with his head down in the blazing sun. No one had bothered to give him a hat, or a coat of grease like the one the little girl and her father wore. It wasn't hard to guess the reasons why a little sunburn more or less wouldn't matter.

And then the boat swerved into a cove, slowed, grated against sand. Tregarth and Jannie were thrown backward as it struck, then jerked forward as strong hands grasped it and pulled it up on the beach. "You can get out now," Corporal Hagland ordered. And as they stumbled out of the boat, almost falling, Tregarth saw a man watching them. He wore Peace Wing khakis and the silver bars of a flight lieutenant.

"What have you got now, Max?" the lieutenant demanded. "A couple more wire-crawlers?"

"They weren't outside the wire," Hagland protested. "They were right up by the launch pads. Had an armored car, too. If it wasn't for Maria suckering them along I dunno if I could've done anything about them."

"Oh?" The lieutenant took a closer look. "Wait a minute, Corporal," he said. "Don't you see this woman's wearing a PanMack Peace Force uniform?"

"I figured she stole it," Hagland said resentfully.

"Well, Commander Ryan is the one who'll have to sort all this out—come on, bring your prisoners up to the commandant's office!"

Tregarth stared at the little settlement as he stumbled along a neatly graveled path. It was nestled in a grove of palm trees. The trees were all dead, of course, but the small buildings tucked under them looked unharmed by the ozone summer. Some of them even were shining with new paint. Over the tops of the palms camouflage netting was strung—the densely patterned kind that would have made a reasonably good sunshade in the worst of the ultraviolet peril. Winds had blown some of it away, but he saw people shinnying up the trees, tugging the missing sections back in place.

The commandant's headquarters was a stone building with a PanMack flag on a staff before it. As they entered Tregarth squinted, thankful to be out of the sun but almost blinded by the dimness inside. Somewhere in the building a diesel was throbbing, and electric lights were combating the gloom.

As Tregarth's eyes adjusted he saw a slim, boyish, redheaded man bent over a computer. The sign on his desk said *Cmdr Wernher Ryan, Commandant.* The man looked up inquiringly as the lieutenant brought the captives in.

"What have you got here?" he asked, and the corporal said eagerly:

"Just a couple more wire-crawlers, sir. They were all the way inside the base." He went on to explain about the armored car and his daughter's part in the capture, but Tregarth hardly heard. He was gazing in astonishment at something on the wall behind the commandant. It was the skin of a huge alligator, six meters at least, so big that the entire width of the commander's office was barely enough to hold it; and in the middle of its forehead, just under the bulbous knobs over its tiny, wicked eyes, there was what looked like an immense gem-quality ruby.

"—don't you hear me?" said a sharp voice. Tregarth shook himself; the commandant was staring at him.

"Sorry," he said. "I was looking at that 'gator skin."

The commandant nodded soberly. "It's worth looking at. It cost us a good many men to kill that one. But I asked the two of you who you are and where you came from. I can't promise it will make any difference, but I want to hear what you have to say."

Tregarth opened his mouth to reply, then hesitated, looking at the commandant. Commander Wernher Ryan was an academy example of an astronaut officer, face strong, posture erect. The only discordant feature was his eyes. They were somber. You could expect justice from a man with eyes like that, Tregarth thought. But never mercy.

The commandant looked around the room, at the prisoners, at the lieutenant who had brought them in, at two other officers who had entered to take part in what was going on.

He sighed. Then he said, "Sergeant Storm, since you are a member of the Peace forces you are now under my command. You will be assigned quarters and duties by the adjutant. Welcome to Base McKen of the Peace Wing."

Jannie Storm said harshly, "What about Captain Tregarth?"

The commandant's didn't respond to Jannie directly. He addressed Tregarth himself, his tone still mild. "Captain Tregarth, we do not have a place for you here. Base McKen is a sensitive post. No one can remain here but military personnel of this detachment and their immediate families. There are no exceptions."

Tregarth said, "I'll go. I just want to find a ship that will take me back to City Atlantica."

"City Atlantica," the commandant repeated thoughtfully. "I'm afraid that would be hardly possible. It is not likely that it still exists. In any case, that does not affect your situation here."

He paused, as though he did not like what he was going to say. "I think you are entitled to know what is at stake in Base McKen. We are the only remaining earthside contingent of General Marcus McKen's space forces. As such, it is our duty to protect this base. We've held it against looters, and guerrilla bands—and worse than that," he said, glancing up at the grinning alligator head above him. "We can't endanger it for any reason."

"I said I would go," Tregarth protested, knowing what the man was about to say.

"I'm afraid not, Captain Tregarth," Ryan said decisively. "We can't risk your coming back with an armed force. Therefore, with regret, I must sentence you to—"

"Hold it right there," cried Jannie Storm. "You said I was in your detachment now! And you said the families were entitled to live here!"

"Watch how you talk to the commandant, Sergeant!" rasped the lieutenant, but Commander Ryan raised his hand.

"You didn't say you were related to this man, Sergeant Storm," he said.

"Related? He's my husband! At least," she went on, not looking at Tregarth, "we've been looking for someone to marry us ever since we left Baltimore." And she turned to Tregarth. "Isn't that right, Ron?" she appealed.

And so it happened that within the hour the chaplain of Base McKen of the Peace Wing said the words over them, and Captain Rodney Everett Tregarth and Staff Sergeant

Janice Phyllis Curzon Storm took the vows of marriage in the commandant's office, with Commander Wernher Ryan and Corporal Max Hagland as witnesses, as the grinning face of the alligator with the ruby jewel in its forehead looked down on them all.

Chapter
16

When Graciela Navarro awoke on the morning of the day the *Atlantica Countess* sailed, the first thing she saw was the portrait cube of Ron Tregarth smiling at her from the bedside table. Now that the new dome was habitable—barely habitable—the refugees from City PanNegra had begun to move in, and she had her room to herself again.

She dressed quickly and skipped breakfast entirely, not wanting to miss the sailing. Life in City Atlantica was nearly back to normal—well, no, not normal. Nothing was normal since Comet Sicara. In City Atlantica the food stocks had been harshly depleted by the task of feeding the PanNegrans; the air changers had been so overworked that each unit had to be taken out of service for maintenance well ahead of schedule. The city simply seemed—well—*tired*.

But at least now there was room to move around. Compared to the surface world, it was paradise. Graciela knew that. The few scraps of information that had come to the undersea cities had been each more horrifying than the last. As she left her room, she turned for one last look at Tregarth's smile. "Please, let them be wrong," she whispered softly, and hurried toward the sailing docks.

To find out whether the stories were entirely wrong was what the *Atlantica Countess* was all about. It wasn't really a City Atlantica ship. It was one of the little fleet that had carried the survivors of City Pan Negra's drowning to the safety of the other dome, and the PanNegrans had been glad enough to donate it to their hosts. Especially for that particular purpose. The *Atlantica Countess* was on a surveillance mission, and the PanNegrans, too, had lost ship's crews that might be somewhere still trapped on the land.

Its crew was mixed. *Very* mixed, for not only were there five PanNegrans and nine Atlanticans, there was also one former PanMack Peace Wing officer, Dennis McKen. And what an argument there had been about including him! Half of City Atlantica, and nearly all the PanNegrans, proclaimed it was madness to trust a lubber on a sensitive mission. It took Mayor Mary Maude McKen's authority to settle the question. "He knows the land better than any of us," she decided. "We don't have any choice but to trust him." So it was ordered.

She had not mentioned that the former Peace Fleet officer was also her son.

Now, as the *Atlantica Countess* was preparing to sail, she was there to see them off with a little speech. And when she had made it, she looked quizzically up at the tall young man to whom she had given birth. "You will come back, won't you, Dennis?" she whispered.

He grinned at her. "I'll come back," he said, and put his arms around her. The crowd of well wishers murmured at the picture, the youth so tall and lean, the woman so short and plump, but with the same pale coloring of skin and hair. "I wouldn't break a promise to you," he told his mother. Then he straightened, and looked across his mother's head to Graciela Navarro.

"Or to you, Graciela," he said.

Even an hour later, when she was already in her pressure suit and heading out on her sea-skid, Graciela still felt the queer tingle Dennis McKen's words had given her. They were almost a declaration, and a very public one at that! And she could not deny that the former PanMack was a good man, as well as an extraordinarily handsome one.

But it was Ron Tregarth she loved, she told herself earnestly. She had pledged to marry him. She meant to keep that pledge. She had no business letting Dennis McKen, or anyone else, think anything else. . . .

But where was Ron Tregarth? Was there really a Ron Tregarth still alive anywhere in the world?

She shook her head inside the two-seventy helmet decisively. She had no time for such personal concerns now; it was the survival of City Atlantica that had to be the first thought of every one of its citizens.

The very first task, of all the urgent tasks, was to ensure the feeding of its people. That meant farming—not just continuing the planting and tending and harvesting, but adding new farms and getting them into production.

That was where her squid would have a chance to prove themselves—if she still had her squid.

The squid school had been harmed more than the rest of the city, because it had been a thousand cubic meters of space that was not urgently needed for the survival of the city, and so it had taken many of the refugees from PanNegra. No squid had practiced its skills in the great squid pool for nearly a year. No squid came there any more. Graciela had seen none of her students, except Triton, in all that time, and Triton only rarely.

Now it was time to get them together again, to use the skills she had so painfully taught them.

If they remembered any of those skills—
If she could find the squid—
If they were still alive.

Four hours later Graciela discovered that Triton, at least, would still come to her—reluctantly and ill at ease, to be sure.

She had tried everywhere—the farms, the undeveloped thermal springs, the power plant, the edges of the deeps. Each time her amplified call had shaken the waters for half a kilometer around, but nothing had responded . . . until, on her way back to the dome, she paused at the sunken wreck of the old surface platform, looming huge and mysterious where it had tumbled to rest.

There were squid there.

She caught a glimpse of them on her radar as she rounded the bulk, a quick flickering motion that disappeared inside the wreck itself. But squid were there! Graciela stopped her sea-skid near the gaping hole in the steel structure and activated her external speaker: "Nessus, come! Triton, come! Holly, come! All squid, come! Graciela here, yes!"

There was no response from inside. She hung in neutral buoyancy for a moment, then decisively moored the skid to a crumpled girder and dismounted. Tethered to the skid, she danced in the slow-motion gait of a walker on the sea bottom toward the gap in the hulk and called again.

Still no answer.

Yet she was sure she had seen squid. It was possible, she told herself, that they were wild squid. There were plenty of those around. Like any sea-bottom wreck, the old surface platform had already attracted the crawling and floating and swimming animals of the bottom, for there was food in plenty inside it. Of course, she told herself quickly, all the bodies of the victims had long since been removed and buried in the level plot beyond the school dome where City Atlantica's dead were laid to rest. Everything salvageable from the platform's stores had been taken away, too, but there were always bits and pieces of spilled food, fuel, anything organic for the smallest creepers to feed on—who themselves would feed the larger ones.

"Squid come!" she called. "Graciela here, yes. Come now, yes!"

No answer—and then, not from inside the wreck but from behind her, a welcome hollow voice. "Triton come, yes. Triton here see Graciela, yes."

In the light from her sea-skid's lamps the squid was an unlovely lavender, its tentacles writhing nervously as it slowly approached; but to Graciela it was a beautiful sight. "Graciela glad, yes!" she cried. "Good Graciela see Triton, yes!"

But what the squid responded was, "Graciela go away this place, yes! Graciela go now, yes!"

It was an unexpected rebuff. Graciela took a deep breath and said, "Graciela go, not! Triton speak Graciela, yes. Squid where?"

The animal did not respond—at least not in words. But two of its tentacles slid forward and grasped the girl around the waist, tugging her toward the sea-skid. "Graciela go now, yes!" the unearthly voice declared.

"Triton, no!" she cried. "Graciela go, not!" She tried to free herself, but there was no strength in her human body to compare with the ten-meter tentacles of the squid. It jammed her against the straps of the skid, while two other tentacles dexterously released the mooring cable, and Triton began to tow her away from the wreck.

"Triton stop now, yes!" she shouted. "Triton speak Graciela, yes! Squid, where? Squid Nessus, where?"

They were already a dozen meters away from the wreck. Triton seemed a little less agitated. It slowed down. Its tentacles writhed indecisively for a moment. Then it brought out a sentence: "Squid Nessus in squid place, yes."

"Nessus not come, why?"

Triton's tentacles moved restlessly, but it had, at least, stopped towing her away. "Tell!" she commanded.

There was a pause, and then the hollow voice boomed, "Nessus like Graciela now, not."

She felt a stab of pain. "Nessus like persons, yes?"

Triton was obviously having trouble explaining himself. "Nessus like squid person, yes. Like Graciela person, not."

"Squid person! Squid person is what?"

But the squid only boomed obstinately, "Squid person is squid person, yes."

But what the squid wanted to say was too complicated for its limited vocabulary. Oh, Nessus, she thought, you were the smartest and best of them all! Why did you turn against me?

And then Triton's tentacles erupted in a flurry of activity, and it began to tow Graciela away again, faster than ever. "Graciela go now, yes!" it boomed. "Go now, go now, yes, yes!"

"Triton, stop!" she cried, hammering against the smooth, remorseless flesh. But the squid only repeated:

"Go go go now now now, yes, yes!" And then it said, "Squid person here, yes! Squid person eat Graciela person, yes! Graciela go, yes, yes!"

And it emitted a great thrust of black fluid to speed them along. . . .

And Graciela Navarro, squirming to see what had upset the squid, got one quick glimpse of something hovering in the shelter of the wrecked platform, seeming to beckon to her. Just one glimpse. Then the black cloud of the squid's jet concealed it; and it wasn't possible that it was what it seemed to be—

But what it seemed to be, what it looked like in that one

quick sight as the squid carried her and her sea-skid frenziedly away, was a human figure.

A naked human figure, nude and unprotected in the killing pressure of the deeps.

The figure of a woman—of the woman who had commanded the lost exploration sub, Vera Doom; and in the middle of her forehead, red and glittering, something that shone like a giant jewel.

It was the first time Graciela Navarro had seen (though she did not know she had seen) the first tiny splinter of the Eternal.

The
Second Year

When I lived in the flesh I lived in a place under a sea on a world. When I lived in the flesh I loved and I worked and I sought knowledge.

Now I live in the Eternal, and I have found all knowledge.

I still love. I love all those who, like me, serve as the arms and the tools of the Eternal, the molluscs and the fish and the crustaceans and the great whales. They are less than me (as I am less than the Eternal) but I love them still, for in the Eternal all are joined.

Forever.

I still love, too, those whom I loved when I lived in the body of Vera Doorn. I will rescue them if I can, and then we will all live in the Eternal. . . .

Forever.

Chapter
17

When Newt Bluestone's van, with its helmeted Peace Police outriders flanking it on their motorcycles, roared through the checkpoints of Quaggerhome, Bluestone felt a curious sense of relief.

The expedition had not been successful. More than half the trucks that lumbered after him were empty. In the second year after Comet Sicara stripped the Earth naked to the searing solar death, all the larders on the planet were empty. So Lord Quagger's "tax collection" expedition had found pathetically little to collect, and often enough they had had to fight for what they brought back.

But within the walls of Quaggerhome was a different world.

Back before the comet, Bluestone had never expected to ever feel glad he was entering Quaggerhome again. Now, however, even the razor-wire barricades looked reassuring; even the barely-seen muzzles of the rocket launchers and machine-guns in the nests in the mountainside that were trained on Bluestone's party were, at least, not intended for loyal servants of Lord Quagger like himself, Bluestone thought wryly. And inside—

Why, inside Quaggerhome the terrible devastation of the past year and more might never have happened! The air was cool and sweet beyond the immense doors. Flowers and shrubs in planters lined the halls he walked through.

The desolation that followed Comet Sicara had hardly touched the people of Quaggerhome . . . except for one.

That was Lord Quagger himself. In the year and more since Comet Sicara, Quagger had sunk in upon himself. He was fatter than ever, so grossly fat that his doctors begged him with tears in their eyes to eat less, take exercise, perhaps even let them try some surgery option that would bypass the stomach; it was not that they loved Lord Quagger so much as that they loved their own lives. They knew what would happen to them if—no, when!—the overtaxed heart began to falter. But the fat no longer creaselessly puffed his face into that of a chubby clown. His face sagged. His chins draped themselves around his neck. His complexion was gray, his eyes dull. Even his braggadocio was gone, along with his wild, empty plans for taking over all the domains of his absent cousins.

When Newt Bluestone was admitted to the audience chamber he found Quagger slumped in his great throne, looking like a puddle of fat in silken robes, while Angie fussed around him, chattering angrily at the servants. But he lifted his face toward Newt Bluestone and looked at him eagerly as he came in.

Angie spat viciously at Bluestone, but Quagger hushed her. He cried dramatically, "My good amanuensis! My valued eyes! Tell me, what is the news of my domain?"

"It is—ah—beginning to recover, Lord Quagger," said Bluestone, trying to find words that were not outright lies. He glossed over his report of ruined Pueblo, Cheyenne and Denver, spoke only briefly of the scoured farms, their topsoil gouged away in the torrential rains that followed the fires. "But there is green coming back here and there, Lord Quagger! Some wild plants are beginning to grow again. I think the ozone layer is beginning to regenerate."

Quagger listened absently, stroking the hideous little Angie, with his eyes gazing mournfully at the pictures on the walls. There was nothing Bluestone had to tell Quagger that others had not already told him, but he maintained the pretense that he did not know how bad things had gotten. "But the tax returns," he complained. "My chamberlain says they were far from complete."

"Lord Quagger," Bluestone said grayly, "there's not much to collect." Taxes! They hadn't been collecting taxes—they were taking away the food people were trying to stay alive on, at gunpoint!

Quagger shook his massive head, the jowls wobbling. "That can't be right. Look at those grain elevators," he commanded, gesturing at the tall, white structures on one of the screens. "Why, they hold enough to feed Quaggerhome for a year!"

"But they're empty! There's nothing there but skeletons of men who fought to steal the grain, or to protect it. There's nothing left to tax! The people are starving."

Quagger didn't seem to hear. "Good, good," he said absently, hardly hearing. "You know how my heart bleeds for my loyal subjects in their ordeal, Newt." Bluestone nodded, trying to keep his face from showing how he felt. "In fact," Quagger declared, rousing himself, "I share all the agonies the whole world suffers. The burns and the blindness, the thirst and despair—above all the hunger," he added, waving irritably at one of the waiting servants to come up with a fresh tray of iced fruit.

Then his expression changed. "This ozone summer," he declaimed, chewing. "It has caused all of us great suffering, to be sure, but now that you've come back with the good news—"

"But, Lord Quagger," Bluestone began, wishing he had been more candid, "all I saw was a few places where weeds are beginning to recover."

"No matter!" Quagger declared, dropping the core of his apple on the floor and reaching for a peach. "Things are beginning to grow. And then—"

He sputtered angrily, taking the fruit from his mouth and staring at it. "Cele!" he cried. "Are you trying to poison me? This is rotten! Why can I not have fresh peaches?" Angie snatched the fruit away and turned it over in her hands, chattering furiously. Then she hurled it away in wrath, narrowly missing Newt Bluestone—not, Bluestone thought, at all accidentally.

"There aren't any fresh peaches left, Lord Quagger," said the girl called Cele. She was one of the three who looked so much like the webfoot woman, Graciela Navarro, that Quagger had been unable to choose among them. He had rechristened them "Grace", "Cele" and "Ella", and attached them all to his personal service. Though the one called Cele spoke bravely, there was fear on her face.

Angie shrieked at the woman, but Quagger decided to be generous. "Ah, these terrible times," he muttered, calming the little creature with his hand. "Yet what we must remember, Newt, is that this terrible year is not merely a trial and a tribulation. It is our opportunity! The ozone cloud may look black, but I am going to give it a silver lining!"

Angie shrieked with pleasure. Quagger stroked her fondly, his spoiled old face looked almost eager as he warmed to his subject. "Order has been destroyed," he declaimed. "The race is at the brink of extinction. I, Simon McKen Quagger, will save it yet. Newt! Do you understand how great your own role in all this is?"

"Why, I think so," Bluestone said despondently, knowing what would come next.

It came. Quagger's voice rose as he cried, "You will record it! You will complete the epic of my life, one that will be remembered by brave men and women for a thousand years, the saga of a savior of humanity. Why, Newt, think about it! Look at the men the world has admired—

Alexander, Caesar, Napoleon, my own revered grandfather, Angus McKen. Not one of them has faced the challenges I dare to confront! Isn't that true, Newt?"

"Things are really in bad shape, Lord Quagger," Bluestone acknowledged.

"So compared to me, all those other great heroes of history will seem to be nothing but pygmies! And it is your task, Newton Bluestone, to emblazon my name in words and tape and film as the dauntless champion who led humanity out of the shadow of the comet, into the splendors of what future historians may well choose to call the Age of Quagger."

He actually stood up at the end of his oration, shouting the words at Bluestone, while Angie, perched on his shoulder, chittered and squawked in triumph and excitement.

Then he fell back. The strain was too much. Angie leaped for safety on the back of the throne, as Quagger's old face slumped again into its pettish flabs of fat. "You've tired yourself, Lord Quagger," cried the girl, Cele.

"Yes, yes," wheezed Quagger faintly. "Bring me wine. No, better still, have my bed prepared and bring the wine there. It's been an exhausting day." He reached out pudgy arms to be helped up, then paused. He looked pleadingly at Newt Bluestone. "You did say things are beginning to grow again?" he said.

Bluestone could not help feeling a little sorry for the old monster. "Indeed I did, Lord Quagger. In fact, there was even a bird—we spotted it just as we were coming through the checkpoints. A wild one, that has somehow survived."

Quagger's eyes lit up. "A bird? A *wild* bird? Flying around outside our mountain?"

"That's right, Lord Quagger," Bluestone said, puzzled. "It's good news that some birds have survived, though heaven knows what it lived on—"

"It's *wonderful* news! Do you know what we're going to

do, Newt? We're going to hunt it," Quagger beamed. "Yes, indeed. Just like the old days! As soon as I've rested a bit I'm going hunting. What do you think of that?"

Bluestone stared at him incredulously. "But— But, Lord Quagger! If any bird has managed to stay alive, it really should be left to reproduce, don't you think? There can't be many of any species left, and to kill even one survivor might just tip the balance—" He stopped, because Quagger was looking at him with anger and suspicion.

"What are you saying, Newt? Don't you think your lord is entitled to a little relaxation for a change?"

"Well, of course, but still—"

Quagger was shaking his head sorrowfully. "You just don't think things through," he chided. "You have no idea what burdens I carry on my shoulders every minute. A little entertainment might make all the difference—just a chance, for a few minutes, to put aside the cares of government, the constant need to keep all of you alive and healthy, the *planning* for the future. No, don't apologize, Newt," he said, smiling again. "I know you weren't thinking it out. Say no more."

As he pulled himself up, leaning heavily on Cele on one side and Ella on the other, Bluestone dared a final protest: "But Lord Quagger, most species of birds are probably already extinct—"

"Forget it, Newt." Tolerant for once, perhaps cheered with the prospect for diversion, Quagger waved a heavy hand to stop him. "Where there's one, there's likely more. If not—if it's the last of the species—what a trophy!" Wheezing for breath, he added almost genially. "You may leave me now. Go to your labors! And I will go to mine!"

With Angie bounding furiously about in his train, he limped away to his bedroom and the only actual labors he was ever likely to undertake.

* * *

Though the second ozone summer was almost over, the stricken land was still far from recovery.

The merciless heat kept on. Little by little the cometary gases were vanishing, being absorbed back into the great, ceaseless back-and-forth exchange of chemical equilibrium that had kept the planet alive for four and a half billion years. Human beings had done their best to wreck that delicate balance with their automobiles and factories and chlorofluorocarbons and forest-clearing, but there were not enough humans left to be a threat now, and the menace of the damage caused by Comet Sicara was dwindling away. Slowly, slowly, high out of sight in the upper atmosphere, the ozone shield was reforming.

But was it too late for life on the surface of the Earth?

As Newt Bluestone waited for his master to join him at the great blastproof gates of Quaggerhome, everything he saw suggested an unhappy answer to that question. But then he heard a step behind him, and when he saw who it was his mood lightened. "Grace," he exclaimed with pleasure.

The girl winced. "Please don't call me that. My name is Doris Calvert. I came to tell you Lord Quagger is on his way."

"Doris, I mean," he said apologetically. "I'm sorry."

She gave him a forgiving look, and then asked eagerly, "What's it like out there now, Newt? I hear there are plants growing—and this wild bird—is it getting better?"

He hesitated. "Yes, a little," he admitted reluctantly. "But whether it's happening fast enough to do any good— that's another question." He shook his head, remembering the dreadful death of Colorado Springs. The last of his PanMack forces had been overwhelmed by a mob of frenzied looters, fighting for a few hoarded stores of canned goods. There were no services any more. No power for lights or to keep the freezers cold, because transformers and generators had been burned out by EMP, and service people had been swept away into the ten thousand little battles that had sped the death throes of the human race.

"I calculate," he told the girl, finishing his account of the trip, "that there are fewer than ten thousand people alive in this whole area, outside of our caves. There used to be fifty million!" He shook his head. "Doris, there were ten billion human beings alive on the Earth two years ago, and now there are nearly that many skeletons. In our district, only one out of five thousand survived—and that is here in the heart of America, with all the livestock and farms. It must have been even worse on the Atlantic coast. Can you imagine what cities like New York and Boston were like? Two-legged animals killing each other for a loaf of bread or a liter of gasoline? And—I don't even want to think about Africa or Asia or South America."

"But you said things are beginning to grow again," the girl offered.

"Only weeds," he said bitterly.

"Of course, Newt, but if things are getting better—well, it's too late this year, I suppose, but next year can't we start planting crops again?"

"If we can live until they ripen. Maybe."

The girl listened to his story intently, her face drawn. Looking at her, Bluestone did not like to think of what the "personal services" Quagger demanded of her might be. The effect his stories were having on her was clear. He asked impulsively, "Do you—have you ever heard anything about, you know, your family back in Santa Fe?"

She said soberly, "I don't have any family there any more, Newt. My husband objected when Quagger's police took me away. They killed him. There wasn't anybody else."

When Lord Simon McKen Quagger appeared, leaning heavily on the arms of his two strongest female servants, Bluestone choked back a sound that was either shocked revulsion or a laugh. Quagger looked not merely ridiculous but almost obscene. He was wearing a red hunting mackinaw and a fisherman's hat with salmon hooks thrust into it, and another female servant carried an ornately embossed double-barreled shotgun. "Well, Newt," he said brightly. "Now how about that hunt?"

But he lingered inside the door for a moment, staring about. It was the first time Simon McKen Quagger had been outside his mountain in nearly two years, and he hesitated inside while his personal guards went out ahead, scouring every bend in the road for possible assassins. Only when they had assured him there was no human being within a mile of the entrance did he uneasily take the first step outside.

"Oh, but it's hot," he gasped petulantly. "You told me the sun wasn't so strong any more, Newt!"

"But it's summer," Bluestone pointed out reasonably. "Still, if you'd rather, we can go back inside."

"Certainly not! I intend to have a shot at this bird, whatever it is. Only where is the confounded thing now?"

His chamberlain spoke into her communications set, and reported, "Surveillance says it was right near the entrance a few minutes ago, headed in this direction."

"Ah!" cried Quagger, his eyes gleaming. "Good! Now, where's my gun? And, remember, no one else is to shoot unless I give the word!"

The woman silently handed him his over-and-under shotgun. One of the guards deferentially started to explain the mechanism to his ruler, but Quagger chided him: "Do you think I don't know how to use a gun, Major? Good heavens! I've killed thousands of birds in my time—yes, and four-legged animals, too. They tell me the trophy grizzly I shot was the last one in Yellowstone Park! A big one—even from the helicopter it looked pretty fierce, I can tell you. And that was with a machine-gun, not a silly little toy like this, so don't worry about my being able to handle it. Now, where is the thing?" he finished, glaring at his chamberlain.

The woman was speaking rapidly into the intercom, and not liking what she heard in return. "It's nearby," she reported. "They say it's a condor, but—"

"A condor," Quagger interrupted, his face puckered up in disappointment. "What's the use of a condor? Whoever heard of eating a condor? I was hoping for a quail, or a wood pigeon, maybe even a wild turkey!"

"Yes, but Lord Quagger," the woman insisted. "Surveillance says there's something strange about it. It's like a kind of—well, they say it's like a jewel in its forehead."

"A *jewel?*"

"That's what they say, Lord Quagger. Like a diamond, and very bright, they say."

"Now, really!" he complained. "Whoever heard of a bird with a jewel? Are they all drunk there in the surveillance room? Get the captain of the guard at once!"

"Lord Quagger," the chamberlain said, "it's the captain I was talking to. He says—oh, there it is!"

And down over the slope sailed a huge condor, its wings half retracted as though diving on prey.

Even in that second Newt Bluestone could see that the surveillance crew had not lied. Jewel or whatever, there was *something* in the feathered head, just over the black, hooded eyes, and it seemed almost to have a light of its own. There were shouts from the guards, a startled squawk from Quagger himself, and Angie seemed to go wild. She was all over Quagger, shrieking piercingly, clinging to his head, tail tight around his throat, screeching into his ear.

Quagger stumbled and fired both barrels at once. The shot missed the great black bird by half a dozen meters, but it kept on coming, diving right down onto Quagger. The Peace Police came charging in, but it was not Quagger the bird was attacking. It was Angie. Squalling, she seemed to wrap her arms around the naked red neck of the bird, releasing Quagger.

Quagger rolled away, flailing the immense arms and legs in frantic fear. "Kill it!" he bawled. "Save Angie! Don't hurt her!"

The guards were already closing in, hand weapons ready, trying to get a shot. When they did three of them fired at once.

The black wings hammered the air for a moment, then sank limply to the roadway.

And Angie, screeching, staggered away, rushing into Quagger's arms. Behind her, the condor lay dead.

And the gem the bird had worn was now blazing in Angie's own brown-furred forehead.

Chapter
18

In the second year of the new world, the *Atlantica Countess* returned to the city.

There was no warning of its arrival. The ship appeared in the middle of the night. The first Graciela Navarro knew of it was when a knock on her door awakened her from the deep, exhausted sleep another day of running farm implements had caused.

When she opened the door Dennis McKen stood there, a videochip in his hand.

"You're back," she said foggily, peering at him. He looked quite different as he gazed down at her compassionately. Tired. Older. More mature. Even—what was it?—yes, kinder.

Dennis had begun to puzzle her. No longer quite the arrogant McKen who had tried to capture his rescuers when they pulled him out of that angry sea, he was different in ways that sometimes disturbed her. What had changed him? She wasn't sure. Life here with the sea-folk? Or, more likely, that first talk with his mother, whom she hadn't seen since he was a baby.

Neither had spoken of their meeting, but she thought it must have begun the healing of their life-long rift. Both had seemed happier since. That bleak bitterness in the mayor's heart was no longer so evident, and she sensed a new warmth in Dennis. He had begun to show a still-reluctant respect for the free people of the sea, and a more surprising regard for her. She still loved Ron Tregarth, yet she couldn't deny her own half-guilty pleasure at the light in his eyes when he looked at her and the tone of his voice when he spoke.

He did not dally now in coming to the point. "There's no sign of him, Gracie," he said at once. "Everybody's dead. I'm sorry."

Graciela shrank away from the words, pulling her robe tighter about her as though it could protect her from their meaning. She blinked up at him, still half asleep—wishing she could believe that she not awakened, that this was just a bad dream.

But it was no dream. She closed her eyes for a moment. Then she whispered, "Come in. Tell me about it."

It didn't take long. "I came right away," McKen said, slipping the chip into Graciela's viewer, "because I wanted you to hear it from me. We covered every port on the

Atlantic seaboard, from Cape Hatteras north to the St. Lawrence. Most of them are simply dead. No one alive at all. Baltimore did have a few thousand people, but they're all PanMack troops—from the Midwest, I think. We couldn't get close."

"But Baltimore's where Ron was going!"

"I know. It looks as though he got there. At least his ship was there; we found that out from a starving fisherman we picked up in the bay. But the *City Atlantica's* crew was taken prisoner by the PanMacks—the fisherman had been one of the guards, until it all fell apart. They were used for slave labor. They died. There's no record of any individuals any more—and hardly anybody alive in Baltimore to remember. But—"

He hesitated, then finished gently, "They're nearly all dead, Graciela. Not just the prisoners. Everybody."

She stood unflinching by her bed, silent, one hand absently touching the portrait cube of Ron Tregarth, gazing up at him.

"I'm sorry, my dear," he said. "Look, here are some pictures. They'll show you what it was like on the land better than I can tell you."

He switched on the viewer.

What it was like on the land, Graciela saw in the first moments, was pure hell. The terrible destruction took many forms, but the end result was always the same: the death of the land.

The first clips were from Norfolk, Virginia, and at first Graciela could not imagine what she was looking at: A sunny beach, littered with odd lumps of things under the sand and projecting out of it—no people, of course; not even any buildings. Then she saw a couple of the crew members of the *Atlantica Countess* digging away at one of the lumps and gradually revealing the shape of a boat. But what was a boat doing buried in the sand? And what was that structure behind it, that looked like the edge of a string of dunes but was too regular to be natural?

"There were some terrible storms," McKen explained. "We couldn't find anybody alive to question—there were people on the mainland, but they hid when they saw our boat approaching. As far as we can tell, there was a really big hurricane that must have come ashore right around here—there's not a building left standing, though there are a few foundations and a couple of walls."

"But Ron was going to Baltimore."

"Baltimore, yes," McKen said patiently. "Here, I'll show you Baltimore."

The viewer zipped through a dozen scenes of desolation, then steadied on a shot from the *Atlantica Countess* as it was coming into the harbor. At first the city looked almost normal. But as the camera zoomed in they could see that all the buildings had staring holes where windows had been; and the rest was desolation.

"We couldn't get very close," McKen apologized, "because we were fired on. We had to run. But you see what's left of Baltimore."

Graciela said drearily, "I see. Turn it off."

McKen said somberly, "Delaware Bay was just as bad— we didn't try going in to Philadelphia. We cruised up the Jersey shore, but we didn't see anybody alive, and New York—" He shook his head, scowling. "It must've been even worse in New York."

Graciela sat staring at the blank screen for a long moment. Then she shook herself and changed the subject, like any hostess making conversation for an unexpected guest. "I'm working on the farms again," she said, her tone quite ordinary. "We need the food, with all the PanNegrans. Luckily, the crops have been good, though we've had some trouble—toolboxes broken into, things stolen."

"Oh? Are the squid doing it?" McKen asked.

She shook her head. "I wish it were the squid. I'm afraid it's that thing that looks like Vera Doorn—oh," she said, recollecting herself. "You don't know about Vera Doorn, do you? That happened after you left." She told McKen about the nude, unprotected figure she had seen the deeps. "Others have seen her since then," she said, still politely making conversation. "So it wasn't just my imagination—"

"My God, Graciela!" McKen snapped. "That's impossible!"

"Yes, I would have thought so, too," she agreed. "But there it is. I think she—or whatever it is that looks like her—is what's been breaking into tool boxes. Maybe what was tapping messages, long and long ago, and what is doing all sorts of other strange things. Others have seen her too, you know. And the squid—they won't come near me any more. And three of our people have disappeared while out in the deeps alone. And something has robbed our farms—none of that is imaginary, Dennis! There is something out there that can dive deeper than we can. It got control of the squid—how, I can't imagine. What it is, I can't guess—but only a fool could doubt that *something* is there!"

She fell silent, as though remembering something.

Then she turned and looked up at Dennis McKen, her eyes flooding with tears. "Dennis? There's no hope that Ron is still alive?" she pleaded.

He shook his head gently. "No hope at all," he said.

There were only a few hours remaining of that night, but Graciela tried to sleep. It wasn't a success. Her dreams were dismal. Ron Tregarth was in half of them, but not the Ron Tregarth she knew. He was floating in the deep sea, almost at the limit of visibility, as naked and unprotected against the murderous pressure of the sea as Vera Doorn—

and, like her, with a gleaming jewel set into his forehead, and his gaze on her icily hostile.

She woke up shivering. As she dressed, she found her eyes wet; she couldn't eat breakfast, for the misery inside her heart as she thought of Ron Tregarth. She forced herself to put him out of her mind as she hurried down to the exit locks.

Dennis McKen was waiting there for her, looking as though he hadn't slept at all. He said, almost bashfully, "I thought I'd go out with you this morning. If you don't mind, I mean."

Graciela was startled. "You're not a farmer," she protested.

"Neither are you. I can learn."

"Yes, but did your mother—I mean, have you asked the mayor—"

He said resentfully, "My mother the mayor has nothing to do with it. There's supposed to be some sort of reception for us, but I'd rather be with you. What's the matter? Don't you want me to come with you?"

She hesitated. "It's not that," she said slowly— "exactly. But after the way you called us webfoot peasants. . . ."

He said firmly, "I haven't changed my mind. I'm PanMack, Graciela. I belong where the human race belongs, on the dry land, and one day I'll go back there. What's wrong with that? I've never lied to you about it. You can't say I haven't done my share of the work here—"

She admitted, "No, that's true enough."

"Then you've got no grounds for complaint, do you? So let me come with you. I've already arranged for a suit."

As the lockmaster's assistants helped them suit up Graciela glanced in perplexity at Dennis McKen. The man was a puzzle. There was no doubt that he hated everything associated with the Eighteen Cities . . . but it was also true that he had set that hatred aside to help in the work the cities needed to survive. He was always a surprise. . . .

The biggest surprise of all came after they were actually out in the sea.

They had left the lock and mounted their sea-skid. Then, when they had their intercoms hooked up, he said suddenly, "Graciela, I've got a question to ask you. Will you marry me?"

His voice was forced, nervous, almost hoarse, the very sound of a man asking something preposterous. But as Graciela turned a startled face to him he could see, illuminated faintly by the glow from the contour charts, her lovely, grave eyes fixed on his, and he did not regret the question.

Inside Graciela Navarro's helmet McKen's voice sounded like the voice of an honest, dependable, sincere man, asking forthrightly for something he had every right to expect.

Yet—what could she tell him? That she still loved Ron Tregarth? (But he knew that.) That she still hoped, somehow, Ron and she would be united again? (But she was as certain as McKen that there was no chance of that.) That this was not a world in which to marry and settle down and have children? (Fine though Dennis McKen's children —and her own—were likely to be!)

And that was only the beginning of the thousand things that flashed through her mind! The squid . . . the PanMack fleet that might attack at any time . . . the mystery of Vera Doom. . . .

She hesitated, trying to sort out what to say, how to say it without giving hurt to this man for whom, in the past year, she had come to care a great deal. And finally she summed it all up in a single sentence:

"Dennis, dear," she said, "I don't know."

That seemed to take care of the subject. McKen didn't speak again. He lay beside her, hugging the holdfasts on the sea-skid, staring unseeingly out into the empty deeps.

Graciela forced her mind to turn away from Dennis McKen, and Ron Tregarth, and every other personal thing. She wanted to keep her wits about her—for his safety, as much as for her own. Every time she saw a shadow at the limit of vision she felt a stab of fear. It wasn't superstition. It was wholly rational, because there had been attacks on single swimmers, and some had been killed. Attacked by what? No one really knew. And yet it was partly superstition, too, or at least a scary, shuddery fear of the unknown, because she had not been the only one who had seen the naked form of Vera Doorn swimming empty-eyed and against all logic in the deep sea.

"One more kilometer to go," she said into the intercom, just to fill that empty silence with some human remark. McKen didn't respond. She half turned to look at him, silent and unseeing in his two-seventy-degree helmet. . . .

Then she gasped and her hand slapped the throttle back hard. Something was boiling into sight in front of them— two somethings, and neither was Vera Doorn.

"They're squid!" cried Dennis McKen, startled out of his silence.

"I think they're friends," Graciela corrected him eagerly, squinting at what the sea-skid's lights revealed. "Do you see the one with the speech implant still in place? That's Triton. And the other is—oh, good heavens! I think it's Nessus! But where is his implant? Nessus! Triton!" she called, leaning over the control panel. "Graciela here, yes! Graciela friend, yes!"

The larger of the squid, the one she had called Nessus, darted ahead of them, reversing his siphon to stop, so near that the force of his jet drove the slowing skid backwards. His tentacles waved dangerously. Then, from the other squid, the one that still had his speech box, an unearthly groaning voice howled at them: "You go back now, yes! This sea squid place, yes! This sea human place, not!"

"But Triton, please! I'm your friend—"

"Squid place friend say human friend, not! Say human go back quick, yes!"

"Squid place friend?" Graciela repeated. "But Triton—"

"You go back now, yes!" howled the unearthly voice, almost deafening in such close proximity. And with twin squirts of black ink the two cephalopods moved in on Graciela and Dennis McKen.

McKen swore under his breath. "What an idiot I am," he groaned. "I came out here without a weapon!"

"No!" cried Graciela. "Even if we had one, these are my friends! I— I— Dennis, we'd better do what they say. We'll straighten this out back at the dome." Already she was spinning the little skid about, sending it back to City Atlantica.

"We can't let *animals* boss us around!" McKen protested furiously.

She said sternly, "*I* can. This is my job, Dennis, not yours. I'm sure it can all be cleared up, but right now—" She didn't finish. She only turned her head to glance at the two immense molluscs, herding them along in silence.

Though she tried a dozen times to speak to him, Dennis McKen remained as silent as the squid, all the way back until the dome of City Atlantica began to loom before them. "So it's quite all right," she chattered reassuringly. "Don't you see, Dennis? They're not trying to harm us. The squid never do anything without a reason, so when we get to the locks I'll talk to them. I'm sure we'll find out what this is all about, and then—"

A startled gasp from Dennis McKen interrupted her. She turned away from him and peered toward the dome. . . .

There were a dozen squid moving slowly away from it. Startlingly, they seemed to be carrying tools of some sort in their tentacles, not the plows and harvesters Graciela had some painfully been teaching them to use, but the torpedo-shaped grippers, cutters, power hammers—the kinds of metal-shaping tools that had been stolen. More startlingly still, among them was a naked human figure.

"It's Vera Doorn," Graciela whispered.

"Vera Doorn!" McKen shouted in rage. "The hell with Vera Doorn! Do you see what they've *done?*"

She did see.

She couldn't miss it, as soon as they were close enough to see details. Those tools had been used. The dome's communications equipment was wrecked. Most of the sea-skids had been destroyed. The long-lines submarines, the *Atlantica Countess* herself and the smaller, older *Atlantica Boy*, had been mutilated, all their external parts wantonly crunched—steering vanes, thrusters, sensors.

City Atlantica had been made blind and deaf and limbless, in one hour's work by the squid.

"Stop now, yes!" groaned the voice of Triton from behind them.

Graciela obeyed without thought, all her attention on the ruin before her. The nude woman turned languidly in the light, regarding them as they floated there. They could see the blazing jewel in her forehead, and the wide-set eyes that seemed to stare at them from somewhere out in the chill of interstellar space.

Vera Doorn raised one slim, pale arm, beckoning.

It was not a gesture meant for Graciela and McKen. The squid Triton soared past them with a rush, stopping at the side of the naked woman. It took something from her hand, and jetted back to deliver it to Graciela.

Trying to fumble at it with her gauntleted hand, trying to make it out through her helmet, Graciela gazed at it in puzzlement. "It's—it's a chart of the sea bottom here," she muttered to Dennis McKen. "I think it was in Vera Doorn's ship when she was—ah—I mean before she— But what do these markings mean?"

For great areas of the chart had been ripped and erased, as though crossed out with a blunt knife—or a woman's fingernails. (But how could a human woman's nails rip through the tough, seaproof fabric of the chart?) All that was left untouched was a few of the nearest farms, and narrow passages to them from the city.

"This your order, yes!" howled Triton in their ears. "You go get food those places, yes! You go other places, not!"

And the naked woman floating there before them, her long, blonde hair streaming in the vagrant currents of the ocean bottom, nodded and gestured toward the dome.

That was it.

A moment later she and the squid were gone, and Graciela and Dennis McKen were gazing in horror at the ruin of so much irreplaceable equipment. From inside the dome they could see the frightened faces of the people of City Atlantica, peering out.

"But we're prisoners," gasped Graciela Navarro, trying to understand. "They've made us prisoners! We're not allowed out except to get food!"

"Let's get inside," snarled Dennis McKen. "Then we'll see about that!"

Chapter
19

By the time the second year of the new world was drawing toward its close Captain Ron Tregarth was pacing nervously back and forth outside his cabin. It was three o'clock in the morning. Overhead a huge white moon lit the streets of Base McKen through the tatters of the old netting and the stark needles of the dead palms. The only lights in the little community came from the headquarters building, where someone was on duty, day and night— often enough Commander Wernher Ryan himself, desperately working to keep his command alive and ready for the day when orders would come from the sky—and from inside Tregarth's own cabin.

He had been there for five hours when Rosita Hagland at last pushed the door open and gazed at him. "My congratulations, Captain Tregarth," she said. "You can come in and see your wife and child now. You have a fine boy."

Tregarth entered the cabin awkwardly; it looked different, almost as though he were an intruder in his own home. But there on the bed they had shared for the past year Jannie looked up at him soberly. Her face was that of a woman who had just done six hours of hard physical labor—as indeed she had. The hair she was beginning to let grow long was matted with sweat, but her expression was relaxed. And next to her, in her arm, was something

wrapped in a sheet that wriggled slightly and made faint
mewing noises. She reached over and pulled a corner of
the sheet away from the tiny face, eyes wrinkled shut, pink
little lips making kissing motions. "There he is, Ron," she
said. "Did I do a good job for you?"

"He's—beautiful," Ron said, lying like any new father.

"He will be," Jannie said absently, turning her head to
gaze at the baby. She adjusted the sheet to keep it from
covering the infinitesimal nose. " Ron? Can we name him
Peter?"

"Of course we can," said Tregarth. "That was our
bargain—you could pick the name for a boy, and I would
name it—*her*—if it was a girl. Peter is a fine name."

Standing in the doorway, Rosita Hagland said indignantly, "Peter? That is too grown-up a name for such a tiny
one! He is Pepito!"

"Pepito it is, then," Tregarth agreed, and did not say the
name that had been in his mind if the child had been
female. But all the same something inside him had very
much wanted that the wounded old Earth should have on
it somewhere a living Graciela Tregarth.

Tregarth did not sleep at all that night. It was his
assignment that week to go out every day and check the
long razor-wire perimeter fence around the old space base,
and as soon as it was light he smeared the heavy petroleum
grease on his face, took a canoe and a rifle and a canteen of
water, and paddled swiftly toward the island. There was
still fuel for the outboard motors, but not much of it;
Commander Ryan had decreed that it be conserved, at
least until one of the scouting parties came back with a
new supply from somewhere. If a new supply existed
anywhere in Florida.

Tregarth walked carefully along the fence, scanning the
swept sand on either side for footprints. There had been
very few wire-crawlers in the past year—none at all for

many months. The reason was not hard to guess: there weren't that many people left alive in Florida, or anywhere else for that matter. And no doubt those few who had survived in some unlikely haven were staying close to it, to protect it against their own version of wire-crawlers. Nevertheless, he studied the ground conscientiously. Three days earlier the previous guard had been surprised by an immense rattlesnake. The man had gotten the snake before the snake got him, but at the cost of three rounds of ammunition—and a tongue-lashing from Commander Ryan, for not killing the thing with a club instead of wasting precious cartridges.

Tregarth slapped irritably at some biting insect, and cursed. Rattlesnakes! Alligators! Mosquitoes! It was good that life was returning, a little of it and not very fast—but why did it have to be those pestilential things which seemed somehow to have survived, when everything that gave joy to life was gone?

And then he was at the beach. The razor-wire continued into the sea itself, just at the low-water mark of the mild Florida tides, but squinting into the rising sun, he could see past it toward the Gulf Stream and the great empty ocean beyond.

City Atlantica lay out there somewhere—or its shattered remains did.

Tregarth sat down on the level sand, gazing at the sea. City Atlantica. What was it like now? Did Graciela's squid now slide in and out of the crushed dome? Did whales still dive down seeking them in the wreckage of the city that had been his home? Did the whales, if there were any alive, still feed on the squid?

And what did the squid feed on?

He shuddered, and then jumped up, grabbing for his gun, as a voice behind him said: "They're all dead, you know."

"Sit down, sit down," said Commander Wernher Ryan wearily. "But if I'd been a wire-crawler, you could have been as dead as your friends in the Eighteen Cities by now."

"If you'd been a wire-crawler I would have seen your footprints in the sand," Tregarth said harshly.

Ryan shrugged, lowering himself to sit beside Tregarth. After a moment, he said, "I don't blame you for daydreaming." Restlessly he caught up a handful of sand, molded it into a ball and threw it at the gentle waves. It flew apart as it went, ending as a patter of sand grains that disappeared into the water. "Did you ever throw a snowball, Ron?" he asked idly. "No, of course not; you're a webfoot. Probably never saw snow, did you? Except maybe on pass in some PanMack city up north. What was it like in the domes?"

"It was," Tregarth began, and hesitated. What could you say that would explain the Eighteen Cities to a lubber? He finished shortly, "—free!"

"Ah, yes," Ryan said, nodding. "Free. Meaning not ruled by the PanMacks and the McKens. You webfeet used to put a lot of value on that, didn't you? And then along comes Comet Sicara, and what difference does it make? We're all free now! Free to starve if we want to!" Then he said, more gently, "I don't blame you for dreaming about the sea, Ron. I have my own sea dreams, only it's the sea of space." He gazed up at the coppery skin, squinting against the sun. "I was up there once," he said, not looking at Tregarth. "Only once. And only in LEO—that's the Low Earth Orbit—"

"I know what LEO means!"

"I suppose so. But you don't know what it's like. You can't. Nobody can who hasn't been there. You're floating around in your lifter vessel, watching the relay ship from lunar orbit coming in to dock with you. Down below is the whole planet Earth, just like a blue beachball, with white patches and the line of the terminator slashing right across it where the sun hasn't reached yet. And outside—there's the stars, Ron! I was hoping some day to reach those stars—but I never even got as far as the habitats."

Tregarth looked at him curiously. "I thought there was only the one habitat, Valhalla."

Ryan stared out at the sea for a moment before he answered. "Actually there were four. Habitat Ley. Habitat Tsiolkovsky Habitat Utopia. And Habitat Valhalla. They're all up there still, in the Lagrange position between us and the Moon. There were even supposed to be two more, Paradise and Olympus, at the L-4 and L-5 positions; but they never even got launched, though the parts are around somewhere in South America or Europe, I guess. And only Valhalla was really ever fully occupied. The Common Europeans and the AfrAsians never finished their two, and the McKens—"

He gave a swift look at Tregarth. "The McKens," he said, "sometimes took bad advice. Someone persuaded them that space habitation wasn't worth what it was going to cost. So they cannibalized Utopia to complete Valhalla. It was the Valhalla observatory that discovered Comet Sicara, you know."

"For all the good it did."

Ryan shrugged. "The ships that blew it apart took off from right here, Ron. It could have been worse. It could have hit in one piece and killed off every living thing in the world at once."

"Instead of ninety-nine percent of us!"

Ryan grinned crookedly. "As long as you and I are in that one percent we don't have much to complain about, do we? Although—" He hesitated. "Well, there was something else. Olympus. If Habitat Olympus had ever been finished it wasn't going to stay in Lagrange orbit, Ron. It was meant to have its own drivers. It was going to move out—not just out to Mars or Venus. Out of the solar system entirely! To start a thousand-year journey to another star, completely self-sufficient, its own farms and oxygen and water—everything! And four thousand people were going to be on it when it left. . . .

"And I was going to be one of them," he said, getting up. "But it didn't happen that way, did it? And now we've got other things on our minds. Like sending out a patrol to find fuel and parts for the radio—I *must* report in to General Marcus McKen! And keeping everybody alive and the Peace Wing base safe. And—oh, yes, Ron," he finished, smiling as he extended his hand. "Congratulations on the new kid."

When Pepito was two weeks old Tregarth kissed the soft, warm, milky-smelling forehead, and then kissed his wife, and left with the foraging expedition. Commander Ryan himself was going along, and they took two trucks and Tregarth's own old armored car.

Their primary concern wasn't food. The seventy-one men, women and children in Peace Wing Base McKen had plenty of food, still fresh in its vacuum-sealed pouches and cans; they had looted—"requisitioned" was the word Wernher Ryan employed—all the vast stocks of the old Peace Wing combat base down the shore. But none of that was alive.

And so, as they crawled along the ruined roads toward the city of Orlando, they kept a vigilant watch on the sides of the road. They were watching for guerrillas, of course; that was the reason for the armored car. But they were also watching for any sprig of green big enough to recognize.

In almost two years of dying, nearly everything had died. Almost every living green thing on the face of the Earth had been scorched to death by the terrible ultraviolet from the sun. But it is hard to kill a seed. A seed is designed by billions of years of evolution to tolerate heat, drought, cold—it is constructed to keep its germ plasm alive inside its hard coat until, sooner or later, there is warmth enough and moisture enough and nutrients enough to trigger its first, tentative little shoot of green.

Even a seed was not, however, designed to allow for intense ultraviolet radiation. As long as the ozone layer was gone, those shoots died, too.

But then as slowly the ozone layer began to reform from the natural reactions of the atmosphere, and the ultraviolet began to weaken again, a few sprouts survived.

So a little vegetation was beginning to come back, now that the slowly reforming ozone layer had begun to shade the surface once more from the killing ultraviolet. Every scrap was studied; the ones that looked as though they might be edible, or useful, or even pretty were dug up at once and placed aboard one of the trucks, to be carefully replanted and tended back at the base. When they found a spindly clump of palms trying to grow along an old drainage ditch Tregarth and four others slid down the muddy banks and began to dig.

The roaring bellow from the edge of the murky water caught them all by surprise.

The alligator was huge, five meters long at least, and it charged at them faster than a man could run. They tried. Slipping frantically in the mud, dropping the precious palms, all five on the detail turned and scrambled away. But they would not have had a chance if Commander Wernher Ryan's rifle hadn't spoken twice. The first shot just caused another bellow of rage from the giant amphibian. The second caught it in the skull. The great tail lashed murderously. The claws scrabbled at the mud. The beast curled and contorted as it died.

But it died.

"Don't touch it!" Ryan shouted furiously from the bank as Tregarth daringly took a step back toward it. "Stay right there!" And Ryan came sliding down to the water's edge, rifle ready, cautiously approaching the animal, peering at its head.

He stepped back, staring around the ditch. "No jewel on this one, anyway," he muttered. "But keep your eyes open! Where there's one there could be more!—and the next one might be one of the devils!"

Tregarth looked at him, perplexed. "Devils, Commander?"

Ryan gazed at him levelly. "Haven't you seen the one in my office? Did you think it was just an ordinary 'gator? That thing killed four of my men—Jesus, Tregarth, you'd think it was human! It stalked them like a cat. The last one was the chaplain—he would've been number five. He was digging behind his house, on his hands and knees, and all of a sudden he felt something breathing on his heels—turned around, and there was that thing! Didn't even have its mouth open! Looked like it was just trying to get close to him."

"Is that what alligators do?" Tregarth asked in puzzlement, remembering the bellowing charge of the dead one at his feet.

"Damn straight they don't! Anyway, Padre yelled, and the guard detail was right there—they shot it dead, and it had that jewel in its forehead. I had it skinned for a warning—but nobody touched that jewel!" He glowered at the corpse. "Ever since then, the word is if you see a 'gator anywhere, kill it!"

He took one more look around, then ordered: "Get a move on with those little palms. I want to get to Orlando while it's still light and see if we can find the parts we need for our comm system!"

There wasn't much left of the old city of Orlando, but once there had been a thriving electronics industry there.

There were still parts to be found. The wrong parts, the technicians complained, but they were all there was.

They loaded up what they could, and when they got back to the base Wernher Ryan and his radio technicians labored to substitute components that had been made for quite other tasks in the destroyed vitals of their equipment. And then, when at last it seemed to be putting out RF power, the next problem was to align the six-meter dish behind the headquarters building. Storms had bent it in one direction then another; the unused guidance machinery had to be recalibrated.

Tregarth helped to do that, and then was sent back to his cabin while the radio technicians made their final adjustments. He ate something, then wearily looked on as Jannie nursed their baby. "What do you think is going to happen, Ron?" she asked fretfully, stroking the soft top of the tiny head. "Is Commander Ryan going to take orders from the PanMacks? Is it all going to start all over again?"

He said, "I wish I knew, Jannie. I know what you mean. If the lubbers let the bad McKens take over again—" He paused, because she was looking at him quizzically.

"I'm a lubber, Ron," she pointed out. "So is Peter."

He flushed. "I didn't mean anything bad," he apologized. "But isn't that what you were asking? Ryan has done miracles here, just keeping the base alive through all this hell. While General Marcus McKen just ran away! McKen doesn't have any right to give us orders any more—he forfeited that through his cowardice. And yet I think Ryan will still take his orders."

"And then what?" she demanded.

Tregarth shook his head. "All I know," he said, "is that we're alive, and it looks as though we've got a good chance of staying that way—long enough to raise Pepito and live out our natural term. And there weren't many people that lucky."

He watched her in silence for a moment longer, and then asked the question he had not been willing to ask. "Peter? your husband? Are you still in love with him?"

She looked up thoughtfully from the child at her breast. She didn't hesitate.

"Ron, there are things you never forget." She waited a moment before asking, "Do you mind?"

It took him a while to answer that, because he had to investigate his own mind to find the answer. At last he said, "No. He must have been a good guy. I'm—I'm proud to have our son bear his name."

"Thank you, Ron," she said softly. "I know I wasn't your first choice, either. You still love Graciela, don't you?"

"Well—" he began, but she was shaking her head.

"It's all right that you do, Ron," she said. "She—she sounds pretty special, too, and it isn't any of our faults that things happened the way they did. You're a good husband to me, and I do my best to be a good wife. If the world had been different you and I would've been different—we wouldn't ever have met, for one thing!" She laid the now-sleeping baby back in his crib. "And now," she said, "let's get some sleep."

And they did . . . but not very much, because even before the sun rose, while the sky over the distant ocean was just beginning to lighten, the camp siren shrilled three harsh blasts.

Contact had been reestablished. General Marcus McKen would speak to his troops.

In the harsh light from the floodlamps Commander Ryan looked exhausted, and something worse than exhausted. There was a look in his eye that Tregarth had never seen before, as he stood in the doorway of the communications shack. The radio techs were busy around him, moving the communications screen out onto the narrow step so that everyone could see.

Everyone in the camp had flocked to see the miracle, and when at last the first shadowy outline of a human face peered out of the screen there was a great sigh of pleasure. It wasn't a good picture. The colors were unrelated to reality, a pale pink officer's cap over the blue and green face of a junior lieutenant—but it was from Valhalla! Nearly to the Moon! To the place where General Marcus McKen himself, Supreme Commander of the Peace Wing, waited in his majesty for his land base to report itself ready for duty.

The lieutenant spoke severely out of the screen. "Attention to orders!" she snapped. "Here is General Marcus McKen!"

The screen flickered into life, with General Marcus McKen's sallow face peering angrily out at them— ludicrously, because the face was almost upside down in the screen, the top of the head in the lower left-hand corner of the screen. "He's in Habitat Valhalla," Tregarth whispered to his wife and child. "He's in free-fall; he's just floating there, so it doesn't matter to him which way is up. Now, listen, he's getting ready to speak!"

And the General did. "Commander Ryan," he snarled, "I am ordering a court of inquiry into your conduct in failing to reestablish contact with command headquarters before this. Your actions are inexcusable, but you will have one chance to redeem yourself—in battle!

"Your base may soon come under attack.

"Our surveillance has shown that the renegade, Simon McKen Quagger, has assembled a large force which has been moving eastward for some months. Because of your negligence in repairing your communications equipment you have not been able to receive our warnings. Now you must face the consequences.

"They are well armed. They have tanks and mobile cannon and rocket launchers in the nearest land force, which is at present in Jacksonville. They also have aircraft;

these are at present concentrated in Virginia and Maryland, where they appear to have conquered the legitimate forces I left in charge of that province. But their occupation there is complete, and it is likely that the air forces will soon move south to join the land spearhead. There are also considerable naval forces now in the Gulf of Mexico; we have not been able to determine their composition, since most of them seem to be transports carrying large machines and what appear to be parts of spacecraft."

There was a gasp from the audience. Commander Ryan frowned and held up his hand. "Listen!" he ordered, as General McKen went on, his expression bitter:

"The renegade, Quagger, has not responded to my messages. I do not know his intentions. But that does not affect your situation.

"Here are your orders. You will fortify your position, Commander Ryan. If Quagger's forces attack, you will engage them, and you will win. It is your duty to defend your base until such time as command headquarters returns to the surface of the Earth—and," he added harshly, leaning forward into the screen until the ludicrous upside-down face filled it, "you will do so successfully or you will face the consequences!"

Ryan nodded to the radio tech, who snapped off the set. Ryan looked around at the members of his detachment.

"Tanks," he said thoughtfully. "Mobile rocket-launchers. Aircraft. Possibly an attack by sea, as well. As you can see, we may be in for a hard fight."

"Commander," called the chaplain. "We can't fight tanks and aircraft, can we?"

Ryan looked at him, then shook his head. "Not with what we have here," he said. "But there are other weapons out there. There was a Peace Force base near Daytona Beach; they had tanks, and maybe some of them still work. At any rate, we've got a little time. We're going to use it.

We're going to send a party to Daytona to see if we can get some more hardware—and then we're going to be ready for this renegade, Quagger, when he attacks!"

The raiding party left before dark that night, twenty men and women with Tregarth's old armored car and the base's one self-propelled cannon.

But they never reached Daytona Beach.

As they passed through the old town called DeLand a helicopter appeared above them. It circled curiously for a few minutes, well out of range of anything Ryan's detachment could throw at it, and then disappeared.

And then, ten kilometers farther along, when they turned a bend in the road, there was a man in a PanMack uniform, but with curious flashes and the insignia of a major, standing before a command car in the middle of the road. He gazed at them benignly, raising his hand like a traffic cop.

Next to the major, a non-com was standing with a hand-speaker. He passed it to the major. "Hold it right there," the major called, his tone harsh through the amplification. "We don't want to hurt you unless we have to."

The ambush was complete. Two tanks crashed through the burned-out vegetation on each side of the little convoy. They did not carry PanMack insignia. Stenciled on their sides was a curious seven-armed star and the words *The Armies of the Eternal*, and their wicked gun barrels were aiming directly at Ryan's vehicles.

Two hours later the captives plodded back into the town of DeLand, disarmed, hot, thirsty—hopeless. Before them their own armored car rolled slowly, the gun turret waving slowly back and forth to cover them. Behind were the tanks, followed by armored personnel carriers and more than two hundred marching foot soldiers.

As prisoners, they were fed—out of their own rations, Tregarth saw glumly. They were herded into the vast parking lot of an old shopping center, where a few rusted wrecks of abandoned cars gave them some shade to huddle into. And they waited and wondered.

For these troops were not PanMack Peace Force. The seven-pointed insignia on their vehicles, the flashings on their uniforms, were utterly unfamiliar. They tried to find out what "The Armies of the Eternal" might be, but the guards would answer no questions.

Then, hours later, a sleek gray jet screamed down from the sky, circled the parking lot, stopped in mid-air on its VTOL thrusters and gently lowered itself to the ground twenty meters away. Its markings were like the others; and when the cabin door opened four giant soldiers leaped out, their guns at the ready. More slowly, a ponderous form appeared in the doorway, blinking out at the light.

Lord Simon McKen Quagger limped wearily out of the plane and peered around.

Tregarth looked at him unbelievingly. This was not the same man who had visited City Atlantica just two years before! Ambassador Quagger had been a comic figure of fat—nasty, dangerous, ill-tempered—all those things, to be sure; but still essentially comic. Now the comic mask had been replaced by the face of tragedy. Quagger's face hung slack from his bones. His eyes were dull, when they were not terrified. He shook with a palsy, and when a moment later a horrid little reddish-brown figure leaped out of the plane onto his shoulder he shrank away. "This is a collection of human trash!" the figure screeched, bounding off Quagger's shoulder and toward the major in command, who seemed to greet it with respect. It perched on top of the command car, screeching and gesticulating to the major, who stood at stiff attention.

Lord Quagger seemed relieved to have the creature's attention elsewhere. He wandered over to the prisoners, idly studying them. "Angie's right," he commented wearily to his guards. "These people are trash, all right. They don't even have decent uniforms. Why, look at that one there! No uniform at all, just—" He paused, studying Tregarth. "Don't I know you?"

Tregarth said, "We met in City Atlantica two years ago."

"Stand at attention!" shouted the guard. "Address him as Lord Quagger!" But Quagger waved him to silence.

"Yes," he said thoughtfully. "You were with Graciela Navarro." Then, eagerly, "Is she here with you?"

"No," said Tregarth, and stopped there, unwilling to follow the guard's orders.

Quagger didn't seem to notice. "Ah, well," he said. "Angie might not let me have her anyway." He gazed toward the little monkey figure, now dancing about excitedly as it examined the captured armored car. "Angie is very strict with me," Quagger confided uneasily. "She's very strict with everybody, these days—she wants us to build a starship, you know."

"A *starship?*" Tregarth cried.

"A ship to go very far away," Quagger explained. "Right out of the solar system—not just to some habitat, like my stupid cousin Marcus. You wouldn't believe the trouble she's put us all to! Finding old machines and parts of spacecraft—repairing barges to bring them here to Florida—why, she's taking over the entire continent," Quagger declared, with both fear and pride in his voice.

"A monkey? Taking over the whole continent?" Tregarth cried.

"Please," Quagger begged, casting a quick look over his shoulder at the brown-furred figure. "Don't call Angie a monkey! Still, I suppose it isn't really just Angie doing it. It's something she calls the Eternal. . . ."

And then he seemed to shrink even smaller inside his gross frame as the creature came bounding back to him; and, as it approached, Tregarth saw the blazing, diamond-like gem in the middle of its tiny, wrinkled forehead.

The Years Between

We all live in the Eternal, though we are so very many, and though we are so very diverse. Though we have lived for long and long, blind and helpless, at the bottom of a water sea, we were never alone. We rejoiced in the sharing of self with self, and the differences between that which some of us had been (air-breathing mammals, tree-dwelling reptiles) and that which had been the first form of others (some of us molluscs, some sand-spiders on a planet with a green sun, most of us harder to image) only enriched the joy and variety of our communion.

Now we have found living things to join us as arms and eyes for the Eternal, and now we can share self with other, newer selves.

Now we can rescue other selves from hunger or fear or destruction or danger. Rescuing them, we can bring them to the endless joy of our existence. We will rescue them from every fear and threat.

We will rescue them from life.

Chapter
20

In the third year after the death of the land, Graciela Navarro was on her way back to the dome of City Atlantica. She could see the great, dim dome of the city before her, most of its lights cut off to conserve the little power they were allowed.

She glanced at her sonar screen. As always, the silent watchers that accompanied everyone everywhere had disappeared from her sonar screen as soon as the dome was in sight.

She sighed and tried to be patient, though there was a meeting she wanted to attend. It was slow going. Her sea-skid labored through the deeps, burdened because it was towing her day's harvest of food in the great, draggy net bag. Besides, the necessary detour had made the trip half again as long as it had to be.

That detour was no decision of Graciela's, or of any human's. It was what was enforced on them by the remorseless watchers that swam slowly with the sled, just at the limits of visibility. Where the people of City Atlantica could go was strictly delimited. They could go to the farms and work them; they could tend the single thermal-power station that was still permitted—in both cases, provided they stuck to the approved routes.

Navigation was harder than it had been, without the

friendly tracery of blue-green laser beams to guide them. But it had to be exact. If they went anywhere else they would be driven back.

That wasn't speculation. It wasn't even a threat. It was an observed fact. It had been tried—as any number of doomed attempts at defiance had failed, from repairing one of the subs to swarming out with spear-guns—and more than a hundred persons were dead as a result.

Dead . . . or something worse than dead; for every now and then one or another of those persons showed up, silently watching the farmers or one of the domes—naked, unprotected and wearing in his forehead the blazing bit of color that marked the change to something other than normal human life.

Graciela turned the skid to the receiving dock, in among the ruined remnants of City Atlantica's fleet of submarines, and gratefully allowed others to take charge of her cargo so that she could go inside.

When Graciela was out of her suit she showered herself clean, but not very—only salt water was permitted for bathing any more, since fresh water was energy-expensive and energy was a stringently rationed commodity now. She picked over the cold leftovers in the floor kitchen and managed to find enough to satisfy her hunger. But not with pleasure; the rationed diet for the people of City Atlantica was enough to keep them fed, but heaven knew it was monotonous. She went to her own room long enough to find a warm sweater and heavy socks—the temperature of City Atlantica had been allowed to drop down a dozen degrees, to save energy, and even that was likely to be cut again.

Then, because she was late, she hurried to the meeting in the mayor's office. There she was lucky. She found an elevator just getting ready to go up to the top level, with a cargo of supplies for the clerical workers there. There was room for her, and so she was spared the eight-level climb on the stairs.

Life in City Atlantica was no longer gracious living.

When Graciela got to the mayor's office she thought the meeting must be over, for she heard no voices from within. But when the mayor admitted her she found the little office full. Dennis McKen was standing by the window, gazing sullenly out at the vast, black deeps. N'Taka Rose, the former PanNegran submarine commander, was sitting with her hands folded and her eyes downcast, silent and sober. Four others were standing or sitting around the little room, but the only one of them who nodded to her was Sven Borg.

Mayor Maude Mary McKen was a lot slimmer than she had been, but a lot older, too. She greeted Graciela with affection. "Did you bring in a full load? Good, good," she said absently. "Have you eaten? Good. Well, you might as well get some rest. I think we're through with our business here."

Dennis McKen turned furiously to confront his mother. "I'm not through!" he snapped. "I want a decision!"

The mayor looked up at him foggily. "But that's not quite true, Dennis," she said. "You've had the council's decision. What you want is for me to overrule it."

"It's a stupid decision!"

The mayor sighed. "The council says that any attempt to repair a submarine will fail. It will simply cost us more lives—that's how we lost Frank Yaro, last time we tried. We can't leave the dome."

"We *must* leave the dome! We'll just die here if we don't! And the *Atlantica Countess* is the only way out. Ask Rose; it was her command when she came from City PanNegra. It's seaworthy! The bow vanes and the thrusters are gone, sure, but we have replacement parts! It still has all its fuel. The damage to the externals can be repaired—"

"Dennis, Dennis," sighed the mayor. "They won't let you do that."

He said stubbornly, "I don't accept the council's orders."

"But I'm not talking about the council, Dennis dear," his mother said reasonably. "It's the others who won't let you."

N'Taka Rose lifted her head and said somberly, "She's right about that, Dennis."

"She's not!" he barked. "Anyway—" He hesitated, then burst out, "Living like a clam in a shell may be all right for the rest of you, you haven't ever known anything else. But I'm used to the wide sky and the sun and the stars. I'm going crazy here! It's—I don't know, call it claustrophobia, call it anything you like, but I can't stand living like this much longer. I've got to get out of here!"

The mayor shook her head. "Out of here where, Dennis?" she asked. "Where is there to go? We haven't had any messages from outside for nearly two years! As far as we know, the rest of the Eighteen Cities may be worse off than we are."

"Or they may not! Anyway, there's more to the world than Eighteen Cities."

Graciela stared at him in surprise. This was something new! "The lubbers?" she said incredulously. Then, flushing, "I mean, are suggesting we go to the land people? But they're all dead; you said so yourself."

"I said *almost* all. It doesn't matter if they are. The ozone layer is bound to come back sooner or later. Hell, Graciela, it could have fixed itself a year ago, for all we know! The whole wonderful surface of our planet may be being reborn, waiting for us to come up out of the deeps and colonize it again—just as the first amphibia did, a billion years ago!"

"Or it may not," she said, copying his own phrasing.

"Or it may not," he mimicked savagely, "but how are we ever going to know if we don't go and look?"

Sven Borg stirred himself. Addressing the mayor, he said, "It is possible, Mary Maude. We have a complete crew right here."

"But even if you did have a crew—" the mayor began reasonably.

He shook his head. "Not 'if'. We do. N'Taka Rose is a qualified ship's captain. Both Dennis and I can navigate—"

"Oh, surely not! Dennis is qualified to navigate aircraft, yes," the mayor conceded. "I suppose you are too—with satellite position-finders and radio beams to guide you. Do you think any of that still exists?"

"Probably not," Borg agreed. "But we can take a star-sighting—"

"There aren't any stars under the sea," she reminded him.

"We can surface for position every night! Trust me, Mary Maude. Dennis and I can get the *Countess* where we need to go! And Graciela can at least relieve the helmsman. And the Ng'Woda brothers are engineers; they were part of Rose's crew in the old days."

"Oh, Sven," the mayor said sadly. "You're talking about a skeleton crew. One person for every duty—don't you think you'll need to sleep once in a while?"

"There are automatic pilots."

"If they still work!"

"We think they do still work, Mary Maude," Borg said gravely. "We've checked out everything we could. Apart from the damage to the externals, the *Countess* is ready to go. We've got the spare parts. All we need to do is cut away the wreckage and hook them up—it's not even a hard job. It's the sort of thing any sub crew would do at sea if it suffered damage."

The mayor looked baffled, even irritated. "But at sea you'll have the squid coming back to wreck you again," she said. "That's where it all falls apart, doesn't it? The minute you send a crew out to the docking area to start repairs they'll be attacked; we know that!"

"Yes, that's true," Borg acknowledged. "If we repair the ship at the docking area. Not if we do the repairs somewhere else."

Weariness forgotten, Graciela sat up straight. There was something going on here that she had not expected! It was clear that the mayor was as surprised as she, and so were the Ng'Woda brothers. Only N'Taka Rose nodded faintly, in resignation, as though she had anticipated this.

Borg turned to Dennis McKen. "Shall I show what we're talking about?"

"Do it," McKen said grimly. Then, as the big meteorologist turned to the mayor's screen, he addressed his mother. "We've worked it all out. Here's the *Countess* the way she is now."

The screen blurred and revealed the *Atlantica Countess*, silent and wounded in its dock, a hundred-meter hulk. The port thrusters were gone entirely, housing and all. So were the bow vanes, but Graciela could see that it was only the vanes themselves that had been chewed off by the attacking machines; the cables and struts were intact. The stern vanes were no worse, and the starboard thrusters lacked only the propellors.

"We're going to repair it, all right," McKen said with satisfaction, "but not here. We'll do it on the surface! We've worked it all out, Sven and Rose and me. We're going to load everything up—then we're going to blow the ballast tanks. We'll pop up to the surface, and we can do emergency repairs there! As you see, everything we need is there already." And in the screen everyone could see that that was so. There on the loading dock lay tools, parts, spares— thrusters to replace the missing ones, vanes, cutting torches, welders. "I calculate," he said, "twelve hours' work. No more. Of course, that's only a jury-rigged job, but it would be enough to get us to, say, some island. Anything with a decent harbor so we can finish the job. In the Grenadines, I think," he said, turning to N'Taka Rose inquiringly.

"Anywhere." She nodded noncommittally. "St. Maarten would be within range at reduced speed, I think."

There was a long silence. Everyone was looking at the mayor.

Finally she emitted a long breath. "You're serious, aren't you?" she asked.

"We're very serious, Mary Maude," Sven Borg told her. "It will work."

"It might," she admitted. Then she thought for a moment. "You'll need help loading all that stuff," she said, and thought some more. "The council will scream. . . . And we won't be able to give you very much food. A six-week supply, at the most."

Dennis McKen glanced at N'Taka Rose, who nodded. "If that's not enough, we're done for anyway," she said.

"Then," said the Mayor soberly, "I'll make an executive decision. You can go, my dear," she said, addressing herself to her son. And then she added, "Funny. This is the second time I've given you up. But it doesn't get any easier."

The loading crews worked almost in darkness, so as not to attract unwelcome attention from outside. But if there were any silent watchers, they didn't show themselves.

The next hours were the hardest work Graciela Navarro had ever done, for everything had to be shifted into the sub—three propellors, each one heavier than her whole body, bow and stern vanes like steel sails, a twelve-meter drive shaft to replace the bobtailed one curled like a watchspring in its housing, a whole portside steering assembly that took a dozen strong men, grunting and straining, to lift and coax through the sub's cargo hatch.

And all to be done over again once they were on the surface! And then to be fitted painfully onto the stubs and remnants the attacking squid had left!

When the biggest parts were somehow aboard and lashed secure N'Taka Rose and Graciela Navarro were relieved from the lift-and-carry to check out the old sub's systems. They entered the pilot room, stumbling in the gloom—their only lights the ones they carried. Rose seated herself at the pilot's chair, looked at Graciela, sighed, crossed her fingers and pressed the power-up key.

There was no response at first, then a faint metallic stirring from the bowels of the *Atlantica Countess*. The old power accumulators still held enough charge to pull control rods from the reactor core. A temperature gauge needle stirred, hesitated, slowly rose as the particles from the uranium-oxide pellets found their way to other pellets no longer entirely blocked, and fission began to speed up. Slowly, carefully, Rose raised the level of reaction until the needle wobbled uncertainly in the eight-hundred-degree range. Her face screwed up in tension, she engaged the generators.

The power needles showed *Charge*. She relaxed and glanced at Graciela. "So far so good," she said absently, as though to herself. She waited a careful minute, then activated the ventilation system.

There was a sigh in the air, and stale old scents to stir around them. "Lights," she ordered, frowning at the board, and Graciela, from the engineer's position, switched on the emergency lighting system.

Lights overhead sprang up. There was a shout from the passages outside, where Dennis McKen and the others were lashing down the huge repair parts. Rose and Graciela looked at each other in the sudden illumination, and Rose smiled. "You know," she said conversationally, "I think the damn thing may run after all. Now we run through the check list. Ballast pumps!"—One by one they tested drive motors, pumps, air regenerators, fresh-water systems, food refrigerators, and communications systems, and the instrumentation showed that every one was in the green.

The old submarine was alive once more, back from its years dead.

"Well," said Rose practically, "that's as far as we can go from here. Let's check out the gear." And when she saw how McKen had lashed down the huge parts she raged, "Do you want to kill us all? All this stuff has to be secure! When we broach the surface this whole sub is going to come clear out of the water and fall back! Do you want those things flying around inside?" And while three of the crew were putting the last stores aboard the rest of them were grunting and straining to secure everything.

As they were finishing there was an angry groan from the galley, where Ng'Woda Eustace was stowing the last of the food. He came out, face furious. "I took a drink from the water supply," he said, "and it was awful! Are we going to have to drink that stuff?"

"We could flush the tanks and refill from the dome supply," Rose said meditatively.

"We don't have the time!" Dennis McKen cried.

She nodded. "We've taken long enough already. All right. We'll blow the fresh-water tanks, too; once we're out of here we can refill through the sea-water deionizers— only nobody will have much to drink for a while." She gazed around thoughtfully. "I wonder what else we've forgotten," she said, almost to herself. Then she shrugged. "We're pressing our luck. Everybody strap in—we're on our way!"

And that was the worst of all for Graciela Navarro. Strapped in beside Rose, with Dennis McKen secure in the radio operator's chair behind her, she obeyed the captain's orders. "Blow stern tanks twenty percent," Rose ordered, and carefully Graciela advanced the lever to the 20% position. The *Atlantica Countess* shuddered resentfully but did not move. "Blow forty," Rose commanded.

That made a difference. There was an angry screech of metal from the bow as the ship lifted slowly at the stern. Graciela could feel her center of gravity shifting forward, pulling her toward the control panel. Rose, scowling at her instruments, said absently, "This is the bad part. If we're stuck at the bow—"

She didn't finish the sentence. She cast one more look out the port and ordered, "Stern tanks sixty percent, bow tanks twenty."

And then there was a terrifying crunching sound from the bow of the ship, and the *Atlantica Countess* lurched— and then they were free.

Through the Nexø port Graciela could see the loading dock spring away from us, and *Atlantica Countess* slid up and away, tail first. "Bow tanks seventy per cent!" Rose cried. "We have to get forward motion!"

If they had had a healthy ship the lightening of the bow would have given them almost as good steerage way as though the thrusters were operating. The *Atlantica Countess* was not a healthy ship. Its external wounds meant that great flaps of metal were sticking out at odd angles from the smooth hull, resisting the easy streamlined flow of water. The ship tried to corkscrew, twisting and lurching as it rose, minute by minute. The depth gauge, steady for so long at twenty-two hundred meters, twitched and moved. Two thousand meters. Eighteen hundred. Fifteen hundred. "Slow us down," Rose commanded. "Stern tanks thirty percent, bow tanks thirty-five!" But even though the tanks obediently refilled the lurching rise of the submarine seemed actually to pick up speed, and the twisting, shuddering motion sent Graciela lunging from side to side against her straps. From the corridor outside she could hear Ng'Woda Everett gagging and swearing—seasick! She stared at Rose, waiting for commands, but there were none. The captain was grimly watching the depth gauge—a thousand meters, seven hundred meters, five hundered.

"We're on our way," she sighed, to no one but herself.

On their way. . . . To what? Graciela tried to remember Ron Tregarth. Strangely, she could barely recall his face—a tall man, yes, and a very dear one. But had his eyes been blue or brown?

And had he eyes at all any more? Or was that dear head now no more than a bleached, eyeless skull on the shores of the distant continent?

She forced herself to put those thoughts out of her mind. At two hundred meters the captain sighed and said, "Ballast all tanks normal." And as Graciela frantically strove to get all the tanks at the surface-flotation level, Rose closed her eyes. "Now we broach," she murmured—

And they did. Graciela felt *Atlantica Countess* leap out of the water, bow first, and braced herself for the fall back.

When it came it was harder and more painful than she had expected, as though she had dropped half a dozen meters into her cushioned chair. There were yells of angry pain and surprise from all over the ship.

Then they were floating on the surface of the sea. There was a slow, surprisingly strong surge as the ship rose and fell in the ocean seas.

Rose opened her eyes and looked around. "Well, what do you know?" she said, sounding astonished. "We made it." She scanned her gauges, nodding. The Nexø hull had taken the shock with ease, and there were no indications of leaks even from the propellor shaft housing or the tank valves.

"So far so good," she said, sounding satisfied. "But now comes the hard part."

Hard it was.

The ship's instruments told them that the air temperature was three degrees Celsius, the water temperature six. The slow, huge waves towered ten or more meters from trough to crest, and *Atlantica Countess* was wallowing helplessly broadside to the waves. Overhead low clouds scudded by, pelting them with icy rain.

Dennis McKen wore an expression of resentful astonishment as he worked the ship's hoists, carefully lowering the bow vanes into position. He had not remembered that it would be winter.

As Graciela strained to stay on the slippery deck and guide the vane with the cable she was holding sleet struck her in the face. The wind was at least forty knots, and colder than she could have imagined. At every roll seas washed over half the sub's tiny deck, and she was drenched through. Ng'Woda Eustace, roped and harnessed as he hung over the ship's side, at least had a wetsuit, though the suit was certainly no protection against the way the waves bashed him against the Nexø hull. When at last he yelled to signal that the vane was made fast, his voice almost inaudible through his mask and above the roaring of the wind, she stood up with relief.

That was a mistake.

The ship rolled abruptly and her chilled, cramped limbs would not support her. She fell heavily . . . as though falling on ice . . . as though falling on a slippery ski slope, her feet sliding out from under her, her body coasting toward the edge of the deck, her head striking heavily against the Nexø hull.

Why, she thought clearly, I'm about to fall overboard and drown.

And then she felt Dennis McKen's arm grab her, just as she lost consciousness. That was very kind of Dennis, she thought dreamily, thinking of how dear he had become to her since that other stormy night when she had fished him from the wreck of his Peace Wing plane. . . .

When she woke up he was leaning over her. "Thank you, Ron dear," she said.

The sudden scowl told her what unforgivable mistake she'd made. "I mean Dennis—dear," she said quickly.

The scowl dissolved slowly, replaced with a look of concern. "Are you all right?" he demanded.

"Oh, yes, I think so," she said vaguely, touching the lump on her head. Then she noticed something. "The engines! They're turning over! And—and we're not rocking any more!"

He sank back on his haunches, regarding her with triumph. "That's right," he said. "We've got the starboard thruster going. The other one will have to wait till we can beach the *Countess,* but we're under weight, a hundred meters down." He stood up, holding to a stanchion as he gazed down at her. "Our next stop," he said, "is the island of St. Maarten. And then—"

He paused, looking at her somberly. "And then we'll see if there's anyone left alive in the world."

Chapter
21

When the Armies of the Eternal had taken over the old Cape it came to life again. Ships! Planes! Convoys of trucks laboring over the potholed, washed-out roads with cargoes of machines and parts and raw materials. They came from everywhere.

Ron Tregarth had not believed there were so many people left alive in the world. The little community that had been no more than a hundred souls was now straining toward a thousand, and more on the way. There were more in Lord Quagger's other bases, two thousand at a factory somewhere near old St. Louis, a couple of thousand in Colorado, nearly five thousand, it was said, in the old PanMack base in Baltimore—and thousands more in ships at sea, and at bases along the lines of communication, and in expeditions to the far reaches of New England and western Canada and as far south as Mexico City. All in all, Quagger's subjects now numbered nearly eighteen thousand human beings! More than half, it was said, of all the people still alive in North America!

Almost as many as any sleepy little crossroads hamlet might have had, in every county of every state . . . before the night of Comet Sicara.

And they were all hard at work in the service of Lord Quagger. Which was to say, the service of the Eternal.

But who, or what, the Eternal was, no one seemed willing to say.

No one had much time to ask questions, either, because as soon as Commander Ryan's little camp had been absorbed into the service of the Eternal everyone was put to work, hard work and desperately hurried, to get everything ready for the arrival of the first ships.

It took a lot of doing, and the first task was housing. The little community under the netting was an order of magnitude too small now. Ron Tregarth was sent with a detachment, half Ryan's own people, the other half the new soldiers of the Eternal, to clean out the homes and hotels of the old town of Cocoa Beach. It was hard work, and dangerous—there were rattlesnakes in the old buildings, surviving on heaven knew what. And it was grisly, besides. Skeletons had to be moved and buried, a score at a time in great open trenches; Ryan's chaplain was kept busy performing funeral services for people whose names he did not know. Beds had to be found for fifteen hundred new people, the ones already on hand and the ones about to arrive. Old buses and cars and boats had to be refurbished to provide transport from the new barracks to where the occupants would serve and work. Then fuel had to be found to make the vehicles run. And food—suddenly there was nowhere near enough food again; as bad, almost, as the worst days of the ozone summer returned once more. So once again foraging parties had to be sent out (another drain on fuel and manpower) to scavenge what little was left in towns and cities as far away as Tampa and Jacksonville and Miami and all the points between; and two hundred people were set to planting farms with quick-growing crops; and then there was the work of repairing the docks, the road to the gantries, the crawler that carried immense objects to the launch sites. . . .

No one rested much. Tregarth hardly slept.

And yet, suddenly, there was a sense of purpose to everything they were doing. They were not merely surviving any more. They had a mission—though no one seemed willing to say just what the mission was.

Even Wernher Ryan began to come out of the shock and depression after his command was captured without a fight, his duty failed. "It's space," he explained to Tregarth as, side by side, they shoveled sand away from the entrance to one of the old assembly buildings. "They wouldn't have come here for any other reason. We're going into space again! I'm sure of it!"

Tregarth paused to wipe sweat off his brow, regarding the former supreme commander of all that remained of General Marcus McKen's Peace Wing on Earth. "And what does General McKen think about that?" he asked.

Ryan flinched. Quagger's first order on reaching the camp had been to seal the transmitter to Habitat Valhalla; there had been no communication with the general since then. "There's a new reality," he said obstinately. "I have to accept it. The big reality is that the Armies of the Eternal are opening up the space frontier again."

"And that's enough for you?" Tregarth asked curiously.

Ryan shook his head. "It's what I was trained for," he said simply. "It's what my whole life is for. Get on with it, Tregarth! They say the first cargo ships may come in tomorrow!"

That night Tregarth was given a few precious hours back in his own cabin. They were meant for sleep, but he took time to help Jannie tend their tiny son.

Pepito was fretful, and Jannie almost as weary as Tregarth himself; she had spent the day in stoop labor, planting seeds in the new farm territory, with Pepito in a shaded spot nearby, watched with the other children by the little girl who had tricked them on arrival, Maria Hagland.

When Pepito was asleep Tregarth whispered to his wife, "Are you all right? You look tired."

She was washing out some of the baby's clothes, but she paused to look at him. "Tired? Cripes, Tregarth, what would I be tired for?" Then she relaxed. "Hang these out for me," she ordered; and then, a moment later, followed him out of the hut with the last of Pepito's things. Standing beside him in the cool of the Florida night she said seriously, "I'm all right, Ron. So's the boy. But I don't know what's going to happen next."

"Nobody else does, either. We're better off than we were, though."

She nodded soberly. "On balance, yes. Do you know what worries me? It's those people with the jewelry in their heads, just like that little monkey—"

"What people?" Tregarth demanded, startled.

"Haven't you seen them? They came in this morning in a van, a dozen of them, anyway. Ron, they're not human! They got out of the van, took a drink of water each and a couple of slices of bread—that's all! After God knows how many days on the road! And then they got right back in the van and headed out for the old launch-pad complex."

"So maybe Ryan was right," Tregarth marveled. "He said space was what this was all about. But I didn't see any people with jewels in their heads."

"Tomorrow," Jannie predicted darkly. "When the ships come in. You'll see."

And indeed Tregarth did. Like every other able-bodied person, he was ordered out to Port Canaveral. Six great ships and barges lay in the port.

It was hard work unloading them, the great, weary old hoists and handling machines chugging and shuddering, but carrying their vast cargoes—great cylindrical hoops of metal the size of a house, precious engines, even more precious capsules that carried the payloads. Tregarth saw them only from a distance; his own ship carried food.

And, yes, Jannie's prediction had come true. Among the crews and passengers was a group of thirty or forty human beings—men and women, young and old, all shapes and sizes and colors; but they had one thing in common. Each one of them wore a gem in his forehead. Like the ones Jannie had seen, they were whisked off to the launch pads at once . . . but everyone had seen them, and the questions flew from person to person among the old-timers at the camp.

Questions only. No one had the answers.

It took two days to sweat all the cargo off the food ship, and then Tregarth, dismissed from that task, had a chance to cross the Banana River to see what the other ships had held.

He halted in shock. A tall, lean rocket was already being put in place against one of the old gantries.

It was not a satellite carrier or the kind that could be used for a manned launch. It was a slim, wicked war rocket, and it was tipped with a nuclear warhead.

As Tregarth stared, he was accosted by a gangling man in Peace Fleet blue, but wearing the star insignia of the Eternal. "Aren't you Ron Tregarth?" he cried. "I'm Newt Bluestone, remember me? It's good to see you!"

Tregarth shook his hand. "But I thought you were—" he began, and stopped.

Bluestone grinned wryly. "You thought I was Quagger's pet trained seal, right?" he finished. "Well, maybe I was. That was while Quagger was running things."

"Isn't he?" Tregarth demanded in surprise.

Bluestone turned and gazed across the water to where Quagger was standing patiently, the weary old head bowed, while Angie screeched and squawked and leaped out, spitting out orders to everyone in sight. "Is he?" Bluestone asked. "Can't you see the way it is now?"

"You mean a *monkey* is running things?"

"Don't call Angie a monkey!" Bluestone ordered sharply. "You don't want to get her mad at you! No, she's not a monkey—exactly—and Quagger's not the boss any more, though he still holds the title. The real power now is the Eternal."

"And what is the Eternal, exactly?" Tregarth demanded. "Is it those people with things stuck on their heads?"

"Not exactly," Bluestone said slowly. "But yes, more or less. They speak for the Eternal—and when they do, you'd better listen!" He shook his head. "Things have changed a lot," he said. "Sometimes for the better, too. Quagger's army has cleaned up a lot of bad situations in the old United States—marauding gangs, vicious local warlords, petty tyrants, murderers—"

"And how many people has he murdered in the process?" Tregarth asked roughly.

Bluestone looked astonished. "Murdered?" Tregarth glanced meaningfully at the wicked war rocket on the launch pad. "Ah," said Bluestone, enlightened. "I see what you mean. That's not meant to kill anyone, Tregarth. I hope not, anyway. Tell me, Tregarth, when Quagger took your people over, how many died?"

"Died? Why—actually none, I guess. They took us by surprise—"

Bluestone nodded. "That's Angie for you. She doesn't like killing. She always knows what's going on, somehow—I guess because the Eternal knows, though they say the birds and the animals tell her! And so the way the Army of the Eternal wins battles is by setting up ambushes, in overwhelming strength. There's no point in fighting back, and hardly anyone tries. Oh, there have been deaths! Sometimes the local chiefs and bandits just won't give up. But that doesn't happen often. . . . And," he finished somberly, "a good thing, too. There aren't enough of us human beings left to be killing each other off!"

Tregarth scowled, wanting to believe what Bluestone

was saying, finding it difficult. "And what about that?" he demanded, jerking a thumb at the nuke.

Bluestone pursed his lips. He turned to glance at Quagger, now coming toward them with a little entourage —Wernher Ryan, a couple of Quagger's own officers and, of course, the ever-present Angie, perched on Quagger's shoulder. *"That* is just about to be explained," Bluestone grinned. "Quagger's been waiting for this moment. Come along, Tregarth. I'll get you into the command post, and you can see the fireworks for yourself!"

The old headquarters and communications shed had been forbidden territory ever since the Armies of the Eternal arrived, but now the guards were gone. A kind of throne had been erected before the big screen, and Wernher Ryan, in his dress uniform but with the new flashes of the Armies of the Eternal on the blouse, waited silently by the cameras.

Puffing, Lord Quagger mounted the steps to the stage and sank gratefully onto the throne, listening attentively as the russet-furred creature named Angie chattered into his ear. "Yes, dear," he said faintly, nodding the ruined old head. "Oh, yes. Exactly." Then he turned to Wernher Ryan. "You're ready, aren't you?" he demanded. "Then what are we waiting for? You in the booth! Haven't you raised Habitat Valhalla yet?"

"Almost ready, Lord Quagger!" called a disembodied voice from the control room. "The general is coming to the transmitter just now. We'll give you the picture." And the screen on the stage lighted up to show General Marcus McKen floating into view, pulling himself hand over hand toward a webwork seat.

He glared out of the screen. "Wernher Ryan?" he growled. "Is that you, Ryan? Can you explain why you've failed to respond to my orders these last months?"

Quagger gave Ryan an irritated little shove, and the

former commandant of the Peace Wing on Earth turned to confront the image. "General McKen," he said flatly, "your authority over this base no longer exists. It is now an installation of the Armies of the Eternal, led by Lord Simon McKen Quagger."

It took a few seconds for General McKen's expression to change, but that was only because it took the light-speed transmission that long to get to the habitat and back. His face flashed from angry to apoplectic. "Quagger?" he roared. "Armies of the Eternal? Man, do you realize you're speaking *treason*? I'll see you hanging from a tree for this!"

Ryan glanced at Quagger, then returned to the screen. "Lord Quagger will speak to you now, General McKen," he said.

The little brown-furred monkey chattered in Quagger's ear. Quagger listened absently, nodding, while the face in the screen grew even angrier. Then, the cameras on him, Quagger said pleasantly, "Hello, Cousin Marcus. I have orders for you. First, you will make no attempt to land any of your forces anywhere on Earth. Second, you will move all of your personnel from Habitat Valhalla to Habitat Tsiolkovsky. I am aware that Habitat Tsiolkovsky has been stripped of some of its mechanisms for your purposes, and so I do not require that this move take place immediately. However, you must begin at once. I require that the transfer be completed within ten days. At the end of that time, Habitat Valhalla will be destroyed." He smiled pleasantly into the screen. "That is all for the present," he said. "Good-by, Cousin Marcus."

That night Tregarth grumbled to his wife, "There's a lubber for you! All they can think of is war, killing, bombs!"

"I'm a lubber, Ron," his wife reminded him gently. "For that matter, so is our son. And what else can these people do? If they don't get General McKen out of that habitat, they're in constant danger from his missiles! No, that's the smartest thing they've done yet."

Tregarth shrugged angrily. But as the days passed he saw other rockets being assembled in the huge fabrication building and carried slowly on the crawlers to launch pads. They were not military. Some were Low Earth Orbit surveillance satellites, and some were one-way instrument carriers, and one was something huge and mysterious that no one seemed to know the mission for. Not even Wernher Ryan. "It's big, Ron," he acknowledged. "It's too big to be a weapon, too big even to carry people to the habitats. Do you want my guess? I think it's going to make a manned mission to another planet! Maybe Mars!"

"Mars?" Tregarth repeated, puzzled. "But nobody has ever gone to Mars."

"The PanMacks didn't bother much with space," Ryan said somberly. "Only the military applications, of course."

"And are the Armies of the Eternal any different?" Tregarth demanded.

Ryan had the consecrated fire of the convert. "You mean Lord Quagger's warning to his cousin? But that was only to *prevent* combat, not to bring it about. General McKen knows that the missile on the pad right now could blow Habitat Valhalla into atoms, so he won't dare start anything. And Habitat Tsiolkovsky, you see, has no weaponry, so there will be no danger of any tricks from General McKen when our own ships lift off—like that baby over there," he said, gazing again at the scaffolding that surrounded the first stage of the mystery spacecraft.

"Mars, you think?" pondered Tregarth, staring at the distant pad.

"I'm sure of it! Or if not Mars, at least some other planet, and you can bet on it," said Ryan positively.

But he was, of course, wrong about that.

Punctually on the tenth day the nuclear war rocket was launched. It took twenty-two hours to reach its target, under acceleration almost all the way, and, when it struck, Habitat Valhalla ceased to exist.

But that, it turned out, was only the beginning of the revival of the old Cape. More was already under way, and new problems were turning up.

The killer rocket had been solid-fueled, and the fuel had come with it. The newer rockets were a different matter. They needed liquid fuel, liquefied gases, hydrogen and oxygen. That fuel didn't exist. The equipment to make it existed—there were great plants to take the gases from the water and the air and chill them down, down toward the temperatures at which they would condense into oily liquids so cold that an incautious finger dipped for a moment into them would freeze, embrittle and, agonizingly, splinter off the hand.

But the equipment had not been used for years, had been left to the depradations of storms and marauders.

Ryan and Tregarth were part of the team that inspected the gas liquefiers and returned sadly to report to the Viceroy of the Eternal, Lord Quagger. Quagger was not in his luxurious suite at the Cocoa Beach Motel; his possessions were being moved to the cruise ship. He wasn't at the ship, either; they found him, finally, in the old encampment under the dead palms, testily barking orders at a work crew disassembling the old communications equipment. He greeted Ryan with a scowl. "Why couldn't you keep things in better order?" he demanded. "We need some of this for spare parts, and most of it is worthless. I'm surprised you ever could make it work at all!"

"So were we," Ryan said shortly. "Parts weren't easy to find, Quagger."

"Humph." The old man licked his lips worriedly. Then he said, "Well, what have you to report? Can you produce rocket fuel?"

"Not a chance. Not with what's out there. The condensers, the electrical systems, the refrigerant—they're all unserviceable. They could be repaired if we had the parts. We don't. We can't make them, either."

"Oh, dear," Quagger sighed. "Angie will be so displeased." He glanced around furtively, but the little creature was nowhere in sight. "I'm afraid we'll have to start up another factory somewhere," he complained. "And you know what that means! More people taken away from the work here to man the new plants—more transportation problems—more time! Angie *insists* that everything move forward as fast as possible!"

"I'm just telling you what's possible," Ryan said. "Believe me, Quagger—" He caught the old man's indignant glare, and amended, "Lord Quagger, I'm as anxious to get back into space as you are."

"Yes, yes," said Quagger unhappily. "I suppose so. Only Angie is so insistent—" He glanced around again. "Where is the little darling?" he demanded. "She must be told of this at once."

And then they heard a sort of faint hiccoughing sob from inside the old headquarters building, and when they hurried in there was Angie. She didn't look up at them. She had pulled the old alligator hide down from the wall, and she was crouched on the floor, cradling the hideous thing in her spidery arms. She was stroking the jewel in its forehead lovingly, despairingly, and there were actual tears matting the fur of her cheeks.

Tregarth's duties were changed to refurbishing the old airstrip south of the town of Cocoa Beach. The instrumentation in the control tower was not so much different from that in a sub—the sub's eyes were mostly sonar, the tower's radio waves, but the screens, the electronic taggers, the communications facilities all used principles familiar enough to a submarine captain. While he was checking out one of the spare consoles Newt Bluestone hailed him from the ground below the tower. "Tregarth?" he called. "You got everything in good shape? I don't want to take any chances with the plane that's due in from Colorado."

Tregarth glanced over at the other screen, where the duty controller was marking the flight. It was the only one on the screen. "Should be down in five minutes," he called back. Bluestone nodded and grinned.

A few moments later he was relieved, and after the new engineer had taken over he found Bluestone pacing up and down, gazing at the sky.

He turned a happy face to Tregarth. "It's my wife who's coming in on that plane," he said proudly. "She was in St. Louis, at the factories making the spacecraft parts, and then she had to go back to Quaggie's base in Colorado for a while. I haven't seen her in months. But she's on that plane coming in now! You'll like her, Tregarth. She's a beauty. She used to be—" He hesitated, then shrugged. "Quagger had some nasty habits. One of them was drafting pretty women to work for him, whether they liked it or not, and he picked Doris just because she looked like someone else. But that doesn't matter any more. After Angie took over, Quagger lost a lot of his nastier habits, and— Here they come!"

The plane came in swiftly and accurately. It roared past them on the landing strip, slowed, turned and began to rumble back. It was a huge transport, with the old Peace Wing insignia covered by the Eternal's star, and as it stopped on a hardstand a couple of hundred meters away Bluestone broke into a run.

Tregarth smiled as he saw the aircraft's doors open and the ladder rolled up to it. The fifth figure out of the plane was small, dark and feminine. Tregarth could not see the woman's face, but there was no doubt from the way Newt Bluestone caught her to him as soon as she reached the bottom step that this was the one he had been waiting for.

Then they approached the cars waiting at the tower.

Tregarth stumbled and almost fell, unable to take his eyes off the woman on Bluestone's arm.

It was *Graciela Navarro*.

But then, as she turned to him to be introduced, the voice was not Graciela's at all. "Hello, Captain Tregarth," she said, voice higher-pitched than Graciela's and with a trace of an accent—a *lubber* accent, the kind Tregarth had learned to recognize as "Texas" in his time among Ryan's people.

He reached out blindly to take the hand that was so much like Graciela Navarro's hand. "Hello, Mrs. Bluestone," he said. "I'm very pleased to meet you."

Chapter
22

The repairs that had taken terrible hours as the *Atlantica Countess* bobbed on the surface of the Atlantic Ocean took nearly two months to do over in the quiet waters of the bay of St. Maarten, but this time they were done right.

The *Countess* lay almost aground in the shallows next to an old cement pier, canted on its starboard side so that the wreck of the port thruster was in the open air. Across the pier was the hulk of a ferry that once had carried tourists to the sister islands, and half a dozen fishing boats and pleasure craft, long since battered into uselessness by storms, had dug themselves into the sandy beach.

It was a pretty bay. Once it had been a joyful one, but now it was simply dead. At first they kept an armed guard squatting on top of the church tower a block away, day and night, watchful for possible marauders, but the only human beings they found in St. Maarten were bone-gnawed skeletons. The rats had survived on St. Maarten longer than its human residents, but now even most of the rats were gone.

It was not only marauders they feared. The lookout in the church tower kept his eyes on the sky and the sea as well, for fear of something coming after them, squid or PanMack.

The hardest job was the port thruster. First they had to clear away the twisted housing, then pull the remains of the old drive shaft and painfully ease the new one into place. When Graciela was not taking her turn splashing in the water or hanging from the pier, sweating and straining as the Ng'Woda brothers burned away the ruined metal and welded the new shaft into place, she, or some other, was listening in the control room to the jumble of radio messages that had once again begun to fill the air. The good part was that none of the transmissions seemed to come from anywhere very near; almost all were from the East Coast of North America, especially around Florida. The bad part was that they were mostly in code.

Then, at first dawn light on a pretty tropical day, they cleared away the wooden scaffolding from pier to boat, boarded and sealed ship. The gentle Caribbean tide was almost full, and when N'Taka Rose applied power the engines easily pulled *Atlantica Countess* out into the deeper waters. They turned and slowly, quarter power, headed into the open sea. When the fathometer showed they had five hundred meters below them Rose submerged the ship for speed trials, gnawing her lip as she watched the instrument panels. But even at full speed the new driveshaft turned true, the engines ran sweetly. Only a flutter from the bow vanes as they dove and rose made Rose frown and chew harder at her lip.

At last she set a course to nowhere, slowed the engines to bare steerageway and called a meeting.

"*Atlantica Countess* is operational," she said without preamble, "but she's a long way from being really seaworthy. The port thruster has no housing, and so there's drag on the port side. The bow vanes have a lot more play than I like. I'd like to see them pulled and rehung. There's a little vibration in the starboard thruster, too; the propeller may need balancing."

Dennis McKen snapped, "What are you trying to say? The ship runs, doesn't it?"

"She runs. She needs more work. And some of the things she needs we don't have," she went on. "Housing for the port thruster; we don't have any."

Ng'Woda Everett, glancing at his elder brother Eustace for permission, asked apologetically, "Where are we going to get Nexø on this island?"

"We aren't, Everett. If we did, I doubt we could find the tools to fabricate it. We'll have to use metal—there'll be some, somewhere—if we're lucky. I think we're talking about weeks, not days. But if we sail as she is now— If we run into any trouble and have to maneuver fast and hard—well, I'd take the chance if I had to, but do we have to?"

"What do you mean?" McKen demanded.

She gazed at him levelly. "What's our mission, Dennis?" she asked.

He blinked at her. "Why, to investigate! To try to make contact with whoever else is still alive!"

"But some of the people who are still alive may not be

friendly," the captain said. "And anyway, where do we go when we go? As far as I can see, we've got three choices. We can try to make contact with these 'Armies of the Eternal'. We can strike out for another one of the Eighteen Cities. Or we can go back to City Atlantica."

"Are you asking for a vote?"

"I think I am, yes. When we're at sea I'm the captain, Dennis. Since this whole thing was your idea, I'll listen to what you say about where we go and what we do. But this involves the safety of everyone, so I want everyone to make the decision." She glanced around and settled on Sven Borg, the oldest of the crew. "Sven?"

The huge man said thoughtfully. "We were lucky to get away, I know. Still, I think we should go back to City Atlantica—not to dock, just to get within range of laser communication, to ask the mayor for orders. I vote for going home."

"No!" shouted Dennis McKen desperately. "Not yet! There's all those radio messages that come from Florida— they may be friendly there!"

Ng'Woda Eustace rumbled, "They may be friendly enough to insist we never leave. But so may the creatures at City Atlantica. I think we should investigate one of the other Eighteen Cities."

His brother nodded. Graciela said quickly, "I think Dennis is right. Let's at least take a look at this place in Florida. What do you call it, Cape Canaveral?"

"That's the hottest spot of all," Ng'Woda Eustace protested.

"And that's the best reason for scouting it," Dennis McKen said eagerly. "We need to know what's going on there, and then, maybe, if it looks like we can make contact with them—"

"The place'll be full of ships and aircraft," Ng'Woda predicted darkly.

The captain sighed. "We can always run away," she said.

"I vote for Florida, too. Only—first we make this ship as perfect as we can!"

The sun was no longer lethal, and, for the first time in her life, Graciela Navarro began to get a sense of why lubbers like Dennis McKen longed for the open, sunlit skies of the surface of the Earth. The basking heat from above was soothing, restoring—physically gratifying, she decided, one morning as she set out with Dennis McKen to forage.

They had found an abandoned car, a great, open, gasoline-powered thing that had neither fuel nor energy in its batteries to start it at first. But when Dennis found a supply of gasoline, and they managed to recharge the battery from the submarine's generators, it started right up. Driving along the highways of St. Maarten, with the wind blowing in her hair and the sparkling sea below them on the coast roads was a wonder in itself, and Graciela cried out in pleasure as McKen found an unobstructed straightaway and opened the car up to a hundred and fifty kilometers an hour, just for a moment.

That was pleasure.

The rest of the exploration of the island was not. So many dead! So terribly, uselessly dead—men and women and children, huddled together in the buildings to escape the terrible solar fire, or scattered one by one where they fell. There was nothing left of any of them but bones and now and then a leathery scrap of skin or skein of hair. Decay had been rapid in the tropics. Almost as rapid as death itself.

They stopped to eat their meager lunch on the French side of the island—not in the center of the port town, for there were the remains of too many tragedies still in plain sight, but on a cliff overlooking the sea, in the shadow of a ruined old building. They laid out their concentrates on a fallen sign.

Graciela gazed at her companion, chewing stolidly, frowning as he gazed out westward over the empty sea. At last she ventured, "Dennis? Are you sure we should go there? To the continent, I mean?"

He blinked at her as though distracted from an important line of thought. "Of course I'm sure," he snapped. "We have to know what's happening there—and what about you? Don't you want to make sure of what became of your runaway lover?"

Graciela felt her face flush, but she controlled her voice. "I know what my reasons are, Dennis. I want to know what yours are."

He sneered, "You think I'm going to turn you all over to the PanMacks, is that it?" Then he relented. "I'm sorry, Graciela. I didn't mean to jump on you. No, I don't want to go back to the PanMacks. But I want to know what happened! You've lost a fiancé somewhere on the land, probably dead. I've lost family, friends, comrades—I've lost my whole life there, Graciela! I want to know what happened to it. Who are these people sending radio messages around? There aren't too many of them—we've only identified about a dozen transmission points on the whole continent. But they're well organized, and I want to know who they are, and what they're doing. It isn't just curiosity! You know what City Atlantica is like now, all those people trapped there by the squid and the zombies—that can't go on forever, can it? And here we are, dawdling over repairs that aren't really necessary, acting like tourists!"

"But the captain's right, too, Dennis," Graciela protested, idly sweeping sand from the twisted metal. It had lettering on it in French, and she tried to make it out as she reasoned with her companion. "We need to get the *Countess* fully operational."

"And how do we do that?" he sneered. "Housing for the thruster! We'll never find the materials and tools for that!

This little island won't have— What's the matter?" he demanded, as she gave a little gasp.

She was staring at the lettering she had uncovered on the fallen sign. "I think we might," she said, pointing.

The sign that had once identified the old shop said:

DuLangue et fils
AutoFabrique

So one problem was solved, for the old vehicle-repair shop had both heavy-gauge sheet metal and machines to form it.

Under the direction of the Ng'Woda brothers, the crew turned to fabricate new housing for the port thruster. First the old machines had to be made to work again. Forms had to be shaped to the contours of the thruster housing. The heavy steel had to be squeezed in the hydraulic press, the metal groaning as it bent. Then the whole thing had to be transported to the port and carefully, accurately, welded to the Nexø hull.

Graciela was spared most of that, because there was another job better suited to her skills.

Food.

It was not, at first, easy to find. What there was not, anywhere on the island that she could discover, was food. Every little store had been looted. Every home had been stripped bare. In the tourist stores along the main street of the port town she found places where delicacies had been sold, but all the shelves that had held patés and preserves and spices were bare. Half a dozen times she found coconuts, worked into souvenirs or mounted on plaques, but every one had been drained dry and the scraps of dried coconut meat inside had been made inedible by age and preservatives and mold. The town had held more restaurants than homes, it seemed, but all the kitchens had been visited before by people whose starvation made them more efficient than Graciela.

There was nothing on the land.

There were, however, a few things in the sea.

When Graciela tried her luck at spearfishing she found a wonderful new joy, more precious even than the spiny lobsters and occasional eel she could catch. She was swimming free in her beloved ocean! Not in a clumsy pressure suit with a great globe of a two-hundred-seventy-degree helmet cutting off the caress of the water, but in the briefest of swimsuits, with only a mask to give her air. It was as easy and natural·as the squid pool had ever been, but with all the wonders of the shallow waters to delight her. Corals and great shells, beds of algae beginning to grow again, long, waving strands of kelp. The kelp was not the edible kind that they grew in City Atlantica's farms, but evidently these shallow seas had denizens of different tastes. There were indeed fishes in the reefs. The biggest and easiest to catch were the eels, great, ugly things that lurked in crevices in the rock until you speared them, and then turned into writhing devils that refused to die until their heads were cut off and their long bodies were thrust, still wriggling, into the carry-nets. But there were other kinds of fish, pretty ones no larger than Graciela's hand, brilliant with red and blue and yellow and green. Graciela didn't have the heart to spear any of them. They were too tiny to be valuable for food, and they were much too beautiful. What she brought back to the crew of the *Atlantica Countess* in her carry-nets were eels and lobsters, crabs and clams, the scavengers and bottom filter-feeders that had profited from the death of so many other things. But what she brought back in her heart, joyously, was the memory of the pretty reef fish.

The land might be dead and hostile, but the sea, the sheltering, mothering sea, was returning to life.

Hostile the land was.

The ceaseless mutter of radio traffic did not dwindle as

the days passed. Though most of it was unintelligible, the ship's instruments had at least been able to locate the major sources—Florida was always active, so were one or two points farther up the American coast, so were other, fainter stations that seemed far toward the interior of the continent.

When the housing was nearly complete Graciela came to get Dennis McKen for a fishing expedition. She found him at the radio, face like stone, listening to the cryptic whines and squeals. "It sounds like military traffic. They're frequency-chopping it," he told her. "Whatever it is they're saying, they don't want anybody to hear."

"Then what's the point of listening?" she asked. He shook his head irritably and didn't answer.

But he came along when she told him what she wanted to do, and the two of them took the little skiff they had found lashed behind one of the waterfront hotels, filled its outboard from the precious stock they'd scavenged, and started out around the coast.

When they reached the cove Graciela had chosen, McKen cut the engine and let the anchor cable drop. He knotted the cable around a fitting, and paused to look at Graciela.

He managed a smile. "Let's dive," he said.

And in the healing water that slid so tenderly and warmly over her skin, Graciela felt the angers and irritations of the surface wash away. The water was glass-clear; she could see the bottom, six meters away, as clearly as the form of Dennis McKen swimming strongly just ahead of her toward the nearest cluster of coral and rock.

He was, after all, a decent man, she told herself. One of the bad McKens, yes. But only on his father's side, and anyway no one chose his ancestors! Dennis McKen had taken his turn at the work of City Atlantica and the *Atlantica Countess* as bravely and effectively as any—and there was no doubt that he was an attractive man, as well. And Ron Tregarth—

She let her mind drift as her body did in the lazy tropic sea, thinking about Ron Tregarth. How long had it been now since they had kissed and parted, as the *Atlantica Queen* left on its one-way voyage? Only two years and a bit?

It seemed forever.

She sucked in a great breath of air from the tank on her back—it was as close as she could come to a sigh in the mask—and dived toward McKen, who had found something worth catching. It was a huge conger, longer than he was tall, and it did not want to be caught. His spear had it in the throat, a few centimeters from the wicked, dangerous jaw, and though it could not snap at him it was lashing about terribly, shaking him through the spear this way and that as the blood poured from its wound in cloudlets of red. Even behind the mask Graciela could see that McKen was grinning with warrior's joy at the struggle. He would not want her help, she reflected, stirring her swim fins idly to keep her level as she watched.

There was a shadow over them, just below the surface.

She looked up and froze. Dennis McKen had found the conger, but something had found Dennis McKen. It was a hammerhead shark. Not a big one—less than two meters, she guessed—but quite large enough to kill, and certainly, in these prey-depleted waters, hungry enough to attack anything that looked edible.

Graciela didn't stop to think. As the hammerhead came down she rose to meet it, her spear before her. The shock when it struck was like running into a wall. She almost lost her grip on the haft of the spear as it sliced into the shark's eye, stabbing into the tiny brain behind it. Sharks do not die easily. There was plenty of life in this one, but the wound was mortal all the same. Graciela held grimly to the spear shaft, so close to the terrible jaws that she could almost count the rows of nail-sharp tearing teeth. It flung her free—

And she felt a thump on her back, and turned in sudden terror—another shark?—but it was Dennis McKen, the conger forgotten, urging her before him toward the boat.

Graciela Navarro had never swum faster than as they raced for the boat, never daring to look back. She could feel the shudderings in the water as the shark whirled about, snapping at its own body in frenzy. At every moment she expected the awful shearing snap of those jaws on her flailing feet. Even when they were at the boat, and McKen was almost throwing her over the gunwale, she lay staring at the sky for a long time, while he hoisted himself aboard.

He was calmer than she. He got up on his knees, shading his eyes from the sun to see where the surface of the little cove was roiled with the struggles of the murdered murderer just below the surface. It took a long time to calm down.

Then he sat down and reached for her. She could feel herself shuddering in his arms.

He was smiling when he looked down at her. "I think you saved my life, Graciela," he said. "Do you know what that means? It means that from now on you're responsible for me."

"Oh, Dennis," she sighed, knowing what would come next.

"I want you to marry me, Graciela. We have a life to live. Don't spend it mourning!"

She was silent for a moment. Then she looked up at him, her face sober. "I will give you an answer when I have seen the land with my own eyes," she said, and would not speak further on the subject.

And then, suddenly, the work was done.

They gathered on the dock, exhausted but content, looking at *Atlantica Countess* as Praxiteles might have looked at the latest Venus when the last rough spur of marble had been chiseled away. It was almost dusk. The port housing was bright red—Sven Borg had found antirust paint to protect it from the sea—and it looked out of place against the milky, smooth Nexø of the rest of the hull. But it was strongly held, and carefully faired into the surrounding surfaces.

"It'll do, I think," said Rose. "Shall we sail for Florida?"

"That's what we agreed, isn't it?" Ng'Woda Eustace said, slapping at his neck. He looked curiously at what was in the palm of his hand. "It's a bug," he said, astonished.

Dennis McKen laughed. "A mosquito," he corrected. "It looks like a lot of things are coming back. Including us!"

Rose N'Taka looked at him thoughtfully, but all she said was, "Is everybody here? Good! Then we're sealing ship right now. Prepare for sailing!"

And slowly, carefully, *Atlantica Countess* slid free of the concrete wharf, slipped out of the harbor and headed for the dark, sheltering deeps.

Six kilometers off the Florida coast they cautiously surfaced.

It was just dawn. The sea was mirror-calm. As soon as the hatch was opened most of the ship's crew scrambled up onto the narrow deck, leaving only Ng'Woda Everett at the engines and Sven Borg manning the main controls.

Graciela Navarro stood by the popup deck controls, gazing eagerly toward the low, distant shore. There was a warm, moist breeze, and the rising sun behind her felt good on her back.

"Looks quiet enough," the captain murmured. "Graciela? What's the radio situation?"

And when Graciela queried Sven Borg, the answer was:

"Lots of traffic. Louder than ever. Some transmission sources are moving—aircraft, I think."

Ng'Woda Eustace was already sweeping the sky with glasses. "They're there, all right," he reported. "There's one to the southwest, just over the shore—and another well south of us."

"They could spot us," Graciela offered.

The captain said thoughtfully, "We're not a very big target—and anybody on the shore would be looking right into the sun. . . . Let's get a little closer."

Graciela gave the signal to the engine room, and the *Countess* moved slowly toward the low, distant shore.

"Stay lively," N'Taka Rose warned. "If we have to duck and run we'll need to do it in a hurry."

But when they stopped again, a couple of kilometers off the beach, there seemed to be nothing to run from. They could see that there were indeed ships there, all moored, all apparently in good condition. Through their glasses they could even see people on deck, and small boats in the water among the ships. As they slowly cruised south, studying every detail on the shore, Graciela gazed yearningly at the sandy shore. She was looking at the largest number of human beings she had seen since they left City Atlantica. If Ron Tregarth were still alive at all, she let herself believe, he might be in some place like this. . . .

But there was really no chance that he was alive, she reminded herself. And this was the day when she had promised Dennis an answer.

Then they came to a part of the beach where tall metal structures reached toward the sky. Dennis McKen caught his breath. "Spacecraft!" he shouted, pointing at the huge gantries. "Look at that! They're going back into space again!"

"Stay down!" Rose warned sharply, and reluctantly

Dennis go back on his knees on the few square meters of deck the captain had allowed above the water. But she was staring a the shoreline herself with grim concern. "That's important," Rose said, half to herself. "If they send up reconnaissance satellites now, it's only a question of time until they start sending out ships and planes. The cities need to be told."

Ng'Woda Eustace looked at his captain in puzzlement. "City Atlantica, you mean?"

"No, no. There's nothing City Atlantica can do, and they're in no special danger from lubber surveillance. I mean the other cities. They need to know that if they do anything on the surface they can be observed."

Graciela, studying the distant shore, was hardly listening to the exchange. She shook her head in wonder. How could it be that these tattered survivors had got themselves into shape to reach out to space again, so soon after the disaster that had destroyed the land?

Then she gasped aloud.

Beside her on the wet deck she heard the captain cry out and Dennis McKen swear unbelievingly. Something was happening around one of those skeletal towers. A puff of white vapor from its base. Then a glow of bright flame.

Then slowly, centimeter by centimeter, something rose alongside the gantry, topped it, soared free, with a great flower of blinding-white fire spewing from its tail. It arced up over their heads and out to sea, and a moment later a huge shock of sound struck their ears, so loud that even at this distance it was painful.

Dennis McKen was on his feet again, hopping up and down in the unsteady footing as he squinted up into the bright sky. "They've launched a rocket!" he cried. "They're really doing it!"

They really were. It was a spacecraft, lifting into orbit.

Behind the rocket a long, irregular cloud of vapor spread across the sky, persisting even after the rocket itself had vanished.

They gazed after it, spellbound, until the captain cried out, "Look at what's coming! Everybody below! Prepare to dive!" —for a ship was bearing down on them from the north, only a couple of kilometers away, coming fast with a white mustache of bow-wave surrounding its wicked, sharp nose. It was no pleasure vessel. It was a ship of war, a gunboat perhaps.

They did not linger to investigate.

The *Atlantica Countess* was a hundred meters deep and ten kilometers away, sliding through the Gulf Stream at maximum speed, before they dared relax.

Then the captain displayed the charts of the Eighteen Cities and leaned back. "We know that PanNegra's gone," she said, "and there's no point in going back to City Atlantica just now. Which way? North or south?"

"South," Sven Borg said firmly. "City Romanche, near the Equator."

Rose looked around the room. "Are we agreed? Then City Romanche it is. Set course southwest by west."

And two hours later, with the ship on autopilot, all the ship's company was present as Captain N'Taka Rose joined Graciela Navarro and Dennis McKen in matrimony.

Chapter
23

Safe in the old reviewing stands, where the PanMack high brass had watched ceremonial launches in days gone by, Ron Tregarth held Pepito up to watch the launch of the first spaceflight to leave Earth's surface since the night of Comet Sicara. The baby didn't like it. The bright light hurt his eyes, and when the thunder of the rockets made the stands shake he cried.

"Ssh, ssh," whispered his mother, leaning to nuzzle against the child's warm head. "It's nothing to be frightened of, little Pepito. Don't you know your daddy will be in one of those things before long?"

"It's not settled yet," Tregarth cautioned his wife, but she shrugged.

"It's certain," she said. "They need space pilots. How many people here have piloting skills? No, Ron, you'll be an astronaut yet."

"Only if the little monkey approves Ryan's proposal," Tregarth said. "And not for a long time—there's a little matter of training, first!"

But in fact, for a person with Ron Tregarth's experience, astronaut training was quick enough. By the time Pepito was two years old, his father had completed as much as could be done using the old simulators.

Compared to navigating a submarine it was child's play; there was no need to memorize charts of channels and reefs and guyots and tides and currents—there weren't any of those in space. The takeoff was nothing—ground control pilots guided that. Maneuvering in orbit was easy enough: you saw where you wanted to go and you got there. It was the return landing that was hard; that took skills Tregarth had never had.

But with Wernher Ryan urging him on, he learned them fast. When Tregarth had made his fifth flawless approach and landing in the simulator Ryan took him to Quagger. "Tregarth has gone as far as he can in the simulator," Ryan reported. "He needs flying time."

"But we don't have any spacecraft for him to fly yet, Ryan," Quagger complained.

"Of course not. But he needs aircraft experience. In a real plane, not a simulator."

"Good, good," Quagger said absently, stroking Angie's fur. The little creature endured it for a moment, the bright little eyes staring at Tregarth. Then it chattered in Quagger's ear and leaped away on an errand of its own.

Quagger followed Angie with his eyes, lovingly. "Don't you think she's losing her hair?" he demanded, his voice worried. "She's slowing down. I'm really concerned about her—but she won't let the doctors look at her. Not that they'd know what to do, I suppose, since she's so—special." He shook his head mournfully. "Now, what was it you wanted? Oh, flight time for Tregarth? Yes, by all means; have him put on the pilots' roster at once, Ryan."

And so a few days later Tregarth got his first flight in an aircraft. He flew copilot with one of Quagger's old personal pilots. It was not like the simulator! The simulator did not give you the sudden rush and the pressure against the back as the great plane swept off the runway, or the uneasy shaking and twisting—like a small sub in tidal currents near the shore—as they passed through regions of turbulence.

Nor had Tregarth ever seen the world from two thousand meters. A blighted toyland. Everything was tiny, and always in somber shades of black, brown and gray. Even the rivers were murky. It was always a surprise, a gratifying one, to complete a flight and return over the Florida shores to the landing strip, and to see the plots of green begin to appear where so much else was dead.

And, of course, to return to his little family.

Tregarth was happy with his wife and child. True, every time he saw the false Graciela, Doris Bluestone, there was a little wrench to his heart. But there was nothing Tregarth could do about that, or wanted to do if he could. His life was stable, and, queerly, full of promise.

There was a definite future for the human race these days!—though, to be sure, he could not see exactly what that future was. Perhaps the growing number of men and women who wore the bright gem of the Eternal on their foreheads could have told the rest of the community more than they knew. They didn't choose to. The gem-marked ones kept to themselves, concentrating, it seemed, on the great new rocket that was slowly growing on its launch pad. . . . But when it would be finished, or why it was taking so long, or what it was meant to do when it was complete, no one ever said.

Pepito had playmates, for the little community was growing. Children were being born. Stragglers were being rounded up and added to the forces of the Armies of the Eternal. There were still bleached bones to be found, but they were retrieved and buried as they turned up, and right around the Cape new palms were beginning to grow, as well as weeds and scrub palmettoes.

Tregarth flew at least once a week, to the factories in St.

Louis, to Baltimore, to Quaggerhome in Colorado, to the outposts in New England and Vancouver and Mexico City and California. As time passed he saw that some of those places, too, were beginning to turn green by themselves, as volunteer seeds at last find an opportunity to grow.

On one stop he picked up an emergency shipment from the Kansas City post of the Armies of the Eternal. The officer was a slim dark woman who might have held his eye even without the great gem blazing on her forehead. She gave him brisk orders to rush his cargo, gestured for him to go, and then spoke again.

"Captain—" Her curt voice caught. He saw her pale lip tremble, saw a flicker of feeling behind her frozen composure. "Captain—"

"Yes?" He waited, startled at the break in her emotionless efficiency. "You have something else to ship?"

"Nothing." Her face and her voice had gone blank again. "You may—" But then she bent toward, pain in her eyes, hoarsely gasping. "Captain, do you know Newton Bluestone?"

"I've met him. Why?"

"I was Judy Rosco." Her racing whisper was almost too faint for him to hear. "We were lovers. We quarreled. Foolishly, when we were not ourselves. I said things I'm sorry for. Now—now I'm afraid he'll think it's too late. I want him to know I'm alive, and I need to know he's alive, because in the Eternal we may have another chance. Will you tell—"

Abruptly, she stiffened and stopped.

"Rush your cargo, Captain." A curt, impersonal command. Her face had gone cold once more, and he saw green fire burning in the stone on her forehead. "You may go."

Puzzling over that on the long flight back to the Cape, Tregarth wondered sadly again how those dreadful jewels could change a woman into a coolly inhuman slave of the Eternal, whatever it was, but he decided not to mention the incident to Newton Bluestone. It was nothing he knew how to explain, and, whatever had happened in the past, Bluestone seemed entirely happy now with the wife who looked so heart-stoppingly like another Graciela Navarro.

Tregarth longed to fly out over the Atlantic, but that was forbidden. Angie had given strict orders.

Sometimes he flew on survey missions, following up reports from the long-distance pilots of smoke, or planted farmland, or moving vehicles. Then they would go out in a VTOL ship on "fishing" expeditions. They would land by a settlement, where two or three or a dozen lean, ragged survivors would greet them, usually, with guns, and inform them that they were now subjects of the Armies of the Eternal. Quagger wanted to tax them, but Angie forbade it. So they were left alone unless some of them had special skills. Then the valued people would be invited to join the community at the Cape. They always accepted—under the guns of the air force of the Armies of the Eternal they had, after all, no choice. Two meteorologists were caught that way, and a tank commander, and, best of all, several dozen farmers.

Crops were growing. In the fourth year after Comet Sicara the remants of the land-living majority of the human race at least no longer feared they would starve. Even a few precious animals had been found, cows and sheep. Each was tended like a champion prizefighter between bouts, brushed and watered and fed, and when the first calf was born it was like a new baby for the whole settlement. The crops were a disappointment in some ways—tiny tomatoes, scraggly pea-pods—for the entire industry of gene-spliced and hybrid seed was no longer there.

But they grew. And so did Pepito, a sturdy young man beginning to speak, and a delight to his father . . .

. . . Who only very rarely wondered what his son would have been like if his son's mother had been Graciela Navarro.

Chapter
24

Half a million kilometers away, General Marcus McKen was working himself up into a sweat as he berated his chief scientist and principal whipping boy, the astronomer Dominic Sicara.

Sicara wasn't sweating. He was cold with fear, because this time the general was furious. "We're *blind!*" the general shouted. "How can I tell what's happening out there? You promised that the sensory systems would work!"

"They were supposed to," Sicara said miserably. "All. the data showed that Habitat Tsiolkovsky had all its equipment mothballed; I had no way of knowing the external optics had never been installed. And, if you remember, I did suggest bringing spare parts with us when we moved—"

"Silence, you fool!" the general roared. "We needed all our cargo space for more important things!"

"Of course, General," Sicara whimpered. "Still, there should be equipment on the other habitats. If our scout can bring the instruments back from Habitat Ley—"

"And how will we know if he's coming back?" McKen sneered. "We can't even see his ship!"

"We just have to be patient, General," the scientist said pleadingly. "He'll be back soon. He has to wait until the habitats are out of sight of the base in Florida, that's all, but he'll make it."

"He'd better," said the general, "because if he doesn't you're the one who will pay." He waved the scientist away, glaring around him.

Habitat Tsiolkovsky was bigger than the abandoned Valhalla (now dust; now only a memory and an occasional heart-stopping scare as a random fragment clanged against Tsiolkovsky's shell). There was nothing else good that could be said for it. Its air stank of mold and rot. Its spin rate was too slow to give it a decent gravity, but too fast for its thermal regulators. The cooling fins that were supposed to pop up on the dark side to radiate excess heat away, like the spined sails of an earthly lizard, had time to get only partly extended before they had spun into the sunlight again and begun to retract. So the heat stayed inside and built up, and the habitat was hot. General Marcus McKen had begun to sweat in the first hour after his enforced move, and he was still sweating—now as much with anger as from the heat of the stifling shell.

This was all that was left of his empire! This vast, echoing, empty shell, with fewer than three hundred persons to serve him—and all because of that arrogant, impudent cousin, Simon McKen Quagger.

"Bring me some food," snarled the general, but the bile in his throat made him doubt he could swallow it.

That was always in doubt, not only when he was in a rage. (But he was often in a rage, anyway.) When the food came he stared at it sullenly for a long time before lifting a forkful of the greasy, gray paste to his lips.

Although the sludge tanks and the algae ponds produced enough food, what food it was! Every day General
McKen had the hapless cooks and food chemists up before
him, stuttering in fear, but nothing helped. Whatever
threats he uttered, whatever exemplary punishments he
imposed, the best they could produce was little loaves of
algal bread that sometimes could be coaxed into tasting,
more or less, like cheese or walnuts instead of moss and
mud. This time it was more a pudding than a loaf, and
tasted, faintly, like fish.

It was not an improvement.

Sighing in resignation, General McKen pushed the mess
away from him and got up to make one more inspection of
the things he had used his cargo space for.

The flight from Habitat Valhalla had been hasty but
there had been time, just time, to load some real essentials
aboard the shuttlecraft. Their sleek, sophisticated food
machines had been left behind. Furnishings of all kinds
were abandoned—half the complement of Habitat Tsiolkovsky shared a sleeping net with someone else, day shift
and night shift. Exercise machines (sorely missed; nearly
everyone was losing bone mass), entertainment spools and
viewers (even books!), amenities of all sorts were only
memories now.

But one thing General Marcus McKen had not abandoned.

Weapons.

There were hand guns and grenade throwers and mor-
tars for twice the strength of his company, and more
ammunition than they could carry. There were rocket
launchers, even now being mounted in the noses of the
scant half-dozen spaceplanes he had insisted on using for
the move, though the shuttlecraft would have been more
efficient. If ever the chance came to return to Earth, he had

the small spaceplanes and two big transports that could make the trip. . . .

But how could he know when the chance might come, when Habitat Tsiolkovsky, without windows, without external optical systems, was blind?

. . . And then he felt the soft, distant clang that meant a berthing.

It was too gentle and too massive to be a simple ricocheting chunk of debris. It had to be the shuttlecraft returning.

And ten minutes later, for the first time in weeks, the docking crews of Habitat Tsiolkovsky saw their commanding general smile.

They lost three casualties from the eva crews, two with crushed and leaky suits when one of the great external eyes got out of control and slashed ponderously into them and the third when somehow she—it was a woman corporal—slipped her tether and went sailing irrecoverably off into space.

It was a cheap price to pay. Not only did Habitat Tsiolkovsky have eyes to see again, but the evas had managed to ease the jammed old radiation fins in their sockets, so that the habitat was slowly returning to a livable temperature.

That was the good news. The rest was bad.

When General McKen pulled himself, hand over hand, into the surveillance room, Colonel Schroeder, his aide, greeted him with worried apologies. "Sorry, sir," the colonel said. "We've scanned every city and base in your protectorate. There's activity in Baltimore, and at the Cape; that's all. Everything else is abandoned. Not a sign of any living thing."

The general's expression did not change. "What about Quaggerhome?"

"Yes, sir," the colonel said quickly, "there's activity there, but all we can see is traffic in and out. The base is inside the mountain, you see, and—"

"I know it's inside the mountain!"

"Yes, sir," Colonel Schroeder said abjectly. "And there are communities in St. Louis and in some of the Gulf ports—and that's about it. Nothing else anywhere on the Earth we can search—up to fifty-five degrees north and south. Except for the Cape, of course."

"Show the Cape," Marcus commanded. "And get Sicara in here."

When the old scientist tottered in the General was gazing angrily at the scene on the vision screen. "What is that?" he demanded.

Sicara glanced fearfully at the screen. "Your Florida base, sir," he reported. "The thing in the center is a launch pad."

"I know it's a launch pad, you fool! What's on it?"

The scientist studied the blurry image. "It appears to be a large launch vehicle. Only I think—" Sicara squinted blurrily at the screen— "yes, I'm quite sure its upper stage is missing. The image isn't really clear enough for details but, yes, there's no payload."

"And what sort of payload could it carry?" McKen asked.

Sicara answered slowly as his eyes studied the image again. "Something very big, to judge from the size of the lifter. If we could get a better picture—"

"And that," General Marcus McKen said sternly, "is exactly why I have summoned you here. Why can't we get a better picture? I must know what they're up to! Aren't you supposed to know something about telescopes? What's wrong with this one?"

"There's nothing wrong with it, sir. It's the best we've got, the best optics, a charge-coupled device hooked in after the last mirror, a photon collector—sir," Sicara said desperately, "you don't understand the technical problems! This is *Florida* we're trying to survey. There's a great deal of water vapor in the air; we can't see at all in visible light half the time because of clouds, and the water vapor cuts our infrared efficiency in half—"

"I've had enough of your excuses," McKen said grimly. "Schroeder! Take this man out and teach him some discipline!"

But, satisfying as·that was to General Marcus McKen, it did not solve his problem. He still could not see what was going on at the base that once had been his own . . . and that he wanted very much to make his own again.

Chapter
25

When Pepito was four years old his mother took him out with her on a fishing trip in the bay. He liked going with her, and this time they went far out—down the channel, past Gator Key, even out to the reef where the waves broke into spray that had a good salt smell. The wind was soft and warm. The bright water had lovely colors of soft blue and green around the reef, and it grew deep and dark beyond; and then there were the fish.

Fish! Strange things that lived in the sea! When Pepito helped his mother haul them in they flopped and struggled, and gazed at him with great staring eyes, and died.

They could not breathe in the air, and that was a wonder to Pepito. "Can people live in the sea?" he asked his mother, and she gazed at him lovingly as she laughed.

"People do," she said. "People did. Your father did, a long time ago, in a city far, far out there—" and she waved to the dark swell of the Atlantic Ocean, out past the white foam of the surf.

"Could he breathe there?" Pepito asked anxiously, and wondered at her answer.

"I think," she said somberly, "that he thinks he breathed better there. Or at least more freely—oh, Pepito! Look!"

And then he saw his first sea bird, a great, wide-winged gull or petrel, skimming the tops of the waves and now and then darting down to catch something. "Birds are coming back!" she cried.

But it did not seem to make her happy. "You see, Pepito," she explained, "in the old days there were millions of birds. Many, many different kinds of them! Pretty ones with colored breasts and necks and tails. Birds that sang— why, when I was small, every morning because their singing would wake me up."

"Did the Eternal let them wake up Lord Quagger, too?" Pepito asked, and his mother frowned.

"I have no idea," she said. "At that time I had never heard of the Eternal—and Quagger was just a guy that gave orders, a long way away from me."

It was clear to Pepito that his mother didn't like Lord Quagger. He didn't know why, but Pepito didn't like him either. Quagger had a shrill, squeaky voice, and he did bad things. What those things were Pepito did not exactly know, but they had something to do with taking Commander Ryan's spaceport, and something to do with his mother's friend, Doris Bluestone. And he made everybody do things that, really, they didn't much want to do, like building that big ship they called a "starship". What that was for no one seemed to know exactly. . . . But Quagger gave his orders, and that was that.

The funny thing, Pepito pondered, was that it didn't seem that it was Quagger's own orders that were followed. He just seemed to be a kind of puppet for that ugly little monkey thing with patchy, dirty-brown colored fur called Angie. She rode on Quagger's fat shoulder, holding to him with a long tail wrapped tight around his throat, and her hard little eyes seemed to shine with their own strange fire. Her eyes had the same cold color as the great blue jewel she wore stuck somehow to her furry forehead. And she *smelled*. When Angie was near Pepito hid behind his mother, or any other friendly grownup, but he couldn't escape the rank scent, so much worse than the ordinary farm animal smells from the barns and the milking pens. And her voice! It was worse than Quagger's, and she screeched and yelled, pointing her bony little doll-fingers this way and that as she gave orders.

When they were home again, Pepito asked his father about Angie. "What is she?" Tregarth pondered, holding his son on his lap. "Who knows? Some people say she's an odd kind of monkey he picked up in India, back before Comet Sicara. There's another story that she's a misbegotten human clone out of some genetics laboratory. The queerest thing is the way she got that jewel. Newt Bluestone says a bird gave it to her!"

"A bird?" Pepito repeated. "But Mother says birds are good."

Tregarth shook his head. "Not this bird," he said grimly. "And they say that after she got that jewel she began controlling Quagger. Maybe the jewel controls her."

Then Jannie came into the room. "Bedtime for you now, Pepito," she said to her son. "And for your father, too, because tomorrow's a big day for him. Tomorrow your father goes into space!"

And so the next day Pepito waited to watch his father's

spacecraft launch from the great gantry, as Tregarth began his first spaceflight. Though Quagger was also watching, his mind was not on the spaceship. "Where's Angie?" he demanded anxiously. "Has anyone seen Angie?"

When the command capsule was sealed Jannie and Pepito got into a little car and retreated down to the shore, two kilometers away. Jannie did not want to be with others while she watched her husband's first perilous venture into the void. Of course, other rockets had been launched, observation and communications satellites; but this was the first with men aboard. Her heart was in her mouth as she saw the great blossom of flame and felt the rolling thunder.

"There he goes, Pepito," she cried, hugging the child to herself. She watched the pale flame cross the sky and dwindle.

"What's the matter with Angie?" Pepito said.

She shook herself and glanced down at her son. He was pointing to the shallows.

Angie was floating there, bobbing gently in the waves, unmoving.

It wasn't Angie any longer. It was just her corpse. And the great jewel was gone from her forehead.

Tregarth chortled with joy. He unsnapped his harness and let himself float free in the tiny control cabin. There had never, ever, not once in the history of the human race been anything like this! It was like floating in a neutral buoyancy suit in the deeps—a little—but without the suit, without the need to suck air from a tank, without the iron grip of water pressure and the two-hundred-seventy-degree helmet! It was—

"It's *flying*," he laughed aloud, and Wernher Ryan was as thrilled and excited as he.

"I knew I'd make it some day, Ron!" the commander exulted. "All these years! All the heartbreaks, and disappointments—No, that's a lie," he corrected himself, grinning. "I didn't know. I thought spaceflight was over! And, oh, Ron, I can't tell you what it's like for me to be here at last!"

But the radio was blaring from the control tower at the Cape, and they had to get back to business. Tregarth cast one look downward at the blue expanse below him, with its graceful curlicues of cloud, and strapped himself down again for the course-correcting burn. By the time they had reached their nominal orbit and all the checks had been completed and reported back to the Cape the signals were growing faint, and what was below them now was the bulge of Africa. "The Sahara," Ryan called, pointing down, and Tregarth nodded. They lost radio contact with the Cape somewhere over the southern shore of the Mediterranean, and a moment later they struck nightfall.

It was all so *fast!* Less than an hour from liftoff, they were half a world away! And it was all so *wonderful!* As the sun disappeared behind them stars sprang out in the sky—what stars! Brighter and more numerous than Tregarth had ever dreamed of seeing!—and a moment later there was the Moon, climbing into the sky before them, ash-white, glowing, huge.

There was not much for them to do except to test the satellite-release mechanisms and open the cargo hatch; Quagger did not waste geostationary satellites where they could not be received from the Cape. They spent the time staring at the dark earth below and the stars above, and marveling to each other. Over India—or was it China?—the photomultiplier cameras picked up faint signals from somewhere. They carefully marked the times and orientation, so that the trackers at the Cape could pinpoint the source . . . but they were not alone in the world, Tregarth realized with a start.

There were other people. . . .

And, of course, he told himself stoutly, there were still

the people of the Eighteen Cities; and it was only then that he realized that, in that first quick look down at the surface of the broad Atlantic, he had been looking directly at the site of City Atlantica.

And down below. . . .

When Jannie was sure that Angie was dead, she stood frowning over the little body. "Somebody should tell Quagger," she said regretfully. "I sure wish I didn't have to be the one." .

Pepito stared at the lifeless thing. He had seen his share of death. The great dying of the ozone summer had left its ugly traces everywhere. Yet, while Pepito had seen plenty of bones gathered up and put underground, he had never seen a human corpse before. If Angie really were human, he corrected himself. Personally, he wasn't a bit sorry that she was not going to be around any more.

"What happened to her jewel?" he wanted to know.

Jannie shrugged unhappily. "That's another thing. I hope Quagger isn't going to think I took it. As though I'd touch the filthy thing—" She broke off, peering out across the surf. "Pepito! Look! That's a *dolphin!*"

"What's a dolphin?" Pepito asked, but then he could see for himself—a thing like a fish, only bigger, sporting on the surface of the sea. It came in toward them, through the surf and into the calmer waters of the channel, and it seemed friendly. Entranced, Pepito waded into the gentle waves. "It wants to play," he exclaimed.

"Careful, baby," his mother whispered, but he wasn't afraid. The dolphin jumped and came down again, lean and silvery and lovely, so close he could see rainbow colors in the water it splashed. Flashing in the sunlight, it looked straight at them. Its queer, long-nosed grin seemed friendly, and he heard it laughing down under the water, a shrill, clickety kind of laugh.

"Pepito!" his mother's voice came after him. "Watch

out!" But he swam out to the animal, and she came after him. The dolphin wheeled around them, very close. Its face came out of the water, smiling at them. The great eyes seemed warm and wise and kind. Its thin nose butted against him under water, then touched his mother. Pepito heard Jannie cry out, as if the touch hurt her, but then she was laughing with the dolphin. They all three dived together. . . .

When they came up, Jannie was riding on the dolphin's back.

They were beautiful together, Pepito thought, and his mother looked suddenly happy. "Come on, son!" Her voice rang with gladness. "It loves us!"

The dolphin brought her to Pepito's side, and she reached to help him climb on in front of her. Its sleek body felt smooth and warm and strong. Pepito felt the quick muscles move under him—and felt something else.

Once in the aircraft maintenance shop, watching his father, he had touched a bare electric wire. The shock stung his fingers and jerked his whole arm, and his father had scolded him for touching things he was not supposed to come near. For just an instant, the dolphin's touch had felt like that bare wire. Pepito cried out, suddenly afraid.

But it didn't happen again, and his mother was crying out gladly, "Hang on, Pepito! It wants to take us riding!"

Her arms came around him. The bad feeling was gone, and the dolphin swam away with them. It leaped thrillingly through the surf, taking them to the pass in the reef. Their ride was as strange as a dream, but it didn't worry Pepito because his mother was not afraid.

When the dolphin leaped again, he saw a jewel on the tip of its curving nose.

The jewel was round and black, with black-shining facets. Flashes of red and green stabbed out of the facets. When the blue flashes struck his eyes they went deep into him.

"Mother!" Pepito cried in sudden panic, because although the jewel was a different color he was sure it was somehow like the one that had disappeared from the forehead of the dead Angie.

But his mother patted him and soothed him. Pepito's dread took a while to leave, for he remembered Angie's jewel and Angie's nasty voice and Angie's unpleasant stench. He shivered in the warm sun, and then the sense of well-being came back and he cried aloud in pleasure as the dolphin leaped, with them hugging tight to its back.

They were through the pass and beyond the surf now, out into the open sea. The ride was exciting. Great bright drops of sparkling seawater splashed against him as the dolphin jumped. Pepito shivered as they struck his bare skin, a shiver of pleasure, because that was exciting, too.

But then the wind picked up. The splashing water felt colder. When Pepito shivered it was not really pleasure any more. It was not just the cold, nor was it, exactly, fear, for after all his mother was with him and her arms held him tight. But it was a bad feeling, for the dolphin had carried them a long way out into the open sea. Overhead the dwindling, twisting tail left by his father's rocket had almost faded away. Behind them the gantries stood tall and stark beyond the white line of surf. But all around was— was nothing Pepito knew—was empty, rolling hills of water, waves that stretched as far as the eye could see.

Pepito began to be afraid.

Then he heard the dolphin talking.

It wasn't a language Pepito had ever heard. It wasn't a language at all, it was just clicks and squeaks and grunts and whistles. It didn't even come from the dolphin's mouth, as a proper language should. It seemed to come from the blowhole in the bulge of its great head. He listened curiously. And then his mother leaned over him, pressing him against the dolphin's back, and she began to speak. "Yes," she said. And, "I see." And, "All right—" just as though she understood.

"Mother?" he said, near to tears, cold, uncomfortably squeezed.

"Sshh, dear," she said absently, listening.

"But *Mother*," he wailed, beginning to cry. But she didn't answer, or at least didn't answer her son. She was listening to the dolphin, and Pepito wept silently for a long time, until he fell asleep.

How long Pepito slept he did not know, but when he was awake again they were back in the surf. The sun was down, only a ruddy glow in the west showing where it had been, and behind them, out over the ocean, a golden full moon had risen. He was cold and afraid and he felt sick, but more than any of the other things he was afraid.

"Mother?" he whispered.

She didn't answer. She wrapped her arms around him and slid off into the shallow water, waist deep, holding him high. She set him down at the edge of the waves and turned back to the sea.

The dolphin was playing in the surf. It opened its mouth as if to smile, and Pepito gasped, for something blue and brilliant twinkled from inside it. It was only a flash of light, gone as the dolphin moved its great head, but it frightened Pepito.

Jannie leaned toward the dolphin, wading out breast-deep into the water, bobbing on tiptoes as the waves passed. She stood before it, face to face. Almost touching. Almost as though they were kissing, Pepito thought.

Then the dolphin rolled away. It turned. It leaped twice in the surf.

It was gone.

Jannie kept watching, gazing straight into the seas dappled with the light of the yellow moon. When it was long out of sight she turned slowly toward her son.

"*Mother,*" Pepito sobbed in sudden terror, for he saw that a blue gem blazed in her forehead.

Jannie looked him over carefully. She didn't speak at first. She studied him, then turned and gazed down the beach, toward the distant lights of Cocoa Beach, then inland toward the gantry towers, then out across the water again. The gem in her forehead blazed a fiery blue. Her eyes were wide and strange, and Pepito caught her hand fearfully.

Jannie looked down at her son. "I remember you," she said, the familiar voice mild and thoughtful. "You are Peter Tregarth. I gave you birth."

"*Mother!*" he yelled again.

She reached down and touched him. Her hand was cold from their long time in the water. "Are you afraid?" she asked, the tone cool and impartial. "It is not necessary. There is no need to be afraid ever again. I promise you that you will be happy and content, for all of us will be happy in the infinite love and grace of the Eternal. But come now, for we have much work to do."

As Tregarth took his seat for the landing he was frowning. For four orbits the radio messages from ground control at the Cape had been terse and even cryptic. The news that the second geostationary satellite had been as successfully launched as the first drew only a, "Roger. Affirmative. Understood," from the communications section, and even on the last pass, as they announced they were ready for the landing next time around got no more than confirmation and a summary of wind direction and velocity and cloud cover.

Tregarth's enthusiasm was dampened. Even Wernher Ryan, still jubilant over at last having achieved his first taste of actual spaceflight, only shrugged and looked noncommital as they strapped in. Yet it had been a glorious flight! Well, Tregarth corrected himself, perhaps spaceflight was glorious only to the people who did it, and maybe even for them only the first time. But it was certainly a *successful* flight. Both satellites had been sent off to do their jobs, and telemetry showed them both in nominal orbits. And there had been a whole host of important observations—the lights they had spotted in China most important of all.

Tregarth had puzzled over that, and at last reasoned out a possible answer. After the night of Comet Sicara, China had had a resource newer, richer countries did not. It was Earth's first life, the anaerobic organisms, that had staged the first comeback. While others starved, they must have feasted in the rivers of China.

The waters most dead had become most alive. The bottoms of the Yellow River and the Yangtze, sludgy with the sewage and runoff of six thousand years of human soil, were fat with food for microscopic scavengers— themselves food for larger ones—ultimately, food for the scarce and starving human survivors with their nets and hooks and traps.

But what it all meant was another living colony of human beings still surviving on the surface of the Earth, and Tregarth waited impatiently for some word of acknowledgement from the tower at the Cape.

None came.

They could at least have wished us happy landings, he thought irritably as they made the first retroburn. Then for a while he had no time to think of anything but the job at hand. He had not fully expected the violence of reentry, thuds and jolts and sickening twisting lurches that nearly made him violently ill; he watched the temperature readouts, biting his lip, as they crawled up to, but did not quite reach, the failure line of the ship's insulation. And then they were flying in air, crossing the neck of Mexico and the Yucatan, descending at a carefully measured rate as they traversed the Gulf, beginning their turn at the long line of the Florida Keys, sweeping around over the wide sea to a perfect touchdown on the long, broad airstrip.

When the spaceplane stopped at last, after rolling more than four kilometers before they dared begin to use the brakes, they had to wait until the service vehicles rolled up to let them out. There was a release inside the door, of course, but also of course the whole hull of the spacecraft was far too hot to touch. They waited for the technicians in their hot-poppa gauntlets to open the door from outside, and then help them step out, carefully touching nothing, onto the debarkation steps that had been rolled out for them.

"How was the flight?" asked Newt Bluestone.

Tregarth, peering around and frowning when he saw that neither Jannie nor Pepito was in the little group that had come to meet them, thought Bluestone's tone was odd, but Ryan was answering for him. "Optimal, Newt," he cried, grinning all over. "You ought to try it some day! It's everything I've dreamed of—or anyway," he went on, as they got into the waiting vehicle, "it's the first step. Now I want more! I want to go farther than Low Earth Orbit, Newt—and I will."

"How bad was the temperature rise coming in?" one of the technicians asked, and for the next few minutes, as the car swept them back to the control tower, both Tregarth and Ryan were busy answering all the questions from the ground crews.

Tregarth was not so busy that he didn't scan the crowd for his wife and son. Sure enough, there was Pepito! Tregarth frowned. Although the boy was waving to him, there was something about the look on his face that disturbed his father—and where was Jannie? For the woman beside Pepito was Bluestone's wife, the false Graciela, Doris.

As he got out of the car he demanded, "Where's Jannie?"

Newt Bluestone coughed. "She's, ah," he began. "She's with Quagger inside the tower. They'll be out in a minute."

"With Quagger?" Tregarth stared at his friend. "What's she doing with Quagger? Newt! Is something wrong with Jannie?"

Bluestone looked wretched. "I, uh— Well, I think— No, look, Ron," he said unhappily, "you'd better just see for yourself. They're coming out now."

And Tregarth turned and saw Lord Quagger, looking older and wearier than ever before; and there beside Quagger, coming toward him without a smile, was his wife, Jannie.

Jannie was naked.

And in the center of her forehead a great blue jewel shone out at him.

"Oh, Ron, dear Ron," whispered Doris Bluestone, her voice charged with sympathetic pain, "we should have warned you. But we didn't know what to say!"

Tregarth, kneeling to hold his sobbing son in his arms, blinked up at her. "What—" He swallowed and started again. "What's Jannie doing now?"

"She's getting Wernher Ryan's report in the tower. I guess it's almost as much of a shock for him as it is for you—no, I don't mean that," she corrected herself, flushing. "Of course it isn't! But—" She stopped, helpless. "She came out of the sea like this, Ron," she said. "She's taken Angie's place, I think. Angie's dead. And Pepito says there was a dolphin that had a jewel, only it was a black one—"

Doris Bluestone's voice went on and on, and her tone was warm and consoling, but Tregarth could hardly take it in. He bent to rest his cheek against his son's soft, warm head. "It's all right, Pepito," he murmured, and knew that it was a lie. But what was the truth? In the years since the coming of Comet Sicara, Tregarth had imagined himself hardened to any misfortune, having seen so many and so awful.

But this—!

He could not find words to say, either to Doris Bluestone or to the boy. And then Newt Bluestone came hurrying over, looking unhappy. "Are you all right, Ron?" he asked. "I'm really sorry. I—" He stopped, wincing at the folly of his own words. "Anyway," he said, "they're through with Ryan now, and they want your report. Can you, ah, can you handle it?"

Tregarth blinked at him. He didn't answer. Truthfully, he didn't know what the answer should be; but he kissed his son, and managed even to smile at him as he returned him to Doris Bluestone's arms.

And then he entered the tower.

"Hello, Ron," mumbled old Quagger, sounding wretched and embarrassed, not looking at him. Tregarth did not look at Quagger, either. All his attention was on his wife—or on the thing that had been his wife, this naked female form that stood silent, regarding him soberly, while the gem in her forehead flashed blue-green rays that chilled him to his soul.

"You are Captain Ron Tregarth," she said. "You are skilled at navigation and pilotage. You are the father of the boy, Peter Tregarth, known as Pepito. You have also been my husband."

"Jannie!" he cried from the depths of his heart. "What's wrong with you?"

The woman who had been Jannie Tregarth looked puzzled. "There is nothing wrong with me." Her voice was curt and calm. "I am an element of the Eternal. I require no medical attention now nor will I later. My physical condition is adequate. It will remain so as long as the services of this element are needed for the work of the Eternal." She turned to glance at Lord Quagger, who quailed and rapidly looked away. "That work must be completed. Commander

Ryan's report of numbers of human beings in China requires special attention, so that they may be rescued with everyone else."

"Rescued?" He blinked at her, uncomprehending, and then cried, "But Jannie! What has been done to you? What about our son? What—" He could not ask another question. It was not because he had none to ask; he had too many, and all of them had answers he feared to hear.

The woman who had been his wife said patiently, "What has happened to me is an apotheosis, Captain Tregarth; that is all you can know for now. What will happen to the boy Pepito is what will happen to all; every one of us will have joy and fulfillment in the embrace of the Eternal. And the time of the Eternal is very near."

Ron Tregarth put his sobbing son to bed alone that night.

It was not the homecoming he had dreamed of. When he took Pepito to the communal dining hall for the evening meal he had felt everyone's eyes on him, but hardly anyone had spoken to him. Only Wernher Ryan had stopped by his table to say unhappily, "Bad news, Ron! Have you heard?"

Tregarth gazed up at him blankly. "About Jannie, you mean?"

"What? Oh, yes, that of course, but I mean that you and I have been demoted. No more spaceflights! All that training, and now we're told there won't be any more!" And then he had hurried off morosely.

Well, that was strange, too, Tregarth pondered, sitting alone in his hut. Everything was too strange for him to take in. He just sat. He was staring blankly into nothingness when the element of the Eternal that once had been his wife opened the door and gazed at him.

The element was a hundred and sixty-one centimeters tall from the soles of its bare feet to the crown of its long,

ragged hair. It weighed sixty-one kilograms. It possessed
the form of a member of the genus Homo, species sapiens,
with the typical coloration of the Euro-American branch of
that species. In a biological sense it was female, possessing
all of the organs, glands and chemical constituents of that
biotype.

Of course, none of that mattered.

It mattered even less that its name had been Jannie
Storm Tregarth, or that in the workings of its biological
past it had delivered a living male child named Pepito. The
only thing that mattered was what it had become, for now
it was an element of the Eternal.

"I recall that this is where I sleep," it said, gazing mildly
at Ron Tregarth.

Tregarth was unaccountably startled. "There—there's
only one bed," he stammered.

"Yes," Jannie agreed. She did not hesitate, but moved
directly to the bed and lay there, eyes vacant, face immo-
bile. Slowly Tregarth followed, his reasoning mind in
shock. He gazed down at her, as unsure as any bride-
groom.

"Jannie?" he whispered.

The eyes turned toward him.

"What has happened to you?" he begged.

"I have been rescued," Jannie said simply. "There is no
need for you to fear. It is time for sleeping; should you not
join me in this bed?"

"But—" Tregarth swallowed, and asked the crazy question that was uppermost in his mind. "Do you still love
me?"

"Love you?" The element named Jannie Storm leaned
back on the hard pillow, one hand thrown behind her
head, frowning at the ceiling. Tregarth caught his breath;
the gesture was so familiar.

"The element of me," she said slowly, "that was Jannie
loved you. There has been no reason for that to change."

He said bitterly, "That's something, anyway."

"And also," the voice went on dreamily, "that same element loved Peter of long ago, and Pepito, there in the next room. Yes. Those feelings are still in my mind, Ron Tregarth. I have many loves. The element in me that was Angie loved Simon Quagger very much. The element in me that was—I'm sorry, this body cannot say the name— that element loved all three of its reproduction partners, on a planet that no longer has anything alive on its surface." The familiar, pretty face turned to search his eyes. "You cannot understand, Ron Tregarth," she said. "I have within this part of me—" she touched the glowing jewel in her forehead—more than forty stored elements, and even we are only a tiny part of that great, wonderful collective that is the Eternal."

"But you're *Jannie!*" he cried.

"I am using the corpus of Jannie," she corrected him serenely. "When we are using the corpus of a creature, we have only that creature's systems to work with. It is not very useful to have a jewel in the head of a shark, or a bird, or an alligator. It can only do what a shark or bird or alligator can do. It is not ideal," she added, "to use the corpus of a human, but that is the best this planet has to offer. Even this corpus, which has been improved, is not enough. To be fully a part of the Eternal, one must surrender the corpus and enter the Eternal."

"I don't understand," he cried in misery, falling to his knees beside the bed.

"There is nothing that you need to understand now," the element told him serenely, reaching out to stroke his head. And this was the woman he had made his wife! With the same warmth of her body, the same touch of her hand.

The element said kindly, "Would it please you to engage in sexual congress with me, Ron Tregarth? There is no reason not. Come, lie down with me in our bed."

Chapter
26

What the crew of the *Atlantica Countess* found at City Scotia was the same as they had found at City Romanche, and what they had found at Romanche was horror. An intact Nexø dome . . . and a drowned city. There were inhabitants in both Scotia and Romanche. But they were only fish, molluscs, crustaceans and holothurians.

Of the humans who had lived and worked in the great undersea cities, there was hardly even a corpse. They were gone.

So Graciela and the rest of the crew of the *Countess* fled south and ever south, praying for a friendly port, with the food running out and always that distant mumble of radio voices that kept them clear of all continents, until they reached the desolate outpost the charts called the Falklands or the Malvinas.

There God lifted His wrathful hand from them, just a bit, just enough to give them a breathing space. For there they found an old military bunker, and in it were supplies of canned and dried and radiation-preserved food.

Why hadn't they been devoured in the awful hunger of the ozone summer? No one on the *Countess* could know that, but the storm-battered bones around the bunker told a story: an attack repulsed, the defenders dying of wounds, no one left alive long enough to find and use the hidden stores.

So they had something to eat.

But that was all they had, and not much of that. Moldy sacks of grain. A freezer that had once held, perhaps, lamb and mutton and beef from the flocks that once had grazed those windswept hills—but now held nothing but leathery lumps and a terrible reek of decay that sent them outside gasping for air.

From the Falklands they sailed west and still south, around the stormy Cape Horn, never surfacing for five thousand kilometers and more, hugging the shelf of the Antarctic continent. "If there is a safe city anywhere," N'Taka Rose declared, "it will be City Gaussberg, on the Kerguelen Ridge."

"And if that one's gone, too?" Dennis McKen demanded. "Then what do we do?"

"Then we die alone," Sven Borg said somberly. "Or we give ourselves up to the lubbers. Which is just another kind of dying. . . ."

But City Gaussberg was intact!

When the *Countess* cautiously crept toward the strengthening blip on their sonar, three lean, fast subs rose to meet them, and down below, through the abyssal haze, they saw the warm and welcoming glow of its Nexø dome.

City Gaussberg was crowded, almost like City Atlantica after the PanNegrans flocked in. It didn't matter. The Gaussbergers easily made room for a few more survivors —they had had plenty of practice.

It did not hurt that the crew of the *Atlantica Countess* were now—had had no choice but to become—tough and resourceful sailors. "Oh, yes," said Aino Direksen, City Gaussberg's port controller, "we have a place for you! Skilled submariners are hard to find—we've lost so many." He was unwrapping the foil from a bottle of sparkling sea-cider as he spoke. He was a big man, taller than Sven Borg but, Graciela thought, looking very like him with those blue eyes and flaxen hair and Viking-pale skin . . . like Borg, or (she thought with a sudden soft and lumpy flip-flop of her heart) like Ron Tregarth.

Who, though surely dead, lived on every night in Graciela's dreams.

There was a whole network of undersea commerce, Direksen explained. As the American colonies had so long ago constructed their secret Committees of Correspondence, so the subsea people had sent their envoys out to reach to the other cities, to see who was still alive and whose cities were crushed, or starved—or worse. And those cities, too, sent out their scouts. They came from the seas south of New Guinea and from the Clarion-Clippterton Fracture Zone in the East Pacific; they came from City Reykjanes, north even of Iceland, and from the poor, crowded cities of the Great Barrier Reef and the Bay of Bengal. And they had horror stories to tell, for not all the cities had survived—and not all that had survived were free.

Direksen listened to their stories of City Atlantica besieged, PanNegra crushed, Scotia and Romanche drowned. "We feared that," he said, his brown furrowed with worry. "We've lost eight good ships in the Atlantic; now we don't go there at all. The Pacific hasn't been hit so hard."

Direksen's wife was as tiny as her husband was tall, but with the same pale look. "Those jewels," she said. "What *are* they? How can they let people live in the sea without suits? *Why* do they?"

But none of the crew of the *Countess* had an answer for that. "We'll have to go back to City Atlantica to find that out," Graciela said, as much to sample the taste of the words in her own mouth as to suggest it to the others.

And, in fact, they did . . . but it took more than two years to get ready.

The Year of
The Eternal

I who was Jannie Storm, and Jannie Tregarth—I who from my loins gave birth to Pepito—I, too, now live in the Eternal, and I am not alone.

Now I am also Angie, soothed from her sad, wicked, fretful life at last. And I am a great, dull-witted bird of prey; and I am a tiny, mindless fish of the deep that the bird had thought to eat; and I am far more than any of these. I am also three creatures who once lived on a planet with a broad red star, and one from a water world that was freezing over, and dozens more from worlds beyond imagining in places too far to tell.

Like them all, I have been rescued from life to Eternity.

Before long I will join with them, and with all the million million other rescued elements, and we will voyage on to rescue others. Our voyage will have no end until all the stars are dust and darkness, for we will live forever in the Eternal.

Chapter
27

For months upon months nothing seemed to change for Ron Tregarth. The Cape showed no more signs of alteration than did an old rock weathering in sun and storm. Tregarth flew his missions in airplanes now, rather than spacecraft, as Jannie had decreed, and Pepito had grown a centimeter or so on each return, and, though work crews were always tinkering with the mysterious spacecraft that stood on Gantry One, the workers were strangers with gems in their foreheads and what they did was internal. As far as anyone outside could see the huge thing just sat there, topless and unexplained.

And then one day, in the twinkling of an eye—actually, it was in the time that Tregarth had spent picking up computer parts in what once had been California—everything was suddenly changed, like the final cleavage of the old rock when at last it splits and shatters and new patterns show.

They were returning from the dead towns of the Pacific coast, Tregarth and Wernher Ryan, in their tiny, long-range surveillance plane with its little cargo space crammed with instruments and four silent, unfamiliar men with gems in their foreheads.

They didn't speak much. Both were exhausted, and they had long ago said everything that needed to be said between them. As they came into the descent pattern for the old space base in Florida it was just beginning to be dawn over the Atlantic Ocean. Tregarth woke Ryan, dozing fitfully in the seat beside him. "We're coming in," he said. "Do you want to take over?"

Ryan opened his eyes and nodded without speaking. He glanced down through the window on his side at the base, there below them as they slipped out over the ocean to come in for the landing. "I'll take it," he said, dropping his hands onto the control wheel. "What's happening? Looks like they're building something down there."

"I wondered what it was," Tregarth confirmed. Across the sands of the old rocket center rectangular patterns had grown in the time they were gone. "They look like barracks."

"Maybe we're all going to move out to the base," Ryan said. "Flaps one quarter."

Tregarth complied with the order. "Will you come to a party tonight?" he asked. "It's for Pepito. Newt and Doris Bluestone promised to get a cake for him, and I've brought back some candy I found—he'll like that."

"Sure I'll come," said Ryan. "Wheels down now. Flaps one half." He glanced at Tregarth thoughtfully, and then added in a reassuring tone, "They love him, Ron. They take good care of him while you're away."

"I know they do," said Tregarth, peering ahead at the land as Ryan wheeled the aircraft back toward the beach for the landing. "Pepito's lucky to have them."

Neither of them mentioned the boy's mother. But when their aircraft was down and they taxied to the control office, there she was. Jannie Storm—even Tregarth himself could no longer think of her as Jannie Tregarth—standing tall and lean and intense, with the bright jewel gleaming in her forehead, was at the end of the strip, directing the unloading of a fat Peace Wing transport plane. Its rear hatch was open, and the ground crews were trundling out great pallets of sacks of rice from the Louisiana paddies.

Pepito came running up to fling himself into his father's arms. "Daddy, Daddy," the boy cried happily. "You're home!"

"Hello, Pepito," Tregarth said, nuzzling his face into the soft, fine hair of the boy's hard little head. Exhausted as he was, he felt a surge of joy at the wonder of this bundle of muscle and energy, squeezing his ribs hard enough to make him gasp. "Here, wait," he said, freeing himself to reach into his haversack. "It isn't your birthday or anything, but I've brought you something."

He found the can of hard candies, discovered under some moldered old newspapers in an abandoned factory canteen, and presented it with a flourish. "For you," he said.

Pepito studied the enameled can, with its brightly colored pictures of cascading lumps of cherry and orange and lime. "Oh, *candy!*" he cried. "I remember candy! I had some once when I was little, didn't I?"

And from behind Ron Tregarth a voice rasped, "Is that food? Hand it over at once!" It was a huge man in the faded undress khaki of the Peace Fleet, with the silver-thread eagle of a lieutenant commander still embroidered on his collar. He snatched the can from the boy's hand and declared, "All foodstuffs have been ordered turned in for the ration authorities. Now, you two, Ryan and Tregarth! Report immediately for debriefing and orders."

Pepito bit his lip and trembled; he had grown too big to cry.

So there was going to be no cake for anybody's party. As the two pilots waited in the hot sun for Jannie Storm to be ready for them, Newt Bluestone came up, looking tired and sunburned. "Yes, it's true," he confirmed when Ryan spoke to him. "All food is rationed now—really starvation rations, too, Ron. Eleven hundred calories a day."

"Eleven *hundred?* But there's all that rice—"

Bluestone gazed wistfully at the trucks bearing away the

sacks from the transport plane. "I know," he said. "Food's been coming in for over a week now, big quantities of it, but— Anyway, they say it's only temporary. Because there are a lot of people coming in, and we need to be ready for them. That's why we're building new quarters for them on the strip, and—oh," he said, glancing around as the Peace Fleet officer began to move toward them, "I've got to get back to work. Pepito can stay here with you; I know you're anxious to be together. We'll see you tonight . . . I hope."

And then Jannie was with them, issuing orders to the gem-wearing men who had helped them find the computer parts. She looked terrible, Tregarth thought. Her hair was waist length and had not had a brush through it for days, and the lines on her face were as though carved with a blunt knife.

She sent the men on their way and turned to her husband and his copilot. "Wernher Ryan," she said, her voice hoarse and uneven. "Your flights are discontinued. Only rescue missions will be flown from now on, and only elements of the Eternal will fly them. You are to join the elements already at work in the computation center. Assist the elements in readying the launch computer. Then you will assist them to plot orbits."

Ryan blinked at her. "Orbits?" he repeated. "Orbits for spacecraft? But—"

Jannie Storm didn't answer him. She made a slight gesture, and the man with the lieutenant commander's insignia grasped Ryan's arm and walked him away as she turned to Tregarth.

Tregarth gazed at his wife. "Hello, Jannie," he said. "You look like hell."

She blinked at him as though surprised. "This corpus is nearing its end," she explained, her tones flat and without regret. "It may be necessary to exchange it one more time before our mission is completed, but the time now is very near. The Starstone of the Eternal is already on its way; the ingathering of the rescued has already commenced. Your flights are terminated, and so you will now be assigned to construction of quarters for new arrivals."

"But don't you want to ask me how I am?" he asked, not in hope of getting a human reaction from that familiar, changed mask, but simply because he couldn't help himself.

"But you are here," she explained. "And it is obvious that you have survived, so what is the need? Carry out your orders. You will join the construction brigades; the first barracks are to be completed this week."

Tregarth opened his mouth, then gave up. "All right, Jannie," he said in resignation. "Can our son work with me?"

The empty eyes turned to gaze at Pepito. "No," she said. "He is not strong enough. He will be assigned to learn how to be a cook's helper." And she turned and walked away, already busily talking to a small, dark man waving blueprints at her.

Tregarth gazed after the creature that had been his wife until he felt his son tugging at his sleeve. "Let's go, Daddy," the boy said nervously. "It's all right, though. Anyway, I'll be sure to get enough to eat . . . and maybe I can get some for you sometimes."

That did not happen, though by the end of the second day Tregarth would have welcomed it. The toil in the hot Florida sun was brutal and never-ending. Up at sunrise. Allowed to return to his own home at dusk, parched and starving . . . and then to line up for the thin gruel, with occasionally a strip of some mystery flesh floating in it; that was all the rationing would permit.

The emergency measures were only temporary, they said. For that matter, so were the barracks. Building materials were scarce along the Florida beaches, and the scavenging teams that had gone into the deserted towns had come back with nothing better than particle board and sheet metal and roofing paper. A row of stakes—reclaimed wood sometimes, more often slotted metal or even lengths of piping—and the paper-thin walls were fastened to it somehow; a few beams to join the walls, and a slapdash roof over all. That was all there was. No windows. No interior partitions. Not even beds—there were pallets filled with dried grass, a sprinkling of thin mattresses, a few air-filled ones found in sporting-goods stores. That was all.

Life was hard for Ron Tregarth and all the rest of the community, to be sure. But he pitied the people who would live in those barracks, all the same. The Florida sun would turn the flat-roofed sheds into instant ovens.

It was certainly good that all this was temporary—but how long, exactly, did "temporary" imply?

When they began roofing in one of the barracks Tregarth discovered that the man next to him was Corporal Max Hagland, once Wernher Ryan's second-in-command when the base still claimed to be part of the Peace Wing. As they finished laying one roll of tar paper and waited for the next to come up on the hoist, Hagland stretched, rubbing the small of his back with a groan. He looked around at the busy, bustling Cape. Across the field the liquid-fuel plants were beginning to shine and look as though they might some day produce actual hydrogen and oxygen again. The stark, headless shape of the mystery rocket was still silhouetted against the hot sky. Out over the ocean a great transport plane, just rising into the sky, was circling onto its course for somewhere across the sea. Hagland glanced at Tregarth humorously. "Sometimes I think I ought to apologize to you," he said, "for getting you into this."

Tregarth had almost forgotten that it was Hagland, with help of his small daughter, Maria, who had captured them in the first place. "You didn't know how it was going to turn out," he said justly.

"I sure didn't," Hagland agreed. "See that plane? That's the third that's left since this morning. They say they're going to China!"

Tregarth blinked at him. "China?"

"Right," Hagland declared. "Somebody heard Jannie Storm talking about rescuing the survivors you and Commander Ryan found there."

"But that's impossible," Tregarth said. "We saw quite a lot of lights—enough to mean a thousand people. Maybe more. They can't move them with just three aircraft." Hagland shrugged. "Well, who's flying them?" Tregarth asked.

The corporal shrugged again. "Strangers to me. They're all wearing the stoneseeds in their heads, though—"

"The what?"

"The stoneseeds. Those things that look like rubies and diamonds and all. That's what they call them; and nobody flies out any more unless he's got one." Hagland glanced around. "And you know something?" he offered. "When the planes come back, the crews all have the stoneseeds. But they're not the same people."

Tregarth stared at him, perplexed. "I don't understand."

"Neither do I. Or at least," Hagland added grimly, "I hope I don't. Here comes the roofing paper—let's get it off the hoist!"

With all the unanswered questions and the worried Tregarth had one comfort. Pepito, at least, was getting by. Almost all the children under twelve had been assigned to help the cooks, and none were so heartless as to begrudge the kids a cooked potato now and then, or a carrot, or even a slice or two of real meat. In the evenings Tregarth and the boy would sit together, resting, gazing out at the sea, and Tregarth would tell stories of City Atlantica and the wonderful, rich farms along the sea bottoms.

And then he couldn't tell those stories any longer,

because to talk about them made far crueler the pangs of his own growing, never-ceasing hunger.

It was a week before the first group of barracks were completed. No tenants were in sight for them, but the crews were immediately ordered to get to work on the next. To Tregarth's surprise, he found himself working side by side with his fellow pilot, Wernher Ryan. "I thought you were calculating orbits for Jannie," he said, as together they raised a length of wallboard to meet its stakes.

"That's over," Ryan grunted, bending his head to wipe sweat off against his forearm. "I couldn't do what she wanted—Ron, you wouldn't *believe* what sort of launch she's planning! Not just into Low Earth Orbit—not even to the Moon, or Mars! No, this spacecraft is going clear out of the solar system entirely."

Tregarth gaped at him. "To where, for God's sake?"

"To I don't know where," Ryan said grimly, "and if you ask me, neither does she. She just wants to pick up all the orbital speed she can—steady acceleration after the launch, flying by the Sun for one gravity assist, then Venus and then Jupiter for others. But when I asked her what sort of delta-vee the propulsion system could produce she simply didn't answer. I don't even know what the propulsion system is! No chemical system could maintain thrust long enough for those maneuvers, and there's nothing nuclear on the launch pad."

"So you told her it wouldn't work?"

"I told her I couldn't compute it for her," Ryan corrected. "What do I know about gravity assists? Or propulsion systems I never heard of? Then she said it was all right, the Starstone had its own propulsion system, and the Eternal would manage the computations when it arrived. That's what all those computer parts we brought back were for, Ron. They're going to automate the launch with it. I couldn't help with that, either, and so she sent me out here to help build these things."

"Whatever *they* are for," Tregarth said bitterly.

"Whatever any of this is for," Ryan agreed, and then looked past Tregarth with almost a smile. "Hello, here's our lunch coming—and, Ron, look who's come along to help serve it!"

And, "Hello, Daddy!" shouted Pepito, proudly waving an enormous spoon as he followed the cart with its steaming tanks of gruel to the serving point.

Time was not to be wasted by standing in unproductive lines, and so the construction crews were released to eat only one at a time.

By the luck of the draw Tregarth's crew was last. But that was good luck, in spite of the added wait for the food his body was craving; it meant that when they had their bowls of rice and boiled beans Pepito, too, was allowed to take time to eat, and they could share the meal together. Since the cook was Max Hagland's daughter Maria, the very one who had tricked Tregarth and Jannie Storm in the first place, they got more than the rationing strictly allowed.

They sat down gratefully to eat. There was no shade. The pitiless sun was almost directly overhead, but they lined up along one free-standing wall, with at least the backs of their heads in its shadow as they sat and ate, the boy between Ryan and his father. It didn't take long to finish the meal. Even with Maria's bounty, there wasn't much of it. Then they sat for a moment in silence, gazing out toward the empty sea, Tregarth almost drowsing as he felt the warm, sweet feeling of his son's shoulder against him.

He woke abruptly as Pepito tugged at his sleeve. "Daddy?" the boy cried. "Is that a ship like yours?"

Tregarth blinked and leaped to his feet. His heart skipped a beat.

Gliding toward them from the open sea was the bright hump of an Eighteen Cities submarine, five hundred meters out. He could see three figures moving about on the weather deck, conning the vessel along the coastline toward the ship channel.

Of course, it wasn't the *Atlantica Queen*. It couldn't have been. Even with only the weather deck visible Tregarth could see that this vessel was half again as big; its popup bridge was flatter and wider than a City Atlantica design. When he could read the registry numbers along the side of the hump he said, "No, Pepito, it's not exactly like mine. I think it's from one of the other Atlantic cities—maybe City Romanche. I wonder what it's doing here?"

"It's coming in, Daddy, see?" the boy cried in excitement. And indeed it was turning to enter the narrow channel. There was a flurry of turbulence at the bow thrusters to stop it short before it turned briskly and surged in on a wave. A fine show of ship-handling, Tregarth observed; and then he got a better look at the figures on the weather deck.

Two women. One man. All short in stature and dark in complexion, and in the forehead of each of them a glowing jewel, two saffron and one an intense and baleful scarlet.

That was the beginning of the ingathering.

The new barracks got their first occupants that night.

There were more than a hundred people jammed into that first submarine from the abandoned cities of the Atlantic, and eighty more on a surface freighter from Galveston the next day. Within the week six more vessels arrived, and a truck convoy from Quaggerhome, and five huge Peace Wing transport aircraft to mop up the scattered settlements in Europe and Latin America. The population of the camp had tripled.

And most of them—in the flights from abroad, every one—wore the bright stoneseeds of the Eternal on their brows.

With so many warm bodies the work was easier; the last batch of barracks went up in two days, and then construction stopped. It was the rocket technicians who were being worked to exhaustion now—checking and finishing the great boosters that sat waiting on the launch pad—and most of all the food services. The hoarded supplies were dwindling visibly.

"With all these people," Tregarth told Wernher Ryan, as they moved up the line to the servers, "even with this rationing, we'll be out of food in a month."

"Jannie Storm knows," Ryan said gloomily. "She says it doesn't matter. We have to launch in three weeks."

"All right, she's talking about that big rocket! But that can't carry more than a fraction of the people here, no matter how you load it! What about the rest of us?"

Ryan shrugged. He said, "She didn't say. Ron, do you know that they've stopped everything but the food flights and the transports of people? Totally! They've destroyed the communications system. They don't even monitor incoming transmissions any more. And there are all these people—nearly a hundred from China this morning, Max Hagland told me. Two planes, and everybody in them Chinese."

Tregarth blinked. "Everybody but the flight crews, you mean."

"Everybody!" Ryan insisted. "Pilots and all, and every one of them wearing a stoneseed jewel. And how are we going to feed them all? They've abandoned the farms, Ron! There are still crops growing, and no one to harvest them; they've brought all the people here!"

"But they've only brought about two hundred in from the farms," Ryan objected. "There were at least a thousand there."

"Not any more," said Wernher Ryan grimly.

Chapter
28

When the *Gaussberg Three* was within a hundred kilometers of the site of City Atlantica they dropped down through the two-hundred-meter level to the depths.

The *Gaussberg* was the first submarine from the still-free cities to venture so far into the Atlantic Ocean, and its mission had two parts. The first was to see what was salvagable in the lost cities, City Atlantica among them. The other was to see what was happening on the land. The crew of fourteen was split down the middle on the question of priorities. The confirmed webfeet would rather have forgotten the landlubbers entirely, concentrating only on what valuables might be found to take back to the cities of the Pacific (and, a wistful hope, what survivors might still be found to rescue); while the pan-humanists were eager to forget old, outmoded rivalries and dare at last to make contact with whoever those people were who were still active on land.

It wasn't just the crew that was split. The question even divided Graciela from her husband. "We shouldn't be wasting time on these drowned cities," he complained irritably. "Florida is where the action is."

Graciela looked at him thoughtfully. "Dennis?" she said. "Suppose Florida really is back to normal. Would you go back?"

He looked at her in astonishment. "Well, of course! That's where people were meant to live."

"We didn't think so," Graciela pointed out. "We wanted freedom."

He frowned. "No," he said decisively, "the land's the place for human beings. I mean, now that PanMack's out of business. And once we get this trouble with the Armies of the Eternal straightened out. And, of course, after things are all growing again, and it's possible to live there. Why bother going back to City Atlantica at all?"

She sighed. "It's my home," she told him—for the thousandth time.

"It's *stupid*," he informed her—also for the thousandth time. "And dangerous! How do we know what those crazy squid of yours have got up to?"

"Dennis," she said patiently, "that's what we have to find out."

He shook his head firmly. "If there's anything left in the world that's worth taking a chance for, it's at the Cape. There are people, ships, planes—even spacecraft! And what's in City Atlantica?"

She said, "Your mother is in City Atlantica."

His face turned pale with sudden anger. "Don't you think I know that?" he grated. "We can't take that sort of thing into consideration! We have to make a mature judgment—reason, not emotion—common sense! But don't you think I *care*?"

"Of course you do," Graciela said, trying—again for the thousandth time—to make peace. As always, it worked. He gave her an angry nod, and that was the end of that conversation. It always was. When Dennis McKen asked her point-blank if she thought he didn't really care about his mother, Graciela always backed off.

But, all the same, she wasn't really sure he did.

City Gaussberg had been more than hospitable to the refugees, and the refugees had done their best for the city. Dennis McKen and his wife had worked like any other citizens, taking their turn on the subsea farms, sailing the perimeter patrols that kept watch on the South Atlantic for any exploration parties—whether Armies of the Eternal or the more sinister and frightening creatures that had taken over the lost domes of the Eighteen Cities. They had sailed to the subsea cities of the Western Pacific—always avoiding the North American coast; they had swum in the lagoons of Fiji and walked the deserted streets of old Singapore.

They were, they thought, like any other citizens of City Gaussberg . . . until the council at last took its courage in its hands and voted approval to the Atlantic Ocean expedition. ·

The decision was not a foregone conclusion. All of the council was hesitant about venturing into such dangerous waters, and nearly half, the mayor among them, was bitterly opposed. When Dennis McKen argued for immediate contact with whoever was running things at the Cape he was silenced. When Graciela urged a look at City Atlantica the mayor shook his head. "But we know what happened to City Atlantica," he pointed out. "They are gone, Graciela. We mourn their loss as much as you do, but there's nothing we can do for them now."

"But, Mayor! We don't know that Atlantica is lost! And even if we did, how do we know that City Gaussberg won't be next?"

"We know that because it hasn't happened," the mayor said soberly. "It's been years since Comet Sicara. All the cities that were taken over were lost in the first year, isn't that true?"

"Yes, but that doesn't mean—"

"It means," said the mayor, "that we aren't being

threatened. Why should we start being aggressive toward
—toward whatever it is you say happened there. Oh, I'm
not denying that something happened! Something strange,
even. But it happened *there*. Whatever was behind it isn't
bothering us, so why should we invite trouble?"

But when a vote was taken, the mayor lost.

"Very well," he said dourly, "we will abide by the will of
the people . . . but I can't pretend that I think it is wise!"

When at last a submarine was provided and a crew was
found, every one of the refugees from the *Atlantica Countess*
begged to join. But only Graciela and her husband were
permitted aboard. "You are only supercargo," the mayor
informed them as they were preparing to board. "You will
follow orders, not give them." And to Dominic Paglieri, the
captain of the ship: "Take no avoidable risks! We must
make sure the ship returns. Carry out your mission. See
what you can find out—and *come back*. Whatever you do,
don't lose the ship!"

So as City Atlantica began to loom large on the sonar
screens, the *Gaussberg Three* circled warily, watching the
doppler radar for any sign of motion as it spiraled in. . . .

And, half an hour later, was speeding away, every
member of the crew shaken, Dennis McKen scowling and
absently beating his fist against the Nexø port in the
control room, Graciela openly in tears.

Nothing had moved. Nothing was there to move. City
Atlantica was only a ghostly Nexø bubble at the bottom of
the sea, the water inside as cold and empty as the water
without; and of all those human beings who had been left
behind when they fled there was no sign at all.

Chapter
29

Three weeks, Jannie Storm had said, three weeks before it was time to launch the mysterious spacecraft. She hadn't seen any necessity to add that those three weeks would be desperately busy. Jannie Storm herself was everywhere on the Cape, urging on the starseed-wearing technicians at the rocket itself, hurrying the crews who were finishing the liquid-fuel plants, pushing the cyberneticians who were racing to get the launch computer ready for its task. Neither Tregarth nor her son saw much of her, but somehow, always, she spared time for Simon McKen Quagger.

For the bag of blubber and guts that was all that was left of the lord of Quaggerhome lay dying. A dozen times a day Jannie looked in on him, no matter what other urgencies were before her, for the part of Angie that survived inside Jannie Storm still piteously loved the old monster. Every time the end was closer at hand.

Quagger's death bed was the best that the colony on the Cape could provide. He lay in what had been Wernher Ryan's own bed, in the days when Ryan ruled the Cape. He was fed with the choicest tidbits. He was given freely of the dwindling stocks of medicines; he had around-the-clock care . . . and not from the ordinary mortals of the Cape. Quagger's nurses all wore a blazing splinter of the

Starstone in their foreheads and, though they sometimes dozed briefly as they sat by his side, his slightest movement was enough to wake them and bring one gliding to him.

And Lord Simon McKen Quagger was terrified.

When he slept he tossed and mumbled. When he woke, he gasped for air and shuddered under the cool, caring touch of his attendants. Out of curiosity Ron Tregarth peered in on him, the day Tregarth was excused from building any more barracks (because there were plenty of newcomers to do the job) and he at last had a day off. Max Hagland was there, standing guard at the door. "You can't go in," he said softly. "Jannie Storm's orders."

"I can see him from here," Tregarth replied. "He looks like he's scared to death."

"He's asleep, I think," Hagland whispered, "but you're right. It's Jannie Storm herself. Every time she comes near him he starts to shake—I don't know why. She keeps telling him that she'll rescue him. Whatever she means by that. . . ."

"Whatever she means by anything," Tregarth muttered, and went back to his hut to try one more time to be both father and mother to the boy whose mother had turned into something incomprehensible and strange.

In the second of the three weeks, four huge floating cranes appeared. They came in with the dawn light, great boxy barges with the steel lattice of the cranes projecting above the hulls like giraffe necks from a railroad car. It was Pepito who saw them first, crying eagerly for his father to come and look at these strange new ships, but then Tregarth saw more of them than he wanted. He and a dozen others were ordered to go over the cranes, checking for rust and corrosion and wear, testing the winches and the cables and the great hydraulic turning gears. "It is essential," insisted she who had been Jannie Storm, "that these machines operate perfectly. The safety of the Eternal depends on it! Everything must be in order. If you need tools, supplies, anything at all, inform me at once; nothing must be spared."

"How about a little extra food?" called Wernher Ryan.

The dark, ruined eyes gazed at him for a moment. "Is additional food of value to you?" the woman asked, as though really in doubt. "Very well. Requisition what you wish, if that is what is necessary to do the work well."

"But what about the rest of our people?" Tregarth put in. "They're hungry! Even our son, Jannie!"

The face of his wife did not change expression. "That is not important," she told him serenely. "The Starstone of the Eternal is on its way! We will launch on schedule. There are sufficient rations on hand to complete the launch, and then everyone will be rescued. At least," she added, her look clouding, "everyone here will be. Perhaps some of the others will have to be abandoned to mortal life, if there are those who your search missions have failed to discover. Now, no more discussion! Proceed at once to your work on the floating cranes!"

And that was all she would say. Most of the others who bore jewels in their foreheads wouldn't speak at all. Even when they worked side by side with ordinary human beings there was no conversation, no sharing of a joke, not even a remark about the unbearable heat of the sun or the desire for a drink. If the "elements" of the Eternal had any physical needs beyond a quick gulp of food or swill of water, they never made them known. At night they trooped into the unbearable hotboxes of their barracks. No lights showed from inside. No sounds of music, or laughter, or song; and in the morning they trooped silently out and set silently to work.

The refugees who came with them, by ship and truck and plane, were another matter entirely. They were willing to speak—volubly and with great passion; but some of them spoke in languages Tregarth had never heard, Japanese and Arabic and Russian and Swahili, and even the ones he could talk to knew no more than himself. The Eighteen Cities? Oh, yes, some of them were from the Eighteen Cities—but there weren't eighteen of them any more. Not eighteen that were inhabited by normal human beings, anyway. Many of the proud undersea domes had been infiltrated and taken over by the "elements" of the Eternal, and most of those cities were now simply lightless, skeletal, drowned hemispheres of Nexø, their air long since bubbled turbulently away, with nothing alive in them at all beyond an occasional venturesome mollusc or shark.

Grieving, Ron Tregarth stopped questioning the new arrivals, because the answers would certainly be statements he did not want to hear. He had no time, anyway. After sixteen-hour days on the floating cranes he barely had the strength to get back to his hut and crawl into bed without waking his sleeping son. But one night he paused at the door, hearing muffled sobbing from within. It was a woman's voice. Jannie? Was it possible that there was enough left of humanity in Jannie Storm to weep?

It wasn't Jannie. It was Maria Hagland, the girl who had tricked them in the first place; she was huddled inside the doorway and when she saw Tregarth she leaped to her feet. "Oh, sorry, *señor*," she said, trying to halt the tears. "I—I came in to be with Pepito, because—" She stopped, biting her lip, her face twisted in misery.

Tregarth felt a sudden wrench of panic. He cried, "Go on! What's the matter? Has something happened to Pepito?"

"Oh, no, *señor!* Not at all. It is simply that I wanted to be with someone, because my father— my father— my father is *gone*, senor! The witch your wife, she has stolen his soul!"

"Jannie has?" Tregarth said numbly, and then the story came out. Old Lord Quagger had at last reached the point of death, and Maria Hagland had been bringing food to her father, on guard outside the deathbed room, when it happened.

"And she cradled him in her arms, *señor*," Maria whispered brokenly, "and then one of those evil ones with the jewels came near and bent down as though to kiss him! And then the evil one's jewel was gone, and it fell dead, and the jewel was in Lord Quagger's head. And then—oh, *señor*," she wailed, "then the witch your wife made my father come in and touch him! And then Lord Quagger was dead, and the jewel—the jewel—the terrible thing was on my father, and when he spoke to me he was not my father any more!"

It took a week's hard work to be sure the floating cranes were in working condition, and the job was finished just in time.

Once again it was Pepito who woke his father up, calling excitedly from outside the hut. Tregarth woke slowly and painfully, wondering at why the sound of his son's voice was punctuated with flat, dull, distant explosions. When he peered out to sea he discovered the answer. The great band of the Milky Way lay across the moonless sky, with a thousand bright stars marking the constellations of a summer night just before the dawn. But something brighter drowned the stars. Out over the ocean great flares like sunbursts were exploding and dropping, with a pale tail of smoke following them down as they fell and died into darkness again.

When Tregarth saw a red flare leap up from the camp he understood that signals had been exchanged. Then it was only a moment before the raucous bleat of the warning horn woke everyone up, as Jannie's voice came over the loudspeakers: "The Starstone of the Eternal is here! All crane crews report immediately to bring it in!"

The mobile cranes were never intended for work in the

open ocean. Fortunately the seas were calm, but even so the great steel giraffes rocked their heads back and forth against the lightening sky. It took an hour to get out to where four huge submarines lay dead in the water, in the corners of a square. Thick steel cables extended from the stern winch of each submarine down into the water, all converging toward something out of sight, something that all four of them had joined to carry up from the bottom of the sea.

It took all of Ron Tregarth's ship-handling skill to keep his crane in position, without fouling the lines of the other cranes or the subs themselves, while all four cranes joined in dropping hooks into the water in the center of that square.

What the hooks were meant to engage Tregarth could not see. He simply deployed his own cable as ordered by the man in the lieutenant commander's uniform, and was surprised to see it slant away from the perpendicular, as though something underwater had taken it and pulled it along.

Something had.

On command, all three crane operators engaged their winches, and slowly, slowly, the great cranes leaned toward the center as something vast and heavy was pulled up to the surface.

As it broke the water Tregarth gasped. Four or five giant squid broke surface at the same time, swarming around a cradle of steel cables that contained a great, multifaceted, glowing jewel. It sparkled like the inside of a geode in rainbow colors, emerald and ruby and diamond and garnet, a thousand times brighter than any stone that ever graced a human woman's finger.

"The Starstone," reverently whispered the gem-bearing crane operator beside him.

As the great burden lifted free of the water, the submarines abandoned their lines and turned away, to make way for the huge pontooned barge with its padded deck that slipped in under the cradle.

Gently, slowly, reverently, the crane operators lowered the glittering mass onto the barge waiting to receive it. As soon as it was down, the operators ordered the floating cranes alongside. "Get on board!" they shouted. "Get the lines free! Secure the Starstone! And hurry—there's another submarine out here somewhere, and we don't know whose it is!"

Tregarth and Ryan were almost the first to obey, judging the rise and fall of the churning bulwarks and making the leap. It was a chancy job, with an excellent prospect of losing a leg—or worse—as penalty for a bad guess; but they both made it.

Tregarth had no time to wonder about the unexpected, unexplained other submarine, whatever it was. He was needed. The cradle of steel cables had fallen away, like the petals opening of a flower, as the crane lines went slack. The squid that had helped guide the lines to the cradle hooks had managed to swim free, all but one. It lay crushed against the Starstone, the siphon at the end of its body almost severed by the cable, but it was still alive. Tregarth could see one of the immense tentacles stirring jerkily, and the huge eye seemed to be staring directly at him.

There was no time for sightseeing. All the cables were thick, cold and stiff; moreover the wires that made them up had sharp edges and stabbing points. Before Tregarth had freed the hooks his hands were bleeding, but he kept on. The sun was high now, and already the barge was beginning to move slowly toward the ship channel, the center of the little flotilla the floating cranes that formed protectively around it as it got under weigh.

When they had thrown padded cables over the immense glowing mass Ron Tregarth stood back and gazed wonderingly at the dying squid and the baleful, glittering thing they called the Starstone of the Eternal.

He did not see the tentacle that wrapped itself around him from behind.

He didn't know it was happening until he felt himself drawn remorselessly toward that staring eye. He shouted in angry fear, struggling against the constricting grip; but the squid was far stronger than he.

Poor Pepito, he thought. . . .

And then, without warning, the tentacle dropped away and he was free. As he stumbled away he saw the tentacle lash out and catch Wernher Ryan, drawing him in as implacably as it had Tregarth a moment before. This time it did not relax its grip. It pulled the struggling, shouting man in—not to the mouth of the squid, but to the point on its body where a glowing orange jewel shone balefully out at the world.

Ryan's forehead touched the jewel.

At once his struggling stopped. The squid's tentacle relaxed, and the body that had been Wernher Ryan stood up, gazed around for a moment, and walked briskly away, the gem now gleaming in his own forehead.

It could have been me, thought Tregarth in sick fear.

But it wasn't. The squid's last twitches had ended. The great eye was glazing sightlessly over in death.

And it was then, as the body convulsed one last time, that Tregarth saw the ragged scar that marked where Graciela Navarro's speaking box had once been attached, and knew what squid it was that, at the last moment, had spared him.

Thank you, Nessus, he said silently, and turned to gaze unseeingly at the nearing shore.

Chapter
30

Two kilometers off shore, Graciela Navarro McKen peered worriedly toward the flares. The *Gaussberg Three* was moving very slowly, no more than keeping steerage way, but the seas offshore were much higher than near the beach; *Gaussberg* was in that tricky bit between Florida coastal waters and the meanders of the Gulf Stream.

Behind them the sky was turning pink, but it was hard to make out anything shoreward. Captain Dominic Paglieri had the night glasses, and Dennis McKen was waiting fretfully for a turn. "What is it?" McKen demanded. "What are they doing?"

The captain shrugged and passed the glasses over. "See for yourself," he said. Graciela, straining her eyes, could see only what looked like the shadows of tall masts, waving gently in the slow rhythm of the sea, and her husband's angry muttering told her she saw little more.

"Get closer," McKen insisted, putting down the glasses, but the captain shook his head. "You *must!*" McKen cried. "We've got to know what they're doing here!"

The captain said doggedly, "You heard my instructions. I'm not risking my ship. We're too close already."

Graciela was hardly listening to the familiar argument. She picked up the glasses her husband had set down and focused on the scene. The outlines were hazy, but the masts, she saw, were cranes, and they seemed to be lifting something that glittered and shimmered in the light from the flares in a way that almost hurt her eyes.

Then the thing was out of sight again, plopped onto a barge. Barge, tugs and floating cranes began to move in a stately procession toward a channel between sections of the long shelter island.

The captain was speaking again, this time in a tone of urgency. He was pointing to the sonar screens. "There are subs there!" he snapped. "Four of them—and if we can see them, they can see us! I'm getting out of here!"

"You can't!" McKen howled, and then, without transition, begged abjectly: "Please! If you won't run in closer, at least let me take a boat in!"

"Yes, please, Captain Paglieri," Graciela added, surprising herself; she had not intended to say anything. "Dennis is right. We've come this far, we should at least send someone in."

"He might not come back," the captain warned.

"I'll come back," McKen boasted. "Anyway, I'll take that risk. I insist! I'll take an inflatable, just to make contact. See if it's safe, if you like—though, honestly, that's a foregone conclusion; the land people are civilized human beings, after all. I'll be back in twenty-four hours."

The captain gnawed a lip. "I can't promise to pick you up, if other subs are in the area."

"I'll take the chance!"

The captain made his decision. "Not alone," he said firmly; and, of course, both of them looked at Graciela. And, of course, Graciela did as was expected of her, though there was something about the glitter of that immense, faceted lump of—something—that had swung from the floating cranes that she did not really want to come near . . . and though something told her that neither she nor her husband would, after all, be back to make the rendezvous in twenty-four hours. . . .

And when Graciela and Dennis McKen pulled their boat out onto the sandy beach they were at once surrounded by silent, scary men and women who wore jewels in the foreheads; so she turned out to be exactly right.

By mid-afternoon the two of them had been fed, questioned, released and left baffled. The bafflement was at the questions the woman with the jewel in her forehead had asked. Such questions! Oh, yes, of course, she had asked about City Gaussberg and City Mahalo and City Arafura and City Bellona and all the other free cities of the Pacific sea bottom—but she did not ask about weapons or defenses or industry. All the questions were about people. Were there poets in City Gaussberg? Were there mathematicians, historians, scholars? How many? Of what traditions?—Oriental, American, Australian Aboriginal, Latin, Eskimo? The questioner sounded more like a collector than a hostile commander, and it was only the gem that glowed from her forehead and the eerily detached intonations of her voice as she spoke that made Graciela's skin crawl as she responded to the interrogation.

Her husband seemed to have no such qualms. He broke off in the middle of a sentence to peer past the tall woman, and then smile in delight. "Look there, it's Wernher Ryan! Commander Ryan! I remember you—you were one of our leading astronaut candidates!"

Graciela could not share her husband's pleasure. The astronaut was also wearing one of those gems, and his tone as he responded to Dennis McKen's greeting was as detached and hollow as the woman's. But the woman made a gesture, and the astronaut led Dennis McKen away. McKen paused as he left to reassure his wife. "Don't worry—that's Commander *Wernher* Ryan! As long as people like him are in charge here, there's nothing to worry about!"

But Graciela did not fail to worry . . . and be baffled,

more than ever when the woman added crisply, "You must call your submarine in so that its crew can be rescued."

"But that's impossible," Graciela said.

"No, it is not impossible," the woman disagreed. "You will know a way. It is the will of the Eternal that all be rescued, you see—those in your vessel at least, though now I fear it is too late for those in the cities you have left behind."

"There really isn't any way," Graciela said desperately. "Please believe me! The submarine won't come in. All they will do is pick us up—if we come out there—if we're alone, and there isn't any other ship or plane nearby."

The woman gazed at her intently for a moment, and then said, "We must find a way. You may go."

And that was the most perplexing thing of all, for then Graciela was abandoned. Not imprisoned. Not told that she must stop where she was, or in any particular place. Her interrogator simply walked away and left her alone.

What she could not do was get back in her boat and flee, for there were guards around it. Even if she had been willing to leave without her husband. . . .

Which, she told herself, making a discovery, she was. She had no complaint against Dennis McKen as a husband, but she had seen the great joy in his eye when he encountered a fellow officer from the old Peace Wing, when he had set foot at last on the mainland of North America—no, he was happier here. He would not have objected if she had gone without him.

It was a curious thought, but of course it did not matter. She couldn't leave.

She picked her way toward the nearest clump of human beings, who were working in a dozen different parties at that huge rocket that squatted ominously on its launch pad. Some of the workers were carefully raising the great glittering thing she had caught a glimpse of to the top of the rocket. At closer range, it was even less inviting, an irregular crystalline object about twenty meters across. Parts of it were glistening clusters of gemlike crystals, parts—parts that looked like remnants of a metal framework—were seared, scorched and pitted.

Graciela shuddered and looked away. On the ground nearby, men in white suits, with thick gauntlets and crystal-visored helmets, were struggling with huge hoses. The hoses led from tank trucks to the great rocket itself, and they were frost-covered. Graciela stayed clear but curiosity kept her close. Were they really fueling this immense rocket, with its glowing, faceted, many-colored upper stage? What was it? Where could they be launching it to?

"Graciela!" shouted a voice that made her heart stop.

She turned and stared. One of the white-suited figures was lumbering toward her. It fumbled at the helmet with the thick-fingered gloves, and when it had pulled the helmet away the face was the face that returned, even now, to her dreams.

"Oh, Ron," she whispered, incredulous, stunned. "You're—alive!"

"And so are you!" he said in sober joy. "Where have you been, Graciela? I used to hope— I never really gave you up. Tell me! How did you survive?"

"I've been in City Gaussberg. I came in off a sub this morning. About yourself? Working here! Since when have you been a rocket technician?"

"I'm whatever they tell me to be. You'd be surprised at all of the things I've been," he said. And paused. And stared at her wordlessly for a moment; and then, still without words, he opened his arms, and silent herself she went to him.

By the time Graciela went to sleep that night, in a barracks with her husband snoring in the bunk below her, her whole world had changed.

Ron Tregarth—alive!

Not only alive, Ron Tregarth with a son! A sturdy young boy who looked quickly to his father for a cue and then warmly, unhesitatingly, put his arms around Graciela's waist in a hug and declared, "It's wonderful you're here, Miss Navarro."

"It's Mrs. McKen now," Graciela corrected him, and did not miss the sudden pain in Tregarth's eyes. But what did the man expect? After all, Pepito had certainly had a mother! And then, as Tregarth began to tell her about what had become of Jannie Storm her own eyes were as filled with pain as his. What a life for the child, with a mother as remote as the stars! And what a life for Ron Tregarth as well. . . .

She could not, however, feel as badly about that as her conscience whispered she should. Yes, of course, since Tregarth had miraculously survived it was only natural he should build a new life for himself. Hadn't she done the same? But it was not altogether unpleasant for Graciela to find that the marriage was—odd.

She was up early the next morning, leaving Dennis McKen asleep. When at last he stumbled out of bed and joined them in the breakfast line he hardly noticed that she was talking to Ron Tregarth. McKen was full of excitement and even pleasure. He barely noticed Graciela's introduction. "Tregarth? Oh, yes—from City Atlantica. Yes, my wife has mentioned you—childhood sweethearts, that sort of thing?" He smiled forgivingly. "But that's a long time ago—and, oh, Graciela," he went on, his expression kindling, "they're building a *starship*. Commander Ryan showed me the whole thing! They're building an automatic launch machine, so the rocket will go off according to preset instructions, without anyone needing to run it once they start the countdown. It's true," he said, his expression changing slightly, "that Commander Ryan's a bit—well—*changed*, if you know what I mean—"

"I know exactly what you mean," said Ron Tregarth. "But what did you say about the computer system? I helped bring the components in, but I can't believe it needs to be fully automated. Wouldn't it be better to have people running it?"

"No, no," said McKen patronizingly, peering ahead as they approached the head of the line. "That's still a kind of webfoot way of looking at things, isn't it? After all these years! But this base was part of the old Peace Wing, Tregarth. We did things right!"

Graciela, half turned away to get the ration of food slopped onto her plate, gazed down at it. "Not always," she sighed.

Somehow she got through the long day. When she reminded her husband that they had failed to meet the submarine at the rendezvous time he only shrugged. "Old Paglieri'll wait around," he said. "When we want him he'll be there—but there's a lot to do here first! I've got to figure out what this starship thing is all about—they're talking about launching it in forty-eight hours, did you know that? And this crazy business with the jewels in people's heads—"

"I told you about that," she pointed out.

He didn't even nod acknowledgement. "I need to know how that works," he went on, oblivious. "I get the idea that when you have one of those things you can work harder and faster and better than ever—haven't you seen that? Maybe there's something there we can use!"

"I'm sure they'll be glad to give you one," Graciela told her husband, and although it was half a joke, it was a grisly one.

And it was even less funny late that night when she was

dragged out of bed by that same wonderful Commander Wernher Ryan and brought to the headquarters cabin. What it was for, Ryan did not say; he only told her in that colorless, detached voice that Jannie Storm required her presence; and when she got there she was surprised to see Ron Tregarth standing, worried and angry, with the woman who had been his wife.

"Captain Ron Tregarth, who was my husband," said Jannie Storm at once, "informs me that he knows of no way to send a message to the wild humans in the undersea cities. I cannot believe this is so."

"I told you, Jannie," Tregarth said roughly, "all communication was destroyed when the comet hit."

"You have told me this, yes," she said serenely, "but much time has passed since then. I do not think it likely that the undersea people have failed to monitor our own radio transmissions, even if they have originated none of their own."

"Well," said Graciela hesitantly, "I suppose that's true—"

"Yes. It therefore follows that if you or Ron Tregarth speaks to the undersea cities on our long-range transmitter they will receive your message."

"But I won't do that," said Tregarth tightly.

His wife looked at him thoughtfully, but only turned to Graciela. "Will you?" she asked. "Will you tell the people of the undersea cities that they can be rescued? There is not much time—less than thirty-six hours before the Starstone of the Eternal must be launched to utilize the best orbits available—but we have transport planes that can reach anywhere in the world in six hours. If your people would come to the surface of the ocean—"

"There's no place to land!" Tregarth barked.

"It isn't necessary to land," Jannie Storm said serenely. "We have other methods. The one by which my own starseed was brought to Quagger's hideaway, for example.

Our planes can hover while birds fly down with starseeds. Commander Ryan has worked out all the details. Other birds will be parachuted to the surface; when the transfers have been effected the rescued ones will yield their starseeds to the birds, who will then fly up to where the transports are hovering—"

"No!" Tregarth shouted. "Don't do it, Graciela! They'll all *die!*"

"They will be rescued from life," Jannie Storm corrected him benignly.

"I won't do it," Graciela said, keeping her voice steady.

"I see," said the calm, emotionless voice of Jannie Storm. She regarded Graciela as thoughtfully as she had studied Tregarth a moment before. "There is a way," she said meditatively. "This corpus is nearing the end of its usefulness. I could transfer to yours—"

"For God's sake, Jannie!" Tregarth yelled in desperation. "Please! Leave us alone! If you want to get in that damn rocket and go, go ahead—but, I beg you, don't make us into things like yourself!"

The unearthly eyes looked mildly surprised. "But, Ron Tregarth," she began, "what I offer you is rescue, rescue from mortal life. How can you deprive your fellow human beings of so great a boon as to live, forever, in the mind of the Eternal?"

"I can," he snarled, and leaped forward to grasp her throat, "and if I have to, I'll kill you to prevent it!"

Jannie Storm did not resist. She simply looked up at him, unafraid. She opened her mouth to speak—

A weird hooting sound interrupted.

For a moment they all stood frozen there, like figures in a wax-museum reconstruction of an ancient crime. Then Tregarth cried, "It's the search radar alarm!" He let go of Jannie Storm, who stumbled away, recovering her balance. Tregarth didn't wait to see what she would do. He ran to the door of her hut, Graciela and Jannie Storm following.

It was dark night outside, overlaid with a thousand bright stars, and all around them other people were tumbling out to gape and query. "You are correct, Ron Tregarth," said Jannie Storm unemotionally. "It is the search radar alarm. We appear to be under attack."

"But nobody's paid any attention to that for years," said Tregarth, staring into the sky. "I'm surprised it's still working."

"But what is it?" asked Graciela.

He tugged at her arm, beginning to run toward the long neglected communications shack. "Let's find out!" he cried; but long before he, or any other, reached the shack shouts from the gathering people made him look up, and the cause of the alarm was visible.

Out over the sea six bright plumes of fire curved down and in toward the settlement.

"They're rockets!" Tregarth cried. "They must be space planes—but where could they be coming from?"

No one could answer that, but what they were doing was instantly clear. Bright glints of light winked out from the nose of each of them, and new trails of fire sped toward the colony. They were firing missiles! Faster far than the ships themselves, the missiles streaked in and down, and where they struck bright balls of flame erupted.

"Protect the Starstone!" called Jannie Storm, her voice carrying over all the hubbub; and

"Pepito!" shouted Ron Tregarth. He ran toward his hut, Graciela following. The boy was already in the doorway, looking dazedly up at the lights, as Tregarth caught him in his arms. "Get *down!*" Tregarth shouted, dragging both Pepito and Graciela with him to the ground. Not all the missiles were incendiary; there were blasts that shook the earth, and the things they hit—the communications shack, the sheds that held much of the community's long-abandoned military vehicles, two of the new barracks—all went up in a shower of fragments.

Then the spaceplanes had done their work. They didn't have the maneuvering ability to turn and strafe again; they dropped to the beach, spread over a mile or more of sand, out of sight.

But they were not alone.

Behind them a huger, slower space transport craft waddled in, this one precisely targeted for the colony's landing strip. It touched down and skidded crazily, and before it had quite stopped its hatches flew open.

Armed men leaped out, stumbling awkwardly as they stretched the ground—falling, many of them, with shouts of pain. Part of the pain was from their surprising clumsiness as they fell; more of it, perhaps, from the glowing sides of the transport, burning hot from the friction of reentry into the earth's atmosphere, that scorched and seared the incautious hands that touched it.

That didn't matter. The armed men lumbered toward hillocks in the sand, crumbling walls, abandoned pillboxes—they took shelter wherever shelter could be found; and if the men were burned and shaken, their weapons were still in fine operating shape.

"We're under attack!" cried Tregarth, as the invaders opened fire. And, even through the wild commotion, they could hear the distant cry of Jannie Storm:

"The Starstone of the Eternal! Preserve the Starstone, at any cost!"

Chapter
31

General Marcus McKen's command craft was thirty minutes behind the troop carriers, which meant that when the attack planes made their first run General Marcus McKen had just finished reentry and was getting his first look at the Mississippi River Delta. When the troop carrier landed the great Tampa Bay Bridge on the West Coast of Florida was just coming into the general's view. Radio contact was forbidden; and in any case it would not have been possible during the reentry. General Marcus McKen, bruised and beaten from the violent reentry buffeting, was strapped in place, crowded between the pilots.

There was no way of knowing whether the assault had succeeded.

Like any spaceplane, the command craft had roughly the flight characteristics of a rock. Once committed, there was nowhere for it to go but down. Win or lose, he would have to land somewhere near the base—either to be welcomed as a conquering hero by his own troops, or to be a hunted fugitive if the attack had failed. He wasn't aware that he was shouting furious, frightened contradictory orders at his pilots. His pilots hardly heard him, for that matter; the three of them were the only ones in the command craft that could see outside at all, and all three were peering into the distance, trying to make out the tall launch vehicle that would tell them where the base was. In the body of the command craft the thirty tough warriors of McKen's personal guard were already slipping their harnesses, checking their weapons, ready for the landing—whatever it might be.

A bellow from the copilot blasted into McKen's ear: "There it is!"

The general hardly heard. He was shouting himself as the fires and smoke hove into view, squinting desperately to try to see through the smoke . . . and when he did he chortled in delight: "We've got them! Total surprise!" For he could see that his transports were down exactly where planned, along the beach, and half the camp was in flames. If there was any resistance it was invisible from his vantage point. His soldiers had taken up positions and were steadily advancing, one echelon at a time, firing as they went.

His exultation was cut short as the craft soared past the camp, reaching out over the ocean for its landing approach. "I can't see," he wailed, straining to peer back through the tiny window. He pounded desperately on the helmet of the pilot. "What's going on?" he shouted. "How can I command the battle if I can't see it?"

"Please, General McKen," the pilot begged, trying to shrink away from his commander's blows. "It'll just be a moment till we turn on the landing leg, then you'll see again."

"Hurry, damn it!" McKen snapped. "If you don't get us down in three minutes you'll never walk away from the landing!"

And, actually, it was nearly that fast. The spaceplane stood on its wingtips to turn, then dived in at high speed, waggling furiously to lose velocity. The pilot, muttering a silent prayer, snapped the flaps to full extension at the last minute. It was like slamming on the brakes; all three of them were thrown forward against their straps, and in the cabin behind them two of the guardsmen slid on top of their neighbors in a snarl of limbs and weapons. When the craft touched the sand it was still going at nearly three hundred kilometers an hour, and the touchdown was more like a controlled—a barely controlled—crash.

But they were down.

As soon as the command ship stopped the guardsmen were up and out, forming a protective line around General Marcus McKen as he followed. His first step back on his own base was far from graceful. He had forgotten what Earth gravity was like. He stumbled and would have fallen, but Colonel Schroeder grabbed him.

There was a steady rattle of shots from the firefight just ahead. But it was all one-sided; hardly anyone was returning the fire. Most of the inhabitants of the camp were flat on their bellies, trying to stay out of the way of the flying rounds.

McKen's troops were weak and wobbly after their years in the habitats, falling, tripping, trying to run and failing; the best they could manage was a limping half-trot, and at least a dozen of them, McKen saw, were on the ground themselves, crying out in pain. The issue might have been in doubt. If there had been any organized resistance it could have gone badly for the forces of General Marcus McKen. . . .

But suddenly a tall woman stood up, raising her arms above her head—not so much a gesture of surrender as the ritual benediction of a priestess.

"Do not harm the Starstone of the Eternal!" she called. "You may stop firing. We will not resist."

And as McKen looked closer, he saw that a glowing gem was embedded in her forehead.

An hour later the victory was complete.

For General Marcus McKen the astonishing thing was

that things were going on that he could not understand. All the inhabitants of the camp were peacefully gathered on a stretch of open land, weaponless, with his best warriors guarding them. But there were so *many* of them! He had not expected nearly three thousand people; and why had they surrendered so tamely? And what were the jewels that so many of them wore glowing from their forehead? And who was this woman, Jannie Storm, who seemed to be in command in this place he had claimed as his own? And where was his despicable cousin, Simon McKen Quagger?

There were more pressing problems for him to deal with. His staunch troops had taken a beating. Few of them had been wounded by weaponry, and most of those seemed to have caught random rounds from one of their comrades; but one was dead, half a dozen were bleeding, and at least a score had dislocated shoulders or shattered collarbones inflicted by the recoil of their own weapons (this was the price paid for the loss of bone mass!), or broken limbs from falls in the forgotten, unforgiving gravity of Earth.

Colonel Schroeder limped toward his general. The colonel was in obvious pain but triumphant as he reported, "The assault zone is secure, sir. Would you like to inspect your prisoners?"

"Have they been disarmed?" General McKen demanded.

The colonel's expression was puzzled. "They didn't have any arms, sir," he reported. "Or only a few—and even they didn't use them. Rotten discipline!" He shrugged in contemptuous disapproval, then barked an order. Two prisoners pushed an electric cart toward them. "We've found this. Perhaps the general would like to ride," he suggested delicately. "Just at first, I mean."

"First," said General McKen grimly, "take me to my

loathsome cousin, Simon Quagger. I have some things to say to him!"

But that was not to be, for the wretch had not only been arrogant and disobedient, he had chosen to die before he could face the righteous wrath of General Marcus McKen.

The general's cheek muscles pulsed with anger. Fate had cheated him of a well deserved revenge! Still, as he rolled in majestic wrath before the ranks of prisoners, his mood mellowed. No one could deny that he had won a great victory! So many healthy, strong captives! They stood, meek as sheep, under the guns of his limping, suffering assault troops. He paused to scowl at a pair of tall, muscular men with blazing jewels inset above their mild and unreproachful eyes. "What are those things they're wearing?" he demanded of Colonel Schroeder.

"I think they're some sort of badge of rank," the colonel offered uncertainly. He gestured with his leather swagger-stick. "See down the line there, sir? There's Commander Ryan, and he's wearing one."

"Ah," the general cried, smiling at last. "Commander *Ryan*, is it? The traitor who delivered my base to Cousin Quagger? Yes, I have some things to say to Commander Ryan!"

But that was a disappointment, too, because Wernher Ryan made no effort to defend himself. He stood, calm and remote, nursing a bleeding shoulder while the general raged. "You're quite right, General," Ryan acknowledged at last. "I have entered the service of the Eternal."

"I'll have you shot!" General McKen roared apoplecti-cally.

"As you wish," Ryan said with indifference. "But we mean you no harm. All we seek is your rescue."

The general glared at him, eyes bulging with rage. "Rescue, is it?" he shouted. "How dare you speak to me of rescue!" He got up from his cart, reaching for Colonel

Schroeder's swagger-stick. He lurched toward Ryan, shouting, raising the stick for a blow. . . .

But that, as it turned out, was a serious mistake of judgment.

For Graciela Navarro, pressed to the ground between Pepito and his father, the firefight was pure horror. It was such a *lubber* thing to do! Human beings, firing at each other with lethal weapons! And when the firing at last stopped it got no better. Graciela could see Jannie Storm and the other "elements of the Eternal" as they turned from surrender to caring for the casualties. And there were so many casualties! Sadly the gem-wearing ones closed the eyes of the half-dozen dead, bearing the wounded away to a makeshift triage area in the shade of the scrubby palms.

Graciela started to scramble to her feet. "We ought to help," she declared, but Ron Tregarth caught her arm.

"No!" he muttered tightly. "Wait! There's something funny going on—"

From behind them the voice of Dennis McKen came clearly. "Funny? Only to a webfoot," he sneered. "Don't you know who that is? That's General Marcus McKen—my uncle! Come on, Graciela. Let me take you up there and introduce you!"

Graciela rose, then hesitated. "I—I think I'd rather stay here with Ron and the boy," she said uncertainly.

"Really?" Her husband shook his head in mock amusement. "Once a webfoot, always a webfoot, I suppose. Well, stay here, then. I'll go talk to my uncle. I'm sure he'll have everything shipshape here in ten minutes—and then we'll see what real Peace Wing organization is like!"

"Wait!" Tregarth shouted, but McKen was already gone.

Graciela gazed worriedly after him. "Shouldn't I go with him? What's happening, Ron?"

"I don't know," Tregarth said, "but I think we ought to get out of here until things settle down. Come on!" And he took raised Pepito from the ground and led the boy and Graciela slowly, inconspicuously away. "Nobody's paying attention to us here," he said softly. "There are some boats by the Banana River—I think this would be a good time to get out of the way."

And then Pepito, craning his neck to look back at General McKen, cried out in shock.

The general was beating Wernher Ryan with an officer's baton. Ryan was not resisting. He did not seem to feel the blows.

"There's your husband, running right up to them," Tregarth reported.

"What's he doing?" Graciela pleaded.

"Nothing yet—the general's busy right now. But he's giving Ryan a hard time, and—oh," said Ron Tregarth softly, "my *God!*"

Graciela caught her breath as she saw what he was looking at. Ryan, face streaming blood, stepped gently forward to enfold General Marcus McKen tenderly in his arms.

Even at that distance, Graciela could see the shock and revulsion in the general's face as he flailed against Wernher Ryan's grasp. It was useless. Ryan was far stronger. . . .

Then Ryan pressed his face against the general's. It looked almost as though they were kissing.

It was a kiss of death. Tregarth made an wordless noise. Pepito sobbed. The actors had switched roles. Now it was the general whose arms were around Wernher Ryan, while Ryan's own arms fell limply away.

Ryan's body sagged slowly backward. Gently, kindly, General Marcus McKen lowered the dead body of his one-time base commander to the cracked old concrete.

And when Marcus McKen straightened, the gem now blazed in his own forehead.

His guards were rushing toward him, shouting. Colonel

Schroeder already had a pistol in his hand, ready to shoot Ryan, stayed only by the fact that Ryan, clearly, was already dead. Even Dennis McKen had sprung toward the group.

General Marcus McKen raised a hand. He seemed taller and stronger, as the jewel blazed out from his brow. "Do not shoot!" he cried clearly. "Stop where you are! Let the elements of the Eternal approach!"

... And already, like the froth of a wavelet sliding inevitably up the sand, the elements of the Eternal were moving toward the Peace Wing soldiers. And they met. And they touched. And as they touched, the conquerors were conquered. Those who had worn the jewels fell, silent and uncomplaining, to their deaths; and those who had been their captors now stood silent and remote, and light radiated from the gems they wore.

Once again the armies of the Eternal ruled unchallenged at the Cape.

Chapter
32

All through the night Graciela woke uneasily to peer out through the undergrowth. The scene on the far side of the river was always the same, the great rocket with its glittering, menacing cargo at the top, stark and shining in the worklights.

The boy, Pepito, rose cautiously to keep from disturbing

his sleeping father. "Mrs. McKen?" he whispered. "What are they doing now?"

Graciela put her arm around him. "I think they're completing the fueling of the rocket," she said. "Can you see?" There was no doubt that he could, for the lights picked out every detail—the men in their white hot-poppa suits guiding the liquid-gas hoses into the fuel tanks, the dozens of technicians checking the explosive bolts that held the rocket coupled to its launch tower, the bustle of activity around the shed that held the countdown computer—most of all, the winking, faceted glitter from the lump of Starstone that sat on top of the great spacecraft. Only part of it was visible, for workmen had dressed it in a heat-resistant shroud of Nexø, with only one section left open—for what reason Graciela could not tell—but even so, it dominated the scene.

"Does that mean they're going away?" the boy asked.

"I hope so, Pepito," she whispered.

"But when Mr. Ryan and my father went into space their ship was almost that big, and there were only two of them. How will all the people fit, Mrs. McKen?"

Graciela shook her head—it was meant as a double negative, first because she didn't have an answer for his question, but also because she was not at all sure that she was still wife to anyone named McKen. The last she had seen of Dennis he was in the grip of one of the star-wearing elements of the Eternal. Was there really still a Dennis McKen at all?

Absently, fondly, she hugged the boy to her. The half-grown scrub was full of noises—other runaways like themselves, some of them; but were all the noises from humans? Graciela had been tucked in with stories of snakes and alligators and all sorts of crawling things that made the land surface of the Earth unfit for decent human habitation—were the stories all lies? She shuddered involuntarily, and realized the boy was straining to stand taller.

"Mrs. McKen?" he whispered. "Isn't that a helicopter?"

It was. She could not only hear the beat of its rotor, she could see the bright searchlights stabbing down from it as it rose from the landing site and fluttered out over the jungle toward them.

A vast voice came from it: "Please, everyone return to the base. Rescue must be complete in two hours!"

Graciela turned to wake Tregarth, but the loudspeaker had done that for her. He rose, groggily peering up at the whirlybird. In the reflections from its own lights he could see a spidery antenna affixed to the bottom of the helicopter. A heat-seeker! An infrared detector, looking for signs of life.

"We've got to get out of here," he whispered.

"Where?" Graciela asked.

"Back to the river, I think. The scrub's thicker there, and the water's warmer than the air—it might confuse their heat sensors."

Tregarth didn't wait for an answer, he simply caught one of Pepito's hands and one of Graciela's in his own and led them, skulking in the doubtful shelter of the scrub, freezing with their faces to the ground when a wandering searchlight beam came near them. Long before they reached the banks of the Banana River the helicopter had taken itself away, but its purpose had been served. Runaways had been located by the heat of their bodies. Searchers on foot were there to finish the job.

Half a dozen times they heard search parties combing the palmetto scrub, and saw the flickering of their handlamps. More than once they found what they were after. Then Graciela heard sudden shouts, scufflings, pleading voices . . . and sudden silences; and the silences were the worst of all.

At the river Tregarth looked around worriedly. "This might be a mistake," he muttered. "The helicopter's gone now, so we don't have to worry about the heat sensors—but here we're pinned."

"The boat we crossed over in is just down the shore," Graciela offered.

He shook his head. "Yes, but—wait! Someone's coming," he whispered tautly. "Lie perfectly still!"

But the people coming were not still at all. They moved purposefully toward the little clump where Tregarth and the others were hiding. He caught a glimpse of them, pausing to peer about.

Then one of them lifted a cone-shaped instrument to its lips and the amplified voice of Jannie Storm said pleadingly:

"Pepito, who was my son! Ron Tregarth, who was my husband! There is no more time, please come and be rescued."

Pepito looked up worriedly at his father. Frowning, Tregarth laid a gentle finger across the boy's lips.

The searchers paused to confer, then split up—two in one direction along the river's edge, one in the other, while that which had been Jannie Storm came directly toward them. She was almost upon them when her son jumped up and stood before her, barring her way, his arms outstretched to keep her from passing. "Mother, please don't," he sobbed, his face twisted in anguish. "Don't make us like you!"

Jannie stopped short, peering soberly at the boy. "But, Pepito," she said reasonably, "to be like us is to become perfect. Don't you know what it means to cling to the animal flesh? It means pain, and sickness, and growing old . . . and in the end it means death, and the rot that follows death. While with us you will live forever, perfectly, in the Eternal. No, Pepito," she went on firmly, "you must be rescued. That is the will of the Eternal. Take my hand."

Jannie reached out toward her son, but Tregarth, suddenly coming to life, pushed him away. "*No*," he shouted, bending to pick up a length of dead, half-grown palmetto trunk from the ground. "Don't listen to her, Pepito! Get into the boat! You too, Graciela! Jannie, I warn you!"

The figure paused, regarding him benignly. "But what I say is true for you too, Ron Tregarth," she said.

"Stop!" he shouted desperately, aware that he was being heard by the others, knowing it would be only moments before the other three would be back to join Jannie, outnumbering him, overpowering him. . . .

Jannie Storm did not stop.

Sobbing, Tregarth struck out blindly with the old club. Fragile with age and parching, it shattered as it struck Jannie's face, but the weight of it drove her stumbling back.

And Ron Tregarth had time to jump into the boat. Thankfully, the motor started. Graciela was already at the controls. As they pulled away Tregarth saw the form of his wife stumble to her feet, face bloody, arms outstretched to him. "But I wanted to give you eternity!" she cried.

"We prefer life!" he shouted back, and turned away to comfort his weeping son.

All the way up the river and out through the channel they were in fear of another, faster boat—of the helicopter returning—of something, anything, preventing their escape. But no one followed. The launch time had come too close.

As day broke Graciela caught her breath. They were passing the launch area. The great floodlighted gantry was in plain view, with the spacecraft of the Eternal tall on its pad.

Hundreds of people were converging on the rocket.

Scowling in perplexity, Tregarth pulled the glasses out of the boat's emergency locker and turned them on the scene. One by one the people were climbing the long steps to the topmost stage of the rocket. They were lined up in single file. And as they reached the top—

"Dear God," Tregarth sighed beside her, putting down the glasses. "I can't believe what they're doing!"

But when Graciela took the glasses there was no doubt. As each starseed-wearing human being reached the top he leaned out to touch his forehead against the great glittering Starstone.

The gem in his forehead touched the stone and was absorbed into it. Then the person stood erect, empty-eyed and waiting—   ·

And then the person next in line, lovingly and tenderly, shoved the abandoned corpus of his predecessor over the side of the little platform to join the growing heap of bodies at the base of the tower.

The line of sacrificial volunteers never ended. As soon as it shortened a group of others abandoned whatever they were doing and strolled over to take their places.

Tregarth glanced at Graciela and the boy and then, without speaking, cut the engine. The little boat rocked gently in the wavelets that came in from the open water.

"Shouldn't we—" Graciela began, but he shook his head.

"Nobody's going to come after us now," he said. "There isn't time. They're going to launch."

"But still—"

He looked at her with compassion. "Getting into that stone," he said, "is whatever there is left of your husband, and whatever is left of my wife. I think I'd like to watch them leave."

It took more than an hour, and the sun was high, when the last person paused on the lip of the top stage.

The person was Jannie Storm.

She turned and gazed out toward the ship channel. Whether she could see them or not Tregarth could not guess, but she stared for a long moment before she turned and pressed her forehead against the exposed Starstone.

Her body fell lifeless to the floor of the platform.

The rest happened by itself. The last panel of shroud for the Starstone lowered itself into place and locked. The umbilicus cords fell away. The platform retreated a meter or so, and as it did the body of Jannie Storm slipped from the metal deck and fell out of sight to the ground. . . .

And there was a shaking of the air, too loud to be called mere sound, and a wash of flame that licked over the little hill of corpses, and a light too bright to look at. . . .

And then the Starstone of the Eternal and the spacecraft that bore it lifted slowly, steadily, remorselessly . . . with increasing speed . . . up and up. . . .

Until it was only a memory of flame, and a curl of smoke that stretched across the sky.

"They're gone," said Ron Tregarth.

"She's never coming back," sobbed Pepito.

"It's what she wanted," Graciela whispered to the boy. "She wanted to give us eternity. We've chosen life—even if some day we must pay for it with death—but she will go on forever."

"Without us," said Tregarth as he started the motor and headed out to the kindly sea, where, sooner or later, *Gaussberg Three* would find them. "I've had enough of this place. I've had enough of the land, for that matter."

"So have I," said Graciela. "I'm never coming back here."

But Pepito, head thrown back to stare at the trail across the morning sky, said thoughtfully, "But, some day when I am older, I might."

I am one element of the Eternal, and I live on. But I no longer live in the Eternal. I stay behind.

I stay behind that the work of the Eternal may be done, for it is I who am entrusted with the brute work of guiding the cold metal machine that computes the thrust and monitors the countdown that launches the Starstone of the Eternal into the next stage of its endless odyssey.

I stay behind, but I mourn.

I mourn the loss of all those elements of the Eternal who have gone before, and left me, alone and unsharing, in a world of sentient animal flesh.

I mourn the loneliness I face; but I do the work of the Eternal.

I do the work of the Eternal now. I will go on doing the work of the Eternal. Long after the Starstone has left the orbit of the last dead planet of this abandoned star, I will go on. For I stay here in the certainty that, one day, some of these mortal bits of animal flesh will join me. . . .

And then we will join the others, and rescue them as well, and rise to meet the rest of the Eternal in some infinitely far place, at some incomprehensibly long time in the future. . . .

Then we will all live truly in the Eternal. Forever.

For the life of Earth has reached its goal.